# A Hundred Thousand Worlds

# A
# Hundred
# Thousand
# Worlds

BOB PROEHL

Viking

VIKING

An imprint of Penguin Random House LLC
375 Hudson Street
New York, New York 10014
penguin.com

ISBN 9780399562211 (hardcover)
ISBN 9780399562228 (ebook)

Printed in the United States of America

1   3   5   7   9   10   8   6   4   2

Set in Warnock Pro
Designed by Alissa Rose Theodor

*For Heather, whose resemblance to Wonder Woman is not coincidental.*
*And for Alex, who taught me to love the ending of* Superman.

He told the man that in America it was nonsense to invent a country—what they ought to do was invent a planet.

—*Jorge Luis Borges*, "Tlön, Uqbar, Orbis Tertius"

People who are lonely, people left alone, sit talking nonsense to the air, imagining beautiful systems dying, old fixed orders spiraling apart . . .

—*Tony Kushner*, Angels in America: Millennium Approaches

They bypassed the death of their reality by becoming fictional in ours.

—*Grant Morrison*, Flex Mentallo: Man of Muscle Mystery

A Hundred Thousand Worlds

# PART ONE

# The Golden Age

I'd be writing a story for Kirby, and Steve Ditko would walk in and say, "Hey, I need some work now." And I'd say, "I can't give it to you now, Steve, I'm finishing Kirby's." But we couldn't afford to keep Steve waiting, because time is money, so I'd have to say, "Look Steve, I can't write a script for you now, but here's the plot we'll use for the next *Spider-Man*. Go home and draw anything you want, as long as it's something like this, and I'll put the copy in later." . . . Okay, it started out as a lazy man's device . . . but we realized this was absolutely the best way to do a comic.

—STANLEY MARTIN LIEBER

If America gave anybody anything it is ambition. Bad things would come out of it because some guys are in a hurry, but that doesn't mean they're evil or anything, it just means they fall into bad grace somehow. It was hard to find work. A friend of mine was going to go out to get a job because his mother told him to get a job, so he said, I'll go out and draw pictures and they'll pay me for them. And his mother said, "No son of mine will become an artist. You'll sit around with berets in Greenwich Village and talk to loose women." Of course, mothers were very conventional, everything was very conventional.

—JACOB KURTZBERG

# Travelogue

Alex Torrey, nine but small for his age, writes the names of the places on the exit signs in his notebook. Below each, he rewrites the name backwards. He reads them aloud, quietly, so his mother can't hear him over the radio. Collections of random syllables. Impossible strings of consonants.

It's tough work. But finding a magic word ought to be. There are useless abracadabras and hocus-poci lying around everywhere, but ones that still have magic in them, that haven't had it all sucked out, are harder to find. Plucky kid reporter Brian Bryson spent days in the dim-lit archives of the Metro City Public Library, eyes bleeding tears behind thick glasses, before he stumbled upon the word that turned him into Captain Wonder, champion of six ancient gods.

"Excelsior!" Alex says. If it worked for Brian Bryson, it might still have a little magic in it. The word uttered, he is still a boy in the backseat of a Honda Civic. He *hmmphs* and returns to his list. Pronunciation and emphasis may be the key.

"Ac-aht-i."

"Olaf-fub."

"Alu-bath-sa."

Nothing.

Most of central Pennsylvania had been dull, but occasionally there were Iroquois place names that sounded magical backward and forward. Alex chewed them like gum that refused to lose its flavor, then asterisked them in his notebook as worthy of further investigation.

Now and then, his mother checks the rearview and sees his lips forming odd shapes, but the sounds are drowned out by one sputtering NPR station after another. Alex cannot understand why she can't bear him talking to her while she drives but she can stand the talk radio prattling on endlessly. As they pass from one station to the next, discussions are repeated, and Alex's mother seems to take comfort in this. She laughs at the jokes again, nods with more insistent agreement at opinions she's already heard.

Alex pages back through the notebook to what he wrote yesterday, about their visit to the Idea Man. *The G train rocks back and forth like a real train*, his notebook says. *The Idea Man's building is like a castle.* And on a page otherwise blank, the thing he'd asked for, his parting gift. An idea. Alex feels special that this one was for him, that Louis didn't write it into the Book like all the others, for anyone who can afford it to read.

*There's a boy. He wakes up in a cave, alone. He doesn't know where he is or who he is. In the cave with him, there's a robot, roughly the size and shape of a man. But it's broken.*

Alex tried to get more information, but the Idea Man clammed up.

"Does the boy know how to fix the robot?" Alex asked, and the Idea Man shrugged.

"I'm wondering that myself," he said to Alex.

Now it's Alex's job to wonder, to ponder on it. Where there was nothing, now there is a boy, and a cave, and a broken robot. They form a still, quiet spot in the center of Alex's mind, a blank made up of information he doesn't have yet. Things he needs to fill in. Alex runs his finger along the words he wrote yesterday. They still feel carved into the page. Soon they'll flatten out, but for now they are still paths across the page, still have depth and curvature.

Alex is aware that they're moving west with some kind of intention, as if they're checking off things on the way. It's not simply a trip for the sake of a trip, but he can't figure what the purpose is. He's tried to glean as much information as he can—from her, from the Idea Man before they left—but it doesn't amount to a full story. Something is missing: a motive, some reason.

A number of times, he's asked her how long they're going for altogether. It's not an important question; there's nothing in New York that won't wait for him. But each time, she changes the subject. Alex's suggestions for things they might do on the drive back, which have included, in no particular order, Mount Rushmore, seeing a cowboy, Old Faithful, seeing a prairie dog, and Canada, have likewise been deflected. It's as if they'll get there and slingshot back to New York in a second, or keep going west, across the ocean until they hit land again, and then make their way around the world to end up once again safe in their apartment in Brooklyn Heights.

Alex thinks of their car traveling across a green sea. *Traveling* is the strongest magic word he knows. That and *home*.

"Ago-hay-uc," he says, knowing it's not right even as he chokes it out. Magic words sound like magic words.

Alex closes the notebook and opens the book he was reading, *Adam Anti & the Book I Read*. It is the first in a series about a boy who grows up in Brooklyn before discovering he has magic powers. He's almost done with it, but he has the second one in his backpack. His mother packed his clothes and then threw open their biggest suitcase in the middle of Alex's room and told him to add anything he wanted, anything he thought he might need. He looked around his room, assessing six years' accumulation of toys, and, closing the suitcase like a great giant clam, he picked two books and some notebooks off the shelf and declared he was ready to go.

Alex dives back into *Adam Anti*, which is exciting, even if his favorite parts were the ones set in Brooklyn. It's amazing when a story brushes up against your real life; it feels as if the characters might pass you on the street. As he reads, he glances up often to keep an eye on the road signs as they zip past, loving the story he's reading, but worried he might miss a magic word as it goes by.

# By Definition

"Mom?" he calls from their bedroom at the Holiday Inn Cleveland. The word soars upward through an octave like a freed bird. Valerie Torrey, in the bathroom with the door open, waits. Sometimes these calls are a kind of sonar, a sounding to confirm her location. She yanks the floss out from between her molars and holds it taut, ready across her thumbs.

"Mom?" he calls again. Higher now and tinged with the beginnings of worry.

"What's up, Rabbit?" she calls back. It's a new nickname between them, inspired by the upper incisors that now outsize the milk teeth in his broad smile, and his always prominent ears, an inheritance from her side.

"What's a vestibool?"

"Vestibule? It's a kind of porch."

"Oh."

She waits to hear if another question is coming, but there's quiet. She goes back to violently working at her teeth and gums. She watches the feral faces she is making in the mirror, faces made entirely of teeth. Maybe when they get to Los Angeles, these are the faces she'll show Andrew. She will bare her teeth like a cornered animal trying to overstate the threat it presents. When the interviewer asks, *How did you protect your child from that awful, awful man, Miss Torrey?* she will smile with her lips pressed firmly together and say quietly, *I showed him my teeth.*

When she is done, she takes a brush out of her travel bag and starts on her hair with similar aggression. The heat in the car has kinked it to the point of knotting. Walking out of a Brooklyn salon two days ago with Alex in tow, she felt like a convincing version of Bethany Frazer, the woman she played on television's *Anomaly* for over a hundred episodes, enough for syndication and the steady checks that came with it. She was the sleek Valerie Torrey of six years ago, whose life had never fallen apart, who'd never kidnapped her own child and run, who'd never been caught. In the glare of the bathroom lights, she looks like a shabby Halloween costume of that woman, the woman she'll be playing again at the convention tomorrow morning. She pulls a lock of hair down in front of her eyes between two fingers and examines the ends. They branch like the ends of neurons. There is no hurry now, no rush to anything. Everything is becoming inevitable, the future coming in like permanent teeth that have always been there, hiding inside the gums waiting, nestled against the skull.

"Mom?" Alex calls, swooping upward again. It brings her back into the world and her heart rises to meet the sound.

"What's up, Rabbit?"

"What's *chivalrous*?"

"Why don't you make a list and we'll go through it together?"

"I need this one now," he says plaintively. "I can't skip over it."

"Gentlemen being kind and polite to ladies," she says.

"Oh." Never *thank you*, just *oh*, as if he would've figured it out in a second anyway. She shakes her hair out and regards her reflection one last time. By the sixth season of the show, she'd internalized an image of what she was supposed to look like and dropped her weight to below her pre-pregnancy level. Her face became sharp and angular, and magazines, when they talked about her, stopped using modifiers meant to gently undermine their compliments. Her mother called after each episode aired that season to be sure she was eating. Now her face is softly rounded, like it was when she first became Bethany Frazer, like it was when she left the Midwest for school in New York, all too aware of every cliché she was embodying. She wonders if, moving across the country toward her point of origin and then away from it, she will transform back into that girl, then into the Hollywood version of herself she briefly became. She wonders what version of herself she'll be when she returns to New York alone.

Leaving the bathroom light on, she stands in the doorway and watches Alex, propped up on the far bed. He's shut the book he was reading and opened his notebook. She listens as he reads aloud what he's written there.

"Ac-aht-i," he says.

"Olaf-fub," he says.

"Alu-bath-sa," he says.

Each one is pronounced deliberately, like an incantation. Sometimes he lets her look through the notebook. The pages are a hoarder's trove of language. Names of pasta shapes and streets in Boerum Hill. Phonetic approximations of the Yiddish phrases passing Hasidim muttered on the sidewalks near their apartment. Lately it had been words plotted out backwards, as if to untie them like knots and release something trapped inside. She asked Alex what he hoped a real magic word might do and he only shrugged.

"Ago-hay-uc," he says. This impossible child. Sometimes she dreams she's made him up, and in the dream she is a woman who lives alone in an apartment in Brooklyn Heights, teaching acting classes to fill her days, putting herself to sleep each night with gin on the rocks because she's forgotten to get tonic and can't be bothered with the ritual of fixing a martini. The dream is not a day in the life of this woman, it is all of her days at once, the flood of years Valerie would be drowning in if she hadn't been thrown this lifesaver, this impossible child. When she wakes up from this dream, she goes to his room and stands in the doorway watching him, like she's doing now.

He looks up from his notebook, fixing her with his eyes—huge, dark, not hers. She wonders how long he's known she's been standing there. How much of her watching he's allowed, tolerated. She is always wondering how much he knows.

"Mom, they have Showtime," he says.

"That's nice, Rabbit," she says, knowing what's coming next.

"Can I watch my dad?" he asks. Last year, Andrew landed a role on a cable sitcom about a washed-up, sexually promiscuous actor. A role he was born to play, Val thought at the time. With a certain amount of schadenfreude, Val let Alex watch the show, even though it was wildly inappropriate for an eight-year-old. It satisfied a need in Alex that Val had come to accept, but now she wonders if this wasn't the door that let Andrew back into their lives.

"Rabbit, it's all reruns till fall. Why don't you read some more?"

"They're all sleeping," he says, patting the book gently.

"You can wake them up," she says. "It's your book." He looks at her as if she's suggested something incredibly rude.

"Okay, Rabbit," she says. "What time is it on?"

"Ten to ten thirty," he says, bouncing on his knees on the bed. The book, forgotten, thumps to the floor.

"Little late," she says, shaking her head as if reconsidering.

"Mo-om." This one dive-bombs, then pulls up at the last second. She forces a grin.

"Only if you're in your PJs by quarter till," she says. "Maybe I'll get prettied up and go down to the bar for half an hour." She's never been able to stand watching the show with him, the way he leans forward toward it. Even when Andrew felt more distant, less of a threat, she couldn't take the feeling of the three of them together. "Maybe I'll meet a prince," she says.

"You're already pretty enough to meet a prince," he says. Like his dark eyes, this quick charm is Andrew's, but it's no less effective for its source. In Alex's eyes, she is ready to play Valerie Torrey, or Bethany Frazer, or whatever role tomorrow offers. She jumps onto the near bed and clambers over it with a flailing of arms and legs. She leaps across the gap between the two beds to Alex, who giggles and cowers. With cartoonish chomping noises, she plays at devouring his ears.

"You are the most delicious rabbit since Easter," she yells, and Alex squeals with joy under her assault.

# Shark Jump

Brett Kazan draws intricate dreams on his bar napkin. He works in from the edges. He uses the constraint of the space to compress concepts into ideas, ideas into images. He is using a Tachikawa .3mm that fell out of his portfolio onto the sidewalk outside of their apartment this morning. When he went to pick up the last of his things. Debra's apartment. Not theirs. Not anymore. Brett likes the .3 for fine line work. With a canvas this small, everything is fine line work.

Across the table from Brett at the bar of the Holiday Inn Cleveland, Fred Marin is still talking. One of the things Brett likes about Fred is his ability to fill space with words. When Brett draws *Lady Stardust*, the comics series they've collaborated on for three years, he leaves acres of negative space on the pages. They come back to him packed with dense verbiage. One of the comic's trademarks, Fred says. Brett's been crashing on Fred's couch in Williamsburg the past few weeks. Fred starts talking when he walks in the door and doesn't stop even after he's fallen asleep. Late at night, Brett can hear Fred muttering full, incoherent sentences into his pillow. It's better, after the almost silent last weeks with Debra, with the two of them speaking only to work out the logistics of never speaking again. Passing each other in the hall silently, or waiting for water to boil for coffee, examining their respective feet. Conversation seems like the one thing every apartment needs.

"What's left in Brooklyn anyway?" says Fred. It's likely he's been talking about Brooklyn for a while now. "You should be looking in the Bronx. There are good things happening in the Bronx." If Fred could afford it, he'd live in Manhattan, in one of those buildings that look like they're made of mercury held in stasis. A building you never see anyone coming or going from. Brett isn't sure Fred *can't* afford it. They don't talk about how Fred can afford to live alone in Williamsburg. They don't talk about money at all. Never have. But somehow Fred has made it through the middle of his twenties living in New York and never needed to hold down a steady job, while Brett has scraped by, augmenting his service industry jobs with the occasional bit of design work and the money Black Sheep Comics pays them for *Lady Stardust*. Combined with owing Debra on the rent most months, it had been a foolproof financial plan.

When he went by this morning before they left, he'd worried there might be a scene. He imagined himself and Debra standing in the kitchen in silence. Early light coming in from the east-facing window. Exactly this, a scene with no script, no dialogue. But everything he'd come to pick up was stacked in the hallway outside the apartment door. He left the keys under the welcome mat. Across the Ohio state line, he sketched the moment of finding his things in the hall. A portfolio, a guitar he didn't know more than three chords on, a Duane Reade bag of assorted T-shirts. They seemed full of meaning once he'd drawn them.

"This place is so abstract," says Fred. Fred says *abstract* when he means *cliché.* Not sure why. "It's like a set for a documentary about the set of *Cheers.* These chandeliers or whatever. Where are the velvet Elvises and sad clowns and jackalopes? What's wrong with dark wood and exposed Edison bulbs?"

"Dark wood and exposed Edison bulbs are abstractions, too," says Brett. He doesn't look up from his drawing. It's easier to adopt Fred's incorrect use of the word than to correct him.

"Elegant abstractions are still elegant," says Fred. He is drinking whiskey, which explains the rhetorical questions. "Why couldn't that be how Cleveland reinvents itself? A citywide commitment to elegance. Public works projects promoting simple lines. Municipal policy enforcing a de Stijl color palette. Who doesn't love red, white, and black?"

"Blue and yellow, too," says Brett. Fred knows art movements only from the album covers they pop up on and the comics artists they influence.

Brett stops and looks at his napkin. It's gotten cluttered. Busy. Last week at New York Comic Con, he and Fred went to Howard Berryman's booth in Artist Alley. Berryman had revolutionized comics in the seventies. Ultrarealistic style, muscles on muscles. Legendary run on *The Ferret* with Porter Coleman writing. Nowadays he couldn't get a steady gig. Berryman was selling commissioned sketches on pieces of paper no bigger than bar napkins. Head shots of the Ferret, Red Emma, the Diviner. Three hundred a pop. Took him three minutes a go, including chitchat with the buyer. A guy known for the obsessive detail of his panels making a living rendering characters with a minimum number of lines. And here's Brett, who prides himself on spacious page layouts, cramping twelve issues' worth of story onto a bar napkin. He wads it up and sets it next to his pint. It soaks up condensation from the glass. Secret blues hidden in the Tachikawa's black ink bleed out. All the lines blur into one another.

"It's Cleveland, I know," says Fred. Brett isn't sure whether he's missed any of this rant. "But Brewer and Loeb are both from Cleveland. Which means the Astounding Family was created here. Which means Metro City was created here. The capital of the Timely Comics Universe. The—I'm going to say this—the greatest fictional location outside of Milton's Hell. Is based on Cleveland."

Brett scans the bar. Not because he's ignoring Fred. Because Brett's mind survives on a diet of visual details. He examines the chandeliers. At first they look identical. Mass-produced. But the lines of leading between the panels of stained glass are shaky. Handmade. The bar is full of people here for Heronomicon. Brett recognizes a lot of them from New York Con last week. Clever T-shirts. The shirts will be cleverer tomorrow. People save the cleverest shirts for day of. It's a mix of fans and professionals. Most of them doing better, moneywise, than Brett and Fred. Freelancers from the Big Two companies, Timely and National, mostly. Fred says he and Brett are retaining their artistic integrity. Brett takes some comfort that while he's on the same rung of the ladder as these guys, he's at least potentially climbing. Devlin over there, for instance. Kung fu T-shirt, bad goatee. Had a hot second three, four years ago. Does fill-ins for National now. Makes more than Brett does, but it's as much as he'll ever make. The industry's only recently created this artistic working class within itself. Fred talks about it all the time. Still, if either of the Big Two came calling with a contract, they'd jump. Part of this trip is about getting discovered. Enough Triple-A ball. Brett thinks that's the appropriate sports metaphor, anyway.

"So the DNA of Metro City is somewhere, dormant, in the genetic material of Cleveland. Levi Loeb was able to find it and grow it into an ideal city. Like Mister Astounding did to create the Perfectional. But now that we have the healthy template, couldn't we start to graft bits of Metro City's DNA back into Cleveland, but active this time? Couldn't we take a broken real city and re-create it as a functioning fictional one?"

At the bar, a redhead orders a drink. In profile, she looks familiar. Line of nose sweeps from brow like a flipped parenthesis. Strong chin, almost masculine but not. She turns away and Brett tries to place her. Something from years ago.

"Isn't that the woman from *Anomaly*?" he asks. Fred is filling the skies over Cleveland with silver dirigibles, but he stops to follow Brett's eyes.

"Valerie Torrey?" he says. "What would she be doing in Cleveland?"

"She'd be a big get for Heronomicon," he says. "Headliner, even."

"She'd be a big get ten years ago," says Fred. He's decided he's too cool for all this. "What's she done since *Anomaly*?"

"Theater, maybe," says Brett, sipping his beer. "Whatever people do after TV."

"*Anomaly* was always overrated," says Fred. "At least half of it objectively sucked." Brett knows Fred is being contrary and he shouldn't engage. He remembers the poster of Frazer and Campbell hanging in their dorm room. On Fred's side. But it's likely Fred will go on regardless. Better a conversation than a monologue.

"Objective suck?" he says.

"Irredeemable suck," says Fred.

"When's the shark jump?"

"The shark jump was ten years ago, I'm saying. Now your Miss Torrey there is past prime."

"Ten years," says Brett. It seems like an overestimate. "What season?" he asks.

"Minutes after the season-three finale," says Fred. "The very moment Frazer and Campbell fuck. The second Campbell's cock—"

"Point made," says Brett. He must have missed Fred ordering a whiskey. Usually it's rhetorical questions after two, swearing after four.

"It's the *Moonlighting* curse," says Fred. "And they never learn."

"I liked season four," says Brett.

"You only think you liked it," says Fred, "because you liked the first three. You were being charitable, hoping it would return to form. Objectively, it sucked." Sometimes Fred informs Brett, in detail, what Brett's opinions are. He's done it since college. He runs at about twenty percent correct. "And it got worse from there. Season six was abominable." Another of Fred's favorite words. Most of them start with *A*. "The end of that show was a mercy killing."

Given the way the show ended, it's an awful thing to say. But Brett downs his last swig of beer in silence. "Another?" Brett asks. Fred nods, almost glumly.

"I'll buy if you go up and talk to her," Fred says. Brett looks over his shoulder at her. She is tracing a circle around the base of her martini glass. Looking at nothing in particular.

"Give me twenty up front," says Brett. "If I chicken out, I'll give it back."

Fred makes a show of extracting his wallet from his back pocket, takes out a twenty. He pauses and shakes his head. "Past prime," he says. "Bet's only worth ten."

Brett snatches the twenty out of Fred's hand and heads to the bar.

Despite Fred's opinion of his opinion, Brett enjoyed all of *Anomaly*.

Even tried to get Debra into it on DVD. She wasn't big on sci-fi. Bad sign. In college, though, they'd plan their Sunday nights around it. He and Fred. Rush back from the dining hall to be settled in by nine. After each episode, they'd get high and come up with time travel stories. Unintelligible, mostly. The trouble with time travel is no rules. The first rule when they'd started working on *Lady Stardust* was rules. They had a bible before Brett drew a panel. The second rule was no working high.

Valerie Torrey, then, is as close to a celebrity as it gets, as far as Brett's concerned. He fingers Fred's twenty in his pocket. He anticipates handing it back over along with their drinks. He's no good at approaching normal girls on his best days. Debra approached him. Before her, not a lot to speak of. By the time he's thought to think about what to say, he's standing next to her. Awkward close. Casting a shadow on her drink in weird colors. Muted browns and oranges.

She turns to him. Eyes light green. *Jade,* he thinks. Television ten years ago must have had terrible picture quality. Her eyes were never this green on the show.

"Hi," she says.

"Hi," he says. Stands there. Somewhere in the final issue, Lady Stardust should wear a jade dress. She should wear it on the cover. Sell a million copies. Green, like that. She's waiting for him to say something. "You're Valerie Torrey," he says. Charmer. Go around informing people of their own names. Worse than Fred.

"I am," she says.

"You're here for the convention," he says. Good. Excellent. Tell her why she's here.

"I am," she says, and waits.

"I am, too," he says, out of breath. Why out of breath? "I'm an artist. *Lady Stardust.*"

"Your name is Lady Stardust?"

"No," he says. "It's the comic I draw. Black Sheep Comics? I thought you might have . . ." Trails off. Of course she hasn't.

"I don't read comics much," she says. Of course she doesn't. Who does? "Is it good?"

He shrugs. "It's a little over the top. Transvestite lounge-singer spy forced to kill her lover a dozen times to save him. My friend over there writes it." He points to Fred, who's been staring at them. Can probably hear Brett wheezing like a fat kid in gym class. Fred waves enthusiastically. Obviously drunk. She waves politely back. "It's glammy," Brett continues. Babbling now. "Which people are still buying. Fluorescent eye shadow. Martian go-go dancers. Sex, hallucinogens, and galactic ennui. Fred's working through his Byron-on-acid phase."

He is willing himself to shut up. He is reminding himself he has won the bet. So shut up.

"So not for kids," she says.

A panel from issue eleven. Lady Stardust, transvestite transplanetary cabaret starlet. Standing behind her lover, David, currently incarnated as a mute clown named Beep Beep. One of her hands points a ray gun over his shoulder and directly at the reader. The other is down the front of his pants. All seen through the ragged bloody hole she's shot through an alien mobster's head.

"No," he says. "Not for kids."

"Huh," she says. She turns away from him a little. Showing her profile. Finishes her drink.

"Can I buy you another?" he asks. She smiles and shakes her head. She moves slowly. Like an actress in an old movie. There's a word. *Languid.*

"I have a gentleman waiting for me upstairs," she says. There is something femme fatale sexy about this.

"I—oh—" Brett stammers. "I wasn't trying to—" Wasn't he? The thought of a chance hadn't occurred to him. Blood rushes to his cheeks. She starts laughing. Not malicious. Languid. Femme fatale gone.

"I'm sorry," she says. "I couldn't resist saying it that way." She smiles at him. Warm. Friendly. Smile that says he never had a chance. "It's my son," she says. "I left him watching TV for a bit, but I have to get back."

She takes a bill out of the small black rectangle of her purse. Puts it on the bar. She stands up to go.

"Your friend," she says, "did he dare you to come up and talk to me? He's been watching us pretty intently."

"He bet me twenty bucks," Brett says. He pulls the twenty out of his pocket. Crumpled and damp with his sweat. Disgusted, he puts it back.

"Twenty bucks to talk to me?"

"Just to talk," Brett says.

She looks at him. Look of a mother, not a lover. She leans over and kisses him on the cheek.

"I'm glad you won your bet," she says. She makes her way past him. Toward the exit.

"Miss Torrey?" Brett says after she's passed him. She turns back.

"I liked season six," he says. She assesses this. Remnant of another conversation. Wreckage from a different ship. She nods and leaves the bar.

# Live-Action Role-Playing

The screen goes black and the credits appear. Andrew Rhodes is Ted Kammen, they say.

Alex's dad is Andrew Rhodes, a television actor who lives in Los Angeles and whom Alex hasn't seen in six years.

Alex's dad is Ted Kammen, a movie actor who lives in Los Angeles whom Alex has spent the past half hour with.

Alex's dad is Ian Campbell, an agent for a secret government organization that tracks threats to the timestream, whom Alex has never met but has heard a lot about.

All of these are true, Alex thinks, even though some of them aren't real. Stories can be true even if they're not real. When Alex thinks about his dad, which he does, often, it's as a knot of these three threads. There are memories of him, which are mostly bits of sensory information: a smell, the feeling of being lifted into the air. There is the image of him on-screen, carrying out actions and storylines Alex can barely comprehend and doesn't feel the need to follow. And there are the stories his mother tells him, which are never about her and his dad directly, but always about the characters they once played on television. None of these on its own is Alex's dad, but the interaction between them makes an outline in his mind, something dad-shaped and of vital importance to Alex.

Alex jots a few of the actors' last names in his notebook for later. There's an actress who plays a Russian maid, and her last name is Gradechenko. It sounds promising, but he doesn't have time to flip it backwards right now.

The credits are almost over. Alex jumps off the bed and goes to shut off the air-conditioning, which he turned up to full blast the minute his mom left. The air conditioner goes silent, leaving a hole in the room's sounds, and in that hole Alex can hear a small metal rattling: his mom's keys in the lock. He never worries. She is always on time.

"Did you meet a prince?" he asks before she is through the door.

"Nope," she says, kicking off her pretty shoes. "No princes tonight." She shuts the door gently behind her, but the lock still makes a loud click.

"Oh."

"It's freezing in here," she says, rubbing her bare arms. Alex pretends not to notice, but of course he wants it freezing in here. Freezing in here increases his chances of being cuddled, possibly under blankets. It's one of the only things he hates about summers in New York. In their apartment with the air conditioner that only cools half of one room, hers, sometimes attempts to cuddle are squirmy and uncomfortable. This hotel has a very good air conditioner.

"How was your father?" she asks him. This reminds him he's left the TV on, and the next show, which he's not allowed to watch, is starting. He finds the remote and turns it off.

"It was a good one," he says. "It was funny and nobody gets sad."

"That does sound good," she says, pushing his hair back to kiss him on the forehead. She stands and smiles at him. She's been doing that a lot lately, and it makes him worried. It's like she's making notes of everything about him so she doesn't forget.

"Tell me a story?" he asks, half because he wants her to stop standing there smiling and half because he wants a story.

"After I get my PJs on?" she says.

"After you get your PJs on," he agrees.

When she comes back, he convinces her to stay in the bed with him while she tells the story and he cuddles her extra. This involves both arms around her waist and the top of his head nuzzled into the hollow below her shoulder.

"What season do you want?" she asks, once they are settled in and the big lights are off.

"What's the first one ever," asks Alex, "storyline or freak of the week?"

His mom thinks about this. Alex has never been allowed to watch *Anomaly,* because his mom says it's graphic. But from his mom's interpretations of the episodes, which Alex suspects she waters down a little for him, he understands that every episode falls into one of two categories: storyline or freak of the week. The freak-of-the-week episodes are more or less interchangeable, although they can be kind of affected by what season they're in, because of the storyline episodes. Like, if it's season three, Campbell and Frazer are never together, even in the freak-of-the-weeks, because Campbell is lost in the timestream and sometimes Frazer is looking for him and sometimes she is doing her job. The storyline episodes have to be in order, from season one to season six, or at least up to season five. Mostly the stuff in season six doesn't make any sense.

She nods, puts her finger on her chin, and scrunches up her whole face. This is her "considering the options" face, and it makes him incredibly happy because it always comes before a story. She clears her throat. Her story voice is a little different from her regular; deeper, more deliberate.

"The first episode I'd have to say is storyline," his mom concludes.

"Good," says Alex. "That's what I want then."

# *Anomaly* Pilot

Tim seeded so much in that first episode. Because she was there the whole time and knows how much the plot changed from season to season, sometimes from week to week, she knows it wasn't a straight line from the beginning to the end. But you could look back from the end and see a straight line to the beginning.

"It all starts with a weird light in the sky above a field in Kansas," she says. She thinks it's Kansas. It might have been Nebraska. "The light gets brighter and brighter, and then there's a flash and a man falls out of the light and lands in the field."

"How far does he fall?" asks Alex.

"Maybe twenty feet. Not far. He's safe when he lands. As soon as he lands, he checks his watch and says, 'Not again!'" She leans in very close to his face to deliver this line with the proper mix of comedy and gravitas. Comedy wins, and he breaks out in giggles. Not one to miss an opportunity, Val yells, "Cue the opening credits," and begins to mercilessly tickle him. A lack of mercy is essential to any good tickle attack. Alex writhes and wriggles and cries "Quit it!" again and again, but Val does not let up until her work is done. This takes roughly as long as *Anomaly*'s opening credits, which featured Daliesque images of melting clocks and watches whose hands spun backwards, then exploded in a mess of innards: escape wheels, springs, and stop levers. Tim always hated the opening sequence, saying it was too literal.

"Next scene!" she says, adjusting Alex's position next to her so they are properly fitted together. "A lecture hall at a major university."

"Harvard?" Alex asks.

"Sure," Val says. "The same man we saw fall into a field is now lecturing a classful of students about the nature of spacetime."

"What's spacetime?" Alex asks, even though he is one of the very few nine-year-olds in the known universe with an understanding of spacetime.

"You should listen to his lecture," she says. She drops her voice into a lower tenor. "'The universe is like a garden full of forking paths. Every time you or I or any of us make a decision, the path splits again. When you decided to come to class today instead of stay in bed with your boyfriend'"—here she tickles him a little—"'you created two possible timelines. One in which you came to class, the timeline we're in, and one in which you didn't. These splits happen a billion trillion times a day; each split creates a different timeline, a different universe. If you look backwards, you'll see one path behind you. The path you've been walking the whole time. Your universe. But if you could hover up above the garden, you'd see billions and billions of paths running parallel to one another. The question is, what keeps them parallel to one another, what keeps them from intersecting? And what would happen if they did?'"

"Mom?" he says. "Is that man my dad?"

"No," she says, "that man is Ian Campbell, a professor of theoretical physics from ten years in our future. But we don't know that yet." She can see he is disappointed by this, but she is careful, when telling these stories, to keep Ian Campbell and Bethany Frazer separate from Andrew Rhodes and Valerie Torrey. The former, after all, get a happier ending.

"Right, then," she says. "Agent Bethany Frazer busts into the lecture hall." Alex always gets excited when Frazer makes her entrance. "'Professor Campbell,' she says, 'your government would like a word with you.'"

"Do they fall in love right away?" Alex asks.

"How do you know they fall in love?" says Val. Alex rolls his eyes at her. It is tough to know what his rules for any given retelling are going to be. Generally, he will listen to one episode as if he's never heard any that come after it, but sometimes he will consider them as a whole, inspecting each episode for possible errors in continuity. "They don't fall in love right then," she tells him. "They don't even like each other at first. He's arrogant and his head's so caught up in spacetime and multiverses that sometimes he doesn't see what's right in front of him. And she's stubborn and literal. And sometimes she doesn't see what's right in front of her, either."

"But they fall in love eventually," he says.

"Don't get ahead of things," she says. "Right now, there's a case she needs to solve. The Statue of Liberty has disappeared, right in front of the eyes of a million New Yorkers. So Agent Frazer is taking Professor Campbell with her to Anomaly Division."

It had been Val who'd dropped out of the sky and Andrew who brought her in. Val had hardly settled into thinking of herself as a proper New Yorker when she'd gone in for the *Anomaly* audition. She was sharing an apartment she couldn't afford, in the Lower East Side, with four other aspiring actresses. Of the five of them, Val had experienced the most artistic success with the least financial reward, having landed a number of serious roles in small theater productions.

Val had landed in Los Angeles the day before the first read-through, her belongings creeping across the country in a Penske van. She'd lain awake on a bare mattress in a barren new apartment in Culver City, listening to the air conditioner buzz. Tired and disoriented, she showed up at the studio to find everyone frantic, for reasons she couldn't determine. She stood in the doorway, afraid that if she stepped into the room she'd be trampled. Andrew strode—there was no other word for it—across the room and extended his hand.

"You're Valerie, right?" he said. She knew of him, mostly from her former roommates, who had told her about his current role as Herc Bronsnan on *Sands in the Hourglass,* but she'd never been around a television in the afternoon to actually see him. Her first impressions of him were of bigness and stillness. He blocked out the entire room with his height and breadth, but also served as a point of calm amid the bustle. She shook his hand, amazed at the smallness of her own hand inside it. "You done much television?" he asked.

"No," she said. "Theater mostly."

"How legitimate," he said. She examined his face to see if this was meant to be a withering comment, but he retained a wide, good-natured smile. He took her by the arm. "Let me introduce you to the circus," he said, which became a running joke over the next few weeks as Andrew, along with his then girlfriend, Nico, who costarred with him on *Sands* as a seductress coincidentally named Nico, integrated Val into a world of actors and actresses who, if they were not more successful than Val's friends in New York, certainly lived as if they were. *Anomaly* had been picked up for thirteen episodes on the basis of the reputation of its creator, Tim Whelan. They shot the first four episodes before the pilot aired, while Val split her free time between tagging along with Andrew and Nico to parties and restaurants and being gently parented by Tim and his wife, Rachel.

She was grateful that Bethany Frazer was such a grounded part: whatever chaos raged around her, she spent her working hours as a precise and efficient agent with little time for distractions. Her friendship with Rachel developed quickly as something separate from her working relationship with Tim. The two of them shared a sense of outsider status, although Rachel had grown up in Los Angeles. Her exclusion was more professional, as the tiny world of L.A. galleries seemed quaint next to the apparatus of cultural production the rest of them toiled away at. She'd spent time in New York in her twenties, when she was the same age as Val, and she'd returned home to L.A. only because she met Tim. By the time Val met her, she'd been back for almost twenty years.

Her work at the time was a thing of large canvases and sprawl, with a sometimes Rothko-level abstraction, but over the years Val knew her, her paintings became smaller and smaller, more intricate and concrete, until by the end her canvases were postcard small and packed with fine detail. Rachel had the strange ability to carry on conversation while she painted, and Val often thought their friendship grew faster because it was incubated under the light of Rachel's work.

After Nico left Andrew, she had called Val up late one night, drunk, and said, "Don't touch him. Keep everything professional or you'll be sorry." Val wasn't sure if it was a warning or a threat. After the call, she never heard from Nico again, and Andrew did indeed keep it professional, now content to say goodnight at the end of a day's shooting. The flirtatious sparring of their characters colored their off-camera conversations, and without writers to script it for her, Val sometimes caught herself trying in her spare time to come up with things to say to him, jokes and exit lines. When this happened, she'd remind herself that the intimacy between them was not a product of their professional relationship; it was the whole of their professional relationship. She thought of Andrew as a friend, but really they were partners, without the romantic or sexual connotations people sometimes heaped onto that word. If it weren't for the show, Andrew wasn't someone whose company she'd ever seek out. He was talented, though not as talented as he imagined, and exasperating, and funny and full of bluster. In another age, when looks and ego weighed in heavier, he might have been not a Grant or a Gable, but a William Holden maybe, a down-at-heel marquee idol, to be dreamed about by women who still dreamed but no longer considered themselves dreamers. Charming, but in a way you couldn't quite trust. Unless you kept your expectations of him low, which she did. Val learned that she could trust him to be Andrew, consistently, for whatever that was worth.

# Secret Identities

"He. Is so. Cute," says the Astounding Woman, who sets down her platinum wig on the table so she can hold Alex's face in her hands, appraising it.

"He's not cute," corrects Red Emma, buttoning a crimson trench coat that ends at the upper part of her thigh. "He's too old to be cute. He's handsome."

There commences a fluttering about Alex that takes Valerie by surprise, so accustomed has she become to Alex's cuteness, the objective fact of it. Her understanding is that children are always attractive to their parents, a preservative quirk of genetics, but there must be parents who know in moments of clarity that their sons and daughters are not the handsomest or prettiest. But here is Alex, who objectively and factually is, and here is the proof: twelve women, each in the revealing costume of a superheroine, each judged attractive enough by someone to carry off said costume, all of them swooning over Alex.

"I'm at a good age," Alex says, "where I'm both cute and handsome."

This sends the women into hysterics, like Alex knew it would. Valerie wonders if there isn't something less dangerous about parenting an unattractive child. Maybe with eyes less deep and dark, lashes less like scimitars, cheekbones less apple-esque, Alex would have a tougher time being liked, would have to work harder at it. How does one build character in a beautiful child, when the world lines up to hand him things? She never worries about him being some pretty little idiot; there has never been a risk of that. She worries he will grow up to be simply charming and nothing more. The kind of person who coasts on a bare minimum of effort and the airy cushion of his looks. Put concisely and inhospitably, she worries he'll grow up to be exactly like his father.

When they first arrived in the convention hall, which was only a ballroom filled with folding tables, Val and Alex were greeted by Randall, who immediately informed them that everything was going great. She would not have guessed from looking around that things were going great. At one end of the room, men who looked like they'd served in at least one world war were schlepping long white boxes full of comic books and setting up racks of comics that were as impossibly old as the men selling them, and often in similar states of decay. The other end looked like the morning after at a frat house, scruffy boys in their twenties and thirties high-fiving and slap-assing as they hung drawings of women in contorted poses on displays where they could lure passersby. Val's signing table, which featured several *Anomaly* posters Randall assured her were vintage, was right in the middle of the room, one in a row of eight. Behind them, clean-cut college kids in brand-new T-shirts strung up big banners that read TIMELY and NATIONAL, one on either side of her.

Randall's exact role in the convention was unclear, but he was the person who contacted Val about appearing. "I know we're still a second-string con," he said on the phone a few weeks earlier, "but we've got some big names." Val wasn't sure that category included her. "I think this year is going to put Heronomicon on the map." She didn't how he'd gotten her number, but it served as a reminder of how very findable she was, how bad at hiding she'd become. It was Randall's offer that had given her the idea to travel west this way. Being paid to appear. She'd called her agent and was informed that while she was too late to get on board for the convention in New York, there was one in Chicago a week after Cleveland, and of course the big one in Los Angeles, where Tiger's Paw Media, who now owned the rights to all the *Anomaly* episodes, would be announcing the release of a remastered box set and was putting together a "major panel" that would feature Andrew Rhodes. Elise made a few calls, and soon Val had a solid appearance fee in Chicago and a relatively ridiculous appearance fee for Los Angeles.

Randall, it turned out, was lumbering, tall, and broad, with a spastic way of moving that was exaggerated by his size. He regularly knocked things off tables as he passed and stopped to apologize to the jostled objects. From the slickness of his hair, Val judged that Randall had not showered since yesterday, and the live-wire staccato of his speech made her wonder if he had slept.

"I ended your afternoon session for tomorrow at three," he said, "so you could catch the Levi Loeb panel if you want. I heard Loeb is here somewhere. I'm not even sure I'd recognize him. No one's taken a picture of him in years. It's a big deal for the con." Val didn't know the name, but she knew there was a lot of excitement around it. It's something she likes quite a bit about this little world: the capability of those within it to get deeply and sincerely excited about things. She wonders how they fare in the real world, where excitement is poorly valued, and she tries to think of things she has been excited about. There are so few.

As the morning progressed, crowds began to show up, and soon there was a line to meet Val. Alex sat quietly behind her with his book as Val faced her fans for the first time in years. They all smiled. Some of them wouldn't look her in the eyes, but some of them looked her in the eyes with a scary intensity, as if they were trying to read something written on the inside of her skull. Many of them called her Ms. Torrey, or Mrs. Torrey. Some of them called her Frazer or even Bethany, and then corrected themselves. The ones who called her Val or Valerie, these were the ones who wanted to touch her in some way, a handshake or a photo with their arm around her.

They had pictures of a version of herself she barely remembered. They had pictures from when she'd made herself too skinny, thinking that was the way television stars were expected to look. They had pictures of her from when she was pregnant with Alex, her face full and round and healthy, when Tim and the other writers scrambled to figure out a plot device that would explain her increasingly apparent pregnancy, until Tim hit upon the perfect one: pregnancy. They had pictures of her with Andrew, her standing in front of him protectively, both of them looking at the camera like it was a threat. For a second she thought, *What a good-looking couple. They should be on television.*

The sameness of it surprised her, the uniformity of interaction. Sometimes one of them would relate a personal anecdote about the show or recount the plot of a favorite episode. Was this how it sounded to Alex when she told him stories at night? By now he knows the plots as well as she ever did. Was he humoring her by listening, the same way she was humoring them?

After an hour or so, when there was a lull in the line, she flagged down Randall and begged for a break. He gave her directions to the women's dressing room, which, he admitted, was actually a kitchenette off the main ballroom, then darted away, likely to inform someone else how great everything was going.

"Alex," she said, tapping him until he looked up from his book. "Let's take a little break." He nodded, put his book in his backpack, slung it over his shoulder, and plodded after her.

Now, surrounded by women, he's rooting in his bag to retrieve it.

"Rabbit," she says, "you want to scope the place out for a bit?"

"Where are you going to be?" he asks.

"I'm going back out to the table to sign autographs," she says. "It won't be very exciting." Alex looks around at the dozen women in the dressing room, and Val senses that in maybe two years there will be no pause: by then nothing will persuade the boy to leave the company of so much exposed female flesh. But now it's not the tight clothes and cooing that are causing the hesitation, it's the umbilical tether, which Val is relieved to know still pulls taut now and then. Alex looks back at her, confirming this.

"I guess I'll walk around a little," he says. They exchange their litany of limits and assurances. He won't go far enough to get lost. He knows exactly where she'll be. All this established, he wriggles into his backpack and leaves the dressing room. The pang as the door shuts behind him is not new, but she hasn't felt it in a while, and in its return, it has changed. It's no longer the pang of a first exit, but the feeling that the number of Alex's departures from her is finite in a way that is new, that is awful.

"You're going to have to keep that one on a leash," says ExSanguina, but she's put her prosthetic fangs in, and the last word sounds more like *leech*. "Or in a glass case." *Glasch kaytch*.

"I'm just glad I didn't bring my daughters," says the Diviner, who has been ready for longer than any of them, since her costume is a purple sateen robe spattered with silver stars, and a blindfold, see-through, which she won't put on until the last minute. She is dark-skinned and her eyes are a peculiarly yellow shade, which Val thinks it a shame to cover up. "A wake of broken hearts behind that one, I can see it."

"You have daughters?" asks Prospera. Her costume can best be described as "sexy magician" or "sexy magician's assistant," which is to say a top hat, tight tuxedo jacket, and fishnet stockings.

The Diviner nods. "Three of them," she says. She reaches into her robe and produces a small photo she's been keeping in her bra, on the left side near her heart. She hands it to OuterGirl. The picture begins to make its way around the room, eliciting *aww*s and other compliments.

"You look so fantastic for someone who's had three kids," says Prospera.

"I think what you meant was 'You look so fantastic,' right?" says the Diviner, with an eyebrow cocked, getting a laugh that is clearly uncomfortable for half the women in the room. There is a lacuna of about ten years in the women's ages. The oldest of the younger set, Iota, whose costume consists of normal clothes sized large enough that they provocatively fall off her in a carefully arranged manner, is twenty-five, and the youngest of the older set is ExSanguina, who is thirty-five. Val wonders if there is something about women in those intervening years deemed undesirable by the culture. Something about a thirty-year-old that falls between the cracks of a high school boy's dream of a girl and a high school boy's dream of a woman, she thinks, wondering why high school boys forever call the tune when it comes to the culture's ideas of attractive women.

"Why don't you bring your daughters?" asks Flail, who, along with her identical twin sister, Flog, is dressed in bondage gear. In what Val sees as another odd choice, the company that hires the costume girls chose real-life twins, even though their masks obscure most of their faces.

"You have to ask me that?" says the Diviner, tousling the cat-o'-nine-tails hanging from Flog's belt.

"I don't think it's problematic to expose young girls to empowering forms of sexuality," says Flail defensively.

"You bring that costume from home?" asks Red Emma. Her hair, a dark, curly mass, has been compacted into a topknot that fits neatly into her fedora.

"And if I did?" Flail asks. "Does that make me some kind of sex freak?"

"Studies show," adds Flog, pulling tight the laces on a black leather boot, "no connection whatsoever between sadomasochistic sexual tendencies and other forms of mental illness."

"That's great news for you guys," says Red Emma.

"I don't think what we're doing is about sex," says Spectacle Girl, whose costume is entirely translucent down to her flesh-colored bodysuit. "It's about imagination."

"That outfit," says OuterGirl, "leaves nothing to the imagination."

"She's right, though," says the Astounding Woman, who might be the oldest of the group. "I used to dream about the Astounding Woman when I was a kid. She was very inspiring. It's kind of a thrill as an adult to actually be her."

"You do mean dress up as her, right?" asked Red Emma.

"She was a real role model to me," the Astounding Woman continues. "She had a family, she was a mother. But she was still her own person, still had adventures, still held her own."

"I'm fine with the role model thing," says OuterGirl. "But why do we have to be busting out of our costumes like this? If I was going to battle aliens or whatever, I'd wear a sports bra rather than a push-up."

"Comics and film are visual industries," says Flail. "The visual is always sexual."

"Male superheroes are no less idealized than female," says Flog. "You could argue that forcing bodies into hyperrealistic shapes has the effect of desexualizing them. "

"I'm sorry," says OuterGirl, tracing the low cut of her top with a finger, "this does not feel desexualized to me."

"What is the male equivalent of cleavage?" asks Ferret Lass, applying heavy black makeup around her eyes.

"I bet in the boys' dressing room," says OuterGirl, "they are not adjusting oversized codpieces right now."

"*That's* the equivalent?" says Ferret Lass. "Gross."

"You're falsely equating sexualization with disempowerment," says Flail. "Very second wave."

"You're falsely equating sexualization with empowerment," says OuterGirl. "Very lipstick feminism."

"The cleavage is a necessary evil," says Spectacle Girl. "It's a fact of life that boys need visual stimulation to be interested in female characters."

"But the reverse isn't true," says Red Emma.

"Women aren't enough of a force in the market to dictate terms," says Spectacle Girl.

"In what market aren't we a force?" asks Red Emma. "Or at least a potential force?"

"Look, y'all," says the Diviner, "I'm saying someday, when I'm playing Lady Macbeth in Central Park, I'll bring the girls to come watch. But as long as I'm spending my summers as Slutty Tiresias on the con circuit, they're staying at home with their dad."

"Lady Macbeth," says Red Emma. "Now there's a role model."

# Artist Alley

The fat man leans over. At any moment, a cold drop of his sweat will drip off him and onto Brett's very own personal neck. Run a wet, alien trail down his back before evaporating into the convention hall's dry, conditioned air. Leave a salty trace of the fat man on Brett's skin.

"You should make her boobs bigger," he says. His breath reeks of a specific sandwich. Cheesesteak.

"You think so?" Brett asks. He stops and examines the drawing he's working on. Medea, a Timely Comics character Brett is often asked to draw at conventions like this. A sword-wielding pose half defensive, half come-hither. Suggests to the buyer of the sketch that she is ready to cut him in twain if he approaches, but secretly she hopes he will. "I always think of her as having more a ninja physique."

"She's a ninja and a witch," the man informs him. Brett is unclear what bearing this has on her cup size.

"But, you know," Brett says, "ninja." Indicates the taut lines of the drawing. "Lithe."

"I think her boobs should be bigger," he says. Brett picks up a lump of eraser from the table. Uncreates most of Medea's torso. With the man still leering over his shoulder, begins sketching the rounded lines that will indicate anatomically improbable breasts.

"You know she wasn't always a ninja," the man explains. "When she was first introduced, she was a witch. But in the early nineties, she was kidnapped by the Finger and Thumb and brainwashed into a ninja." He says this the way you might tell a stranger about your mother's Lasik surgery. Brett nods. Focus on the drawing. On the cash the man will hand him when he's finished.

It's around two. Brett has been working on this sketch for twenty minutes. This is the first person who's talked to him all day. When Brett asked him if he was a fan of his work, the man said he'd never seen any of it before. Describing the plot of *Lady Stardust* to him nearly cost Brett the commission.

"Sounds a little . . . queer," said the man. But he still pays. He walks away very happy with the augmented drawing of a comic book character far more popular than Brett and Fred's creation could ever be.

Brett turns to a blank page. Thinks about getting some work done on the final issue. Then he notices there's a kid, a real kid, paging through his portfolio. Dark hair flopping over dark eyes. Upper teeth resting on lower lip like socked feet on a coffee table. Clean pair of jeans and a T-shirt that says THE BOOK WAS BETTER.

"How's it going?" he asks the kid. This seems like an all-ages-appropriate question. Brett has very little experience with kids. Williamsburg, you can avoid them almost entirely. Although less so every year.

"It's going well," says the kid. Brett is impressed by the grammatical correctness of the answer. "Who was that guy?" he asks.

"Someone who probably lives with his mother," says Brett. Quietly, though. There may be several people within earshot who also cohabit with their mothers. Brett can't afford to lose a potential customer.

"I live with my mother," says the kid defensively. He taps on a stack of *Lady Stardust* comics. "Did you draw all these? They're really good."

"Thanks," Brett says. It's possible kids are easily impressed in general. Or this kid in particular. Brett isn't sure. The kid continues flipping through the portfolio. Doesn't seem put off or taken aback by any of the nudity or violence, but doesn't seem pruriently interested, either. Brett expects the kid will see a character he recognizes, maybe the Mister Astounding sketch, then quickly lose interest. But the kid continues through the portfolio as if he wants to see how it all ends.

Turning the last page, the kid looks up at Brett. Eyes wide and so dark the pupils are indistinguishable from the irises.

"Do you ever draw robots?" the kid asks.

"You looking for a commission?" Brett asks, smiling.

"Yes," says the kid after mulling it over. "We should totally do a co-mission." Something strange in the way he says it. Like hearing your voice echoing back at you but saying something different. The kid sticks his hand across the table. "My name's Alex," he says. Brett takes his hands and shakes it.

"Brett," he says. Alex nods. He spots the chair next to Brett.

"Do you think I can take that?" he asks.

"My partner might be back in a little bit," says Brett. "It's technically his chair."

"Your partner?"

"My writer," says Brett.

"Oh," says Alex. "I'm a writer, too." He comes around the table and sits next to Brett. "So there's a boy and a robot in a cave," he says. He looks at Brett, waiting.

"Okay," says Brett. Picks up his pages and pencil. "Tell me about the boy."

"He's older than me," Alex says, "but younger than you. Like high school age. And he has blond hair." He taps the blank page as he says this. It must be important somehow. Brett sketches the skeleton of a figure. Pauses.

"Long or short hair?"

"Long," he says. On top of the vague boy's head, a mop of hair appears.

"What's he wearing?" Brett asks.

Alex nods and chews on his lower lip. "Regular clothes," he says. Brett eyeballs what Alex is wearing and outfits the boy in a T-shirt and jeans. "They should be dirty, but not raggedy," says Alex. Brett nods and adds stains to the shirt and pants.

"What about the robot?" Brett asks. While he waits for Alex to answer, he creates a cave behind the boy, darkening in crags and shadows. When it's done, he looks up. Alex is gnawing on his lip again, his brow creasing. "Is he like R2-D2 or C-3PO?" asks Brett.

"He's short," says Alex. Tentative. Finding out, learning it for himself as he talks. "Like R2-D2 height. But he's shaped like a person. And he's silver, not gold. But not shiny silver, more like gray and metal."

"Does he have any buttons or dials?" asks Brett.

"He does," says Alex, "but they're on the inside. He has a big panel on his chest and it opens up to show all his buttons and dials."

Brett nods and draws the robot, which takes less time than drawing the boy. There are fewer lines, less detail. The robot's body is a cylinder. Brett draws it in three lines, plus more for the panel and lots of little lines for the buttons and dials. Its arms and legs are weird and thin and bendy, but its hands and feet look like people's hands and feet. Brett pauses before drawing the head.

"How realistic is the face?" he asks. "How much like a person?"

"If you make it too much like a person, there's no point in it even being a robot," says Alex, scratching his chin. "But it has to have some kind of face so the boy will know where to look when he's talking to it." He looks up at Brett, excited. "That means the robot can talk! I didn't know that before." Alex examines the headless robot. "He should have eyes," he says. "And a mouth. But that's it."

Brett obliges, drawing two perfectly round eyes and a rectangular slit of a mouth. He touches up a few details, erasing stray lines here and there, then shows Alex the drawing.

"There you go, Alex," says Brett. "I'll tell you what: it's on the house." He rips the page out of his sketchbook and hands it to Alex, but Alex is looking at the blank page underneath.

"Are you done?" Alex asks. Brett looks at him, unsure why he seems so disappointed. "I thought we were doing a co-mission," Alex says.

"I know, but I'm not going to charge you, kid," says Brett. "This was kind of fun."

"We have to figure out what happens next," says Alex, pointing to the blank page.

"Nothing happens next," says Brett. "It's a picture."

Alex glares at him. "It's a story," he says. "It's just starting, so it looks like a picture."

"Okay, so what happens next?" asks Brett.

Alex looks at the picture again. "Well, no one wants to hear a story about a boy sitting in a cave," he says.

"That does sound pretty boring," Brett agrees.

Alex bites his lip, scratches his chin. "I'm going to think about it and I'll meet you back here tomorrow," he says. He rolls up the drawing carefully. Then jumps out of the chair and takes off, running a few feet. He skids to a stop, comes back over to Brett, and shakes his hand one more time before turning, dashing, and disappearing into the crowd.

# Secret Origin of Captain Wonder

*They call you names. Crip. Gimp. Crutch. The word for it is* metonymy. *The part comes to stand for the whole. The crown becomes the kingdom. The piece of wood that stands in for your flawed leg becomes all of you. Your brokenness becomes all of you.*

*You know the word because your entire world is words. You can move through words deftly, you can run and jump and fly through them. You can lift mighty sentences, shoulder paragraphs. In the basement of the Metro City Public Library, you run through a labyrinth of words, through arcane documents detailing the weird occult history of Metro City. You run through it looking for your sister, calling her name into the dust-thick air.*

*This too is why they hate you: tragedy. It runs like a virus in your blood. None of them have lost their parents in a plane crash. None of them have had a sister simply disappear from the house your parents left to you both, the one even the Metro City Department of Social Services couldn't tear you away from. You are a carrier of weird misfortune, and to touch you might mean catching it.*

*When you find the word, it is puzzling. It stands out on the page, glistening under the flickering fluorescents. Maybe that's why you read it out loud. Maybe that's why the lightning comes. It courses through you. You are made of its etheric energy, it burns away* crip *and* gimp *and* crutch *until you are no longer a boy but a man. A man made out of lightning.*

*Now you run and jump and fly through the streets of Metro City. You stop bullets, they thud against your barrel-broad chest. You search for your sister now not in books but in dark rooms full of killers, in abandoned churches taken over by would-be wizards.*

*And when you say the word, the lightning goes away. Leaves behind it a boy. A crip. A gimp. A crutch. Until you summon it back.*

*As the days and the nights pass, you spend more and more of your time as a man made of lightning with a child in his mind. The thought of your original body becomes more repellent. You begin to associate it with the names the other kids call it. You dream of being trapped in it forever and wake up, sweating and shaking, in the body of a man made of lightning.*

*There are things about this body you don't understand. The workings of it. Feelings it has that can't be yours. But whose can they be? In a runic circle out in the Fawcett Flats, you grapple with Cerridwen, an enchantress who may know where your sister is, and there's something this body wants from her, but you don't know what it is. It's a want that lingers after the fight is over, after the police have taken her to a cell she's sure to escape from. The want floats through your dreams, but you can't name it. It feels like an enchantment, but it comes from this body. If it's not your want, whose is it, and what is it for?*

*You are aware you are sacrificing your childhood. This bothers you less as time goes on.*

*Alone at night, a little closer to finding your sister than you were the night before, but still she feels so distant, you think of the word that will change you back into a boy, a crip, a gimp, a crutch. You try to forget it. You picture it, hold it in your mind, and then attack it with fists and scrub brushes. But it's still there. Puzzling. Glistening. And you fall asleep in the bed of a child, in the body of a man made of lightning.*

# Role Models

Gail Pope subjects her spine to a series of stretches and twists, trying to wring out the knots and kinks that have accumulated in the course of a cramped bus ride across New York State and a night's sleep on a less-than-stellar hotel bed. She makes yawning and creaking noises, cracks knuckles, rotates shoulders, straightens her T-shirt. She plays the theme from *Rocky* in her head. Then she sits down in the metal folding chair in front of the National Comics banner, and her back quickly resumes its normal shape, that of a gooseneck desk lamp. On the table there are back-issue stacks some National intern must have laid out at dawn: *The Speck & Iota, OuterGirl* ongoings, *The Perfectional* miniseries. She got to meet the interns at the New York office the other day. They are spritely little geek elves. She imagines if she left one of her worn sneakers outside her hotel room tonight, it would be shiny and repaired in the morning.

She scans the room for them, but, true to their elfin heritage, they have vanished now that their work is done. From her duffel bag Gail extracts copies of *Fountain Ethics* and slides them to the front of the table. It's a creator-owned book she wrote for Black Sheep Comics years ago, before she got her first gig at National. It's dirty stuff, full of sex and violence, and when she asked the publicity people at National if she should bring copies to the signing, there was a lot of wincing and floor examination that served as her answer. She pages through the first issue, thinking that it reads like a tryout for a career path she never took, one where she worked on sexually fraught characters like ExSanguina rather than the quirky heteronormative scientist couple that was the Speck and Iota. But it never sold well, and she has boxes of comp copies that clutter her apartment. If she can't give them away here, she'll probably be buried with them.

It's strange for Gail to be at a convention as an object of fandom rather than as a fan, but she's glad she chose to start with Cleveland rather than jumping right into one of the bigger cons. Cleveland is also nice because it's all comics: no movies or video games or any of the other noisy, flashy things that are ancillary to her job but which she's not all that into. Of course she likes stories in any form they take, but for her it's all about twenty-four pages in full color every month. Last year, she hadn't been one of the writers National tapped to represent the company on the con circuit, but recently Gail has developed a fan base that is, if not as large as those of some of the other writers in the National stable, more vocal. And let's face facts: it's good publicity to have a female writer standing out front. It makes National look progressive and obscures the fact that Gail is the only female writer they currently employ full-time. She hits that sweet spot between talent and tokenism that earns one a seat on a Greyhound and a single bed at the Holiday Inn. She can't complain. Three years ago, she was attending cons as a fan journalist, entirely on her own dime. Crashing on the couches of other fans she barely knew. Missing out on the high-end industry parties to drink Schlitz with the comic book dealers and cosplayers. Not that she's been to any high-end industry parties. Not that she is going to, or that there even are any. But in the pocket universe of comics, Gail has risen from the bottom to a firmly ensconced place in the upper middle. She is no longer a fangirl; she is a name on the poster. She is a draw.

Valerie Torrey's line is, of course, double the size of Gail's. Gail knew she was going to be here, but she had no idea they'd be right next to each other. If Gail had her choice, she'd be in the line rather than sitting ten feet away from her and not talking. She's waiting for her chance, a moment when their lulls overlap. Except Valerie's line is lull-less. There is not a break, nary an opening, and Gail can imagine the two of them like co-workers who sit in adjacent cubicles for years without saying hello or learning each other's names. It's unacceptable.

For the moment, there is no one in Gail's line. No one eyeing her up or getting ready to approach. She reaches into her duffel and grabs a small stack of comics, then walks over and stands over Valerie's shoulder in a way she hopes isn't menacing. Valerie is talking to a man in his forties who is well dressed and fidgets with his hands.

"I have a time travel joke," he says.

"That's great," says Valerie. "Let's hear it."

"The bartender says, 'We don't serve faster-than-light particles here.' A tachyon walks into a bar." He pauses. Valerie chuckles. But Gail, for whom knowledge of crazy sciency things is a job requirement, busts out laughing. Valerie turns to look at Gail over her shoulder.

"Hi," says Gail, giving a little wave.

"Hi," says Valerie. She doesn't look too weirded out. Maybe a little.

"I didn't want to interrupt," says Gail.

"Do you want to sit?" says Valerie. She pulls out the chair next to her and Gail takes a seat.

"This is so weird," says Gail. "I am so generally not a fangirl." She shakes her head. "I mean, obviously, yes, a fangirl. But I don't usually get nervous. And you have people." She points to the man with the time travel joke.

"I've been waiting in line," he says.

"And that was the best material you came up with?" says Gail.

"Tachyons can theoretically travel through time," he says to Valerie.

"No, yeah, I'm sorry," says Gail.

"I know," Valerie tells the man. She's very polite. "I was listening to a *Radiolab* about them on the drive yesterday."

"Oh," says the man, seeming a little deflated. It's unclear to Gail whether he hoped the joke would go over Valerie's head or not. She signs a glossy photo for him and he runs away.

"You wouldn't know me, but my name is Gail Pope," says Gail.

"Val," says Valerie. Says Val. Gail hands Val the stack of comics like a business card. On the cover of the top one is a drawing of Frazer and Campbell, guns drawn. "I wrote that," Gail says. She must sound like an elementary schooler showing off her artwork. "It was my first job. A six-issue mini for Black Sheep Comics."

"I haven't read them," Val says.

"It's not very good," says Gail. "I never got the voice of Bethany Frazer. I was young and I wrote it like it was me running around with Campbell, solving cases. Nobody liked it. I'm surprised I ever got another job."

Val hands back the stack of comics, but Gail waves her off.

"They're for you," she says. "The story's set in season three. It's a lost episode."

Val thanks her and sets them aside. The woman at the front of the line is doing the International Dance of Impatience, shifting from one foot to the other with her arms folded.

"I wanted to tell you how great it was you were there," Gail says, staring at her hands. "That you existed. I was a big geek growing up. Big as in geeky and big as in heavy. The girls I read about, or the ones on the covers of the books I was reading, they weren't anything like me. They were prettier, but they also weren't smart, and they weren't badass. They were sexy—or the good ones were plucky. Fucking plucky. And then there was Frazer, and she was smart and badass. She was badass by being smart. It was the first time I saw a woman in any of these worlds I was spending all my time in and thought she was someone I could be, or would want to be. I was twenty-one when the show started and I'd been reading comic books all my life. You were my first hero."

"Thank you," says Val. She's blushing, and now Gail feels bad, having made her blush. The woman in the front of the line clears her throat.

"Your adoring public," says Gail. She stands up and starts to back away, then pauses. As someone who makes her living manipulating words, she's always surprised how often they prove inadequate or inappropriate, how frequently the only way to say something sounds clunky and immature. "Do you," she says, "want to hang out later?" It is the kind of thing a middle school boy would mutter staring at his shoes. She and Val look at each other for a second, as if they are trying to find the adult translation for *Hey, want to be friends?*

"I'd like that," says Val.

"Great," Gail says. She turns to go, then realizes her chair is still only ten feet away from Val's. "Or we could just start now."

# Long Distance

V al drives a half hour each way to pick up food she considers reasonably healthy from the nearest Whole Foods. That Alex ate Froot Loops for breakfast and God knows what from the hotel restaurant for lunch should make this matter less, but it makes it matter so much more. She wants to know that even when she isn't with him, her voice will be in his head saying things like *Eat something green with that* or *Do they have it in organic?*

At a red light, she discreetly picks up her phone and dials her agent, Elise at Diverse Talent in Los Angeles. She's always claimed Val is the easiest client she's ever worked with, since Val came to her as soon as she moved to L.A., contract in hand and three days of shooting already complete. But she more than earned her keep after Val disappeared. For Val's first year in New York, Elise was the only person on the West Coast who knew how to find her; she wrapped up all of Val's affairs, including getting Val out of the last year of her second *Anomaly* contract. By then, there was no show to be under contract to, but there were, all the same, legal issues to be put to rest, and it was a relief when Elise called to tell Val that the remainder of the contract had been voided, and any money Val had been paid in advance of the upcoming season that was never to be shot was hers to keep—Tiger's Paw Media was anxious to forget the whole thing and not about to sweat small change. Since then, Val's made her work for her money in dribs and drabs, arranging auditions for theater parts in New York, a world Elise claims to know nothing about. But she's proven good at it, and doesn't get upset when Val turns down a more lucrative role for one with a more manageable rehearsal schedule.

"Val," says Elise, "where the hell are you?"

"Cleveland," she says.

"Is it terrible? I imagine it's terrible."

"It's fine," says Val. "I've only seen the Holiday Inn and the Whole Foods."

"So you've hit the high points already," says Elise. "I've been meaning to call you. Houston Grant is calling me at least three times a day. *Perestroika* is going into rehearsals in six weeks, and if you're not going to do it, he needs to recast."

"Can you put him off a little longer?"

"I can try putting him off till opening night, but I can't guarantee he'll hold the part for you," says Elise. "You want other news?"

"Is it good news?"

"I never know with you," says Elise. "It's an offer. For most of my clients, an offer is good news. For you, an offer is like a box full of snakes."

Val snorts out a little laugh. "What's the offer?"

"Gertrude," says Elise.

"*Gertrude* Gertrude?" says Val. "Who the hell is doing *Hamlet*?"

"Royal Shakespeare. In London. Starting in January."

"Holy shit," says Val.

"I told them you were too young," says Elise.

"You didn't."

"I didn't."

"What did you tell them?"

"I told them I'd talk you into it," says Elise.

"Wouldn't take much talking into," says Val.

"With you, everything's an argument," Elise says. "You think you could move that kid of yours to London for six months?"

Val winces. "Let me worry about that," she says.

"So what should I tell them?"

"Put them off a little while."

"Val," says Elise, "you know I don't know what I'm doing when it comes to the theater stuff, but it seems to me, the Royal Shakespeare Company is not something you put off for a little while."

"Can we talk about it when I get to L.A.?" says Val. "I'd like to talk about it in person."

"Your wish is my et cetera, et cetera," says Elise. "So how is your road trip going? How's Alex?"

"He's fine. Everything's good here."

"You're lying."

"I'm driving, Elise," says Val. "I'll call you when I'm in L.A." Never taking her eyes off the road, she fumbles around on the passenger seat until she finds the phone and hangs it up.

She's made it to the hallway on their floor with dinner in one paper grocery bag, the old kind, without handles, when her phone begins to buzz in her pocket. She shifts the bag onto her hip to grab it. The number is unfamiliar, but it's got a California area code; Andrew changes phones so often these days. What if he's doing it to avoid a dangerous stalker, she thinks, someone who might hurt Alex? But she dismisses this as too obvious. In real life there are no reruns.

"How's it going?" he asks. There is the sound of wind in the background; he's driving with the windows open. Val thinks of smog, traffic fatalities.

"We're fine," she says. "We're in Cleveland."

"I thought you were going to call me when you guys got on the road," he says.

"I couldn't," she says. "I was driving." A second passes and the wind noise stops. He hasn't stopped the car, she knows, but he has rolled up the windows.

"I've been thinking," he says, which has always been the precursor to him going back on his word. "Maybe I should meet up with you guys in Chicago. If you're doing a signing anyway, I could be at the signing and then we could all come to Los Angeles together. Fly right out of Chicago to Los Angeles, maybe spend a few days together before the convention. What do you think?"

"You promised me Chicago," she says. "We agreed."

"It's funny," he says. "You talking about agreements as if they're binding." She can't decide if he sounds hostile or if he's musing on it. "It's funny."

"When you say something's funny twice, it makes you sound like an idiot," she says. "It's like saying 'It is what it is.'"

"That's my character's tagline," he says. "On the show."

"I haven't seen the show," she says, which is technically true, but it doesn't mean she hasn't done a little Web surfing. She's told Alex on a number of occasions, "Only idiots say 'It is what it is.' Not that that makes your father an idiot." Anyway, what kind of person does taglines?

"Valerie," he says, "I'm trying to make this easier on everyone. On Alex."

She hates the sound of Alex's name coming from him, because it forces her to remember that Andrew is the one who named him, when she was blissed out on whatever weird concoction of hormones her body cooked up to apologize for the pain she'd been through. "You could make it easier by staying the fuck out of our lives," she says.

"I wish you wouldn't think of it like that," he says. She's breathing fast now. She worries he can hear it on the other end of the phone. She sets her groceries down and leans hard against the wall. She has to remind herself that this toxicity is only between them, that it has nothing to do with Alex. That he was a bad husband will not make him a bad father. People change, and it has been a long time. She has to remind herself not to hate him. She fails.

"If you show up in Chicago," she says, "I will take him and run. I will run to someplace where no one has ever heard of you, or me. I will start from scratch and I will wait tables in a diner and you will never see Alex or me ever again."

There is a silence, and in the silence she can hear her heart beating and she can hear his car running. She knows his taste in cars and knows he must be going very fast for his car to make any noise at all. Valerie thinks again of traffic fatalities.

"Fine," he says. This is such an important word between them because it can sound like approval and wellness and so many other things when it's only shorthand for *final*. He hangs up the phone and Val holds her breath, thinking it will ring again and he will say *I've been thinking* and she and Alex will have to disappear. The phone doesn't ring, so she picks up the bags of microgreens and whole wheat pasta and the organic rotisserie chicken and walks down the hall to feed her child.

# Glass Ceiling

Trying to decide if it makes her feel more like a waitress or more like one of the boys, Gail maneuvers her way to the table holding their beers above her head. She's known Geoff and Ed since her blogging days, and both of them have regularly praised the hell out of her work, but it's tough not to feel like their little sister. Not to imagine herself judged by how different, how lacking, she is physically, compared with the anatomically ideal women they all write. When she went to her first con as a fan, she'd played at dressing sexy, but she'd nearly been tossed by security for giving, let's say, an enthusiastic lecture to a group of college-age boys who took a break from catcalling a woman dressed as the Minx long enough to offer Gail dieting advice. Now she sports the same worn jeans and Northwestern University hoodie she wears while writing. Her outfit for tomorrow is a variation on the same. The winning move is not to play.

She carefully sets the beers on the table. Ed predictably tips his fedora, and Geoff thanks her and raises his glass to cheers the three of them.

"So have you had offers?" Gail asks Geoff, picking up the conversation where it left off.

"Are we talking about this?" Ed says. His voice is rapid and gruff, and very few people in the industry other than Gail know it's not natural. When Ed got his start writing fill-in issues of *GigaDroids,* a comic derived from a cartoon show derived from a toy line, he was spunky and spoke in the ringing tones you would expect from someone who'd been in his college's glee club, which, although he'd never admit it to anyone, Ed had. She'd interviewed him by phone back then, holding the receiver away from her ear to buffer the treble. But when he'd made his major breakthrough with the detective series *Cleave,* which followed the investigation into the murder of a minor National Comics superhero, he'd taken on a public persona inspired by Dashiell Hammett, and now that he'd taken over *Red Emma* at Timely and been hailed as the founder of the "New Grit" aesthetic by PanelAddict.com, his private-dick act, which included the fedora and a pack of Lucky Strikes poking carefully out from the pocket of his vintage shirt, had become dominant. "I was under the impression we had agreed we were not talking about this."

"So you've had offers," Gail says. Ed's currently writing three monthly books for Timely. Only *Red Emma*'s in the top twenty, but all three have "vocal fans," meaning fans who spend a lot of time commenting on the Internet and would be likely to make an editor's life unpleasant if any of the books were to get canceled. Geoff writes two titles for National and consults on four others, while remaining tight-lipped as to what it means to consult. Or what it pays.

Gail's situation is a little dicier. For three years, she's been writing *The Speck & Iota.* Thinking about it, she's written a whole lot of *The Speck & Iota.* Twenty pages a month for thirty-six months, for a total of seven hundred twenty pages about a pair of scientists who can shrink down to the size of dust motes. That's a Tolstoy kind of page count. And she could have done more.

Gail hasn't told either of them that National is moving her off *The Speck & Iota* in three months. "On to bigger and better things," her editor quipped, his desiccated sense of humor explaining how so many of Gail's best jokes end up butchered before they make it into print. They didn't tell her where she'd land, but she was given three issues to wrap up the storylines she's been working on so the title can be handed off.

"I don't think I could jump," says Geoff.

"Don't start," says Gail, "You could write for anybody." Before she was hired at National, Gail ran a feminist and sometimes misandrist website called BrainsOverBreasts.com. In the comments sections, Geoff would add to her teardowns of a particular comic by pointing out continuity errors, moments when a story contradicted a story published ten, twenty years ago. National had originally hired him as a kind of fact-checker before giving him a tryout on *The Galactioneer*, about a dashing space pirate who'd appeared in one issue of *OuterMan* in 1978. Back then, Geoff and Gail would run into each other in hotel bars like this at small-time conventions like this and compare the day's haul of autographs and sketches. They even made out once, in Pittsburgh, one evening when Gail had enough beer to dip her toe back into the tepid pool of heterosexuality, but luckily it hadn't gone any further than that. When she was toured around the National office in New York for the first time after she'd been hired, Geoff was hiding in the men's room. She still likes to bring up "that time you took advantage of me," to see him go sheepish.

"That's not true," Geoff says. "That's not. *You* could. You're more versatile than I am."

"Less distinctive is what he's saying," she explains to Ed, who laughs grimly. Ed does many things grimly.

"You have a very distinctive style," Geoff insists, a little too strenuously.

"Female is not a distinctive style," says Gail.

"You bring a real compassion to your characters," Geoff says.

"It's my mothering impulse," says Gail.

"So why couldn't you write for Timely?" Ed asks Geoff. Ed has taken a cigarette from his pack and is using it to play a safer version of mumblety-peg, tapping it nimbly in the spaces between his fingers.

"*Couldn't* might be strong," Geoff admits. "I could."

"Have you had offers?" Gail asks again.

"Can we admit," Ed says, spreading his hands out to quiet them both, although Gail was the only one talking, "that we've all had offers? That we've all been flirted with by the competition at this point?"

No one responds, no one makes eye contact.

"Good," says Ed. He turns his attention back to Geoff. "Now why can't you come write for Timely? What about the Ferret? You love the Ferret."

Each time he says "Ferret," he reaches across the table and hits Geoff lightly on the shoulder. This kind of casual physical contact is one of the things that make Gail feel like an outsider. Out of a respect she's never requested, very few male colleagues ever touch her in any way that isn't formal and earnest, mostly hugs and handshakes.

"The universes work differently," Geoff says.

"The universes?" asks Gail.

"Timely and National."

"The universes work the way the writers write them," says Ed, returning to his cigarette tapping.

"You say that, but it's because you don't have to worry about it," says Geoff. "You do this street-level ass-kicking stuff and it doesn't matter if it's the mean streets of Metro City or the mean streets of New York."

"Thank you," says Ed, "for so elegantly belittling my work."

"Who's belittling?" says Geoff, throwing his arms outward. "I'm saying they work differently because they were built different. National publishes *OuterMan* in thirty-eight, but he's alone for years, until they add OuterGirl, who's basically OuterMan in a skirt. Early forties, National sues Stunning Comics for copyright infringement over Captain Wonder, then ends up owning Captain Wonder. Blue Torch, the Perfectional, and the Speck were all bought from Heston after the war, and ExSanguina and the Diviner were bought from Femme Fatale after the Senate obscenity hearings put them out of business in '55. But none of the characters interacted until the late sixties, when they formed Vengeance Troop."

"They fixed all that with *Conflux Across Timespace*," says Gail.

"Have you guys ever read *Conflux*?" Geoff asks.

"No," says Ed.

"I've read the wiki," says Gail. *Conflux* was a twelve-issue series from the dawn of the eighties that featured every National character ever and a plot so convolutedly cosmic that even Gail, who loved all things intergalactic, had to put it down.

"It's kind of brilliant," Geoff says. "It's so precise. But it incorporates everything. It fits all these stories together like a watch made out of scrap metal. And so it needs constant tending and adjustment. Retcons and explanations."

"It's true," says Gail. "I spend at least one page each issue of *The Speck & Iota* trying to explain the crazy bullshit some other writer had them do a decade ago."

"But Timely has a birth moment, and parents. Everything grows out of Brewer and Loeb creating the Astounding Family. The Astounding Family discovers the totem that gives the Ferret his powers. The Ferret discovers the Visigoth trapped in ice during a battle with the Wailing Wendigo, and Doctor Right uses the Visigoth's DNA to create the R-Squad. Red Emma's family is killed in a fight between the R-Squad and the Perilous Pentad, which starts her war on crime. The Timely Universe grows and accretes. Each writer adds to it, but they don't have to fix what's come before. They work with the universe; it's an organism."

"You're romanticizing," Ed tells him, "with your mechanisms and organisms. You're talking about two massive corporations, neither of which give two shits about how their little comic book universes operate as long as they have characters to put into movies and on T-shirts."

"Red Emma's not in any movies," says Geoff, "and you're still outselling me on *OuterMan* and *The Blue Torch*."

"Why is a man writing *Red Emma* anyway?" asks Gail. Most female characters have male writers, but it's always offended Gail that *Red Emma*, which is as close as the industry comes to portraying an ass-kicking lesbian, even if they never admit it, is written by a Sam Spade impersonator.

"It's due to my lack of compassion," Ed says.

"It's due to *my* lack of a cock," Gail says. "Which is why, incidentally, I have not had offers."

"You're shitting me," says Ed, banging his beer on the table for emphasis.

"Why would you leave anyway?" asks Geoff, sounding a little hurt.

Geoff is old enough to have been in the wars, the old days when National fans hated all things Timely and vice versa. It's a partisanship he's never shaken off.

"I don't *want* to leave," says Gail.

"I can't believe they haven't made an offer," says Ed.

"Besides which," she continues, making sure to sound like all of this is theoretical, "what if National decides they don't want me anymore? That I don't understand how the universe works? I'm back working full-time creator-owned—*if* I can get somebody to publish it."

"You working on ideas of your own?" Geoff asks.

"I like to think all my ideas are my own," says Gail. Creator-owned work holds a weird place of reverence among the three of them. Steady superhero work pays more reliably and affords a comfortable living, not to mention that all three of them are established enough to have a certain amount of creative freedom in their work. But they are playing with someone else's toys. The rarity of a successful creator-owned project is daunting, and the path is littered with bodies, but at the end of the path: complete creative control, complete rights. Gail talks about it as if she's equating it with financial ruin, but part of her hopes she might be forced off that cliff, might begin to float midfall.

"I bet by the end of con season," Ed says to her, "Timely offers you a book."

"Maybe they'll offer me *Red Emma*," she says, grinning maliciously at him.

"We could cowrite an arc," he suggests.

"I would destroy you with my skills," Gail says, waving at him dismissively.

"He would drink you under at every story meeting," Geoff says. Ed looks directly at him as he finishes his beer, then turns back to Gail.

"By Los Angeles," he says, "Timely offers you a book."

"You putting the word in with Weinrobe?" she asks. Gail has never attempted contact with Philip Weinrobe, Timely's editor in chief. He has a reputation for being preternaturally nice, and is loved by everyone who works for him. But none of that changes the fact that he took over Timely when it was in bankruptcy in the mid-nineties with the expectation he'd oversee the demise of the Timely Universe, selling off its intellectual properties and bringing the publishing side of things to an end. Instead, he managed to bring a long-standing court case between Timely and Levi Loeb to a favorable conclusion, then set to clearing out all the dead weight, guys who'd been hacks in the seventies but had kept steadily churning out rehashed plots as long as they pulled a paycheck. He headhunted young talent, he declared that nothing was sacred. And he turned Timely, which had in its stable some of the most recognizable fictional characters in the world but was squandering them, into the top publisher in the industry.

"You want a word in," says Ed, "I'll put a word in. Who do you want to write?"

"Tell him we should change the Ferret into a woman and I'll write her," says Gail.

"Ferret's in movie development," Geoff says, always aware of various characters' licensing statuses. "They'll never let you gender-bend him." Here, a rule of comic book writing: the more money a character is worth as a property, the less the writer is allowed to deviate from that character's status quo or core concept. All three of them are, in a way, blessed that none of the characters under their current control are being considered for Hollywood treatment.

"Who *will* they let me gender-bend?" Gail asks.

"You can gender-bend me any day of the week," Ed says, leaning in and fixing her with his best fanboy leer.

"There's not enough compassion in all of Metro City for me to mercy-fuck you, dear," Gail says, and dusts off her beer.

# Eating Habits

The book is too good to put down for something as minor as food, so Alex sits cross-legged on the floor and devours the last chapter of *Adam Anti & the Wild Wild Life* simultaneously with a small bucket of microgreens.

When it's over, he slams the book shut, which is one of his favorite things to do. He prefers hardcover books for this reason; although they are bulkier and harder to carry around, they make a much more satisfying noise when slammed.

"I'm done," he says proudly. He gives his mother a huge, toothy grin. Bits of microgreens have filled every possible space between his teeth, and she makes a disgusted face.

"Oh my God, go brush right now," she says, laughing. Alex rushes to the bathroom and makes the same face at himself in the mirror he's made for his mother. He looks like a hideous monster that lives at the bottom of the sea. It's one of the main reasons to eat microgreens, although it doesn't work unless you eat them in huge, chomping mouthfuls. His mother, he knows, has been expert at using disgusting biological quirks to get him to eat things most kids find repellent. He eats asparagus because it makes his pee smell funny, beets because they make him poop red, and microgreens because they make him look like a hideous monster that lives at the bottom of the sea. Alex vigorously brushes his teeth and watches the lime-colored spit, thick with chunks, swirl down the drain.

"So tell me about your day," his mom says as he comes back into the room and starts putting on pajamas. It's a silly request, since he's spent most of the day rocking back and forth on the folding chair next to hers or sitting on the floor against the wall, writing in his notebook.

He shrugs. "I finished my book," he says. He thinks about showing her the picture Brett drew for him, but he worries about trying to tell her the beginning of a story when he doesn't know the rest. He wants to wait and share it with her when it's done.

"Nothing exciting?" she asks. He shrugs again and jumps onto her bed. "What do you think you're doing?" she says.

"Cuddling with you," he says, wedging himself under her arm.

"What if I wanted to read?" she asks. This is a silly question, because the whole time he's been reading, she hasn't picked up her book. He can't blame her: it doesn't look very interesting. It's very long, and it's a history of dancing. Not fun dancing, but theater dancing. It has a ballerina on the cover, and even she doesn't look like she's having a good time.

"I don't think it would be very fair," he says, "for you to read when I don't have a book."

"So I should stare off into space until you fall asleep?" She's basically been staring into space for the past twenty minutes, so he can't imagine why she's upset about it all of a sudden.

"You should tell me a story," he says, wriggling in, resting his head on her stomach so that her breath lifts and lowers it.

"What season do you want?" she asks.

"When do Frazer and Campbell become friends?" asks Alex. His meeting with Brett earlier has him thinking about friendship, about how it can be a process or a becoming. He has friends in New York, but it just happens. Put two kids in a room, or in a park, and they're friends right away. Sometimes his mother will take him to a playground and say, "Go make friends," and it's that easy. At least it was when he was littler, but that, like everything else, was bound to change.

"Season two," she says. "They were friends in season two."

"Then that's what I want," he says. She sighs, as if she's about to do something difficult, and Alex focuses his attention on her voice.

# *Anomaly* S02E01

"So you remember at the end of season one," she says, "everybody in the world knew about Anomaly Division."

"Because they turned the Statue of Liberty back after it looked like Hitler for a while," says Alex, which is exactly right. In the first season, Tim had an obsession with the Statue of Liberty. Three episodes featured the statue as a central plot point, including one about the assassination of Frédéric Auguste Bartholdi before he could design it, and the season finale, in which history was altered so that the statue was of Hitler, still in a toga and holding a copy of *Mein Kampf*. But usually when Frazer and Campbell fixed some crime against the timestream, no one in the present was aware anything had happened. For reasons that wouldn't be revealed until season three, because Tim hadn't come up with them yet, everyone remembered the Statue of Liberty turning into Hitler, and everyone knew it was Frazer and Campbell and Anomaly Division who'd turned it back.

It was an inspired move on Tim's part and helped set the show even further apart from other procedurals. It let the outside world in. "I was thinking about the Astounding Family," he'd said when he handed Val and Andrew the scripts. "How they exist both as a critical force for good and as an object of celebrity worship. How that might affect their inner dynamics." It was also incredibly prescient. By the time they reconvened on set for the second season, the show, which had barely hit the ratings numbers needed for renewal, had taken on a previously unheard-of after-life on the Internet. Episodes shot to the top of download lists at legal and illegal sites, and the phrase "digital tipping point" was used repeatedly, although it seemed to Val it meant something different each time she heard it. *Anomaly*, they'd been assured, still wasn't making the network any money, but it was being watched by more people in the key demographics than any other scripted genre show on television. From the network point of view, the show was worth keeping alive as an experiment.

The first episodes of the second season had Frazer and Campbell appearing on talk shows and being offered endorsement contracts for luxury watches. For Campbell, who claimed he was a Neil deGrasse Tyson–style celebrity intellectual before falling through the time portal, it was a welcome return to the public eye. For Frazer, it was mortifying. She spent those episodes practically unable to work, feeling brutally exposed, culminating in episode five's stalker storyline, done because it felt inevitable for a female in the spotlight. The episode, titled "Eratomania," saw Frazer attacked in her home by a man who thought he'd met her in the future where he was from. It would later be pulled from syndication and from the DVD, but Val had already seen bootleg copies of it for sale at the con. She'd thought of buying them and destroying them, one by one, as if she could chisel away at the actual thing by eliminating the physical evidence of it.

In real life, neither Andrew nor Val adjusted well to their new celebrity status. Andrew might have been better prepped for it, having been something of a heartthrob in the world of soap operas, but it was quickly apparent that *Anomaly* fans had no interest in Andrew Rhodes; their love centered entirely on Ian Campbell. It was true of both male and female fans he encountered: in their minds, Andrew Rhodes was a nonentity, and Ian Campbell was real.

More than that, in his soap days, a whole two years past, there were fewer media outlets to deal with. In a given month, you could do two or three interviews and feel you'd done the work. Now there were daily requests from websites and video blogs, and to refuse was to risk alienating whatever subset of the fan base that site serviced. The network made it abundantly clear to Val and Andrew that they were to make themselves available to any fan who made any claim to being part of the media—new, old, social, or otherwise.

The resulting emotional burnout had little effect on Val's life outside of work; she already spent most of her nights at home, or at Tim and Rachel's. But for Andrew it was catastrophic. At the end of a day's work and the interviews that followed, he couldn't summon up the energy to appear at a restaurant, much less a club or a party. The steady stream of girls who appeared on the set at the end of the day, partly so they could be impressed by a real television set and partly so the crew could be impressed by Andrew's prowess, slowed to a trickle and then dried up.

Andrew was not shy about public lamentation, but after a few weeks Val began to see the edges of a real loneliness rising up from under the shiny surface he presented to her and the rest of the crew. He became a regular at Tim and Rachel's weekly dinner parties, which he'd once begged off with a string of excuses so creative and far-fetched even Tim had to be impressed. The Andrew who showed up at their house in Laurel Canyon ("Manson country," Rachel would say after a few glasses of zin) wasn't the blustery star who showed up on set, but a polite young man who'd grown up poor in North Texas and had buried his accent when he ran off forever at seventeen. Who'd been applying to graduate programs in English when a casting agent for *Sands in the Hourglass* either cruised or discovered him at a coffee shop near UCLA. He talked about his good looks as a resource he was slowly squandering and had insightful praise for the talents of every other member of the cast, especially Val. This Andrew was trying less hard to be liked, and as a result was much more likable.

Against this backdrop, the show told some of the weirdest stories of its entire run. The woman who had July 12, 1982, as a pet, in a birdcage in her living room, and kept it alive by playing nothing but Duran Duran and the Clash on her record player. The widower whose tears stopped time, who'd park his car in front of a bank, sit in the driver's seat, and stare at a picture of his dead wife until he wept. Then, sobbing, he'd rob the bank while everyone else was suspended like fruit in a Jell-O mold. The historical romance writer with a half dozen pen names whose bodice-ripping heroes and swooning heroines began bleeding into real history, distracting John Wilkes Booth backstage at Ford's Theatre or seducing Torquemada and ending the Spanish Inquisition.

"My favorite," says Val, "was episode seven. A whole neighborhood in Queens—"

"Which one?" says Alex. He has never been to Queens, and really the episode took place outside Boston, but it seems like a way to give him a sense of context without too much distraction.

"In Astoria," she says. "The whole neighborhood turns back to the way it was in the fifties. All the stores, and all the cars."

"And the people?"

"The people are still the same people, but they dress and act like it's the fifties. The episode starts with a woman from Brooklyn taking the subway to see her sister. She gets off at the Astoria stop and all the men are tipping their fedoras at her. When she arrives at her sister's apartment," Val says, "her sister, who as we've heard her talking about on the phone has blue hair and nose rings—"

"She was punk rock?" says Alex.

"Exactly," says Val. It's a kind of catchall term Alex uses to describe the hipsters who hang out near Tim's place in Greenpoint, scaring the old Polish ladies; the tattooed punkers who loll about Washington Square Park waiting for 1987 to come around again; and, maybe most correctly, the three young black kids who play a beautiful and, to Val, incomprehensible sprawling of instrumental metal out front of the Forty-second Street stop. "Her punk rock sister is wearing an apron and baking a pie," she says. Val remembers the girl who played the sister, her blue Mohawk tamped into a bizarre approximation of a poodle cut, perfect midwestern teeth glimmering out between a zipper of lip piercings. She'd knit between takes, stabbing the sock she was working on with her needles to avoid anything resembling downtime.

"Pies can't be punk rock?" Alex asks.

"Maybe," says Val. "But I'm pretty sure aprons can't be. I'm probably not the best resource on what's punk rock."

"You're regular rock," says Alex, as if stating a fact.

"I'm more easy listening," says Val.

"So what happens when her sister is baking pies?" says Alex.

"The woman calls Anomaly. Frazer and Campbell have to go undercover." To demonstrate, she pulls the covers over her head and waits for a laugh that doesn't come. She peeks back out, and Alex is waiting for her.

"Do they have secret identities?" he says.

"Donald and Alicia Stone," she says. Tim thought this was very clever, a gender reversal of the leads on *The Donna Reed Show*, Donna and Alex. Val had assured him no one would get it, but since their fandom existed in a universe of linked signifiers, his little joke killed.

"They're pretending to be married?" says Alex.

"They're pretending they're in the fifties so they can blend in," she says. "When they're out in public. When they're alone, they're normal."

By the time they shot this episode, Val and Andrew had taken to hiding out after the crew left, ordering Chinese from Century Dragon and eating it on set. Andrew was tired of going out into the real world, and for Val this world was as much her home as her apartment was. Andrew got chicken lo mein, every time. Val would pick the dishes whose names best obscured their content. Planet Chicken. Art of Dragon. Four Happiness. Some of it was inedible and some of it was overwhelmingly delicious, but she never kept track. Sometimes she'd open the carton and know this was something she'd had and hated before, but she'd eat it all the same. Andrew would try a bite of most of them, if they didn't look too intimidating. He filled his iPod with classical music, which they both wished they knew more about, and each night they'd listen to a new composer and discuss. In the beginning it was dull, because what can you say about Beethoven or Bach? But as it progressed, their opinions diverged and deepened. He liked Shostakovich and she liked Prokofiev. They both hated Mahler. The music seeped into their work lives: he'd whistle a snatch of a Chopin mazurka after they'd nailed a scene. She'd hum Ravel's "Bolero" when they seemed stuck in an endless repetition of takes.

"After a few days, though," she says, "the fifties start to creep in on them. Campbell starts smoking a pipe and listening to Bing Crosby."

"Who's Bing Crosby?" says Alex.

"A fifties singer who smoked a pipe," says Val. *And beat his children,* she thinks. "Frazer starts wearing aprons and cooking. Even though she doesn't know how."

"Does she bake pies?" Alex asks.

"No," she says, "she doesn't make it that far. She's in the middle of trussing a chicken when she realizes what's going on."

"Why does she trust a chicken?" he asks.

"Truss," she says. "It means 'tie up.'"

"Oh," he says. "So what is going on?"

Always more perceptive than Val, Rachel asked the same thing while putting extra touches to a piece that was already beautiful but evidently not beautiful enough.

"Nothing," Val assured her. "Nothing."

"She remembers," says Val, "that they've been there before. There was a rip in time, in the first season, and a biker gang from 1958 had been terrorizing the neighborhood. They'd managed to get the bikers back where they belonged, but they couldn't seal the rip."

"Something came through it?" says Alex.

"A zeitgeist," she says. Before he can ask what that is, she adds, "The spirit of an age." He still looks at her quizzically. "The way people, generally, thought and felt about things. The way they imagined themselves."

He considers this. "Was it like a ghost?" he says.

"Yes," she says, relieved. "It was like the ghost of the fifties."

"What did it look like?"

"In a way," she says, "it looks like the whole neighborhood. It looks like fedoras and aprons. Pies and trussed chickens. But we couldn't have Frazer and Campbell fighting a pie. So the ghost looks like a dad from an old TV show. A sweater vest and smoking a pipe. He calls Frazer 'little lady' and he's all black and white, and lines of static run up and down him all the time."

"What did she do?" he says.

"She tries to reason with him," she says. "To get him to go back to where he came from. But he didn't want to. He knew if he went back there, he'd die. He'd seen it when the bikers came through, that he only had a few years left before he was replaced. So he came here, and he was determined to stay here, in this little place, forever. He had Campbell try to attack her."

Alex gasps, and Val regrets choosing this episode. "What'd she do?" he asks, nervous.

"There was a pop song," she says. "He kept singing it the whole way they were driving up. All through the start of the episode. The song of the summer. She sings it to him and he snaps out of it."

"That's it?" says Alex, obviously disappointed.

"It makes sense," she says, a little too insistent. "It reminds him of the modern world."

"How does it go?" he asks.

"You're not serious."

"Sing it," he says, crossing his arms defiantly.

"I can't sing," she says. This should be a point of understanding between them. She doesn't do lullabies; she does stories.

"Could Frazer?" he says.

"Not really," she says. "That's what made it funny. She even did a little dance." As soon as she's said this, she knows it's a mistake.

"Do it!" he says, sitting up.

"I don't remember it."

"You're lying."

"I am not," she says.

"Teach it to me," he says. She thinks of all the things it would be better to teach him in this limited time they have left.

"All right," she says, "get up." She swings her feet out of the bed and he clambers over her. "Put your feet like this," she says, adopting a wide stance with her knees pointed slightly in. He follows. "It's not a good dance," she says. "That was kind of the point. But put your fists up." Like a tiny boxer, he does. "And then it goes like this."

# Convincing Arguments

B rett is on a planet orbiting Proxima Centauri, a red dwarf 4.24 light-years from Earth. It's never been called anything but Proxima Centauri, this planet. Life here exists only in cities under massive protective domes. The domes were found abandoned and in ruinous disrepair when Earth explorers made landfall centuries ago.

Brett wants *Lady Stardust* to end here, because this is where it began. A bar called Clandestino where Lady Stardust works as a dancer for the Syndicate. She meets David Jones. Newly hired bartender. They fall desperately in love. Her boss, Ocelot Spider, the color of a melted orange Creamsicle, spindle fingers striped and spotted, makes plans to sell her contract to his cousin, Manatee Spider, on Mars. David reveals he's an undercover agent of Factor Max. Before they can escape, he's betrayed. Captured by the Spiders. The two of them are brought to the basement of Clandestino. Ocelot injects David with the Persona virus, an alien organism that throws its victim's personality and appearance into a state of flux. As they carry him away, David takes on a half-dozen faces. A panel apiece. Each one from her point of view. That night, before she's shipped to Mars, Lady Stardust is recruited into Factor Max by Ron Marxon, David's former partner. He tells her that by killing each of the identities David changes into, she has a chance at purging the virus from his system. Restore his original self. The last page is a close-up. Teeth together, lips apart. Barrel of a ray gun resting against temple. Tear trailing mascara down cheek.

The sprawl and space opera are all Fred. In the details, Brett can read the story of his own life, barely transformed. He'd been working as a barback at Clandestino, on the Lower East Side, when he met Debra. Fred hadn't even bothered to give their space bar a different name. He and Debra felt star-crossed. Her a lawyer for a large firm uptown. Him not hip enough to work the bars closer to his apartment, not qualified to do more than barback in Manhattan.

She was a master of disguise. Slick and professional uptown. Classy but fast downtown. Trashily hip in Brooklyn. These changes were even more amazing to Brett once they'd moved in together. From his drafting table in the bedroom, he'd watch her enter the bathroom a high-powered corporate lawyer and emerge moments later a Greenpoint hipster.

Brett puts his pencil down on the still-blank page. The convention hall is starting to bustle. In a corner of the hotel's double ballroom, a sound guy checks mics that won't be used until the panel tomorrow. Interns lay out swag for Timely and National on the signing tables that line one long side of the room.

Brett sets up the offerings at his table. Issues of *Lady Stardust* in stacks plentiful enough to assure they don't look like a rinky-dink operation, but not so plentiful that they suggest a surplus. Brett's portfolio open to reasonably priced sketches, recognizable characters. Toward the back, the covers of issues two through eleven. Priced significantly higher. Brett doesn't want to sell them. The prices reflect the point where money outweighs his sentimental attachment. He was surprised how low those numbers turned out to be. The pencils for the cover of issue one he gave to Debra for her birthday last year. Fred has not let him forget this. Brett wonders if Debra's thrown it out by now, or if it's rolled up in a tube in their old apartment. Sometimes he checks eBay to see if she's put it up for sale, at a price that reflects the point where money outweighs her sentimental attachment.

His display enticingly arranged, Brett wanders away from his table to check out his neighbors. There's a hierarchy to Artist Alley. Those on the lowest rungs, who've brought work samples and self-published comics in the hopes of being discovered, stay bolted to their tables. The fear someone might show up the moment you get up to use the bathroom or get a

sandwich is paralyzing. They smell like the nearest Kinko's, and their fingertips are black with toner. At the end of the day, the items they've handed
out will float on top of overflowing trash cans near the exits, or skitter
across the parking lot. The next day they'll be back before anyone else arrives. Suffer through it all again.

The artists at the top show up late. Disheveled. Hungover. Bored.
Their tables are waiting for them at the far end of the Alley. Everything
set up by interns who appear throughout the day to offer coffee, sandwiches, beer. Artists are contracted to appear for stints of two or three
hours. They stay exactly that long. They leave with fans still in line and
clutching pivotal issues to their chests.

Then there are those in the middle. Like Brett. They hover near their
tables but don't need to constantly attend them. They have fans. Sparse,
but dedicated. There's money to be made selling pencils or taking short
commissions. If an opportunity presents, they visit the tables of artists
higher up the food chain, converse while the more prominent artist dis-
tractedly signs autographs, tosses off hundred-dollar pencil sketches.

The midlevel artists also serve as ambassadors for the bracket of success they inhabit. The realm of the reasonably achievable. In this capacity,
Brett looks over the sketchbook of a local artist two tables down. A sense
of anatomy learned solely from reading comics. Women with hourglass
waists and volleyball breasts. Men as broad across the shoulders as they are
tall. But the kid has an eye for facial expressions. A Viking shield-maiden's
face contorts with rage as she brings a sword down. A cleric, hooded,
sneers with contempt, and the contours of the lip form a line like the edge
of a violin. Brett nods approvingly. Then spots Alex headed toward the
*Lady Stardust* table.

"Robot boy!" says Brett.

"I'm not the boy with the robot," Alex says calmly as Brett comes over.
"He doesn't know what his name is yet, but it's not Alex. Plus we made
him blond, remember?"

"Sorry about that," says Brett.

"It's okay. I'm not insulted." Brett watches him fiddle with things on the table. Picking up comics and putting them down. Organizing Brett's pens and pencils into straight lines. He feels confronted with an alien intelligence. He has no idea what is going on in this kid's head. But he remembers being a kid. He tries to remember how he thought about things. Not what he thought, but the method by which he reached his conclusions. He comes up empty.

"I have a favor to ask you," says Alex, his hands folded in front of him.

"Another commission?" Brett asks.

"Exactly," says Alex. "A bigger one this time. A field trip." Brett's not sure he likes the sound of that. But Alex barrels on. "Have you read any of the Adam Anti books?" he asks.

"I did," says Brett. "My girlfriend gave them to me for Christmas a couple years ago."

Debra had intended it as a pretty major gesture. She was trying to like things he liked. It was how much make-believe she'd be willing to swallow. There was no way she could have known it wasn't *his* type of make-believe. "Of course *those* are the kind of books she likes," said Fred contemptuously when Brett told him. It was like pouring bourbon for a Scotch drinker to prove you liked whiskey. It occurs to him now that he should have valued the attempt more than he did. But it is too late for all that.

"I finished the second one last night," says Alex.

"The second one, that's *Adam Anti & the Wild Wild Life*?"

"Exactly," says Alex. "It's where Adam and Matilda and James are on summer break and they're experimenting with magic outside of school even though they're not supposed to."

"And Adam finds out his parents aren't his parents," says Brett.

"Is that a rule in stories?" asks Alex. "That your parents are never your parents? It's like that for Mister Astounding, and for Adam. But for Moses, too, in the Bible, and Dorothy in *Oz*."

"I think it's a thing a lot of kids think about," says Brett. "What if their life wasn't their life. When I was a kid, sometimes I felt like I had so little in common with my parents that I must have been adopted."

"I finished that one," Alex says, "and now I need to get the third one."

"The third one's no good," says Brett. "They go off to fairyland. They never say it's fairyland. But it's full of tiny people with wings. The cool thing about the *Adam Anti* books is that they're regular magic stories but they take place in Brooklyn."

"He lives right in my neighborhood," Alex says.

"You live in Brooklyn?" says Brett. Alex nods. Proud. "Me, too." They look at each other a little differently. There's something about when you meet someone from home abroad. How there's an instant bond you'd never feel if you met the person at home. "Anyway," he continues, "the third one felt like anyone could have written it," Brett continues. "It's my least favorite book in the series."

"But it's the next one," says Alex. Kind of shrugging. *You know how it is* look about him. "So I need to read it."

Brett nods. "I guess the rest of the books don't make much sense if you don't read the third."

"So I need you to take me to this bookstore," says Alex. "It's called Loganberry Books. A loganberry is a cross between a blackberry and a raspberry. I called already and they're holding a copy for me. It's not that far."

Brett does not know the ins and outs of hanging around children, but he's pretty sure this idea is not okay.

"Can't your mom take you?" he asks.

"She's signing autographs," says Alex. "There's a big line. She said it was okay."

"Maybe I should go check with her," says Brett.

"I told her I knew you already," says Alex. "See, look." He climbs up onto Brett's chair, turns toward the tables at the head of the room, and starts waving his arm broadly. Like he's trying to flag down a plane, or say goodbye to someone on her way to sea. Trying to attract someone's attention. Brett can't see who through the crowds. Then he sees a hand, definitely female, returning Alex's wave.

"Is your mom a writer?" he asks. Guessing from where the table is.

"No, she's just my mom," says Alex. "I wouldn't ask you except you don't have a line right now."

He tries to figure out if the kid is actually being tactful. The way Alex says "right now" implies he knows that Brett will be swamped with fans. Later. Soon.

"The lady at the desk printed me a map," Alex says. He pulls a crumpled piece of paper out of the back pocket of his jeans. Shows it to Brett. "It's close enough we can walk." The whole idea seems increasingly bad to Brett. It feels more and more like kidnapping. Some arrest-worthy offense.

"We can talk about the boy and the robot on the way," Alex says. "It's perfect."

Brett wants to see the Levi Loeb panel that's in less than an hour. He needs to work on the last issue. He should be trying to pick up a few more commissions. But he remembers Sunday afternoons when he was nine. Begging his father for a ride to the comic book store to buy the issue where OuterMan dies. On the TV, the Steelers ran up the score on the Bills. *After the game,* his father said, *right after the game.* Even though the comic book store would be closed by then. By the time his dad stopped by on his way home from work the next day, they'd be sold out. He'd needed to know how it happened.

"Is your mom going to be okay with this?" Brett asks. He knows he's already lost the argument. He's already given in.

"I told you," Alex says brightly, "she said it was okay. She understands I need to get it right now."

Any kid would understand. Anyone who can remember what it's like when a story stops in its middle. That's how it is for Brett with *Lady Stardust* right now. He's pretty sure that the kid's mother won't understand at all. But in the kid's voice, Brett hears a language he used to speak fluently and has almost forgotten.

Brett calls to Devlin. Next table over.

"Watch my shit for me, hey?" he says. Devlin nods enthusiastically. Because this is a favor, and favors create bonds. "C'mon, robot boy," he says to the kid. "Let's make it quick."

# Women in Refrigerators

"I'm sorry," Gail says. "I thought this was the ladies' room."

"You could not be more correct," says the Diviner, sitting on a stool with one of those electronic cigarettes. "Over half of the ladies at this convention are in this room right here."

"You'd think we'd get a bigger room," says OuterGirl from behind a folding panel screen in the corner.

"They do have you crammed in here," Gail says. It's so crowded that Flail is on Flog's lap, although this may be by choice. In the corner, Gail spots Val and waves.

"Hey," says Val, and Gail takes a moment to assess whether Val is genuinely glad to see her or is being gracious. "You looking for a place to hide out?"

"I'm being chased by a mansplainer," says Gail.

"Come sit," says Val, patting the arm of her chair. Gail balances herself next to Val, not quite sitting.

"So this is where the magic happens?" she asks, somewhat awkwardly.

"These girls are better with makeup than anyone I've ever worked with," says Val. "It was much easier to make me look young and glamorous ten years ago. Those guys didn't know how good they had it."

"She's being modest," says the Astounding Woman, removing her wig so she can re-pin her hair. "She could roll out of bed and go right out there with that face."

Gail teeters a bit, and Val steadies her. "I should leave you guys to it, then," she says.

"No, stay," says Val. "There's room."

"Be glad Ferret Lass isn't here," Red Emma says. "The girl cannot seem to register the fact she's wearing an erect three-foot-long tail."

"Do you need to get changed, hon?" OuterGirl asks Gail.

Gail looks at what they're all wearing. She's never delved into cosplay herself, but her friends who have lament that commercial spandex has an inability to mimic the sheen of superhero costumes and ends up making the wearer look more like a Tour de France rider than an alien warrior princess or ninja psychic. Or was it psychic ninja? Those who were into it and had the budget relied on vinyls and thermoplastics for high-gloss, form-fitting—or form-enhancing—costumes. The costume-making process often involved wrapping one's torso in Saran wrap or aluminum foil, then heating a sheet of space-age polymer over oneself with a hair dryer or heat gun until it molded into shape. Ideally, this was done with the help of a friend, but some of them had burn scars to show for their solo efforts.

These ladies' costumes, though, were professionally made, custom jobs. Either the girls sank a lot of money commissioning their outfits or someone else paid for them. The material of most of their outfits is high-gloss Milliskin, a fabric Gail has heard described as the Cadillac of cloth polymers. It clings to them as if it were painted on and shines like the scales of a freshly caught fish. The ones who aren't decked out in tights, or in actual leather and vinyl, wear what appears to be normal clothes, but smaller or shorter or lower-cut, or ripped and frayed in particularly alluring ways. What remains is held on only by willpower or decency. Or, more likely, spirit gum.

Then she looks at what she's wearing. The jeans she left New York in. Brown shoes she thought of as dressy, but which her brother Ron referred to as "old-lady librarian shoes." The pair of glasses that had come free with a nicer pair of glasses that she fell asleep wearing six months ago and irreparably bent. A National Comics T-shirt a size too big that she'd been given as her signing bonus five years ago. The logo, with NATIONAL in alternating red and blue letters, hadn't been updated since the early eighties and was derided by the fans as a symbol of National's overall dated aesthetic. Gail believed it would soon take on a retro cool, or that the aging fan base would realize they themselves were a little on the dated side, and there was nothing sadder than middle-agers trying to look hip. Anyway, she was waiting it out.

"You're going out there in that?" asks Spectacle Girl.

"They'll eat her alive," says Flail.

"No," says Flog, stifling a giggle, "they won't." This gets a laugh out of the younger girls and a glare out of the older women. Gail feels playground division lines have been drawn and there may be no team for her to join.

"She's a writer," says Val.

They all examine Gail, inspecting her costume to decide if it's convincing.

"Of comic books?" the Diviner asks. Gail nods.

"I didn't know they had women writers in comics," says Iota.

"They don't have many," Gail tells her.

"What a surprise," says Red Emma.

"I write *you*," says Gail, approaching Iota slowly and with a sense of wonder. The costume is intended to look like Iota is mid-shrink: a white lab coat huge at the shoulders but short enough to show off her legs, practically falling off her. It's a problem Gail has tried to address during her run on the book: Iota's powers often lead to her ending up tiny, naked, and struggling to cover herself up with a gum wrapper or ginkgo leaf. Gail had Iota create a costume for herself out of unstable molecules, an unexplained but vaguely sciency-sounding substance that would shrink with her whenever she got little. But when Iota is drawn for covers or pinups, she's clutching some odd piece of minuscule detritus over her unmentionables.

Gail thinks about Geoff's stories of visiting the set of the Blue Torch movie, seeing a character he'd written for years come to life. This might not be on such a grand scale, but the girl is perfect—it's like she stepped right out of a panel and off the page. She knows it's weird to address this woman as if she is Iota, but she can't seem to help it.

"I mean, I write the series you're currently in," Gail says. "You don't have your own series."

"I don't?" Iota asks.

Gail looks around at the other women in the room, taking stock. "Most of you don't," she says. "The Astounding Woman is part of the Astounding Family, which is a group book that hasn't been published in twenty years. The Diviner and Medea are both in team books, too. OuterGirl shows up in the *OuterMan* books occasionally. Flail and Flog are villains."

"We're misunderstood," says Flog.

"Demonized for our sexuality," says Flail.

"ExSanguina is in *Sinister,* which is a horror anthology, but she's only in a couple times a year. The only one of you who has her own title is Red Emma."

"Suck it, bitches," says Red Emma.

"But I used to, at least," says Iota.

"All of you used to," Gail says. "Even Flail and Flog. Back in the nineties, early two thousands." She has the feeling she's in a waiting room between series cancellation and cultural disappearance. Like a scantily clad terminal ward. "They were mostly awful. All tits and ass. But tits and ass sold back then."

"Tits and ass always sell," says Flail. Or possibly Flog. Gail adjusts her glasses but still can't tell them apart.

"Well," she says, "the supply of tits and ass went up, so the price went down."

"Fucking Internet," says Red Emma.

"In a lot of ways," Gail continues, "things are better now. Female characters are stronger, like Red Emma—"

"Again I say, suck it," Red Emma says to the room.

"And less explicitly sexualized." Here they all examine Red Emma, who is fixing the lapels of her trench coat so they reveal only a PG-13 level of cleavage. "But there are fewer female-fronted titles. Even *Red Emma*'s written by a guy."

"What the fuck?" says Red Emma.

"So why don't I have my own series anymore?" asks Iota.

"It got canceled four years ago, just before I came on. Editorial decided to fold you into *The Speck*'s regular cast."

"He's my boyfriend, right?"

"You read the comics?" Gail asks.

"They give us dossiers," explains the Diviner. "I, for instance, am an archaeologist who becomes possessed by the prophetic Greek goddess Cassandra."

"Cassandra's not a goddess," says Flog.

"Is that so?" says the Diviner, clearly not interested.

"She's the daughter of Priam," says Flail.

"She's in the *Iliad*," says Flog, "and she's murdered in *Agamemnon*."

"Congratulations, you both pass Who the Hell Cares with straight A's," says the Diviner. "I'm telling you what's in my dossier. I'd love to know what yours say."

"Did National Comics hire you?" Gail asks Iota.

"The convention organizers hire us," says Spectacle Girl.

"If you could get any of us a meeting with someone at National," says OuterGirl, "that'd be amazing."

"You think some writer is going to get you cast in the next *Vengeance Troop* movie?" says Red Emma. "No offense," she adds, to Gail.

"I'm so sorry," says Gail. She looks at Val for help, but Val doesn't know what's going on. Gail puts her hand on Iota's shoulder. "They're killing you off. In . . . maybe five issues. Just after I leave the book. You get beaten to death by Quietus the Quisling."

The girl looks horrified. "Why are they killing me off?" she asks. "Do people not like me?"

"It's for the Speck," Gail says. "Editorial thinks he's goofy. Dated. They want to give him motivation. Make him more driven."

"But what does that have to do with me?" It has nothing to do with this girl who is not Iota the Incredible Shrinking Girl only a passable iteration thereof. But she is in real pain at the thought of her impending death, less than a hundred pages away.

"It's a fridging. It's how you motivate a male character," says Gail, feeling like a mother explaining some of the less pleasant parts of sex to her daughter. "You kill off the woman he loves, then he swears revenge. Maybe her death keeps coming up in flashback, a kind of emotional touchstone moment. But after ten, twelve issues, he meets somebody new and moves on."

"And what about me?" asks Iota.

"You'll come back eventually," Gail assures her. "Dead's never dead in comics. If you were a male character, you'd fight your way back from the nether-whatever. For you? I'd guess resurrected by scientists after a year, year and a half. Heel turn for six months, then saved by your love for the Speck."

"Heel turn?" asks OuterGirl.

"You'll come back evil," says Gail. "But only for a little bit."

"You wrote this story?" says Red Emma.

"It hasn't been written yet," Gail says. "I'm saying that's how it's likely to go down. They informed me of the new editorial direction. I told them I didn't want to write *The Speck* without Iota in the book. So they took me off the book."

"But you're the writer," says Iota.

"Only as long as they let me be," says Gail.

"They ever kill off a guy to give a female character motivation?" asks Red Emma, putting the last word in air quotes.

"I've never read a story like that," Gail says.

Red Emma nods and pulls her fedora down over her eyes. She tries to lean back like a weary private detective about to catch some sleep, but there's no room, and the attempt knocks over the Astounding Woman's wig stand. Red Emma pretends not to notice. "Maybe you should write one," she tells Gail.

"That's just not how it works," says Gail. "We work in tropes. Broad, familiar strokes. Women are in the story to get the men where they need to be. Dead lovers and mothers, mostly."

Through the chair, Gail feels Val give a little shudder.

"Have any of you seen Alex this afternoon?" Val asks.

# Welcome Party

"So tell me more about the boy and his robot," says Brett. They are heading back from the bookstore, Alex with a copy of *Adam Anti & Nothing but Flowers* tucked under one arm and a too large paper cup of loganberry soda, slick with condensation, gripped in his other hand. When they got to the store, it became clear to Brett that while the kid knew, intellectually, what a loganberry was, he'd never had a loganberry soda. They stopped at a corner store to remedy that, and now the kid's lips are a vampiric shade of maroon and his teeth pale pink.

"It's not *his* robot," Alex says. "It doesn't belong to him."

"But he fixed it," Brett says.

"Just because you fix something," Alex says, "doesn't make it yours." He slurps up the last of his soda. Rattles the straw around to see if there are any dregs left, then lets it hang at the end of his arm. "The boy and the robot," he says, "go out of the cave and they're by the ocean. Have you ever been to the ocean?"

"My girlfriend and I went last year," Brett says. It occurs to him that the kid is making this up as he goes along. He tries to remember if it was like that when he was a kid, if stories came about in real time. They always seemed as if they were fully formed, but maybe it was only that the details, laid one on top of the other over time, became instantly set and immutable.

"You talk about your girlfriend a lot," the kid says. "What's she like?"

"She's actually my ex-girlfriend," says Brett.

"Do you ever talk to her?"

"Sometimes."

"Do you miss her?"

Brett shrugs. "Sometimes."

"Oh."

As they pass a trash can, Alex drops the cup into it like an afterthought. "What was the ocean like where you went?" he asks.

"It was big," says Brett. "Biggest thing I've ever seen. We were still within sight of New York. But the city looked so small. Like it could fall into the ocean and the ocean wouldn't notice."

"That's a good description," says Alex. "That's what it's like for them, too. And the city is in the distance, just like you said."

"Which city?" Brett asks. This is the first mention of a city.

"They don't know," Alex says. "But they can't cross the ocean and they can't go back to the cave." He pauses at a corner. Brett knows the way back from here, but he waits. Let the kid figure it out himself. Correct him if he goes wrong. But he picks the right way, and they start down the last block back to the hotel. "Can you do a robot voice?" the kid asks.

Brett stops. No one has ever asked him to do a robot voice before. But it turns out it's the kind of question he's always wanted someone to ask him. "Does not compute, does not compute," says Brett in a monotone. Alex considers.

"That's not what he sounds like," he says. "Do another one."

Brett thinks for a minute, then begins flailing his arms wildly and spinning around, yelling, "Danger, Will Robinson, danger!" Alex has to duck to dodge, running around Brett in a circle.

"No!" he says, laughing. "Do a different one."

"I'm afraid I can't do that, Dave," says Brett. It's not a particularly good HAL impersonation, but it's unlikely the kid knows that.

"That was scary," Alex says. They cross the street to the hotel. "Do robots have to sound like robots?"

"I don't think there's a rule," says Brett.

"Then this one doesn't," says Alex, pulling open the heavy door to the hotel lobby. "He sounds regular. But he knows stuff. He knows lots of stuff about the city."

Alex has just started to describe the layout and design of the city the boy and his robot have arrived at, its abandoned golden spires that the boy dimly remembers, when they are attacked by a mob of women, all but one of them in superhero costumes. The one who is not in costume grabs Alex and swoops him into her arms. Clutches him tightly to her. Turns away from the rest of them. Brett recognizes her immediately.

"You're Alex's mom," he says.

"Where have you been?" she says to Alex. Ignores Brett.

"I went to get a book," he says. Her shoulder muffles the sound.

"You had everyone in a panic," she says. She rocks him back and forth the way mothers do to get their babies to sleep. Like she's going through the motions of calming Alex down to calm herself.

"I was at the bookstore," Alex says.

"Where?" she says. Alex tries to get the map out of his back pocket, but his arms are pinned by her embrace.

"It's on Larchmere," says Brett. Half of the costumed women glare at him. Even the Diviner, through her blindfold. He looks at the girl dressed as Ferret Lass for sympathy. She bites her darkened lower lip nervously.

"We were about to call the police," Val says. Not to anyone in particular, but loudly enough that everyone in the lobby hears.

"I was okay, though," says Alex. "I was with Brett." He still sounds bright and happy. But Brett begins to see the severity of the situation. He would back away, but two women in bondage gear stand behind him, arms crossed authoritatively.

"What were you thinking?" Val demands of Brett. She sets Alex down and steps in front of him protectively.

"He said you said it was okay," says Brett. Now he can't remember if this is exactly what Alex said.

"And you didn't think to check?"

Brett thinks of the moment before they left. The wave. He'd read approval into it, but there'd been nothing there. He wonders if the kid tricked him, and if so how willing to be tricked he had been. He looks at Val, wanting to apologize. Two nights ago, he was flirting with her in the hotel bar. Badly, but still. She bears down on him as if she were his own mother, and Brett feels like he's shrinking. Regressing to Alex's age in front of an audience he notices now includes Fred, who watches over Ferret Lass's furry shoulder pad.

"I should have you arrested," Val says.

"He didn't do anything," says Alex from behind her.

"You could have gotten him killed."

"It seems like everybody's okay," says Ferret Lass, not quite stepping in front of Brett, but putting a hand on his chest and pulling him away from Val.

"Stay out of it," warns the Diviner.

"I'm sorry," says Brett. "I didn't think—"

"It's okay," Ferret Lass says to him quietly.

"He didn't *do* anything," says Alex. He steps between Val and Brett. His cheeks are flushed, and his huge brown eyes are full. They glisten like glass marbles in a fishbowl. "He took me to the bookstore to get my book. Because *you wouldn't*." He throws this at her like an accusation.

"Alex, go upstairs," she says softly, still looking at Brett.

"He's my *friend*," says Alex, crying now, "and he's helping me with my story." He is such an abject little thing that Brett wants to pick him up and hold him. He knows that if Val would look at Alex right now, her heart would break the same way Brett's is breaking and everything would be all right.

"Alex, go upstairs," she says again, louder. Alex stands there for a second. Still below her line of vision. He stares at her, then at Brett, then runs off. Once he is gone, the fight goes out of Val. When she speaks, her voice is quiet. Without panic or malice.

"I don't want you talking to him again, do you understand? I know you were trying to help him. I know. But we're fine. We're fine, and we don't need any help." She walks past Brett. She very softly thanks the other women, who form a buffer between Brett and Val. Keeping the two of them apart. None of them look angry with him, just pitying. It's a basic rule of nature: you don't come between a mama bear and her cub. The looks they give him call him out for not knowing that, or not remembering. Sometimes the simplest rules are the hardest to remember, proscriptions grow vague and milky from a lifetime of disuse. Over shoulders bare and caped, he can see Val making her slow and deliberate way up the stairs.

## Secret Origin of the Blue Torch

*Not only are you jobless, but you are fine with it. Fucking fine with it. Fuck your friends and their "graphic design" gigs. Graphic design is for fuckers who used to think they were artists. Graphic design is where creativity goes to die. Fuck those guys.*

*The girl behind the bar, ack. If you were single, oh my God. But you're not single, and also you're broke. So you hope that picture of her you drew on the bar napkin and left as a tip doesn't make her think you're a cheapshit. Because you're not a cheapshit. You're just broke.*

*And you have to piss. Like a racehorse. Like your molars are swimming. And of course there's some asshole making out in the men's room. There is always some asshole making out in the men's room on a Friday night, as if that's worth everyone else's inconvenience. As if you couldn't just make out in the bar, for fuck's sake, without denying everyone else a place to piss.*

*So you take it out in the alley. Which smells of trash that hasn't been picked up in two weeks and two weeks of other fuckers' piss. One more sign you're not having an original idea. But something rustles in the trash bags, in the piles of garbage, and once you've emptied your bladder you climb over to see.*

*Dropped into the black vinyl of the garbage bags is a man, no bigger than a nine-year-old and the color of fresh-cut grass. He is leaking blaze-orange blood from his nostrils, which are disproportionately large and weirdly close to his eyes. He holds out a flashlight to you, royal blue.*

*"Take this torch," he says, "and carry the blue light of justice throughout your sector. Protect the oppressed, defend the innocent, punish the—"*

*And he dies. He just fucking dies. So there's this torch that's all about protecting the innocent, and it's in the hands of this little green dude. Who wants you to take it. Who told you to take it.*

*So you take the fucking torch.*

*Little do you know, there's a whole thing. That it's basically the intergalactic police. There's a whole training module the torch downloads directly into your fucking brain. And now, because you picked this thing up, you are an officer in the Blue Torch Armada. By virtue of plucking something out of the garbage. And it doesn't pay shit.*

*The weird thing is, it's great. You fly off to other planets and stop civil wars between the purple people and the orange people or whatever. Because it's always really clear that either the orange people or the purple people are total fuckers and whoever isn't total fuckers, you side with them. When you're active, when you're out there, it's great.*

*Of course there are down times. There are days, sometimes weeks or months, where no one is fighting a war in space. And you're just living in your neighborhood, where the women cross the street to avoid you, sometimes. And the men mutter "lowlife" and "scumbag" under their breath, sometimes. Gallery owners don't return your calls, even though you diverted an asteroid from destroying the fucking planet and some gratitude is maybe in order. A freelance client stiffs you on your fee, even though you could incinerate her with a thought. The time away, the secrecy, is fucking your relationship. You give it another week, maybe. And you look to the stars, waiting to go to war.*

# The Sense of an Ending

A bar is a wonderful place to work. So long as you're willing to look standoffish, which Gail most certainly is. She feels the aberrant blue glow of a laptop screen in a dimly lit hotel bar is like the bright coloration of a poisonous insect, warning off those who might think it a good idea to talk to her. There's a script page that's been nagging at her all day, a story beat that's missing. It's tougher when you're moving things to an ending. Beginnings are so much simpler—everything can sprawl out. But endings have to winnow to a point, and it's easier to trip and stumble into it than to smoothly spiral downward.

Part of the problem is that it's not her ending she's moving toward. It's the first time Gail's encountered this, but there's a problem that may be unique to comic book writers, which is that the story will go on without you. With only three months to go, everything had to move faster than she'd planned, stories that would have played out over six issues compressed to five pages, foreshadowings foreshortened. Mostly it isn't that hard. But there was a tack she'd wanted to take with the Iota's professional life, establishing her not just as the Speck's girlfriend but as a scientist in her own right. After all, he'd only discovered how to shrink himself and then rashly decided to try the process out; she was the one who'd figured out how to return him to actual size. Iota was going to finish her degree and take a job at Metro City University, where, over time, she'd come to outrank the Speck, who would never get tenure as long as he was skipping office hours to go help the Vengeance Troop by entering someone's bloodstream or defusing a nuclear bomb by stabilizing the uranium iso-topes at its core.

She'd decided to skip a lot of the necessary steps and have the university hire Iota straight away. It would have been hard to get action-packed storylines out of Iota toiling on her dissertation anyway. But the scene between Iota and the Dean, where he knows she's secretly Iota and she knows he's secretly Ominus, but neither knows the other knows, isn't playing out right.

She shuts her laptop and spins on her barstool to survey the room. Sometimes the background noise of a dozen conversations can stimulate whatever part of the brain writes dialogue. But tonight the words are lying flat on the page, and the scene comes off like a bad high school production of *Oleanna*. She sips her beer. None of this has to be done now. She's already a month ahead on scripts, and she planned these weeks as dead time. But still, that scene. It's not right. The characters keep running their lines in her head and not clicking.

She spots him in the corner of the bar, at a table by himself. There's a whiskey in front of him that hasn't been touched. The ceiling lights conveniently avoid falling on him, and if she hadn't seen him at the panel today, she wouldn't recognize him, but it's him for sure. Gail packs her laptop into her bag, then hesitates. What does she possibly have to say to Levi Loeb? It'd be weirdly like meeting God.

But how many chances do you get to meet God?

"Mr. Loeb," she says. He looks up from the stain on the table he's been examining. His eyes are milky blue behind thick lenses. "My name's Gail Pope. I'm a comic book writer."

"Miss Pope," he says in a voice rasped by a half-century of smoking, "if you know a thing about me, you know that's about the worst way you could introduce yourself. Terrible way to make a living." She winces. Maybe she should mention that she's German while she's at it—that'd go over real hot.

"Well," she says, "it beats my old job clubbing baby seals to death."

He chuckles. "That pay by the hour?"

"By the seal," she says.

"Siddown, kid," he says. He makes a feeble attempt to kick out a stool for her. She pulls it out and takes a seat. "Who do you write for?"

"National."

"*Pfft.*" The noise generates a small cloud of spittle. "Queers."

Gail smirks. "Some of us, yeah."

Loeb puts his hand over his eyes and shakes his head. It might be a gesture to indicate she's too sensitive, but it looks like genuine remorse. "I didn't mean it like that," he says. "My age, you forget which words have become awful. You like girls then?" As casually as he might have asked if she liked the Cleveland Browns or pinot grigio.

"Who wouldn't?" she says.

"Good for you," says Loeb. "Find a nice girl, settle down. Why not? It worked for me." The weird, lazy bigotry of the Greatest Generation.

"Who do you write?" Loeb asks.

"The Speck and Iota," she says. "And the Perfectional."

"Huh," says Loeb. "Those are all Jersey Sapolski's characters. I was still at Heston when he came up with them." Gail is ashamed to admit she's never read the old Heston issues. She bets Geoff has. "Sapolski was queer, too," Loeb says. "Homosexual, I mean."

"He was?" says Gail.

"We all knew," Loeb says. "Not that any of us cared. Christ, the office of every comic book office in New York was full of people no one wanted. Jews, Italians, Greeks, queers. Everything except women, to be honest with you. Well, there were the secretaries." Loeb's eyes drift away, probably imagining some toothsome piece long since passed away. "I remember Jersey, though. Sharp dresser, like they are. Ran around with so many women you'd think he was putting a softball team together. But you could tell. We all spent so much time together, you knew guys like you'd gone to war with them." He nods to himself, spins his whiskey glass around slowly, twice. "I always liked Jersey."

"I didn't know you worked at Heston," says Gail. She wishes Geoff were here, except that later she'll get to tell Geoff about this and he'll be achingly jealous. Still, he would be able to cite any comic Loeb had ever worked on.

"Before I went to Timely," he says. "Before I paired up with Brewster. It was hack work. All of it was hack work back then, but the Heston stuff, ach." He turns his head away from the table as if he's been served some entrée that disgusts him. "No spark, you know?"

Gail thinks about Iota and Ominus engaging in dry contract negotiations, debating dental plans and sabbaticals. "Yeah, I know."

"National was the same way," he says. "All brains and no heart. Except at Heston there were no brains, either."

"So you left Heston for Timely?" she asks.

"No, I was working both," says Loeb. "When we came up with the Astounding Family, I was still drawing *Krazy Kritters* and *Friday Night's for Heartbreak* at Heston." Gail has never heard of either title. She is aware that there were whole genres of comics that got swept away in the second wave of superheroes, the wave Loeb was mostly responsible for. She imagines an alternate comics industry in which talking-animal comics are ubiquitous. "Once *Astounding* was a hit," says Loeb, "Brew convinced me to hitch my cart to Timely. Told me we'd make millions." He shakes his head. "He was half right."

"So why are you here?" asks Gail, somewhat gingerly.

"My son's picking me up," Loeb says. He glances around the bar to make sure his son isn't already here. "He doesn't get off shift till late. Figured I'd have a drink, but this stuff burns my guts." He tilts the whiskey glass backward, then forward.

"No, I mean why are you at the convention?" says Gail.

"Well, they're paying me, for one," says Loeb, chuckling that low lung rumble. "I don't know. Burying the hatchet, I guess? Better than being buried with it. Fifty years. It's a long time to be angry." At this he takes a sip of his drink and, if his face is any indication, regrets it instantly. "And they're putting my name back on the books," he adds. "Phil Weinrobe, he's a good enough guy. He's trying to do right by me. More than Brew ever did."

"Is it enough?" asks Gail. He looks so broken, she can't imagine anything would be enough. She wants to sign over her paychecks to him and bake him a cake.

"No," he says flatly. "If I ever see Brewster Brewer again, I'll—" He stops, and Gail watches the anger slip away from him. "I'll probably buy him a drink," he admits. "He's the last of us left alive. Jersey killed himself in seventy-eight; Eisler and Dysart, they were at National, but we used to drink together at Bemelmans when we were flush. They both went with cancer twenty years ago. Stanchek was an asshole, but he died broke and half blind in some shitty home. He created the Flag Bearer. Brew didn't have a thing to do with it, even if he took all the credit. Poor Stanchek."

Again, she thinks how Geoff would know all these names, but she also thinks about her own position. She's paid by the issue, no long-term contract. She makes rent, but she's not saving anything, and the freelancers' union charges multiple limbs for minimal health insurance. Fifty years on and she's not sure anything's gotten better but the page rates.

"It's great, though," he says, "to see what it all looks like now. It's another planet, isn't it? Kids in their costumes and all. Good for them."

"It is, you know," she says. "The capes and the spandex and all. They protect you. They make you believe you can be better."

He nods and muses on this. "Me," he says, "I'm tired and I don't believe in superheroes anymore." He and Gail sit quietly for a minute. "You got the time?" Loeb asks.

She checks her phone. "Nine thirty."

"Bries is late," he says with a sense of inevitability. "We named him after Brewer. Did you know that was Brew's real name? Bries Borowitz. His secret identity. He wanted me to change my name, too. Something less Jewy, he said. Something alliterative and goyim. Bries, my Bries, was ten when they kicked me out of Timely. I'm ashamed to admit, I took it out on him for years. We're only now speaking again. So it's okay he's late, I guess."

Gail thinks about putting a hand on his shoulder, or patting him on the back. Any of the gestures she's seen her male colleagues do, the ones that say *Buck up* or *Walk it off.* Because he's not of a generation you can hug, unless you're related to him, and maybe not even then. There is too much space and time between them to connect properly. "You mind if I keep you company?" she asks.

"Sure thing, kid," says Loeb. "If I nod off, check my pulse."

# Male Bonding

"I cannot believe you fucked Ferret Lass," says Fred. "In her costume. In her fucking costume! Does that make you a furry or something? Because I have dibs on all sexual deviance in this friendship."

Brett snuck back into their room early this morning, sheepish and surprised to find Fred already awake. Last night at the bar, Fred said he wanted them on the road by eight. So they could make Chicago at a reasonable hour and rest up for their signing at Quimby's. Brett dimly remembers this. He can recall a moment before he was talking to Ferret Lass. Staring at her as she talked to Iota and ExSanguina. In a state where he was slightly too drunk to be clever, but sober enough to know he couldn't be clever. Every so often, Ferret Lass turned and looked at Brett, then looked down at her drink. Finally she said, "I don't think it's fair the way that woman was yelling at you."

Brett shrugged. "She's looking out for her kid," he said. Ferret Lass scooted over to discuss, and someone must have turned the volume down on Fred, because Brett doesn't remember him saying another thing all night.

"The sad thing is," Fred says, "I don't even know enough about ferrets to make a proper string of ferret jokes. Do they have scent glands? I feel like I should mention something about her scent glands."

After Brett left the hotel bar with her last night, this is likely the kind of conversation that ensued among the all-male corps of artists he'd left behind. If he'd watched one of his fellows leave with Ferret Lass, he might even have participated. Something about boys in aggregate leads to a locker room ethic. But he and Fred are not those kinds of guys. Being not that kind of guy is not only a defining aspect of who he is, or how he thinks of himself; it's also one of the only pieces of leverage he has with women. When he and Debra first got together, she made it clear she'd chosen him because he was "not like most guys she met." Over time this became not a virtue but a problem. Ferret Lass had picked him out of a crowd at a moment he was more broken than anyone else in the room. More vulnerable. If he ever sees her again, he'll ask her why that was.

For now he helps Fred pack up the van. He submits to a brand of masculine ribbing that seems like it was written for two other characters. He is too tired to protest. He wonders if he should call Debra. This is the first girl he's slept with since her. Meaning the only non-Debra sexual partner he's had in almost three years. It's not that he can't think what he'd say; he can't even determine what his tone would be. Calling to brag? Apologize?

But thinking about it, last night didn't have anything to do with Debra. It wasn't revenge or a final severing of ties. Maybe that was the best sign that things with her are over—the fact that Brett could hook up with someone else and it didn't involve Debra at all.

He loads his sketchbook, with some of the drawings he did of Ferret Lass last night. He remembers something she said as he left this morning. How all the cosplay girls are carpooling to Chicago together. And he realizes he never found out her secret identity.

# Ministry of Transportation

In the morning, she has stopped being mad. He knows this because he asks her, "Have you stopped being mad yet?"

"It's okay, Rabbit," she says. "I'm not mad at you."

"Are you still mad at Brett?" he asks. She doesn't answer, which means yes, she is still mad at Brett. They pack up the things in their hotel room, and Alex helps, looking around to make sure they got everything. He offers to carry her bags, but she says he can just take care of his.

On their way to check out, they pass the ballroom where Heronomicon was held, but now the ballroom is empty. The city it once contained has moved on and will be waiting for them in Chicago, bigger, better. Now that it's gone, Alex finds it easier to think about the things he liked about it, which mostly is that it had little pockets of quiet where he could read his book and not be in anyone's way, and that from anywhere in it he could usually spot his mother. He knows this makes it a little bit worse that he didn't find her before he went off to the bookstore with Brett, but there was something in him that wanted to keep a secret from her. He knows there's one she's keeping from him, too; the longer hugs and the seconds where she goes quiet and looks at him are all part of hiding something, and he wants to ask, but instead he tried to build a little secret for himself. Of course it didn't work. Secrets never work out the way you want them to.

While his mother stands at the front desk, talking to the same woman who gave Alex the map the day before, he surveys the crowd, hoping he will see Brett before they leave. The lobby is full of people Brett's age, who look and dress a lot like him, but none of them are him.

In the backseat, Alex arranges his things for the trip. He wedges a pillow against the door, for leaning, not for sleeping. He brings *Adam Anti & Nothing but Flowers* out of his backpack and sets it on the seat, then covers it with his notebook. Last night in the hotel room, after he'd shut off the lights, he could feel it calling to him, pulsating the way a star might. There is a gravity between him and the book, but he'll wait until they're on the road, not wanting his mother to see it and get upset all over again. Instead he takes out a couple of comics and opens an issue of *OuterMan* to somewhere in the middle. OuterMan has a car triumphantly hoisted over his head, its passengers staring down at him in amazement.

"How far is it to Chicago?" he asks as his mother straightens mirrors.

"Five hours," she says. "But we're going to Babu's house down in Normal, so that adds a couple hours."

So seven. Alex figures he reads about a page every two minutes. So thirty pages an hour, times seven. If he starts soon, he should be able to finish half the book by the time they arrive.

His mother starts the car and it lurches, like it's trying to jump out of itself. It makes a coughing noise and the radio flickers on and off, as if the announcer is stuttering. She tries this a couple of times, and he watches how turning the key, a motion that's usually carried out by her wrist, becomes a full-body action, leaning her shoulder toward the dashboard like she's going to push the car to start.

"Stay here, okay, Rabbit?" she says. She reaches under the steering wheel and pulls something that makes the front of the car go *ka-chunk*. Then she gets out of the car and goes around to the hood. "Fuck, fuck, fuck!" screams Alex's mother. He cannot see her, because she's opened up the hood, but smoke is pouring from the front of the Honda Civic.

"Piece of shit motherfucker!" she screams. Alex gets out of the backseat and comes around the front of the car to watch. Casual profanity is mildly entertaining for him, but this kind of dedicated and emphatic swearing is a real treat. She is shaking out her hands and blowing on them, because the hood must have been hot when she opened it. After a few more strings of curses, listening to his mom swear stops being fun. Alex wishes he could help.

"Hey, Alex," someone calls from across the parking lot, and Alex turns to see Brett heading toward them, doing something between running and walking. He looks frumpy, like he's still in his pajamas. Alex knows that for some grown-ups, their clothes are their pajamas.

"Get away from there!" Brett yells. "What if it hits the gas tank?"

"The gas tank's in the back," says Alex calmly. The smoke coming from the engine is starting to taper off, and if there was an emergency, it looks like it's passed. He's happy to see Brett again, but he wishes there were still an emergency. Without one, his mom will have nothing to focus on except Brett. Alex waits for the explosion.

"Do you guys need help?" Brett asks, more to Alex than to his mother.

"Not from you," says his mother. She slams the hood back down. Alex doesn't know much about cars, but he's pretty sure that when your car starts smoking, it's not going anywhere for a while. There is some kind of fluid coming out of the bottom of the car and pooling around his mother's feet.

"That's radiator fluid," says Brett, pointing at the green-black liquid. "It's . . . better if it's on the inside."

"You're an amateur mechanic now?" his mother asks, stepping out of the puddle. Alex wants there to be a way to make her not so mad.

"I know radiator fluid when I see it," says Brett. "Something like this happened with my old car. We had to put her down." He looks sad about this, and for a minute Alex is confused. Then he remembers the movie *Old Yeller* and how they say they're gonna have to put Yeller down. It looks like they're going to have to shoot the Civic.

"What's the car, late nineties?" asks Brett. "If it's the radiator, it's not even worth it to get it fixed. You'll put a thousand dollars in and then wait to see what blows out next."

Alex's mom is crying, the worst kind of crying. When she's sobbing, he knows he can hug her and it'll get a little better, but this is the kind where her face is very still and has tears running down it, and if he goes to her now, she'll push him away.

"We can take you to Chicago," Brett says. He turns back toward his van, where his friend is standing there waiting for him. "We've got room in the van. It smells like boys a little, but there's room. And it's only a day's drive."

Alex looks at his mom to see if she has heard this, expecting her to say no, or something worse than no. It's like the moment in a play where the main actress is about to sing her big number. Everyone else on stage is watching, and the stage lights go dim and the spotlight is on his mom, standing all by herself. Smoke wraps around her like arms.

## Secret Origin of the Idea Man

*Alex follows his mother up the spiral staircase. He doesn't need to hold her hand, but he does. He keeps his books tucked under his other arm and lets that hand slide lightly up the railing, which is made of wood so old it no longer feels like wood. It is the color of metal and feels like dried newspaper. Splinters of it try to grab his hand, but they can't find purchase. Skin is the best thing for keeping the world outside of you.*

    *At the top of the stairs, they come to the Idea Man's door, a huge slab of dark and polished wood. Alex is a step or two behind his mom, and for a second, as he looks up at her framed by the bulk of the door, she looks small to him. It's not all right when parents look small—it means something somewhere has come loose. Lately, Alex has seen more and more of these small moments: his mother tiny at the dining room table or sitting shrunken and slouched at the edge of her bed. When he's asked what's wrong, the answer is always* Nothing, Rabbit, *and the moment is over; she is mom-sized again. The way she is now.*

    *"You want to open it?" she says, because she knows he does. Alex turns the brass knob with both hands and lays his shoulder into the door, pushing it with his full weight. There is magic in opening doors, and the heavier the door, the greater the possibilities. It creaks open on ancient hinges, its bottom edge scraping against the floor with the fricative sound of wood against wood. A pale quarter-circle has been traced in the varnish by the door's slow-swinging path.*

    *In the living room, Louis is already rushing to greet them. Alex likes Louis, but he's never been sure if Louis likes him. He's never been sure if Louis likes anything. He seems too busy to have time for opinions about things. When Louis appeared, Alex thought he might be the Idea Man's boyfriend. Then he thought he might be the Idea Man's butler. Alex's mother finally explained that Louis was a Man Who Ends This, which means he writes things down.*

*Louis lays his hands gently on Alex's mother's shoulders, rises onto his toes, and kisses her on both cheeks.*

*"I'm so sorry," he says. "I was clearing duplicates out of the Book and didn't hear you come in."*

*"It's fine, Louis," she says, drawing him into a hug that he responds to by patting her lightly on her shoulder blades. "How is he today?"*

*Louis rolls his eyes and sighs dramatically. Alex remembers his babu used to do the same thing when they went to visit her in Illinois that time Dedulya was sick. If you roll your eyes and sigh, it means* Don't get me started. *When his babu did it, it meant things were bad, because Dedulya was dying. When Louis did it, it meant more like things were the same as they always were.*

*"Valerie!" There are four doors into the living room, not counting the one they've come through, and the Idea Man's voice could be coming from behind any of them. Alex makes a guess. He has a one-out-of-four chance of being right, which is twenty-five percent.*

*"Alex!" says the Idea Man, and Alex almost changes his mind, convinced for a moment that the voice is coming from the kitchen. But then the Idea Man emerges from where Alex thought he would. He is, as usual, half dressed, wearing sweatpants, a T-shirt for a band Alex has never heard of, and one sock. His hair, ghost white as long as Alex can remember, springs like an exclamation point from his forehead.*

*"Like Athena from the head of Zeus," Alex declared during the months he and* D'Aulaires' Book of Greek Myths *had been inseparable. He'd gone on to describe how the sprout of hair must be bursting from the Idea Man's head in super slow motion and how one morning it would escape into the kitchen to help Louis make breakfast.*

"Did you just get here?" the Idea Man asks. "Has Lawrence offered you anything?"

"Louis," corrects Louis. The Idea Man hasn't looked at Louis since he made his entrance, and his botching Louis's name is a funny little routine between them, played out, Alex thinks, largely for Alex's amusement. He enjoys it, but not as much as he did a year ago, and now his enjoyment is tinged with the tolerance of a child who knows he's being condescended to, if only a little, and sweetly.

The Idea Man grabs Alex under the armpits and sweeps him up into an embrace with surprisingly easy strength. Alex grips the Idea Man's neck. He thinks of the Idea Man as being so fragile, but he is perhaps the most physically solid person in Alex's life. Alex's mother says that before he became a television director, the Idea Man was a surfer, and even now, when he's neither, his body retains its old muscles, as if some rogue wave could hit his castle in Greenpoint any day, and better to be ready.

"We're fine," Alex's mother says to Louis, who is standing by, ready to cater to their every desire.

"I'll have a ginger ale," says Alex, still in the Idea Man's hug, which is beginning now to feel too long.

"Lance," says the Idea Man, holding Alex out at arm's length and a few feet above the ground as if to appraise him, "a ginger ale."

"I don't think we have any ginger ale," says Louis.

"It's lucky, then, that we live in the most civilized city in the universe," says the Idea Man. "Get the boy a ginger ale." Without another word, Louis leaves. Alex wonders why anyone would be so mean to someone who helps him. Again he thinks of his dedulya barking orders at Babu in his hoarse and whispery shout, and how there was some kind of love in his unkindness and some other kind of love in her enduring it.

"So Alex," says the Idea Man, settling into the large and very old chair where he likes to sit, the one the windows cast a light across in the afternoon, "tell me about your trip."

*Alex considers this. "I don't know anything about it yet," he says, "since we haven't even left."*

*"But you know the plan," says the Idea Man. "You know where you'll be going."*

*"I was thinking about that," says Alex, "but I've been reading this book where the character thinks he's going to a regular high school, but it turns out to be a high school for magicians. So maybe it's not a good idea to think you know where you're going until after you've been there."*

*The Idea Man is smiling and nodding at him, but a look of confusion is starting to spread down his face. "A high school for magicians," he says absently. "Val, is that one of mine?"*

*"I hope not," says Alex's mother. "If it is, you didn't get paid enough for it. It's a book series.* Adam Anti. *You must have read at least one of them."*

*"I can't read books anymore," says the Idea Man. Alex looks around the room, which is lined with bookshelves not full but overfull, stacked two deep in places.*

*"You and I must be the last people who haven't read them," says Alex's mother. "There are more copies of it on the subway than there are rats. Even some of the rats are reading it."*

*For some reason, the popularity of the* Adam Anti *books had convinced Alex's mother she shouldn't let him read them. The girl working in the bookstore in Park Slope had to persuade her it was age appropriate. Of all the stories Alex consumes—plays, movies, TV—his mother is most protective when it comes to books. This makes sense to Alex, because books make you create something in your head, which means the bad stuff is even worse. He's on to the second one now, although he's a little overwhelmed that there are seven books altogether. It's almost too much of one story. Like if you ate candy bars all day.*

*The door creaks open and Louis returns, holding a can of ginger ale out like he's recovered a treasure.*

*"That took long enough," says the Idea Man. Alex walks across the room*

*and takes the can, and as he turns, he sees his mother giving him the face and turns back.*

*"Thank you, Louis," he says, then opens the can, marveling at how much it sounds like saying "kiss," inviting you to put your lips up to it.*

*"Louis," she says, "have you read the* Adam Anti *books?"*

*"I'm not sure," says Louis. "Is that something we're allowed to admit in public yet?"*

*"You were only out there for five minutes, Lucas," says the Idea Man. "Did you catch some sort of hipster credibility virus?" As he says this, the Idea Man's face crumples, not like before, when the confused look started at the top and dribbled down like wax off the sides of a candle, but like a soda can crushed underfoot, like his eyebrows are trying to jump into his mouth. "A serial killer," says the Idea Man. "A hipster serial killer."*

*"Hold on a second," says Louis, rushing out of the room.*

*"Hurry," says the Idea Man. "Fucking hurry." He's beginning to twitch, as if an electric current is running through him. In a way, Alex thinks, it is. The Idea Man only gets like this when an idea is coming to him, like a broadcast only he can pick up. Louis rushes back into the room with a notebook exactly like the one Alex brought with him, only this one is black, not green, and this one is the Book, where Louis writes down the Idea Man's ideas as they come. People from television and the movies pay a lot to come and pick one page out of the Book. Part of Louis's job is to make sure they only ever use the one idea they've paid for. Sometimes when Alex and his mom are watching TV, which isn't often, she'll say, "That's one of Tim's," even though the Idea Man's name never appears anywhere in the credits.*

*"A hipster serial killer," the Idea Man repeats. He looks as if he's trying to remember something. "He targets the inauthentic. Poseurs. Fakers. Liars. Storytellers." The Idea Man's head shakes back and forth. "He's hunting novelists in Brooklyn. He's hunting anyone who creates fictions."*

*The Idea Man's expression is becoming pained.*

*"This," says Alex's mother, "seems like not a great idea."*

"You're right," says the Idea Man, his face opening up again like a bloom. "Did you start a page?" he asks Louis.

"Yes."

"Tear it out."

Louis tears out the page, crumples it into a ball, and makes it disappear into a pocket. Alex wonders how many times a day this happens and if at night Louis empties dozens of abandoned ideas out of his pants.

"I've read them all," Louis says, as though the last few minutes never happened. "Most of them twice."

"So you know how it ends?" Alex asks.

"I do," says Louis. "You want to know?"

Alex panics for a second; then he realizes Louis has no intention of spoiling the ending of the books for him and is, in fact, messing with him. Louis has never messed with Alex before. He's not sure he likes it; it feels like being mean. Alex thinks it must have something to do with how the Idea Man is mean to Louis, but he can't figure out how the two things relate.

"So are you ready for your trip?" Louis asks Alex's mom. Alex is tempted to answer, because he's been thinking a lot about the trip and about readiness. This will be the first time he's left New York since he and his mother moved here six years ago, which he knows but doesn't remember. And California is about as far away from New York as you can get, even if it is where Alex was born. He remembers nothing about it and feels unprepared for it. He wonders how he could be ready and worries he isn't, that he doesn't even know how to start getting ready and wouldn't know when he'd arrived at readiness, a state that seems nearly as far as California.

His mother answers for him.

"We're as ready as we're liable to get, which probably isn't ready enough."

This is a good way to put it, so Alex takes another swig of ginger ale.

"I talked to the woman at the correctional facility in Lincoln," says Louis. "It's about two hours outside of Chicago." Louis is apparently more prepared for their trip than they are.

"I know where Lincoln Correctional is," says Alex's mother in that sharp tone Alex knows means she doesn't want to talk about whatever is being discussed. "My mom lives forty minutes from there."

"The warden's name is Iris something or other. They're ready for your visit. She said she'd rather you came to the parole hearing, but—"

"That's enough," says the Idea Man. "No talking about the middle before the beginning. In a minute there is time for decisions or revisions which a minute will reverse."

"You're quoting 'Prufrock' now?" asks Alex's mother. Alex imagines how a proof rock might work. Either you put your hand on it and it tells if you are telling the truth, or it records evidence somehow: sounds and voices that it can play back.

"I grow old," says the Idea Man. "I grow old."

"Don't be maudlin, Tim," says Alex's mother. He grins at her. When he smiles, he doesn't look old at all.

"I've been too much indoors," he says. "Eliot's like Whitman's asthmatic little brother. But lately I find my thoughts drawn to him."

"Why don't you and Alex go read for a bit?" says Alex's mother, addressing both of them like they're children. "Since you won't be seeing each other for a while. Give Louis and me a chance to talk some things out."

The Idea Man springs from the couch and plucks Alex out of the chair with arms like taut cables of wire.

"Let us go then, you and I," he says in a weird British accent. He tucks Alex under his arm like a giggling briefcase and whisks him away. Once they are in the hallway and Alex is set properly on his feet, Alex heads toward the reading room, a sunny and spacious spot in the back of the apartment where he and the Idea Man have spent hours sharing the adventures of the Ferret, the Astounding Family, OuterGirl, and dozens of other brightly costumed heroes. But this time the Idea Man calls for him to wait, and Alex stops in front of a door halfway down the hall, the only one in the house that is perpetually closed. The Idea Man moves Alex a little off to the side and pulls the keys out of his pocket.

*"Have I ever shown you what's in here?" the Idea Man asks. He hasn't, but Alex has always wondered.*

*The Idea Man opens the door. "It's a time machine," he says. Alex steps in.*

*On the inside, it's bigger than Alex would have predicted, or even thought possible. The ceilings are higher than anywhere else in the apartment, and bookcases and file cabinets climb up all of the walls, so high the bookcases have ladders on runners that slide across them and some of the file cabinets have other ladders propped against them.*

*"The present's nearest the ceiling," says the Idea Man, pointing up, "and the past is closer to the floor. Comics in the file cabinets, books and photos on the shelves. It should probably be the other way, so the past is harder to get to, but usually it's the past I'm in here looking for."*

*Alex puts his hand on the handle of one of the file cabinets and gives it a tentative pull, testing its give.*

*"Go ahead," says the Idea Man. Alex yanks the drawer open. It makes a metallic scraping noise, very different from the wood-on-wood sound of the Idea Man's front door. Inside, as promised, are dozens of very old comic books. The Visigoth. The Blue Torch. The Astounding Family. The Idea Man has offered him issues at random over the years, but here they are meticulously sorted and cataloged, month by month. The thing that's strange to Alex is that all of them were once new, when the Idea Man was young. The thought of their newness implies a time before they existed, before they were made, and times before are always troubling to Alex.*

*"You should take a couple with you," says the Idea Man. "You're traveling into a foreign country, and it's good to have some sense of the language." Alex isn't sure what this means. They are going to Cleveland. They are going to Chicago. They are going to Los Angeles. All of them well inside the United States. "Besides," says the Idea Man, "it'll be a while before we get to read together again."*

*"It's only three weeks," says Alex, delicately turning the pages of* Captain Wonder, *one of the Idea Man's favorite characters. Alex looks up from the*

*comic to see the Idea Man staring at him as if Alex has fallen and bruised his knee.*

*"It could be a while longer than that," says the Idea Man. "California's a long ways away."*

*He's not sure what the Idea Man means by this, but then sometimes the things the Idea Man says don't make a lot of sense. Alex has checked and done the math: you can drive from New York to Los Angeles in two days, if you drive all day and all night. But there are so many things to see between here and there, Alex can imagine the trip taking longer, their path back across the country strange and snaking. They can take all the time they need.*

*"I'm coming back," he says, surprised how small his voice sounds in the big room.*

*"You're going back," says the Idea Man. "California's where you're from, after all. But that doesn't make it your home. Only you can decide where your home is. And every good story is about finding your way there."*

*Alex thinks about all the stories that end up with the main character arriving home, and how there's something disappointing about the story ending where it began, but how there's something satisfying about it, too.*

*"Is New York your home?"*

*"No," says the Idea Man. "California's my home at the end of the day."*
*He has taken a picture off the shelf and is looking at it, wearing that same expression he gets before an idea comes to him, his almost remembering face. Alex can see the picture: in it are the Idea Man, Alex's mom and dad, and another lady Alex doesn't recognize. They're wearing tuxedos and fancy dresses. His mom and the Idea Man are holding up gold statues and they all look very happy. "This is a nice place to hide, but I have the Pacific in my blood. I have heard the mermaids singing, each to each."*

*"Are there mermaids in California?"*

*"The realest mermaids I know."*

*Alex has not until now thought about the Pacific, but he's heard that it's the blue color of oceans in picture books. He thinks about the ocean you can see at Coney Island, which is gray like the railing out in the stairwell, and how his mother took him to the Mermaid Parade there one year, where not many of the mermaids had tails at all, just turquoise skirts and no tops. He wonders what realer mermaids look like, but before he can imagine one, he hears his mom calling from the next room.*

*"Sounds like they're done plotting and scheming," says the Idea Man. He opens another drawer and skims through, extracting a comic. He gets up on a short stepladder and opens a different, more recent drawer to get another. He does this a half-dozen times, flitting about the room, then straightens them into a stack and hands them to Alex. "Basic vocabulary," he says. "Dónde está la cabina telefónica? With great power comes great responsibility. To be continued."*

*Alex and the Idea Man go back to the living room, where Alex's mom and Louis are standing near enough to the doorway to indicate it is time to go. But Alex doesn't want to go. The Idea Man is the last thing they've scheduled to say goodbye to in New York, but what about the Alice in Wonderland statue, or the Whispering Gallery in Grand Central? What about Elizabeth at Peas n' Pickles, who sneaks him candy while his mom shops for groceries, or the Brooklyn Heights Promenade? There was no last pizza at Frankie's, no final ride on the Staten Island Ferry to wave good-bye to the statue. Alex wants to mention these things, to list them off to his mother as things they need to do before they can leave. But something about the way she's been worrying keeps him from sharing his worries with her.*

*"When will you leave?" the Idea Man asks Alex's mother.*

*"Tomorrow," she says, and all Alex can think is that he is not ready. "How long does it take to drive to Cleveland?"*

*"I should know this?" says the Idea Man. "Who ever has to drive to Cleveland? Leonard. How long does it take to drive to Cleveland?"*

*"I've never driven to Cleveland," says Louis.*

*"No one's ever driven to Cleveland," replies the Idea Man. "But there must be some way to calculate it or something."*

*Alex's mother intervenes in this argument by pulling the Idea Man away and into a hug. "It'll take how long it takes," she tells him. "You'll take care of him?" she says to Louis, turning her back to the Idea Man.*

*"As best I can," Louis says, as if she has asked him to juggle chainsaws while on a unicycle.*

*"You're fantastic and he loves you dearly," she tells Louis. He bows his head. Louis gets embarrassed whenever anyone says something nice to him, probably because it happens so rarely.*

*"Alex," the Idea Man says, shaking Alex's hand up and down sternly, "it was very good to see you."*

*"It was nice to see you, too," says Alex. He pauses. He is deciding something, and after a moment he decides yes. "Can I have one?" he asks.*

*The Idea Man, who bent over a little to shake Alex's hand, straightens up and strokes his chin. "Hmm. People usually have to pay."*

*"I don't have any money," says Alex, although this is not entirely true. His mom makes sure he has ten dollars in his pocket at all times, for emergencies. It's been the same ten-dollar bill for two years, and Alex has come to think of this money as talismanic rather than spendable.*

*"Tell you what," the Idea Man says. "I'll give you one, but if you make a story out of it, you have to tell it to me when it's done."*

*"I thought you didn't like stories," says Alex.*

*"I like stories very much," the Idea Man says. "I just can't come up with them anymore."*

*"Okay," says Alex, putting his hand out to be shaken again, this time on business. "If I make a story out of it, I'll tell it to you next time I see you."*

*"All right," the Idea Man says, shaking Alex's hand once, twice, three times, the number of anything magic. He squats down. He lowers his voice until it is not reverse yelling but secret quiet. And he speaks.*

PART TWO

# The Silver Age

I had to work fast. I would draw three pages a day, maybe more. I would have to vary the panels, balance the page. I took care of everything on that page—the expressions of the characters, the motivation of the characters—it all ran through my mind. I wrote my own stories. Nobody ever wrote a story for me. I told in every story what was really inside my gut, and it came out that way. My stories began to get noticed because the average reader could associate with them.

—JACOB KURTZBERG

What did Doctor Doom really want? He wanted to rule the world. Now, think about this. You could walk across the street against a traffic light and get a summons for jaywalking, but you could walk up to a police officer and say "I want to rule the world," and there's nothing he can do about it, that is not a crime. Anybody can want to rule the world. So, even though he was the Fantastic Four's greatest menace, in my mind, he was never a criminal!

—STANLEY MARTIN LIEBER

# On the Road

"We should add more characters," says Brett. He shovels another handful of corn chips into his mouth. Fred wanted to make the trip without stopping. But Alex spotted a Road Ranger outside of South Bend and they'd stocked up on provisions, none of which Valerie approved of. At Alex's request, she agreed to sit up front with Fred so Brett and Alex could work. Fred's been monologuing at her the entire time, on what Brett can't imagine. He hopes Fred's not sharing his opinions on the decline of *Anomaly* across the last half of its run. But Brett's sure it has at least been mentioned. In the backseat of the van, Brett and Alex race to the bottom of the bag of Fritos. Alex leads.

"Iwa finken at," says Alex, spraying wet crumbs. Rather than elaborate with his mouth full, he gestures for Brett to offer ideas.

Until now, Brett has only confirmed or clarified Alex's ideas. Drawn them. Made them one degree more real on the page. He hasn't contributed any new concepts. At best he's refined some. The story isn't his. It's a bauble of thin glass. Now Alex hands it to him to carry.

"They leave the city," Brett says. He looks at Alex to see if this is correct. Alex nods. "Outside the city, there's—" He stops. They haven't discussed what's outside the abandoned city. There's the stretch of beach behind them. Past that, the cave. But he can't move the story backwards. "There's nothing," he says.

"Desert," says Alex. Tears off a piece of beef jerky with his molars. Val had complained that these were basically pure salt. "It's okay, though," Alex tells Brett as he chaws away. "The robot knows where to find water."

Every now and then, Val cranes around from her seat in the front and looks with a kind of horror at what they're eating. Brett looks up at her, and she takes a breath as if to speak, then bites her lip and turns her attention away, back to the road. Alex seems to enjoy food to an extent inverse to how much his mother disapproves of it. Brett's mother was less invested in what he ate than Val is. As a result, he probably never attacked a piece of beef jerky with the feral joy Alex demonstrates.

"They walk through the desert all day," says Brett. "When it's getting to be night—"

"When night falls," says Alex. "In stories, night always falls."

"Have you ever seen night fall?" asks Brett. Scowls with his eyes, then grins. Alex grins back and shakes his head. "When it's getting to be night, they come to a hut."

"Shouldn't it be a tent? I think desert nomads have tents."

"Are you telling this or am I?" asks Brett.

"No, no, go, with your huts," Alex says, rummaging in a bag of chips.

"I never said there were nomads," says Brett.

"It's a desert; it should maybe have nomads, I'm saying," Alex says, shrugging and pursing his lips.

"No nomads," says Brett.

"No-no, nomads!" says Alex. As if he's chastising some desert tribe for packing up their tents too soon. This cracks him up. His laughter consists of trying not to inhale whatever combination of junk foods currently fills his mouth. "Hut is good," he concludes.

"There's a girl who lives in the hut. About the boy's age."

This stops Alex cold. For the first time since they've started talking about it, he speaks with an empty mouth, crisp and clear.

"Are they going to end up boyfriend/girlfriend?"

Brett hasn't thought about this. "It's a girl in a hut," he says.

"You can't give him a girlfriend when he doesn't even have a name," Alex says. This is what Brett was worried about when he took over. That he'd ruin it somehow.

"I didn't say she was going to be his girlfriend," he says.

"She isn't," Alex decides. "She's from the city. The next city."

"That's what I was thinking," says Brett, although he hadn't been. He pauses to see if Alex is going to take the narrative back. He doesn't. So, tentatively, Brett continues. "She was thrown out of the city," he says. "Because of her powers."

"She has powers," Alex says. Less a question than a first bite. Chews this idea to see how it tastes.

"She's a shape-shifter," says Brett. Alex looks unsure about this.

"Like a mutant?"

"Are there mutants in this story?" Brett asks. He wishes there was a set of rules he could follow to avoid moments like this. Alex considers. Then shakes his head. "So, not a mutant," Brett says. He is stumped. He decides the best thing to do is ask. "Where does she get her powers from?"

"She doesn't know," Alex says. "She wasn't born with them. At some point she just had them."

"There's a lot of things in this story people don't know," Brett says. Takes a small piece of jerky and grinds it between his teeth. Val is right: it's like a piece of leather designed to carry salt. But as he gnaws on it, his mouth floods with the overwhelming salinity of it. It is painfully good. The kind of good that induces discomfort.

"That's what the story is for," Alex says. "For finding out."

"She doesn't want to go with them," Brett says. "She doesn't want to go back to the city that threw her out."

"The boy and the robot need her help," says Alex. "There are guards at the city gates. They need her help to get through. But she doesn't want to help them. Because what you said. The city, it threw her away. So why should she go back?"

Brett makes a first attempt. "Do they have anything they can give her? Can they pay her for her help?" Alex shakes his head. Obviously wrong. Can't give the boy and the robot pocketfuls of treasure at this point, because it'd be convenient. What good would treasure be to a shape-shifting girl who lives in a hut in the desert? What could she possibly want that they, or anyone, could offer?

"The boy tells her," Alex says. "He explains he doesn't know his name. And the girl, because she's a shape-shifter, she doesn't have a name, either. She did, but they took it away from her."

"That's good," says Brett. Draws the girl, listening. Sadness settling over her face. A nameless boy and a nameless girl, explaining themselves to each other. The boy's hands are out, pleading. Once the figures are rendered, he pauses, wishing they hadn't set this scene in the desert. Nothing to work with. No background. But then he can see it. A living, moving thing. Octopal arms of sand, drifts that have undulated for a hundred years. Lines come forward, wrap around the boy and the girl, float between them. It obscures them from the viewer and from themselves. They can hardly see each other through the sand.

# Home-Cooked Meal

There are apps you can buy that track the progress of someone traveling long-distance to visit you, or track your own progress toward someone. Valerie's mother must have come with this software pre-installed. Val could have called from the road to say they'd be there in an hour, but she didn't, and her mother is still standing on the porch when the van pulls into her driveway. Fred cuts the engine, and the front door of the house shoots open, firing two border collies toward the new arrivals.

"A van now?" her mother says, shouting to be heard over the enthusiasm of the dogs. "Are you one of the soccer moms?"

"The Civic died in Cleveland," Val says, climbing down from the van to be greeted by Eero and Eliel, who demand her full and immediate attention. Eero, younger by five years, jumps up to greet her face to face, while Eliel nudges somewhat pathetically at her knees. Val retains a soft spot for the older dog, whom she associates more closely with her father, and after gently deflecting Eero's attentions, she kneels down to embrace Eliel around the neck.

The house is a two-story A-frame her father built when Val was eight and his architecture firm was enjoying a string of boom years. It's simple and intentionally rustic, with none of the self-conscious flourishes that adorned their house in Chicago, which had always seemed to Val more like an advertisement for her father's professional skills than a real home. It had been intended as a summer retreat, but when her father got sick and left the firm, he and Val's mother had moved here permanently so he wouldn't be constantly faced with reminders of the person he'd been as his faculties quickly dwindled. Her mother lives here by herself now with the dogs, and the house forms a perfect backdrop for her, its angularity complementing her roundness. Val thinks of her father constructing it this way: a circle inscribed in a triangle, floated onto a field of deep green. The image is one of a protective sigil, something arcane drawn for protection.

A little warily, the dogs go to investigate Brett and Fred as they load out of the van. They are not used to strangers and—since Val's father died four years ago and her brothers, as her mother is quick to point out, never come around anymore—unaccustomed to men. Eero hangs back a second, then jumps up onto Brett, while Eliel waits patiently for attention from Fred.

"And these boys?" says her mother, easing her weight down the porch steps as if she's testing the stairs for creaks. She has some vague complaint regarding her knees, but Val's been unable to pin her down on which knee is ailing, much less force her mother to see a doctor. She looks quizzically at Fred and Brett. "I remember my Shura being smaller. And there only being one of him."

"Babu!" yells Alex as he jumps out of the van. It's a word he might grow out of any day, and Val holds the sound of it tightly in her mind, taking an impression of it to play back later. Alex runs across the gravel drive, Eero at his heels, and flings himself at his grandmother. With impressive stalwartness, she catches him in her thick arms and lifts him with an easy strength.

"Now this is my Shura!" she says, holding her head back to inspect him. "You've gotten big! Not *so* big"—she indicates Brett and Fred as baseline measures of bigness—"but big." She sets Alex down, and the dogs are on him immediately, licking and pawing. "Who are your bodyguards, Lera?" her mother asks.

"These boys gave us a ride from Cleveland," Val says. "Mom, this is Brett and Fred."

"It's nice to meet you, Mrs. Torrey," says Brett, setting down his bag and going to shake her hand.

"'Mrs. Torrey' he calls me," she says, swatting his hand away and pulling him into a brief but firm hug. Fred must understand this is protocol and steps forward to receive the same. "Toropov is our name. Too ethnic for television, my Lera decided."

"Give it a rest, Mom," calls Val as she pulls one of her bags from the trunk. "You sound like the fiddler on the roof."

"Your boy gets none of his own culture fifty-one weeks out of the year," says her mother, louder than she needs to. "The few days I see him, I have to overwhelm him with Russianness." She reaches down and grabs a hank of Alex's hair, shakes it affectionately. "I'm going to read him Pushkin to put him to sleep."

"You hate Pushkin," says Val as she carries her bags up the porch steps.

"Bite your tongue," hisses her mother, following her. "Aren't you going to invite your bodyguards to stay for dinner?"

Since their hugs, Brett and Fred have been standing on either side of the van. It isn't clear whether they're waiting to make their exit or to receive further instructions. Val is aware that everyone is looking at her to see what will happen next, particularly Alex, who is giving her the same face he has when he wants to keep pigeons he's found in the park as pets.

"They can't stay, Mom," she says. "They've got to be in Chicago tomorrow morning."

Her mother looks at her with fierce disappointment. "It's a long drive to Chicago, and getting dark already." Val realizes the decision was never hers to make. "They drive you all the way from Cleveland and you'd put them back on the road in the dark?" She waits for her mother to add a scathing *This is the way I raised you?* but thankfully it doesn't come. "We'll feed them and they can sleep in the attic." She looks at Brett and Fred, making some inscrutable calculation in her mind. "Are you two . . . *goluboy*?"

Brett looks at Val, then back at her mother. "I'm not sure," he says. From somewhere in her teenage past, a spring of mortification wells up in Val. The house and the commanding presence of her mother have worked an awful magic: she is fifteen again.

"She's asking if you're gay," says Val, realizing she doesn't know the answer to this.

"I am, Mrs. Toropov," says Fred. Val is surprised less by the answer, which is news to her, than by the graciousness and openness with which it's given. It is possible he is one of those boys who are especially good with mothers. "But Brett here is as straight as they come."

"Hmm," her mother says, heading into the house. "Only asking. With Lera's friends . . ." She throws her hands in the air. New developments in the world like acknowledged homosexuality she's taken to treating with a bemused curiosity that points itself toward acceptance rather than under-standing. She seems to think of them the way she thinks of the Internet: fascinated that it is there but utterly uninterested in how it might work.

As if she's leading them in a parade, they all follow her into the house: one daughter, three boys, and two dogs. "There's an extra mattress down the hall. It's musty a little."

"We can't stay, Mrs. Toropov," says Brett, but it's a halfhearted decla-ration, and would have carried more weight if he'd tried it from the win-dow of the van. Now that her mother has gotten them into the house, it will be impossible for them to leave.

"You'll stay, and you'll stop calling me that," orders her mother. "No one wants handsome young men to call her an old lady's name. It's Hildy, and I'm hearing no more debate this evening. Shura, tell me about your trip." She and Alex disappear into the kitchen, where Val is sure she is feeding him terrible things, things she has stockpiled for this visit. Val stands in the living room with Brett and Fred, the three of them able now for the first time to assess what has happened, the manner in which their lives have been hijacked by a senior citizen in drawstring pants.

"I'm sorry," Val says. "She wasn't always like this. She was born in De-catur." The change happened sometime in the year after Val's father died. Val sometimes thinks that when her mother lost the role of supportive housewife and, later, caretaker, she replaced it with a kind of stock char-acter, a bit of comic relief. But when she does, she becomes aware of how often she imposes ideas about herself on her mother, and the unfairness of doing so.

"She seems great," says Brett, smiling.

"If she's feeding us," says Fred, "you don't need to apologize."

Even as an adult, Val doesn't want to hear that her mother is great; she wants her mortification to be confirmed so it is not something in her head. But it's an inhospitable sentiment, and it reminds Val how unkind she's been since the hotel parking lot in Cleveland.

"Also, thank you," she says, her head lowered. "I should have said before. You didn't have to drive us all this way." This she addresses to both of them, but then she turns to Brett. "I know you must have better things to do than draw pictures for a nine-year-old the whole trip."

"He's a cool kid," Brett says. Val wonders why the feeling this elicits is the inverse of being told her mother is great. It's as if she wants to be credited for everything good about Alex despite everything that's wrong with her own mother, as if she's the fulcrum on which the balance of three generations shifts.

"And thank *you*, Fred," says Fred, "for keeping me entertained even though you were driving the whole time."

"He likes you," Val says to Brett. "And I shouldn't have bitten your head off yesterday."

"You're a riveting conversationalist," Fred continues to no one but himself, "and all around a real catch."

"I get overprotective," says Val.

This moment of reconciliation is curtailed as Val's mother emerges from the kitchen. "You, the skinny one," she says, pointing to Brett, who is no skinnier than Fred. "My Shura says you're a fancy comic book artist. You know how to cut potatoes?"

"Yes, ma'am," says Brett.

"You call me ma'am again, I break your fingers. For you I have two jobs. You cut potatoes and you keep Lera out of my kitchen. And you, with the face."

"Me?" asks Fred.

"Shura," she says to Alex, "show him where the mattress is in Dedul-ya's study and help him lug it upstairs." Val feels a twinge from hearing the room at the end of the first-floor hall still referred to as her father's study, even though it serves now as a storage closet for unneeded house-hold things and items she and her brothers have never bothered to reclaim or remove from their parents' house. "You," says her mother, pointing at her menacingly. "Sit yourself on that couch and don't get up until dinner is ready. Never do I get to take care of my own daughter."

# Sibling Revelry

Gail loves Ron's neighborhood in Chicago, dotted as it is with Eastern European churches that look like they've been delivered from some outdated version of the future. When he first moved here ten years ago, right after their parents had kicked him out, the streets of Ukrainian Village had been full of little babushka ladies and bearded Cossack-looking gentlemen. Now it was changing, smoothing out like wrinkles in a shirt until there was nothing left but the middle class. But the churches are still there, foreign, unsettling, and strange.

A plastic bag of Chinese food in one hand and a six-pack of Goose Islands in the other, she trudges up the back stairs of Mac's American Pub to Ron's apartment. The food at Mac's is lackluster, the clientele are mostly White Sox fans, and the bar vomits loud drunks into the street at last call, but Ron figures living above a bar is saving him a couple hundred a month in rent. He's on the phone when she gets there, still at work hours after he's gotten home.

"Well, we're not going to cede them that point," he says as he opens the door. Once Gail's inside, he continues pacing, gesticulating as if the person on the other end can see him. "We're not going to cede them any points, we're not giving them an inch." Not for the first time, Gail's heart breaks a little at the sheer bigness of Ron's apartment. There ought to be a law against one person having this much living space.

"I've got to go," says Ron. "My sister's here. Don't do anything until tomorrow. Okay? Okay." He hangs up the phone, sets it on the counter, and then puts up his hands as if it might be covered in herpes.

"I work with idiots, is what it is," he explains. "The firm should be called Mouthbreather, Moron and Manchild."

"Mouthbreather, Moron, Manchild and Pope," says Gail. "If you're fantasizing, at least give yourself a partnership." She puts the beer and food down on the counter. "I brought provisions."

They hug, Gail trying to assess whether or not he's bonier than last time she saw him. He looks healthy, but it's a stretched kind of healthy. It has an intensity and determination to it that she doesn't like.

"How was the train?" he says, holding tight to her. "I'm sorry I couldn't meet you at the station."

"You've got fancy lawyer things to do," she says. "I can take the L. I'm a big girl."

"You're getting to be," he says.

"Don't start on me, Jack Sprat."

"Is this why you brought food? You assume I don't eat?"

"You think any of this is for you?" she says. "Get plates."

"Plates," he says. "You New Yorkers are so uptight."

Ron's the youngest, three years younger than Gail. He'd still been living with them when Gail came out to their parents in a letter written in her University of Chicago dorm room, drunk on bad wine and Frank O'Hara poems. When they told him Gail would no longer be welcome in the house since she had chosen a life of sodomy and debauchery, Ron first explained to them that lesbians didn't engage in sodomy, and then informed them that he, on the other hand, did. Four hours later, he showed up at Gail's dorm with a black eye and a suitcase.

"I went to the place on Division," she says, "and got a slew of stuff. I should have let you pick."

"You've got to go to the South Side for decent Chinese," he says. He opens a beer and hands it to her, then one for himself. "We should go to Won Kow while you're here, sit in Al Capone's booth."

"Al Capone died of syphilis," says Gail.

"I'm sure they've cleaned it since." He dumps half the container of lo mein onto a plate; it slumps out like a dead octopus. "Do you think this place uses MSG?"

"No," says Gail. "I don't think about it at all."

"So tell me about the life of the mind," he says, once they've settled into the couch and are picking apart various dishes with chopsticks.

"I'm getting dumped off *The Speck*," she says, carefully choosing a crab Rangoon.

"No shit?"

"Zero shit," she says, taking a swig.

"What are they moving you on to?"

Gail shrugs. *"Admiral Animorph & His Danger Rangers*?"

"You'd be great on that," he says. "Lesbian lemurs."

"Sapphic sea otters."

"Dyked-out dugongs."

"What the fuck is a dugong?" she asks.

"It's like a manatee."

"So why not say manatee?"

"I thought we were doing alliterative."

"Forget all that shit, how's your superhero life?"

He blushes. One of the things she loves about her little brother is that he actually blushes. As much as she knows it's not true, part of Gail has always thought of her own sexual orientation as a natural result of growing up in a house full of boys. Their older brothers are scrappers, three-sport athletes, and mighty chasers of women. But Ron has always been the family's resident alien, kind in a family that values toughness, quiet among men who bellow. When he started at a law firm that specialized in blocking deportations, he proudly declared to Gail that "being a rich lawyer is probably the only thing that would get me back into that house. So I'm going to be a poor lawyer forever." And if he didn't manage to dodge at least a modest amount of money, he could always say he fought on behalf of Mexicans and the like, which would kill any chance of reconciliation.

"Everything's terrible and everyone is awful," he says. "At least once a week, I have to remind myself how much progress has been made, and that we're not shooting people as they hop the fence, and that there's a million kids in schools who will never get deported. Then I get to work and someone has made it his mission in life to kick some poor cabdriver out of the country. Has dedicated himself to ruining this guy's life in the service of some abstract idea of I don't even know what."

"Tin-pot Hitlers," she says.

"Don't go Hitler," he says, sighing. "I spend all day trying not to think of them in terms of Hitler."

"You're doing good work," she says, holding out the neck of her beer to be clinked.

"I'm shoveling shit against the tide," he says, clinking.

For a while, they stare out the window at the intersection. His apartment has a pseudo-turret, a bubble in the northwest corner of the room that hangs out onto the street. It's perfect for people watching, especially after a sporting event. Tonight the corner is quiet. The people heading into the bar aren't drunk enough to be interesting yet, and neither are the people leaving this early. Later, this corner will be bro-tacular, and they'll be through the six-pack and into whatever else he has on hand, commenting on each drunken hookup or faux fight.

"You talk to Mom?" asks Gail. Independent of each other, they both got back in touch with their mother two years ago around Christmas. Neither of them admitted it to the other for a year, and even more surprising, their mother never mentioned to Gail that she'd heard from Ron, or vice versa. They both had excuses for why they'd broken down and made contact, Gail's involving rum and Prince's "Another Lonely Christmas" playing on Hot 97.

Ron takes a long swig of beer, then holds the bottle against the side of his face. "Two months ago," he says.

"Three," says Gail.

"I'm in the lead," Ron says.

"She say anything remarkably awful?"

"No," he says. "It's better when I'm not dating anyone. I feel this weird compulsion to tell her about it. You ever get that?"

"I've never dated anyone."

"Drama queen."

"I've never been dating anyone when I've talked to Mom."

"But would you tell her?"

"Maybe," says Gail. "Maybe I'd tell her in totally gender-neutral terms. Maybe I'd date someone named Pat or Terry and tell Mom all about her so she could have dreams about me and a banker in a Brooks Brothers suit when in reality I'm banging some Sarah Lawrence prof I met at Cubbyhole."

"Sarah Lawrence prof?" says Ron, scooting forward.

"It was hypothetical," says Gail. There'd been an M.F.A. student from Hunter, briefly, but that was hardly the same thing. "You know Mom reads all my comics?" she says, changing the subject.

"So do I," says Ron, defensive. "I've got a whole long box of them."

"Aw, you even know the word 'long box.'" Ron had never been her kind of geeky when they were growing up. It was her older brother Tom who had gotten her into comics, giving her his issues of *R-Squad* when he was done with them.

"But Mom?" says Ron.

"It's all we talk about," Gail says. "She talks about the Speck and Iota like they're real people. She asks me how they're doing. She's going to be crushed I'm not writing it anymore."

"You'll have to tell National to give you another hetero fantasy couple to write," Ron says, hauling himself up from the couch. "You want another?" he asks, which is not really a question at this early stage of the night.

# Summering

The room is a small right triangle, and once it was his mom's. The bed is tucked into one of the vertices, a sixty-degree angle. This means the wall meets the other wall at a thirty-degree angle, and that wall meets the floor at ninety degrees. This year, they've been doing geometry on Tuesdays and Thursdays. Although it's his mother's least favorite subject to teach, Alex loves the language of it, every hypotenuse, arc, and sector.

Eliel is wedged between Alex and his mother, asleep. He has the stink of an older dog, meaty, not unpleasant, and coming from somewhere no bath or hose can reach. Alex leans on him slightly, careful not to apply too much weight.

"Why doesn't Babu want you in her kitchen?" Alex asks. There are so many things to understand about the room, beginning with its shape. In Alex's mind, the only rooms that are not cubic are found in museums, and they aren't simply rooms, they're *about* rooms. They say something about what it means to be a room, instead of just being rooms themselves. Then there's the idea that his mother did not grow up in this room but "summered" here. Alex knows the transitional seasons can be used as verbs— he's been known to spring and fall himself—but he's never summered or wintered. Home is supposed to be a singular thing, something that exists in one place and persists in time. It doesn't sound like a luxury to Alex to have a summer home and a winter home; it sounds confusing. He imagines he would always miss whichever home he wasn't in and worry if it was okay without him.

"She doesn't want me in there because she knows I'll check the labels," Val says.

"Check them for what?"

"For things that are bad for you."

"Babu wouldn't feed me anything that's bad for me."

"Sometimes Babu doesn't know any better," she says. He likes it here, he likes coming to stay here, but sometimes he feels as though his mother and grandmother are fighting over him, tugging at both his arms. This wouldn't be so bad except that he thinks the fighting is not about him so much as it's about something that came before, or something that was always there and still is.

"You didn't tell me a story last night," he says.

"I was upset," she says. This is not an apology, only an explanation.

"I didn't mean to scare you," says Alex. This too only explains.

"I know, Rabbit," she says. "I'm not used to you being so big you can run off by yourself."

"I wasn't by myself. I was with Brett." Alex regrets this after he's said it.

"He's nice, huh?" she asks. There is something resigned in her voice that calms Alex's fears. Brett is no longer the enemy; he's paid for his mistakes.

"He's my friend," Alex says.

She rolls over to face him, half her face visible over the sleeping border collie. "Tell me about what you guys are working on."

Alex shakes his head vigorously. "You owe *me* a story," he says. "An extra one. Two episodes." His mother rolls back over and looks back up at the ceiling.

"Storyline again?" He nods, and he's not sure if she sees it out of the corner of her eye or knows from the way the bed shakes, but she nods, too. "Which season?"

"I want to hear how Frazer and Campbell fell in love," he says.

"Huh," says his mother. "There's not an episode for that." She always stares off into space when she's telling about storyline episodes. Freak-of-the-week episodes, she pays extra attention to his face to make sure she's not scaring him, but when she tells storyline episodes, it's like the words are written very faintly somewhere and she's straining to read them.

Alex pulls himself closer to her, displacing Eliel, who moves some-what grudgingly around Alex's legs and situates himself behind Alex. Alex wants to tell her he's not so big he can run off by himself, but the words get caught and he puzzles over them. He tries to decide if they're true, and whether or not he wants them to be.

Undecided, he curls into the angle described by the wall and the bed, tangential to curves described by mother and dog.

## *Anomaly* S03E12

"It started in season three," she says. "There's something in TV called the *Moonlighting* effect. It's where there's a couple that doesn't get along, but the audience wants them to fall in love. Or they think they do. So the writers make it happen, and then the audience decides it's not what they wanted and then the show gets canceled."

"This happens because of the moon?" Alex says.

"No, that's just what it's called." She remembers the insistent match-making of the fans. On the Internet, people wrote shockingly explicit pieces of erotica featuring Frazer and Campbell. There is a weird disconnect reading someone else's writing about what you're like in bed, but she and Andrew used to recite some of the racier ones for the amusement of the guys in the writing room. Not acting them out, of course. Sometimes she'd even read them to herself and think it wouldn't be like that at all. The fantasies tended to be either violent or tender, the former all lust with no love, the latter all love with no lust. It wouldn't be like that, Val would think. It would be both at once.

"All season, there have been clues that everything they've dealt with, all the problems in time, have been caused by someone called the Leader," she explains. "But no one knows anything about him. Until Frazer and Campbell catch some bad guys trying to tamper with the NIST-F1, which is our master clock."

"What's a master clock?" asks Alex.

"It's the clock every other clock is set to," she says. "Like if your watch said nine thirty, and mine said nine thirty-two, and we wanted to know which was right, we could check them against the NIST-F1."

"Oh."

"So these bad guys tell Frazer and Campbell that the Leader is planning on altering the FOCS-1, which is the master clock of all master clocks, so that all of the clocks fall out of sync."

"Why would the Leader do that?" asks Alex.

Even Tim hadn't had a good answer for that. The network wanted the show to have a big bad, so Tim complied with the biggest bad he could muster: a vague threat that tied every other plotline together. But the plotlines were so diverse and resistant to the idea of a single motive that when the Leader showed up, he had to remain part cipher, part trickster god. There had been hints dropped for eleven episodes before he finally made his appearance. Going into shooting, they had a fabricated mask and a vocoder, but no actor to play the villain. At the very last minute, Tim had grabbed one of the gaffers, put the mask on him, and told him to stand "in a menacing way."

"They finally catch the Leader in Switzerland, where the FOCS-1 is kept. They have him at gunpoint, and he tells them he's actually one of them from the future."

"You said 'he,'" Alex says. "So the Leader is Campbell."

"I said 'he,'" she explains, "because the Leader has a deep robot voice that sounds like a 'he.' But it could be either of them. Anyway, before they can figure it out, *the Leader*"—she says this with emphasis, avoiding any gendered pronouns—"zaps Campbell and he disappears to somewhere in time."

"What does he zap him with?"

"By 'he,' do you mean *the Leader*?" she asks. Alex giggles. "A time ray, I guess?" she says. Tim was never big on the science behind things. "The Leader is from the future, so the Leader has all kinds of future technology."

Andrew had actually been zapped by the movie gun. His agent convinced him he'd never make the jump from television to leading man, so, with his contract coming up at the end of season three, he'd started taking roles in smaller films. "Big parts in little movies," he'd told Val. What worried him was that, more than anything he'd done before, these parts called for legitimate acting, something closer to Val's career experience than his own. "They're going to realize I'm a mug," he told her. He asked her about classes she'd taken. He borrowed her copy of *An Actor Prepares*, by Stanislavski, because he'd heard of it. She'd grinned and told him he didn't have enough pathos to be a Method actor, and a week later, when he returned the book and admitted she was right, she introduced him to some Meisner exercises. The moment rather than the method, being present with another actor rather than being deep in your own character's head. The two of them stood in her living room, sizing each other up, then finding one thing about the other to speak out loud.

"You look unhappy with me right now," she said.

"*I* look unhappy with *you*?" he said. This was always the rookie response, to overstress the pronouns.

"You do; you look unhappy with me. Right now."

"I look unhappy with you *right now*," he said, moving the emphasis. Back and forth like that, feeling the words shift and morph through their repetition. Their attention so focused on one another that it was indistinguishable from attraction. In the classes she'd taken at the Acting Studio, in New York, a good exercise ended with you wanting—needing, almost— to either punch or fuck your partner. This tension usually escalated into laughter, breaking the scene, and the same held for Andrew and Val, aided no doubt by the fact that Andrew always brought a bottle of wine to the sessions. And then there was a Friday, late, when Val started the exercise with "You have big teeth," a standard opening, but one that brought all of her attention to his mouth. She stared at it as the words bounced back and forth between them, and as he said, for the seventh time, "I have big—" she stopped him with a kiss, and he repeated it back at her, escalating. When she paused for a breath, she pulled back and examined his face, worried, frantic that this had only been part of the exercise. Then he kissed her, something new. As she pulled him toward the couch, something her acting coach used to say at the beginning of each class popped into her head and she giggled into Andrew's neck as his kisses moved down her shoulder.

"What is it?" he said.

"The moment," she said, "is a tricky fucker."

In the morning, she woke up to the sound of coffee grinding and Andrew whistling the overture to *Love for Three Oranges*. She found him in the kitchen, adorable in boxers and socks, pouring two cups.

"This is good," he said, tentative, half asking.

"This is good," she said.

The producers were determined to keep Andrew around, so the writers had to construct the second half of season three as "Campbell light," with Andrew appearing in the minimum number of episodes his contract required. At first, Val had looked forward to carrying the show on her own. Frazer had become a sidekick, and this was her opportunity to retake the reins. Fans responded well, but Val had trouble finding Frazer's character without Andrew to play off of. On her own, Bethany Frazer seemed not efficient and professional but cold and hard.

"Through season three," Val says, "Frazer is at Anomaly all alone. She was working alone before Campbell showed up, but now she realizes she's alone. And Campbell, he's been zapped into the past. And he was used to being alone, too, because he'd used his time ray to zap himself around time before. But sometimes being alone is okay until you realize you're alone, and sometimes it takes being not alone to figure that out. While Frazer's trying to find all these clues to where in the timestream Campbell is, and Campbell's trying to find time portals the Leader left behind so he can get back to the present, they're both starting to figure out how much they need each other."

Tim wrote two scripts for the finale: one that would serve as a series finale and one that would set up season four. Val signed on to do *Othello* with Shakespeare in the Park at the end of the summer, even though it might mean she'd be in New York when shooting was supposed to start for the new season. But then the advance reviews started to trickle in on two of Andrew's movies. Not only had they been panned, but he had been singled out for abuse. Critics called him arrogant and flat. "Attractive cardboard," said one. He showed up at her apartment, looking as if the air had gone out of him. She cooked him dinner, although she hadn't had any appetite for days. She poured him wine, but none for herself. Earlier that day, she'd done the math and calculated that by the time *Othello* was in production, she'd be showing, and no one wanted a pregnant Desdemona. But that conversation could wait.

"Let's sign," she said, as if it was what she wanted. He offered hollow protests, but he was obviously relieved. It was important she never let him think that she'd given something up for him. It was important that he hadn't had to ask.

That night, they invented lists of demands to submit to the network, to justify having held out as long as they had. The network gave them everything they wanted. The show was saved.

"So they fall in love while they're not around one another?" Alex says. He's curled up next to the dog now, the two of them like a pair of parentheses.

"Something like that," Val says. She wonders if children can ever understand the way their parents are in love, or that their love could possibly exist outside of the children themselves. It would require the child to look at her parents as people completely separate from herself. And if Val is unable to think of her mother that way, she wonders if it is even possible for her to understand herself as separate from Alex, now that he is here, now that he is the inexorable thing in her life.

She continues a summary of that season, a plot so convoluted that when they were shooting the episodes, she'd sometimes have to have Tim explain to her what was going on, but Alex either understands it all on his own or is losing interest, because his questions and interruptions taper off, and by the time Frazer and Campbell are reunited in the season finale, his breathing is tinged with a soft, gentle snore.

Val quietly climbs out of the bed and makes her way downstairs. Brett and Fred have already retired, and her mother is sitting on the couch with an afghan covering her legs and Eero covering her bare feet. The living room smells of spices Val could not name and is the temperature particular to rural summer evenings. In New York right now, the day's heat would be struggling and failing to dissipate, trapped like a bug under a jar, but here, where there is nothing but space, the heat leaves behind it a cool that feels like an absence rather than an imposition.

"Is he asleep?" her mother asks.

"More or less," says Val. Her mother curls her legs under her, displacing the dog and making room for Val on the couch. Val sits, and for a second Eero looks up at her beseechingly. But when Val doesn't pat the couch or her lap to invite him up, he retreats to his own bed.

"It's nice having a house full of boys again," her mother says. "It makes the place feel heavier. Less likely to blow away." What Val remembers a house full of boys feeling like is loud: her father preferring to bellow from the next room rather than come find the person he was talking to, and her brothers racing around outside yelling in the voices of whatever breed of mortal enemies they happened to be that day: cowboys and Indians, Martians and astronauts, commies and G-men.

"You should sell the house, Mom," she says, not for the first time. "Come live in New York."

"New York is no place for dogs," her mother says. She has a list of complaints about New York, reasons for not moving. For years, Val's asked her mother to come live in New York because it would make Alex happy and because it would be better for her mother than living in the woods and because Val wouldn't have to worry about her anymore. But this time, it's that Val wants her mother with her, who doesn't want to be alone. Her mother seems to know this, although it doesn't change her answer. "I like my house," her mother says, "especially when my family's in it." She puts her hand on Val's knee. "Honey," she says, "what are you doing here?"

"There are things I need to do here," Val says. "We're booked at the convention in Chicago this weekend. It's one of the bigger ones." She can see now all of the tasks she's put in front of her, how she's made a line, a mechanism to move her forward, a conveyor belt that will gnash her up at its end. "We have to be in Los Angeles in two weeks. Not even. A week and a half."

"No, you don't," her mother says, angry with her, *for* her. "It's as simple as you don't go. You stay here. With me. Or you go somewhere else."

"I can't, Mom. I should have known when I took Alex this was going to happen. Sooner or later, Andrew would decide he'd look good as a father."

"So let him go knock someone else's daughter up and leave mine out of it." Val smiles at this. Her mother never liked Andrew, as much as he poured on the charm. It had driven him nuts, which made him act even more charming, which made her like him even less. Even during the time she loved Andrew, she got a kick out of seeing him struggle to rope in those few people who didn't succumb. It was an obsession with him, being universally liked, something he'd been able to talk about but never get over. Andrew told her once that when his mother had remarried, when Andrew was ten, his new stepfather sat him down and told him that while he'd never love Andrew like a father loved a son, he wanted them to be friends. But despite Andrew's constant efforts, his stepfather never treated him as much more than a roommate and was palpably relieved when, at seventeen, Andrew announced his intention to move out. During the run of *Anomaly,* Andrew had been a regular checker of discussion boards, and still kept boxes of letters from his time on *Sands in the Hourglass,* often handwritten, both fan and hate mail, soap opera watchers being apparently more traditional than sci-fi fans in the way they relayed their opinions to actors.

"I don't think he wants the whole mother/child package at this point." What Valerie suspects is that Andrew has reached a point where he needs a gimmick to continue going after younger girls, and Alex is cute enough to induce womb-ache in Andrew's target demographic. Maybe if he were an ugly child, she wouldn't be in danger of losing him. It's not a charitable thought, but charity is for people with things to give away.

"What happens if you don't go?" her mother asks, as if the question has never occurred to Val, as if she didn't ask it with every exhale. "If you say you're staying in the middle of nowhere with your mother in the house where you were raised. Where Alex will have two dogs to wrestle with and woods to play in and he'll never eat sushi till he goes to college."

"They'll take him from me," Val says. This is the conclusion of all paths that don't take her and Alex to Los Angeles, a point where rational thought brings its boot down on every hope, every emotion. "I violated the custody agreement. I completely fucking ignored the custody agreement. They'll take him away from me." It makes no sense to her that now only her mistakes count for anything and the statute of limitations has run out on all of Andrew's sins. But her lawyer has assured her it's true. At best, they'll award Andrew lost time: all the days that should have been his to spend with Alex for the past six years. At worst, they'll remove Alex from her custody. Months of sleepless nights have reduced it to a brutal mathematic, a heart and a feather on a scale.

"I can give him up for two years," she says, "or I can lose him forever."

# Secret Origin of OuterMan

*Everyone like you is dead. They've been dead forever. No one is like you. No one is like you at all.*

*Not only is this true, but you're reminded of it constantly. Every time you look at anyone, your eyes move right through the skin, like yours but as easily rent as tissue paper, to the fragile bird-like bones underneath. To muscles that cannot hoist cars in the air, much less change the direction of planets. You see the differences between them and yourself as easily as they see the differences among themselves, the meaningless divisions of race and ethnicity they hold all-important.*

*So breakable. They are like glass, like china. How is it you come from a race made of such sturdier stuff than they, and yet your people are dead and these people with their bones of spun sugar thrive?*

*You avoid touching them, as much as possible. Your grip can crush coal into diamonds; the potential to casually shatter one of them, to accidentally rip and tear and break, is overwhelming. Even with the woman who raised you, whose embrace had a fierceness to it, who squeezed your indestructible body until tears welled in your impossible eyes, you could never chance it. You could only stand stock-still, arms at your sides while her love for you crashed against skin that could never be cut, never bleed.*

*When you walk among them, you take on the affect of someone clumsy and gun-shy. The words* contact inhibition *loom large in your mental landscape, the way a cell knows to stop growing the moment it touches another cell. You seem to bumble. In the near-lost language of the woman who raised you, you act the schlemiel. But you are always under control, every muscle of you. To truly bumble into that wall might destroy it.*

*Unless they need you. Unless some certain death is barreling down upon them. Only then can you swoop in and pick them up, as gently as you would a baby bird. In those moments, you can cradle them in your hands, soft as they are, slight as they are. In those moments, they can break through your skin and save you.*

# Visiting Hours

*If it is as difficult to get out as it is to get in, there's no risk of the Woman escaping,* Val thinks as the guard hands back her ID. Although Val called from New York to arrange this visit two weeks ago, the clearance procedure still takes up most of the morning. So much work to get into a place she doesn't want to go.

Val walks across the yard that separates the guard tower from the ring of cells. A basketball game stops to observe her. It is not the individual players who stop, but the collective organism of the game, casting twenty of its eyes on her. Along the edges of the wall, cigarettes dangle from hands, the ripe cherries at their ends winking as a warm-hot breeze moves lackadaisically across the yard. Val is led by a corrections officer named Iris. Iris a messenger of the gods, frequent guide into the underworld. Into but not through. Iris also a flower, and goddess of the rainbow. Colorful name in a gray place, and in a gray uniform. Etymologies and theogonies clatter and clang in Val's head and she wishes she was not here. Anywhere else. She will take back her promise. She cannot do this, not for Tim or Rachel or herself. She is not strong enough. Even her hate is not strong enough. But everyone is watching her—from the guard tower, from the cells, from the yard, Iris a few feet ahead, wondering why Val has paused. Val wants to go, exit, but after all, this is a prison and it's not like they just let you leave.

"I know you," the Woman says. Jittery, scratching at an irritated spot on the back of her neck. "Or I did know you? Or will? It gets so confusing. They don't tell you that in training. There ought to be a course for verb tenses and knowing. Epistemology of tense. *I knew you. I will have known you.* I've told them this, but I think the training is woefully inadequate when it comes to the psychological impacts of nonlinearity. But who's an expert? Who's been there and back? Nonlinear is forever. Nonlinear is for life."

Her skin is fish-belly pale, and her hair, long, brown, is a mess of matting and knots on the left side, like a section of a lawn that's never been cut or tended. But while her body judders, her eyes fix on Val's with the empty calm Val remembers from the trial.

"We think of time as if it's a straight line," she continues, "but it's more like a bubble. Except that's not exactly right, either. It is to a bubble what a bubble is to a circle drawn on the ground. The last part isn't as important, but if you can begin to think in terms of the bubble, you can abandon the idea of time passing. You can sit out the dance of now and then. Even causality. It doesn't disappear; it becomes myriad. Everything causes everything all the time."

"It's going to be you," whispers Rachel, grasping Val's hand in the dark and squeezing it. "I can feel it."

The theater is filled with the mix of professionalism and fraternity common at office holiday parties. The awards shows are an attempt to convince the public that movies stars, television stars, pop stars, are all one big group of co-workers, punching the clock, churning out culture the same way other companies churn out marketing reports or widgets. In-jokes and backslapping. Gleeful hugs and affectionate kisses on cheeks. The illusion of community is important.

"She's right," says Tim, leaning across his wife to whisper, too loud, to Val. "Mothers are big this year. Look at the Oscars. Mothers cleaned up." His tuxedo, picked out by Rachel, tailored by a team of Eastern Europeans whose ancestors outfitted czars and archdukes, must be lined with bees. He twitches and winces inside it as if being repeatedly stung. Any time Val sees him in anything other than T-shirt and jeans, it feels as if something has gone wrong with the world. This is Val's third nomination and Andrew's second, but the academy seems to have finally discovered Tim, who is up for Best Director of a Dramatic Series, along with nods for Best Writing and Best Series. Rachel insisted he dress up.

Rachel pushes Tim back into his seat. "It's not going to be you because you're a mother," she tells Val. It hurts to talk about motherhood in front of Rachel. She and Tim tried for years, and it was only this winter that the doctors told her it was highly unlikely they'd be able to conceive. They've been like parents to Alex, who spends many shooting days in Rachel's painting studio and whose first burblings sounded a lot more like "ray-ray" than "mama." "It's going to be you because you've earned it," she says. "And this is the year they're going to get over their snobbish aversion to science fiction." There is something amazing about the way Rachel says "snobbish aversion," as though the words themselves are things not to be touched.

"What about fathers?" Andrew asks no one in particular. He's been distant since they wrapped the season. It's taken awhile for Val to find her way back to her own personality, to pack Bethany Frazer in the closet, but slowly, she's remembered who she is when she's not being someone else. Alex helps; he has held his mother in his mind, never changing.

Andrew has taken longer to come back to the real world. He watches each episode as it airs, then takes to the fan sites to see the reaction. He's constructed a number of aliases so he can comment without being recognized. He hasn't hidden it from her; sometimes over dinner he tells her what they're saying, talking about commenters as if they're actual people. She hoped that this hiatus between seasons would be their chance to recalibrate as a couple, to redraw the map for all three of them, but Andrew hasn't played the role of father with the commitment he brings to his character on-screen. His performance is stiff and unconvincing, and sometimes seems like it's cribbed from fifties sitcoms.

Unlike Tim's, Andrew's tux fits him like a second skin. He has been working out excessively this year, to the point that Tim had to ask him to tone it down; his new physique was dangerously close to becoming a plot point. He had too much to drink and not enough to eat at dinner, but Val didn't say anything. In the lobby, she simply pointed him at people and stood slightly behind as he chatted them up. But she's also happy the television awards come early in the proceedings, since his face has a slackness that might signal nodding off in the near future.

"Real fathers are never big," Tim explains. "Oedipus rears his eyeless head. Surrogate fathers, stepfathers, sure. Stepfathers are hot this year, maybe because there's not a cultural archetype for—" Rachel puts her hand to his lips, then turns to Val.

"It's going to be you," she says.


"Another way. Subjectively we experience three dimensions of space and one of time. But time also has more than one dimension. You need to think of timespace as one thing, a multidimensional system, a geometric supersolid. You're thinking about the shooting, but where is it? Why can't you point to it? It exists, but where? Nonlinearity gives you this, lets you think this way. It jumps you up from the surface of timespace so you can see the past and future as a single object. Not up, really. But think of the circle again and draw an arrow up from it. Then think of standing on the drawing of the circle, and now where is up? You see? When the airplane was invented, we learned for the first time to think in three spatial dimensions. When nonlinearity was invented, we were freed from a one-dimensional reckoning of time."


Rachel is covered in blood. It spreads across the sky blue of her dress, her pretty dress, like some awful sunset. It drips onto the star of Montgomery Clift. It is splattered across the stars of Harold Lloyd and Fay Wray and Gene Autry. Is Tim screaming? Someone is screaming, and it's not

Andrew. Andrew is standing constellations away. On the star of Hattie McDaniel or the star of Rod Serling. His mouth opens and closes like a fish's. Val will remember this later: that it is Tim screaming and Andrew silent like a trout. Two men have grabbed the Woman by the arms, and the gun has fallen onto the star of Clint Eastwood. Such a little gun. So much blood to come from such a little gun. Val cannot hear what the Woman is yelling as they pull her away, but there are words to it. Words are what makes it yelling. Screaming is the sounds Tim makes. Feral sounds with size but no shape. His shoulder is bloody, but it is not Rachel's blood, which pools in handprints pressed into concrete in a golden age. Tim has been shot as well, but he is only screaming for her, for Rachel. A pop star new to the charts this year in a dress cut nearly to her navel holds Tim back, improbably strong despite her waifish frame. The ground is littered with golden statuettes, dropped in a panic. Val and Rachel were holding hands when the shots were fired, so now they are on the same star, and people are pushed back from them, gravity in reverse. Val is holding Rachel's head in her lap and pressing on the blood as if she can push it back into Rachel's heart, but no, it's too much, or she's pushed too hard. Bubbles form on Rachel's lips, paler than her lipstick. "I want to look like the evil queen in a Disney cartoon," she'd told Val in the car, but no makeup could hide the kindness in her face. Her eyes dart frantically, looking for someone who isn't Val, blind to Val's presence with her in this broken moment.

"You're her. But you're older. Are you from the future? Are we in the future now? I've wanted so much to talk to you. To tell you how sorry I am. Or I was. Has it happened yet? I think it's happened for me already and you were younger then. It all feels present. It always feels like right now, so when five minutes from now is ten years ago and last week was twenty years after that, it's all right now. I'm here and I'm talking to you but also right now I'm shooting her. Because if you can't tell if it's future or past, then it's right now. It all happens at once, all the time."

At the trial, the Woman calls Andrew Ian, or sometimes Agent Campbell. She apologizes to the court that she's broken agency protocol; relationships between agents are strictly forbidden. It's important to her they understand that Agent Campbell deserves none of the blame. She pursued him. Even knowing it could cost her her place in Anomaly, she couldn't stay away. She followed him for weeks, sitting two barstools down from him at Wood & Vine, running on the treadmill behind him at the gym. He was the one who broke it off, a week before the shooting, because it was wrong for a senior officer to take advantage of a junior agent like her. She had recorded that phone call, him explaining that the preservation of the time continuum was more important than their feelings for each other, him choosing his duty to Anomaly over his love for her. In the recordings, he sounds more like Campbell than like Andrew; there's a way he used to deepen his voice a quarter-octave and slow down its cadence as soon as the cameras were on, and Val can hear it here. She details the ways he took advantage, the places and times. Her testimony is like the juiciest parts of a Harlequin romance, and it doesn't hurt that she's in her early twenties, built like an aerobics instructor, and exuding the feverish sexual energy of a true manic. The judge allows it, leans pruriently toward the witness stand as the Woman speaks. It would seem like she's role-playing if not for the obvious conviction in her eyes. She is an agent of Anomaly, an international organization dedicated to stopping threats to the timestream. For the past several months, she has been romantically involved with Special Agent Ian Campbell.

There is so much evidence. The Woman kept copious notes. She saved hotel receipts. Took pictures on her phone. Even recorded calls from Andrew, sometimes on his way to see her, laying out the things he would do to her when he arrived. She says maintaining evidence is an essential part of training for all Anomaly agents.

The defense insisted on a competency evaluation, but the law only asks that the person on trial be able to understand that she is on trial. The Woman assured the evaluator that she understands early-twenty-first-century law and that, even though she is not from this time, she is subject to the jurisdiction of the time she currently inhabits. The defense pleads not guilty by reason of insanity, but the people on television all say it won't work. Things are different since John Hinckley, they say. Your delusions cannot necessarily protect you in a court of law. The Woman is aware of what she did and why she did it. She saw another woman with her lover and, in a jealous rage, tried to kill her. Unfortunately, she missed.

While the Woman's delusions may have no legal bearing, the press is fascinated, and the trial drags on for weeks, even though the salient facts are quickly established. Val skips days to visit Tim in the hospital, although he does not talk, just stares into space. The doctors say he will not eat, and the skin of his face hangs limply off the bones like clothes draped over the back of a chair. They say they are quieting his mind so it can heal. This does not fit with Val's conception of how a mind works. It is a nice way to get around saying that when Tim is not full of Thorazine, he is screaming.

There are news vans parked outside their house all the time. For the first three weeks after the shooting, even as information about his affair surfaces, Andrew does not move out of the house. It isn't so much a matter of him refusing to leave as it is the shock of Rachel's death keeping them both in a kind of stasis. Although Val wants him gone, she also doesn't want to be alone, and, strung between those two desires, she does nothing to kick him out. They occupy opposite poles, Andrew sleeping on the couch in his office, Val in Alex's room, their bedroom empty. He is usually up and out of the house before she and Alex are awake. But one morning, during jury selection, they find themselves at the breakfast table together, through some accident of scheduling. In the living room,

Alex crashes trucks together. Andrew says how there are couples that get through things like this.

"We're not one of those couples," she says, realizing it's true as she says it.

The next day, he's gone.

"You can understand, then, how I was jealous, how easy it is to be jealous when it's all now. Because what I saw was him with you. But what it was is he had been with you. It was like I was watching something on television, something that was already over. Had happened. But it is happening, too."

Val has followed the Woman's progress as she's been shunted from one facility to another like Goldilocks sampling porridges and beds, across four states in the first year. Each facility she ends up in, she refuses antipsychotic medication. Some facilities insist more strongly than others, Coffee Creek Correctional Facility in Oregon even appealing to the Ninth Circuit for the right to compel her to take haloperidol, which, coincidentally, Tim was being treated with at the time of the case. When Coffee Creek lost the appeal, they sent her here to Normal, Illinois, where no one is interested in advancing her treatment. This is a place where you put things no one cares about and forget them.

Should Val feel better that this woman, whose name she has struck from her memory, is now a ruined husk? Does she thrill to think of the woman whose frenetic beauty jittered on the witness stand, promising burn scars, cuts, and abrasions to a tabloid audience that wanted her by the bowlful, and how little this woman, chewing on her split ends, resembles her? Her skeleton threatens to tear the sallow paper of her skin and caper about like a drunken marionette. Does it make Val happy to know that the Woman must live in this room, a space without windows or time, or that the cell reeks of acrid, panicked sweat? As the Woman babbles, displaying for Val the shards of a mind that was once at least a warped mirror, is there a victory to be claimed?

Tim insisted Val come to see the Woman. As proof that she was locked up. He said he'd been having dreams where she was spirited away. He said he'd seen her on the street in Greenpoint, from out his window, only it wasn't her. Fantasy stuff, episode fodder. But he insisted and she agreed. She knows how different it is for him. There were times, in the first months after the shooting, that Val had envied him his hospital bed and his catatonia. As if he was taking a vacation from the reality of what had happened and it would all be cleaned up when he came back. But even more than Val, Tim lives in that moment permanently. Part of him will always be there on the sidewalk, screaming.

Val's navy blue suit is crisply pressed, but she can feel the heat of this place, its dank, wearing the edges off it, threatening to eat through the shield of it and curl itself, wet and somehow cool like a fish, like the tentacle of some mollusk, against her skin, against her belly. The sight of this woman, the little that is left of her, the ugly stain that remains, does not make Val happy, or angry, even though parts of her want these things. It is something worse than hate, because it goes not simply outward, from Val to the woman like a rain of arrows. It snakes and twists and goes in every direction at once, until Val's life is permanently entwined with the Woman's and it is impossible to blame her for Rachel's death and Tim's shattered psyche and her own ruined marriage, without crediting her for the last six years of raising Alex on her own. Val can't go back in time to the moment, erase it, and imagine a life for herself as good as the one she's led. Maybe it's a failure of imagination on her part, but she can't picture that version of herself, six years older: still married, still working in television and having dinner at Tim and Rachel's once a week. It might have been a lovely life the Woman destroyed, but Val doesn't pine for it, which leaves her in this terrible place and wondering if she doesn't owe this woman gratitude, a thank-you for destroying everything Val ever thought she wanted.

"I'm glad I'm being debriefed. Although I'm surprised they called you in, given your personal connection to the case. It's important the agency get as much information from me as they can. And it gives me time to reflect. It's funny to think of time as something to give or take. Any day, they'll be done with me. Not any day: tomorrow. As soon as the today loop stops. As soon as they shut it off."

The divorce proceedings proceed. There's nothing Val wants, so there's nothing to argue about. All assets are neatly divided like a pie neither of them wants to taste.

Regarding Alex, it comes down to the Solomonic slice. She wants sole custody with supervised visitations, but her lawyer wards her off. The State of California does not consider adultery a factor in determining custody, she tells Val. Even the demonstrable craziness of the Woman is a nonfactor. If the relationship was ongoing, it would be, certainly. But the Woman is locked away, and there's no chance of her doing Alex any harm. If anything, her incarceration is to Andrew's advantage.

Meeting in her lawyer's office, Andrew says "I'm still his father" at least a half-dozen times, as if it's a catchphrase he's trying out. This seems to be his major justification for joint custody, but it's a legally valid one. Val tries to write out descriptions of Andrew as a father that make him seem unsuitable, but it's all absences and omissions. He wasn't there when Alex rolled over for the first time. He doesn't know what breakfast cereal Alex likes. Her lawyer says Andrew will never exercise the joint custody agreement even if they give it to him. She says Val will end up with sole custody in fact if not on paper, and that in the end, Andrew will only want a weekend here or there, the trips to the zoo and the beach rather than the committed work of a parent. Her lawyer has seen all this before; she knows the type.

There are stacks of papers to be signed. For days, Val goes to the lawyer's office and signs until her wrist aches and her hand is cramped into a talon, but finally it is done. Val reaches the last signature without knowing it and spends the first few moments of her divorced life waiting for another piece of paperwork to appear in front of her. She and Andrew shake hands as if there are cameras watching. They choose a time on Friday afternoons for him to pick up Alex and a time on Sunday evenings to drop him off, and Val realizes with a measure of disgust that all this paperwork has not removed Andrew from her life. They are tied together, and Alex is the knot that does it.

It goes on for a month, for two. Val begins to understand that the show will never start up again, that they should have been on set weeks ago. Tim is still in the hospital, and no one from the network has contacted her. The seasonal rhythm that has structured the past six years of her life is broken, the last tether to snap. She wants to mourn Bethany Frazer, but it would be such an insult to Rachel, the kind she would have suffered through with quiet grace if she were alive. Val begins making the adjustments necessary to being a single mother, which center around carving out pockets of Alex-less time to get other things done. Andrew mentions that he is always available to help, but she doesn't want his help. Once a week is the most she can stand to see him.

It's during one of these Alex-less hours, while he is being watched by the teenage girl from across the hall and Val is stopping by her lawyer's office because some little bit of money has been released from escrow, that she is approached by a woman from the district attorney's office. Val remembers seeing her in the courtroom. She wears her hair the way Val used to, back in season one. Val remembers her because when she first saw the woman, she thought it was Bethany Frazer, haunting the trial. She was worried for that split second that she had cracked, and in the next second she reasoned that it would be okay if she did, and that no one could blame her. But details asserted themselves: the too-sharpness of the nose, the too-slightness of the body. The woman became someone else, someone who wasn't Val.

She hands Val a manila envelope. She is shaking her head, and Val isn't sure what she's recriminating herself for. There was a picture that was not shown at the trial, the woman from the district attorney's office explains. She'd held it back, because there had been so much evidence already, and there had been leaks out of their office. Val knew this, of course; on one of the days she'd skipped the trial, she sat in Tim's hospital room and watched pictures of Andrew and the Woman pop up on Court TV. There on the sidewalk, the woman from the district attorney's office explains that celebrities open themselves up to this kind of thing, they paint targets on themselves when they step in front of a camera, but the kids, the kids should be off-limits. It's in the envelope. Val has only to open it and look.

Val goes to a coffee shop near her lawyer's office. She doesn't order anything, just sits at a table alone. People type on their laptops and check their phones. There is the general clatter that reaffirms to all of them they are living in a city and it is important they are right here, all of them. Val takes out the photo as if it's an X-ray or a CAT scan. Good news does not come out of manila envelopes. Good news is never extracted.

The photo is grainy and pixelated, taken by a cell phone. She recognizes the Woman, and from the position of the photo she can tell that Andrew took it, and that the Woman is on top of him, shirtless, head thrown back. Val recognizes their house, their living room. The windows looking out onto the park, the William Eggleston print of a bicycle fallen over on the sidewalk that she'd bought for an unreasonable price without telling Andrew, and that sat now in a bank vault waiting for the last of the papers to be signed.

And over the Woman's bare shoulder, in the doorway, framed by the darkness of his bedroom, is Alex, in his banana-colored pajamas, his expression lost in the low resolution of the digital image, excluded in the space between yes and no, zero and one.

With no appointment, with a mixture of rage and vindication, Val takes the photo to her lawyer's office. She demands to see her right away, which, as she says it, she realizes is a ridiculous thing to demand. Instead, she waits. She calls the girl watching Alex and says she'll be late, another hour or so. It's three hours before her lawyer returns from court, but it feels like it's worth it when she takes the picture out of the envelope.

The lawyer looks at her sadly. "It doesn't change anything," she says. "We could submit it as evidence of abuse, but we never alleged abuse."

"It's endangerment," says Val, pointing to the picture as if it's self-evident. "He let that woman near Alex." And while her lawyer assures her there's nothing that can be done, Val knows she will never let Alex be hurt, she will never risk handing him over to someone who could so casually let him near something so dangerous, so evil.

"I've been thinking about it, though, and I think it's okay. Because your friend, she was always dead. She always had been dead. Right now she's dead and even then before it happens, she had been dead now. The training has helped me to see that, which is why I'm ready to go home."

Hands are shaken, shoulders are slapped. Flashbulbs fire, spark, explode. Tim is giddy, and Rachel, who is a moon to his sun, beams with the light of him. Andrew, the only loser among them, is playing at being sore, muttering "always a bridesmaid," but it's a role. When no one is looking, some second in between, he whispers in her ear, "You earned it, Valerie." Later she will think, *That was the last moment he was . . .* and find there's no word to finish the sentence.

He tells Rachel that since they're the only ones with free hands, they should ditch the other two and go dancing. He demonstrates with the little dance from season two. Then he grabs Rachel, spins her around, and dips her in the overcrowded lobby and the cameras fire again.

Val looks at her award. She's spent so long saying that things like this don't matter. It's difficult to admit how badly she was wrong. It does matter. Now that it's in her hands, it matters very much.

"You two should go first," says Rachel. "Andrew and I will follow behind you, bowing and scraping."

Tim links arms with Rachel and gestures for Val and Andrew to do the same. Andrew takes Rachel's arm: the awards on the outside, like a border, like a guard.

"Off to see the wizard," says Andrew.

"We all go out together," says Tim.

# Me and My Eero

The trailhead opens like a mouth. Eero, on the leash, hangs back, looking to Alex for courage. Let the woods swallow me, Alex thinks and, giving the leash a tug, plunges in.

"It's funny I'm going into the woods from Grandma's house," Alex had told his grandmother as he put his shoes on.

"That's the safest way," she said. "When Little Red Riding Hood headed back home after bringing the basket to her grandmother, the woods were wolf-free."

"No wolves in these woods?" said Alex. He was not nervous, but like many kids who grow up in cities, he secretly believes all woods are full of wolves and bears and so on.

"Eero'll be the closest thing to a wolf in there," she said. At the sound of his name, Eero looked up and gave Alex a decidedly unwolfish grin. "You'll need to keep him on leash," his grandmother said. "Otherwise he'll go running after everything that moves. There's some deer in these woods, and I'd rather not have them harassed." She was packing him a little bag with trail mix and apples. It should have been a basket, he thought.

"And stay on the path," she said. "Your grandfather cut a very nice path through the woods. It'll be overgrown a bit. No one's seen to it in years. But you'll be able to follow it easy enough. It'll lead you in and around and back here home."

It was important that a journey like this be preceded by rules and by warnings. Part of the job of adults was to set limits. But the last rule, the unspoken rule of any story or journey, is that all limits are suspect. All warnings show only the point where the last story stopped, the boundary past which the map is unmapped. The kingdom of *Here There Be Dragons* is the province of explorers, magicians, and kids.

After only a few minutes walking down the throat of the trail, Alex knows he has been gulped. The trail takes a couple of turns right at its start, so the entrance disappears quickly behind him. Eero sniffs at everything and strains at the leash every time there is a noise. There is always noise. Alex hears the arrhythmic woodblock clacking of the upper parts of trees knocking together in the wind, tittering and chirruping of birds, scuttle of small things across leaves.

Alex listens, but there is nothing except the chirrups and titters and scuttles. Sitting behind him, Eero whines, unhappy to be still when everything else in the woods is moving. Alex looks down and sees that the shadow of the tree points away from the trail, down a naturally occurring channel of space running perpendicular to his grandfather's path.

"Come on, Eero," he says, and the two of them tromp along the long shadow the tree casts along the bed of leaves.

At some point before being lost becomes terrifying, it is raw and thrilling. When they stayed on the path, Alex and Eero walked slowly, stopping to smell this or examine that. Now they run and bound, leap over hurdleous logs and swing from trapezal branches. The sun comes through the upper leaves in yellow slats that slap Alex playfully across the eyes. He has left his grandparents' woods and entered his own. If there are bears here, they will be bears that dance and know old Russian songs they've overheard Babu singing while she cooks. If there are wolves, they will be the kind that invite you to ride on their backs, burying your hands in the soft white blankets of their fur.

Alex rushes unscathed through bushes and brambles. Ahead is a hill, and because there is no point in breaking only some rules, Alex lets Eero off the leash to race ahead. As Alex pistons his legs to scale the hill, blissfully aware of the hindrance of his own weight, Eero stands at the top, barking encouragement, beckoning Alex to come see what he sees.

Out of breath, Alex crests the hill and immediately turns to look back the way he came. The woods spread out below him and he can see the trail his grandfather carved out, snaking through them like a crooked scar.

Eero barks again to call Alex's attention forward, so Alex turns to see what they've found, what Eero has been waiting to show him. On the other side of the hill is a lea, grassy and free of trees, circled by the woods. Grazing there are deer, dozens maybe, or a dozen at least. They mill about, becoming impossible to count. The deer do not notice Alex and Eero watching them from the top of the hill. Eero runs excited circles around Alex, and Alex wonders if the dog's impulses are playful or predatory. Eero barks once, louder than before, and all the deer, all dozens or dozen of them, turn their heads as one to regard Eero and Alex. Eero stares back at them, his whole body tensed, coiled, ready to strike.

Alex lays his hand on the back of Eero's neck, feeling the taut muscles beneath his wiry fur. He can't see his grandmother's house, and certainly he can't see New York. New York is becoming harder to think about, and sometimes he has to check his notebook to remember the specifics of things. But there's nothing wrong with here, and this moment of not knowing where he's been or where he's going.

Tomorrow they'll leave for Chicago and another hotel and another convention. Everything, the whole trip, has seemed like a ceremony, like a long way to say goodbye. Alex thinks about what could be in California that could change things so radically, but the only thing he knows about California is that his father lives there. And in that moment, he knows that his father is waiting for him in Los Angeles. His mother is taking him to his father, to stay. His first thought, figuring this out, is a bright blue thing: *I'm going to see my dad.* His heart leaps up at the thought, in that second before it's pulled back into his chest with missing New York, and then into his stomach by wondering where his mom will be in all of this, why she hasn't told him before now what's going to happen, and what it means, to stay. For how long? Forever?

The dog gives out a little huff, followed by a low growl. "Stay, Eero," he says. "Let them be, Eero." With a resigned whimper, the dog's body goes slack and he sits, then lies down in the grass. Alex sits, then lies down too, in the grass, at the top of the hill, in the summer sun. The deer lose interest in them and return to grazing. Alex eats some trail mix and feeds a treat or two to Eero, who accepts them as a consolation prize. After a while, by mutual decision, they all head back into the woods.

After a dinner that makes Alex feel heavy and woozy, he and his grandmother play checkers at the kitchen table. The first couple games she very obviously lets him win, but then he manages to goad her into playing for serious and she wins the next four. He likes watching her win: she lights up like she's a kid herself. She talks trash, says things like "Bet you didn't see *that* coming!" as she double-jumps his men. The sky behind the trees goes fiery orange and his attention begins to drift away from the game. He is thinking about the robot. When they left off, the boy and the girl from the desert and the robot had gone into the city. They were standing outside the gates of the factory, watching the other robots going in to work. He is wondering where his mother is, and decides it's worth trying to ask.

"She had grown-up stuff to do, Shura," she says. He can tell from her tone that he won't get any more information out of her, so he begins to act tired, yawning and stretching. His mother told him once that yawning is contagious, and as evidence of this, Eliel begins to yawn and stretch along with him.

"Babu?" he says. "Is it all right if I go to bed?"

She smiles at him. "This is what good country air does for you. It keeps you awake when you should be awake, then knocks you right out when it's time to sleep." She offers to tuck him in, but he declines, so she kisses him on both cheeks and his forehead, says, "Goodnight, Shura," and pats him on the butt to send him on his way. Eliel trods along after him, while Eero lets out one last mournful whine. Alex stops, goes back into the kitchen, and gives the younger dog a vigorous rub behind the ears.

"You were a good dog today," Alex whispers. He presses his forehead against Eero's forehead and thinks those same words at him: *You were a good dog.*

They reach the room Alex is staying in, and Alex has to help Eliel up onto the bed. The old dog is asleep in moments, snoring loudly and occasionally releasing farts that are audible but seem to drift away from Alex, mercifully.

He tries reading some of *Adam Anti & Nothing but Flowers*, but he keeps thinking about what he knows now. Turning the fact over in his mind to find a crack in it, some way for it not to be true. He returns the book to his backpack and takes out an issue of *The Astounding Family* that the Idea Man gave him. The pages are yellowed and crispy. The colors, which must have jumped off the page once, are badly faded, printed so that if you bring the comic closer to your face, they stop being colors and become a collection of little dots pressed together between the thick black lines. When Alex's mother comes in, he is not so much reading the comic as examining it, as if it were an object from an archaeological dig, a journal of one family's strange adventures.

"Hey, Rabbit," she says, "I thought you'd be asleep. Babu said she'd tuckered you out."

"I waited for you," he says. She looks like she's lost a hundred games of checkers in a row. She's doing that thing where she puts her fingers on her eyes and presses, like she's pushing them back into her brain.

Tomorrow he will ask her. They will talk about California and what's going to happen, like they should have already. It will be easier if they can share it. It's getting harder for her, carrying the secret of it. He should have known what it was sooner. But right now she is tired, and he scoots over so she can lie down on the bed. He holds on to her and presses his head against her shoulder.

He can feel, through his forehead, through her shoulder, that she's in California already, that maybe she's been in California since before they left New York. She's in a place they're not together anymore. He doesn't know how to bring her back here, to this room where she used to sleep as a kid, where there's a dog and him and California is still in the future and not now, not here. Since he doesn't know how to bring her here, all he can do is ask her to meet him somewhere else. "Tell me a story?" he asks quietly.

"Not tonight, Rabbit," she says, her voice barely there.

# *Anomaly* S04E03

After the casual, loosely structured weekend at Cleveland's Hero-nomicon, Val assumed the role of celebrities at these things was to sit in an assigned place for a certain amount of time, and not much else. But when she arrives at Chicago's McCormick Place convention center with Alex in tow, she's handed a booklet titled "Windy City Comic Con Talent Code of Conduct" and assigned a handler who goes over the code in detail as he whisks her away from the main convention floor and down a side hallway.

"The most important thing," he says, "is that we try, as much as possible, to discourage non-official photography." He is short, balding, and pudgy, with an officious air, a clipboard, and a red windbreaker with WCCC STAFF emblazoned on the back. Val is beginning to form the thought that he reminds her of the White Rabbit when she hears Alex softly singing, "I'm late, I'm late, for a very important date." Moments like this confirm for her that he could be no one's child but hers.

"Of course," the White Rabbit says, "complete containment is impossible. But if someone asks to take a picture with you, respectfully decline and suggest they purchase a ticket for one of the photo ops. Someone will be making the rounds at the signing tables selling them."

"Purchase a ticket?" says Val.

"It's all in your contract," the White Rabbit says. Val hasn't read the contract. Everything was set up by Elise, who's in the business of reading contracts and must have thought this was all perfectly normal. "You'll receive thirty percent of net on all ticket sales, over and above your flat-rate fee."

"How much are tickets?" says Val, not so she can figure out her cut, but because the entire thing sounds preposterous.

"Fifty dollars," says the White Rabbit.

"Fifty dollars?" she says, shocked.

"Listen, I know, all right?" says the White Rabbit. They've arrived at a door that seems to be their destination, and he takes a moment to give her a patronizing eye roll. "Talent always thinks theirs should be higher," he says. "But we've been doing this for quite a while, and we put a lot of thought into the price points. Trust me, we'll all make more money with you at fifty than we would at seventy-five."

"People are going to pay fifty dollars to get their picture taken with her?" asks Alex. The White Rabbit nods enthusiastically.

"We've sold—" He checks his clipboard. "Eighty-three tickets so far."

Alex looks impressed. "Being your kid has saved me hundreds of dollars," he says. The White Rabbit lets them into the room, where a trio of photographers and a trio of assistants putter with equipment. Diffused flashbulbs go off at random intervals, and the White Rabbit is soon distracted by some other crisis. Val stands somewhat dazed until one of the photographers' assistants grabs her and says, "Torrey."

"Yes," she and Alex say simultaneously. The assistant ignores Alex.

"Stand here," he says, pointing to a spot in front of a backdrop bearing the *Anomaly* logo: a highly italicized *A* leaning over a tightly packed, sans serif grouping of the remaining letters. Val does as she's told. The assistant runs a light meter over her like a Geiger counter, then barks, "Two's a go" over his shoulder and flits off.

"You're a go, Mom," says Alex.

"For now, Rabbit," she says. "Later I'll be a went." He laughs at her little grammar joke. He's in better spirits this morning than he has been. They borrowed her mother's truck and drove up last night, checking into the hotel near the convention center late. Both of them had been exhausted from the sheer amount of food her mother had compelled them to eat, stuffing them as if they were headed for a food desert rather than the financial district of Chicago. Once they were settled in, there was a feeling they'd returned to the path, a place where they knew better how to behave toward each other. But there was something forced or off about it. All of her jokes seemed strained, and sometimes she could tell he wasn't reading his book, but using it to shield himself from her attention.

An older man, well into his sixties, dressed in a red crushed-velvet three-piece suit, approaches Val and Alex.

"Excuse me, miss," he says with a crisp, upper-class British accent. "Might I trouble you?" An untied bowtie hangs limply over his neck, and he holds up the useless ends of it in his fingertips.

"I don't know how to tie one," says Val. He has a great plume of white hair and sparkling blue eyes. His teeth are straight, but his smile is crooked, leaning to the left as if his mouth wants to make room for an absent pipe or cigarette.

"They're ridiculous," he says, dropping the end. "But no one recognizes me if I don't wear it. 'Give the people what they want' and all."

"He's the Curator," says Alex. He's looking up at the man, wide-eyed.

"Indeed I am," he says. "You're a little young to have seen my era of the show, though."

"My friend let me watch some," Alex says. He turns to his mother. "The Idea Man has them all on DVD. Shelves and shelves of them. He says you're the best one," he tells the man.

"Then your friend has excellent taste," the man says.

"I don't think I know what either of you is talking about," says Val.

"*The Curator.* It's a British TV show," Alex says. "He used to be on it."

"Long before you were born," says the man. "Probably before your mother was born as well." Slowly and carefully, he lowers himself to one knee so he's at eye level with Alex. "Would you mind helping me?" he says.

"Sure," says Alex.

"First cross left over right," says the man. Alex takes the ends of the bowtie and crosses them. "Then bring that one under and up. And the other gets folded. That's it. Now bring the first over and through and fold it behind.

Now we pull the whole thing tight. There!" Val watches as Alex goes through the complex series of movements with surety, then finally pulls the whole thing taut into a perfect bow. And once the bowtie is on, she does recognize the man, from afternoon reruns on WTTW on days she was home sick from school. Painted fabric sets that occasionally billowed breezily. Rubber monster suits and plots with fever-dream logic. "So much easier when it's someone else's hands," he says. "Mine shake something awful these days. My jazz hands, my wife calls them. But now we're ready to play wax museum, eh?" He smooths out bits of his suit and straightens the tie.

"You've done these before?" Val asks.

"I hardly do anything else," he says. "It seems seven years of playing a beloved hero has made me unqualified to play any other character."

"I'm familiar," says Val. But is she? She's never tried to go back into television, and in the world of little New York theater, her time as Bethany Frazer has been irrelevant. It certainly hasn't prevented her from getting roles; it even opened certain doors for her. Grant, her director on *Millennium Approaches,* told her once that Valerie Torrey helped the play work, but Bethany Frazer helped it sell tickets.

"Yours was the American time travel show?" he asks.

*"Anomaly,"* says Val.

"Couldn't wrap my head around it," he says, apologetic and not unkind. "Audiences in my day required much less science in their science fiction. Whenever we needed to explain something, we'd say *particle* this or *morphogenic* that. Introduce some machine with *tron* at the end of it. The episodes they're doing now, you need to be Stephen Hawking to follow them."

"They still make the show?" Val asks. The old man laughs.

*"The Curator*'s a British institution," he says. "Fifty years on Auntie Beeb. Which makes me something of a museum piece, I guess." At the far end of the room, the White Rabbit has returned. He's leading a line of people, each of them with tickets in hand, and reading another long list of rules off his clipboard.

"Talent will spend as much time at their table as possible," he says. "Please remember that talent, like you, need time to rest, recharge, eat, et cetera, so please be respectful of their need to take breaks. Head shots will be available at the table for signing, or bring your own item! Cash is the only method of payment accepted. Talent reserves the right to refuse to autograph any item they deem inappropriate. Bootleg merchandise is not allowed."

The old man looks at the oncoming crowd wearily. "The Internet's made Lazaruses of all us old television hacks," he says. "Or zombies, perhaps."

"It feels a little exploitative, doesn't it? Charging people to take a picture with you?" says Val. She inspects her outfit, unsure if it's photo-op worthy, but it's too late to change now.

"A little monetary sacrifice at the altar of the television gods, it's all right," the old man says in a grand, airy tone. "Pays for the wife and I to pop over once a summer. Our daughter's at University of Chicago. She's getting a doctorate in economics."

"That's great," says Val, because it's the kind of thing you say when someone's child is getting an advanced degree.

"This from two parents who could never balance a checkbook," he says.

"You must miss her," says Val, looking at Alex, who has staked out a corner of the room to sit and read in.

"They don't stay his size forever, you know," says the man. "You there," he calls to Alex, who looks up immediately. "Stop growing. You'll end up breaking your mother's heart." Alex smiles the way you would at a child who's trying to be cute, then returns to his book. "It's one thing I liked about *The Curator,*" the man says. "The idea that every few years, he becomes a completely different person. And the audience has to decide whether they like this new person or not."

Later, when there is a lull, Val goes over to the corner and slides down the wall to sit next to Alex. "Hey, Rabbit," she says, "how about that story I owe you?" Alex doesn't say anything, but he closes his book and tucks it in his backpack. For a moment it looks as though he's trying to figure how to position himself. As if he doesn't know how to listen to a story unless they're curled up in bed. He folds his hands in his lap and looks at her expectantly.

"Frazer is eight weeks pregnant," she says. "This is season four. She hasn't told anyone yet, not even Campbell. Anomaly Division gets called in on a series of couples who claim their pregnancies have been sped up. You know how long a pregnancy is supposed to be?"

"Nine months," says Alex.

"Some of these are lasting three weeks, but the babies are being born perfectly healthy. Not premature at all. And once they're born, they're growing up too fast. Walking at one month. Talking at nine weeks.

"It's funny," says Val, wandering off the story's path a little, "because we all think that. That it's happening too fast, maybe even that something might be wrong. But we think time is passing quicker than it should, not that the child is actually growing up faster than they ought to, even though that's how we say it: *They grow up so fast.* Looking back, I'm amazed at how Tim nailed that feeling, even though he and Rachel never had kids. It was before you were even around."

She finds it easier to remember Andrew during the pregnancy than to remember herself. He attacked the pregnancy like it was a problem to be solved. He brought home bags of prenatal vitamins, of lotions and creams. He read half a dozen books and took notes on all of them; she'd find Post-its around the apartment that read "folic acid supplements" or "increased levels of prolactin." She began to feel like the sole patient in an overly specialized hospital, but didn't notice that as this went on, Andrew became more interested in the pregnancy than in her: the two became oddly separated. They talked about the varying effects pregnancy could have on a couple's sex life, but never noted the effect it had on theirs, which was to bring it to a mutually and tacitly agreed-upon halt. He looked at her now like the mother of his child and touched her gently as if she might break. She was so grateful for his help, his solicitous assistance, that she assumed the physical bond between them would be easily repaired after, later. That it hadn't been severed but only put aside.

"There were weeks of the pregnancy that stretched out into months," she says, "or felt like they did. Nausea and backaches and constant trips to the bathroom. And then I was huge and I couldn't remember getting huge, or being a little big. All of the interim states had passed me by before I had time to notice them.

"And then you were there," she says.

He leans in against her, tucking his head into her armpit. There was a moment, that first day in the hospital, when Tim and Rachel had left and Andrew was asleep in the chair in the corner. Val and her baby, whose name they hadn't decided yet, alone for the first time; his heart, which had a day before been inside her, beating next to hers, and she felt as if she was returning to herself after a long time away. *Everything will be different now,* she remembers thinking, with no idea what would be different or how, whether it would be better or worse.

The major difference in those first few weeks was a break from everything outside of herself and Alex, one enforced by the sheer exhaustion resulting from Alex's constant need for attention, for feeding, for holding. Val had continued shooting right up to the day before she went into labor, even though she moved with all the grace of a zeppelin. Tim and the other writers had come up with a couple of Frazer-free scripts they'd shoot after the baby was born, and he held things off as long as he could so Andrew could have time away from the set, but a week and a half after Alex was born, Andrew had to go back to shooting, working longer-than-normal days to make up for the time they'd lost, until the longer-than-normal days became the norm. Each week, Tim would drop by to see Alex and ask Val if she felt ready to come back, and each week she said no, not yet. When she saw Andrew, he was usually asleep on the couch as she passed through to the kitchen to get water or a snack during one of Alex's brief periods of quiet.

When Val and Andrew found time to talk, it was like they were speaking in different languages. Val would report on Alex's moods, digestive issues, minor developmental milestones. Andrew would recount plot details and rumors going around the set. In some ways, she was aware she was making a little world sufficient unto itself and that she was waiting for Andrew to find his way in. But in those weeks, he became even further invested in the show, spending time in the writers' room contributing ideas, bringing home books on multiversal theory and the epistemology of time travel, most of which would end up dropped on the floor by the couch, barely read.

After a month, the attention Alex needed no longer felt constant and, as promised, Tim arranged for a babysitter near enough to the soundstage that Val could check in on Alex between takes. She reentered the world of *Anomaly* begrudgingly, shocked that nothing else had changed when everything for her was different, as she'd known in that first moment it would be. But once there, she could feel the relief of it, to be lost in someone else's imaginary story, only a thing in Tim's dream.

The line is starting to fill in again. The White Rabbit makes sure he stays in her field of vision as he paces back and forth, checking the time on his watch, on his phone. He can wait. Everyone else can wait.

"It gets worse," she says. "Maybe Tim already knew that by intuition or empathy, but I didn't, then. In the episode, it's the Leader. He's stealing time from them, stealing days and weeks and months to use elsewhere. I look at you and I think that. And whoever'd done it replaced that little person with a version of you that was even better; they did it over and over again, and every time I was so happy for what I'd been given, and so sad for what I'd given up. And every time, I knew that I'd be losing this one, too, any second now, the moment I blinked."

# Island of Misfit Toys

Alex's superpower may be invisibility, he thinks as he darts unseen among convention-goers. It is a good superpower if you're interested in sneaking, but Alex is not big on sneaking.

McCormick Place convention center could probably hold four or five Heronomicons inside it, he estimates. Not only is it much bigger in terms of floor space, but the ceilings are so high you could fly planes in here, if they weren't full of ductwork and metal supports. Where Cleveland had chandeliers, Chicago has industrial drop lighting. Where Cleveland had velvety wallpaper, Chicago has concrete. Overall, Alex prefers Chicago.

The rules are different here, though. He is not supposed to leave the main hall. He has to check in once an hour, either with his mom or with one of the costume ladies, who are all really nice and all have his mom's phone number. "If there's trouble," his mother told him, "find a sexy lady in a superhero costume."

He imagines a network, a team of superheroines watching over him, patrolling this little imaginary city to keep track of him. It should make him feel good, but it doesn't. It makes him feel like his mom doesn't trust him anymore, because he made one mistake. At first, she'd said he wasn't allowed out of her sight, but it was boring in the photo room, and even the Curator didn't have time to talk to him. When he insisted, she set up the rules. He asked if he had to check in because he was being punished and she said, "No, it's just because." It's not really an answer, and it makes Alex think about other questions he's asked that haven't gotten real answers, either.

Alex is on his way to Artist Alley when he sees Brett with a girl dressed as a kind of half person, half weasel. Alex calls out to him excitedly.

"Alex!" says Brett, happy to see him. He puts up a hand for Alex to high-five him. This is something a lot of adults do to kids, and Alex actually is a little over high fives. He enjoys fist bumps and thinks handshakes will be better once his hands are bigger. But he obliges, then looks at the girl to see if she wants a high five as well.

"Is this your son?" she asks Brett.

"How old do you think I am?" he says. She shrugs, indicating not just that she doesn't know but that she doesn't care.

"I like your costume," Alex says to her.

"Thanks," she replies. "Anyone ever tell you you've got great eyelashes?"

"Everybody does," he says.

"It's tough when they only want you for your looks, huh?" she says. With her pinkie finger, she carefully removes a bit of dark makeup that is attempting to find its way into her eye.

"I was hoping we could work on our story," Alex says to Brett. He kind of whispers '*our* story' so the girl doesn't hear. "I've been thinking about the robot factory, and I think it has sensors that detect humans, so the robot has to go in alone."

"What are you guys talking about?" asks the girl.

"Nothing," Brett tells her. He turns back to Alex. "We're going to go get something to eat," he says. "Maybe you and I can meet up later to work on the story? When I get back to the booth?"

Alex knows there are real *later*s and fake *later*s, and this one is a real *later*. It still hurts to be put off. "I'll go wait for you," he says.

"Great," says Brett. "I'll be maybe twenty minutes." The girl looks at him funny when he says this, but Brett doesn't see it. They head off toward the food court, and Alex walks toward Brett's booth, less motivated now.

Artist Alley, which in Cleveland was just that, is a flourishing neighborhood here, a small village of people, almost all of them boys, who all look roughly like Brett. It's like they got every possible Brett from every possible alternate dimension and put them right here. After crisscrossing the neighborhood several times and finally asking Brett-If-He-Were-Fatter-and-Had-a-Goatee if he knows where Brett's table is, Alex finds Fred there by himself.

"Hey, kid," says Fred. Fred has not yet called him anything other than "kid." "Brett's not here. He's out hunting ferrets," Fred says.

"Huh," says Alex. "She's a ferret."

A man stands next to Alex paging through Brett's portfolio, kind of Brett-If-He-Dressed-in-Nicer-Clothes-and-Was-from-Jamaica-or-Somewhere-Like-That.

"These are great," he says to Fred. "Do you do commission pieces?"

Fred sighs loudly again and rolls his eyes. "I'm the writer," he says, pointing to his name on the cover of an issue of *Lady Stardust*. "We are distinguishable from artists in that we show up on time."

The man walks away without another word.

"You weren't very nice to him," says Alex.

"I'm not feeling very nice today," says Fred.

"How come?"

Fred sits up and looks directly at Alex for the first time. Alex can tell he's deciding if whatever he's about to say is worth saying to a kid. He has seen people make that decision a hundred times before.

"Look," he says, "I don't want to badmouth Brett, because it looks like you guys have this whole OuterMan-and-OuterKid thing going on. It's adorable. But he's got certain responsibilities, and he's shirking them to go shtup his lady friend."

"What's *stup*?" says Alex.

"*Shtup, shtup,* kid," says Fred. "It's Yiddish—you've got to get the *sh* sound back here." He raises his chin and pinches right under his jawbone.

"So what's *shtupping*?"

"I'm not sure I should be talking to you about this," says Fred, and from that Alex knows exactly what *shtupping* means.

"They're having sex," he says, less interested now that the mystery's solved. He tries to lean his chair back like Fred's, but it doesn't feel safe and he puts all four legs back on the ground.

"Like right now: he's supposed to be here to watch the table so I can go see the Mad Brit talk."

"What's the Mad Brit?"

Again the eyes roll, and this time they stay pinned to the ceiling. "He's the greatest writer in the history of comics. He's a personal hero of mine, and I am not a person who has personal heroes. He's also speaking right over there"—Fred points to the other end of the convention hall—"right now. And I'm stuck here, being asked if I'll do a drawing of Ferret Lass for ten bucks, which is ironic, because Brett is currently—" Fred looks back down at Alex. "Never mind."

"Did you ask him to stay?"

"No, but he knows how important this is to me."

"So you told him it was important to you."

"He should just know."

"Can I say something mean?"

"Go nuts, kid."

"That's stupid. It's one of the stupidest things adults do. Things are broken and things are important and they don't say anything. They don't say anything and nothing gets fixed."

Without waiting for a response, Alex walks away, too, just like the man looking at the drawings did. He's mad at Fred, even if there's nothing to be mad at Fred about. Walking away with a really angry face helps a little, but the fact that there's nothing to be mad at Fred about makes it harder to stop. Alex considers finding a spot to sit and read *Adam Anti & Nothing but Flowers*, but for some reason he feels angry at the book. He thinks about going to talk to his mom, but then his angry feeling gets even worse. So he just wanders around the convention hall, which seems like a big empty space now, the ceilings too high and the concrete floors slapping against the bottoms of his feet and everything loud and echoing.

There are practically no other kids here, which is stupid, because there's so much stuff for kids here. There are card games and action figures, there are bobblehead dolls and stuffed superheroes, but there are no kids anywhere to play with them. It makes Alex feel bad for the toys, and it makes him think of his toys back in their apartment in New York. What will happen to all the things he didn't bring? Will she throw them out? Will she keep his room like a shrine and never go in there, never dust it or anything so it's like one of the dioramas at the Museum of Natural History? There are things in his room he still wants: most of his books, a couple of the toys, his Mets hat. Why did he not bring them?

# Three May Keep a Secret

"You met with him or you had a meeting?" Gail asks. Whatever the answer is, she's annoyed. Ed does not have a face made for smiling. There's something unsettling about him when he smiles. He looks like a predatory animal wearing a funny hat.

"I don't know what the difference is," he says, setting a round of beers on the table. And then there's this: Ed buying two rounds in a row without being asked. Usually, Ed skips out after the second round or begrudgingly buys the third after all three of them have sat dry for at least five minutes. This despite the fact that he's making more than both of them. Or at least more than she is. There has been some body-snatching, mind-wiping foofaraw going on here in Chicago.

It's late and they're at a bar on Chicago's South Side that Ed picked out. It is a perfect bar for Ed to have picked out, because it gives the impression of being divey without actually being a dive. Ed showed up an hour and a half late because Phil Weinrobe, Timely Comics' editor in chief, had asked him to grab a drink.

"If you're not sure, then you met with him," she says.

"I can't talk about it," says Ed, beaming like he's just gotten laid.

"Then it was a meeting," concludes Gail, picking up her beer and trying to consume as much of it as she can before the real Ed returns and asks for it back.

"You can't talk about it?" asks Geoff, sounding hurt. Geoff has a face made for smiling. When he smiles, he looks like an adorable animal wearing a funny hat. Gail decides she is drunk.

"You guys are the competition!" says Ed. "You're the enemy."

Gail slaps the table and points at Ed. "Exclusive contract," she says. Ed smiles coyly. "Three years." Ed smiles coyly. "Five years!" Ed smiles coyly. "Truckful of money," she yells. People are starting to look at them.

"They gave you the Ferret," says Geoff. Gail realizes that she and Geoff, who is also drunk, are projecting their own desires onto Ed's meeting.

"I wouldn't want the Ferret," Ed says dismissively. Then he gives them that grin again, that sharklike grin. A shark wearing a fez, maybe. "It's bigger than the Ferret."

"The Ferret movie grossed half a billion," says Geoff, who for one thing thinks about comic book characters in terms of their dollar value as intellectual property but also probably writes fanfic about the Ferret in his spare time. "What's bigger than the Ferret?"

"'Death of the Ferret,'" Gail says, muttering it into her beer. Everyone pauses, like when a gymnast vaults into the air and you're waiting to see if she'll stick the landing. Gail takes a deep breath. "The Gentleman kills the Ferret," she explains. "Lures him into a trap and beats him to death with his bare fists. Ferret Lass goes crazy and seeks revenge. Kills the Gentleman, takes over the whole criminal empire of New York." She realizes both of them are looking at her and not speaking. The same thing happened at one of their bullshit sessions years ago, when Geoff offhandedly said, "Wouldn't it be cool if there had been a cruise ship full of people from OuterMan's home planet of Nebulon who'd been light-years away when the planet exploded and they showed up on Earth, a hundred aristocratic cruise-goers, all with the powers of OuterMan?" It was a silence and a stare that meant a real idea had been thrown on the table like a rummy card and they were waiting to see if the person who'd tossed it was going to pick it back up. She's stuck the landing.

"You gender-bended the Ferret," says Geoff.

"No, I didn't," Gail says. "I killed the Ferret."

"But Ferret Lass, she'd drop the 'Lass.' She'd be the new Ferret."

"You could run with that for at least three years," says Ed.

"Next Ferret movie's in two," Geoff says. "He comes back from the dead before the movie drops. Fights the new Ferret."

"She fights *him*," says Gail. "He comes back bad."

"You'd gender-bend and heel-turn the Ferret," says Geoff, clearly impressed.

"You should pitch that," says Ed.

"I'd need a meeting first," Gail says, taking a deep swallow of beer to indicate the conversation is over. But the three of them are still mulling the idea, and Gail fights to keep herself from writing it on a bar napkin. She hopes she is not too drunk to remember it.

"It's a crossover," says Geoff, going back to playing twenty questions with Ed.

"Timely doesn't do crossovers," Ed says. "We do events."

"You said 'we,'" Gail points out. "You never say 'we.' You're all Team Corporate Overlord now?"

"So it's an event," says Geoff.

"You are bursting. You are bursting to tell us." She notices a little *sh* in her esses.

"I have been sworn to secrecy," says Ed, putting his hand in the air. "All will be revealed in time."

Remedial grinning lessons. Japanese smiling schools where they put a pencil behind your eyeteeth until your face learns the feeling of a natural smile.

"In time for the next round?" asks Gail, who is surprised to find her glass is empty.

"Los Angeles," Ed says gravely. This is better. Gravely is better. It's more Ed.

"This is the Los Angeles announcement," says Geoff. There have been rumors for months that Timely will be announcing something big in Los Angeles. All the blogs have been running wild speculation about it. Gail was convinced Timely had hired the Mad Brit back, but when she saw him wandering the convention floor that morning, Phil Weinrobe wasn't holding his beard for him.

"It relates to the Los Angeles announcement," says Ed.

"You are a terrible person for not telling us," Gail says. "You are worse than a hundred Hitlers for not telling us what this is."

"Don't you want to be surprised?" says Ed, sounding a lot like Geoff. "Just once, don't you want to go into something unspoiled?"

# *Anomaly* Hiatus

T he hotel restaurant's menu attempts to serve all comers. It is a culinary United Nations. Along with hot dogs and steaks, there is an extensive offering of pastas and curries. An entire page details stir-fry options; another, falafel, kibbeh, and tabbouleh. Val and Alex sit there for an hour, and Alex doesn't eat. Not *won't* but *doesn't*.

It's a savvy trick on Alex's part that in these situations he doesn't present resistance or declare his intentions not to do something. He simply *doesn't*.

*Won't* she could break down. *Doesn't* is a reed that bends with wind. When the waitress comes around and Val insists that he order something, he chooses a hamburger, plain, which goes cold on the plate while Val works her way through a massive Cobb salad.

She asks if anything is wrong, and he makes a noise that resembles the letter *M*.

Missed, skipped, and refused meals have always been crises for Val. Alex is an engine, burning through calories at an alarming rate. The caloric intake required for sustenance, let alone growth, is daunting to her, and most meals barely end before she's contemplating the next one. On the occasions Alex will not eat, she finds herself less interested in the cause than obsessed with the idea that without food he will grind to a halt, or collapse like a puppet with cut strings. In the past, she's tried to force the issue, over stomachaches and queasiness, over the rare claim that he doesn't like this food or that. But the amount consumed ends up outweighed by the effort expended in its consumption. Her current defeatist strategy is to let it go and leave the food around, trusting he will find his way to it when he needs it, but part of her wants to reach across the table and stuff the hamburger into him like stolen goods into a burglar's sack.

The waitress asks him if everything is okay, and he nods. She boxes it up for them to cram into the tiny hotel fridge, hopefully to be eaten cold later.

Upstairs, Alex gets into his pajamas and brushes his teeth wordlessly, without being asked. It's a bad sign, because he is fastidious about not eating after he's brushed his teeth. Once he's out of the bathroom, Val goes in, shuts the door, and sits on the edge of the tub, sweatpants gripped in her right hand. It's a testament to what an agreeable child Alex is that she has so few coping strategies for when he's not. Negative emotions usually float through Alex like ducks down a stream. She's thought that his basic mood has something melancholic about it, but real sadness and pronounced anger come upon him rarely. When they do, they strike quickly and dissipate just as fast. She tries to think of times he's been this recalcitrant and can only think of the car ride from California to New York when he was three. She'd left her lawyer's office that day, the manila envelope gripped in her hand, and walked to a copy shop a few blocks over. Scanning to make sure she wasn't being watched, she took the picture out and copied it once, in black and white. The result was grainier than the original, and it was harder to make out Alex in the doorway. She thought for a second that she could copy this one, then the result, spiraling down into lower and lower resolutions until Alex was no longer in the picture at all, and that somehow that would fix everything; it would keep Alex safe and erase or at least obscure Andrew's sin. But she slipped the copy and the original back into the envelope and went home, sending the babysitter on her way with a generous tip. Andrew wouldn't be home until the following day. He was on a shoot up in Vancouver, the shift from L.A. to a cheaper location being a sure sign that the movie was running over budget. She found boxes in the back of a closet from when they'd moved in and packed as much as she could. Then, with the last of the packing tape, she affixed the copy of the photo to the door, layering strip upon strip of tape over it so he'd have to claw and scrape the last little bits of it off the door with his fingernails.

She made so many mistakes those first few days. In deciding to run and not walk away, she'd left too much behind. Too many of Alex's things, jobs left unfinished, friendships severed. Tim.

Alex refused to eat and wouldn't leave the car. Although he'd been potty-trained for over a year, he regressed, forcing Val to stop at a Walmart in the southern tip of Nevada to buy diapers. He screamed bloody murder in the parking lot as she forced them on, convinced someone was going to call the cops, who would arrest her for kidnapping. When she had to haul him out of the car to go into the motel they ended up at the first night, he'd kicked and flailed at her, making inchoate noises so loud the desk clerk gave Val the key card to the room without payment, suggesting Val come back "when the little guy's calmed down." That night, he slept in the bath-tub with the door closed, refusing to come out, refusing to talk to her. Thankfully the lock was too high and too elaborate for him to work it, but Val let him stay in there alone and, exhausted, fell asleep sitting outside the door, listening to him cry.

The next morning, all that rage had been spent. Silently, he ate a muf-fin from the continental breakfast and got into the car. He'd consented to being diapered, but mumbled "Gotta go" when he needed to for the rest of the drive, and on the third day he went without them. On the fourth, she threw them away at a rest stop in Pennsylvania, not wanting to bring them with her into whatever new life awaited her and Alex in New York.

This feels like an echo of that: he punished her for taking him away from Andrew, even though he couldn't have known what was going on, and now he's punishing her for taking him back to Andrew. Val stands up and pulls on her sweatpants, leaving her skirt on the bathroom floor. She ventures back into the room. Alex sits cross-legged on the unused bed, his book open on his lap.

"Hey, Rabbit," she says, "how about a story?"

"No, thanks," he says quietly, not looking up.

"You sure?" she says. "There was an episode I had in mind." He doesn't respond. Val isn't sure Alex has ever refused a story before. A curious thing about being a mother is how little newness it involves. Routines may at times feel oppressive, but the entry of newness is disruptive, frightening.

"You want to cuddle?" she says, sounding to her own ear desperate and weak.

"I want to read my book," he says. Rebuked, she goes to the other bed, pulls the sheets out of their tight tuck, and slips herself in like a letter into an envelope. She turns off her light and lies on her side watching him, but when he looks up and sees her, she rolls to the other side and stares at the blinds. They are lit buttery yellow from the lamp next to Alex's bed, and although he doesn't shut off the light, she never hears him turn a page.

# Living Arrangements

The sun is coming in at a steep angle through the slats of the hotel window blinds. That means it's late. Not the New York sun. Heartier, more robust, a midwestern sun. Surprised he didn't notice it before now. The clock next to the bed reads 11:11. Seems like it should be significant.

"Let's not get out of bed," says Ferret Lass. Rolls and throws her arm over him. Not sure if she means today or ever. He is fine with either.

"Fred will be angry with me," he says. The past week with Fred has been strained, and it's not anyone's fault. It's been a team effort. Ferret Lass called Tuesday to get together. Brett tells himself he wouldn't have gone if there'd been work to do. But Fred hadn't given him more than three script pages to pencil, and that included one that read "Full-page spread: vast barren starscape." Brett told him they didn't have room for full-page establishing shots at this point, and Fred sulked for an hour. In the absence of work, spending time with Ferret Lass seemed permissible and preferable to watching Fred sit at the hotel room desk and affect the postures of the tortured writer, trying to mine bits of genius from his skull. But when Brett returned early the next morning to accusations that he'd broken the creative flow, he turned right around and called Ferret Lass to see about going out for breakfast.

Things had gotten better, and by Friday morning they were almost at the halfway point they'd promised to Russell at the beginning of the week, due in no small part to Brett's advancing the plot on his own late Thursday night while Fred slept. He presented the pages, still in sketch rather than finished pencils, to Fred the next morning, before coffee had been acquired. "We can work with it," Fred muttered, and Brett resisted the urge to tell him to fuck off and draw it himself.

"Fred's not your girlfriend," she says. The first time this word has been used. By either of them. It makes him nervous.

"Are you my girlfriend?" he asks. Tentative. He'd be fine with either answer. She laughs. She is so pretty. He always thought of Debra as pretty. She is, but in an everyday, meet-you-at-a-bar way. Here is this impossible kind of pretty. If he drew her into the comic, Fred would tell him to draw someone more realistic. "Aren't you supposed to be working?" he asks.

"I called Iota and told her I was sick," she says. "The organizer can't keep track of us. Every time he sees one of us up close, all the blood rushes from his brain to his dick. Besides, there's so many cosplayers here, they barely need us."

"What exactly is it you're supposed to do?" Brett asks.

"I asked about this," she says. Raises one finger. She is about to deliver a thorough answer. "It used to be the comic book companies would hire girls like me to come and work cheesecake. Hang around the booth attracting attention. But some of the female fans called bullshit, and rightly so. Because objectification. But at the same time, guys who show up at a con have certain expectations of what they're going to see. So the people running the convention hire us to do the same thing the comic companies used to hire us to do. Because capitalism."

"What difference does it make if you're hired by the company or the con?"

"We never say we're hired by the con," she says. "We never say we're hired at all. No one ever gets angry directly at us. But they don't know who they should get angry at. So no one gets hurt."

It's the longest he's ever heard her talk. Her voice is the only thing about her that is more attractive when she's in the costume than out of it. Impressed by her assessment of things, he realizes she hasn't answered his question about what they're hired to do. It isn't important.

"You should come to Los Angeles," she says. Out of the blue. "After the convention."

"What's in Los Angeles?" he asks.

"Me." This is something he didn't know. That she lives in Los Angeles. Two lists: Things He Knows on the left and Things He Doesn't Know on the right. He finally has something in the left column.

"You mean to visit?" he asks.

"If you want to visit," she says. Sounds a little disappointed. "Or you could come live with me." He looks at her to see if she's joking. He hasn't known her long enough to know what she looks like when she's joking. "I have a big apartment on La Cienega," she says. "It gets good light in the morning. There's a room you could draw in."

"What would we do?" he asks. He has no idea what he wants the answer to be. What the question is. She shrugs.

"You could draw. I'd keep looking for modeling work. We'd fuck a lot. Same thing we're doing right now. Or I could move to New York. New York's the same as L.A., as far as I'm concerned."

"You'd move to New York to be with me?"

"I'd move to New York to be in New York. If I was moving to New York, it'd be nice to have someone to stay with. And to sleep with. Or, if I stay in L.A., it'd be nice to have someone to share my rent and my bed." She looks at him as if she's explained something incredibly simple.

"Is this a West Coast thing?" he asks. "People don't do this in New York."

"I'm sure people do this in New York all the time," she says. He wonders if this is something West Coast people assume. That people in New York are not uptight. But they are. "I'm not asking you to marry me. I'm not even asking you to sign a lease. I'm asking you to come to L.A. for a while, and if you get tired of it, leave. Or if I get tired of you, I'll ask you to leave. Or maybe we both get tired of fucking each other and we end up roommates." He gets the impression all of these endpoints are essentially the same to her in terms of desirability.

"It sounds weird."

"It's easy," she says. Draws out both syllables. Makes the word a patch of smooth road. "That's why it sounds weird. Because you're used to things being hard, and this is easy. You're used to things being complicated, and this is not complicated."

He can think of a hundred problems. Thousand ways for it to go wrong. Screaming scenarios play out in his head. Crying jags. Thrown plates. "It seems complicated."

"Think about it," she says. She is there in bed with him. She is this impossible kind of pretty. "Here," she says. Moves toward him. "I'll make a convincing argument."

# Career Opportunities

After spending all morning in the recycled air and manufactured sunlight of the convention center, stepping out onto the street is overwhelming. The thick, damp heat of Chicago's summer is weirdly refreshing, or maybe it's the body's natural need for sun. Gail holds her face up to the light for a few seconds before thoughts of skin cancer pop into her head and she shades her eyes with her hands.

From out here, you can see the convention's effect on the outside world. Robots are waiting for cabs. The lines for the hot dog vendors include angels, aliens, mutants. But even among the general population, clothes are getting tighter and shinier. It occurs to Gail that she might be the only one here without an alter ego; most of the people who pass must have Twitter handles or DJ names or online personas that mask or reveal. Even Val is Bethany Frazer when she's here. She's often thought of the con as a throwback to adolescence. But what if it's a prediction, or a pupal stage? Is it possible the culture of the outside world is becoming more paranormal, or that this subculture being celebrated inside is bubbling up, bleeding through?

"I'm buying," says Gail as Val reaches for her wallet. The hot dog vendor hands them two, and Gail begins liberally applying mustard to hers. She gently grabs Val's wrist when Val reaches for the ketchup.

"You want everyone to know you're a tourist?" says Gail.

"I don't know what I was thinking," says Val. "My father would have been mortified."

"You were thinking it was a New York City cart dog and you'd have to smother it so it'd taste like something," says Gail. "This is one complaint you can file against New York: our street food is for crap." With glee she tears into her hot dog, wads the bite into the side of her mouth, and asks, "You grow up here?"

"Around here," says Val. "In Bucktown for a while, then up to Evanston. We had a summer house in Normal; my mom still lives out there." Gail has never met anyone who would admit to having had a summer house growing up. "You?"

Gail shakes her head, then nods and swallows. "Ames, Iowa. Home of the Iowa State Cyclones. You know what Gertrude Stein said about where she grew up?"

"I don't, actually."

"There is no there there," says Gail, complete with poetic pauses. "True of Gert's hometown, true of mine. I left when I was seventeen, came to school at U of C. First lesson I learned: mustard only. Chicagoans take their condiments very seriously." She chomps on the hot dog again and continues with her mouth full. "It ended up being a big advantage, having lived here. Most New York comics writers don't know the first thing about Chicago. But Center City is the National analog of Chicago, so when I started writing *The Speck & Iota,* I was able to give it some local color."

"I have no idea what you're talking about," says Val, smiling genuinely for the first time all day. It's the perfect opposite of how she smiles at the convention: the forced smile draws the memory of happiness out of the body and pushes it into the face; a real smile feeds happiness back into the body, radiating it out from a point.

"National Comics set their books in fictional cities," says Gail. "Metro City is clearly New York, but they don't call it New York. Pearl City is San Francisco, complete with the Pearl Gate Bridge, which, for some reason, is bright blue. And Center City, which is where the Speck and Iota are headquartered, is completely and obviously Chicago."

"Why not use real cities?" Val asks.

"In the beginning I think it was because they wanted OuterMan to have a futuristic city to have adventures in. Metro City is New York, but it's more like New York in Corbusier's wet dreams. Highways spiraling through the air, tram cars on a web of invisible wires. Once your main city is fictional, it's easier to stick with fictional cities, for the sake of consistency. There's also the fact that comic book cities get blown up a lot. The past couple years, it's nice not to have to be blowing up New York or Boston or Chicago. I mean, who wants to knock down the Empire State Building now?"

"But you live in New York?" she says.

"Where else is a person going to live?" says Gail. "I miss Chicago, but a girl can't live on hot dogs alone." The zeal with which she's eating gives the lie to her statement.

"You couldn't live here and write?" asks Val.

"I could," she says. "I probably should. There's maybe a half-dozen writers I see regularly in New York. And my company's editorial office is there, but they never want to see me." There was probably a time when everyone who worked in comics lived in New York, but now National is the only major publisher whose offices are in Manhattan. If there's a city where the comics industry lives, it's this traveling city, the cons, that moves westward every summer like a tent revival show. "What about you?" she asks Val. "You couldn't live here and act?"

"New York convinces you it's the place you have to be," Val says.

"Must be a weird place to raise a kid, though."

"He adapts," Val says. "He's thrived. He's more of a New Yorker than I'll ever be."

"Subway maps in the brain, and lungs that can process exhaust fumes," says Gail. "Superpowers." She and Geoff sometimes make lists of the gifts that would make living in New York easier. The power to make yourself visible. Able to leap from Flatbush to the Lower East Side in a single bound.

"You have kids?" Val asks.

"Oh, no," says Gail. "No, no. I'm a few rungs lower on the ladder of stability than the having-kids one. I have cats. Multiple cats. I am a single New York lesbian with cats. Living the dream." Val looks a little surprised. "Don't worry," Gail says, "this isn't a come-hither hot dog."

"You seeing anyone?" says Val.

Gail chuckles. "I spend my days thinking about a woman who can fly faster than the speed of sound and can hear heartbeats a planet away. Dating prospects pale in comparison."

"Standards too high," Val says. "I'm familiar."

"Being married to Ian Campbell was that great?"

"No," she says, laughing. "It was awful."

"People are, it turns out, largely awful," says Gail. "One more thing that makes dating a challenge."

"Plus I've already got the perfect man in my life."

"Sometimes I leave my desk after writing all afternoon and I can't bring myself to talk to anybody," Gail says. "No one seems as real as the people in my head. It's isolating. It keeps you apart from people."

"It keeps you from getting hurt," says Val.

"Getting hurt's not so bad," says Gail. "Builds character or something."

"Character can fuck itself," says Val, dabbing mustard from her chin. Gail can tell from the way she says it that she's not used to swearing. Having a kid, you must get out of practice.

"Yeah, fuck character," says Gail, trying to encourage her.

"I worry about going back to it full-time," Val says. "I'm not sure I can start being other people again."

"What's stopping you?"

"It feels so selfish," she says. "All that energy put into making things up."

"*Selfish* gets a bad rap," says Gail. "You could also see it as you're giving up all that other stuff and all those other people to create something, and that something you create is as much for everybody else as it is for you. It's kind of self-*less* when you look at it like that."

"Is that how you look at it?" says Val.

"No," says Gail. "I like writing about flying girls in spandex. That and a job I can do in my pajamas."

# *Anomaly* S06E23

Alex finds Fred and not Brett manning the table in Artist Alley. He's got his feet up, tipping his chair precariously backwards, face obscured by a copy of *Adam Anti & Life During Wartime.* The way he's sitting, the way he's holding the book, too close to actually read it, all broadcast the message that Fred doesn't want to talk to anybody, and the message is being received. People glance at Brett's portfolios or the covers of *Lady Stardust,* then quietly move away.

Alex comes around the table behind Fred, looking over his shoulder but not at the words so he doesn't ruin it for himself.

"You like those, too?" he says. He tried to sneak up, but it must not have worked, because Fred isn't startled at all.

"Nope," says Fred, snapping the book shut. "I've seen the movies. I found this one in Brett's bag. I thought I'd give it a try. The prose is flat and the story is a warmed-over mix of Arthurian legend and rock opera. But it's far from charmless. And it reads quickly."

"You can't start with the last one," says Alex defensively. He hasn't understood most of what Fred said, but he grasps that it's a negative review. He likes it that Fred doesn't take the time to make sure Alex gets it. It's the same lack of respect Fred shows everybody, and in that way it's kind of respectful.

"I'm sorry I yelled at you yesterday," Alex says. Fred puts down the book and stares at him a second.

"Thanks, kid," he says. "That's very stand-up of you. Here, pull up a chair. You can help me not sell any of Brett's artwork." Alex drags a chair over. "So what's it like having a mother who's famous?" says Fred.

"She's not that famous," Alex says. Famous people belong a little bit to everybody, and his mother belongs just to him.

"Within a certain demographic," says Fred, "she's quite famous. Iconic, almost. And we happen to be surrounded by the members of that demographic. I bet everyone here has seen at least a full season of *Anomaly*. It's like required watching for a certain generation of geek."

"Have you?"

"I, for better or worse, have seen them all. Every episode. I can't tell you why I kept watching after they jumped the shark, but I did. Stockholm syndrome, I guess."

Alex thinks about getting out his notebook to write down some of the words Fred is using so he can look them up later, but he's worried he would look stupid. He's interested, though, to get to talk to someone who's seen all of *Anomaly*.

"So you know how it ends," he says.

"Mercifully," says Fred, "like an elderly patient expiring after prolonged illness."

"But what happens?" says Alex.

Fred puts his chair back on the ground and leans toward Alex. "You want me to spoil the ending?" Alex nods. Fred looks excited about this, and Alex realizes he's excited, too. He's always tried to avoid knowing endings, but there's something about skipping to the last page that feels empowering.

"How much do you know?" Fred asks.

"My mom's told me a lot of it."

"You know the big bad is the Leader."

"Uh-huh," says Alex. "And no one knows who he is. But he's from the future."

"The final season," Fred says, "they're throwing out clues left and right. Only they're not clues, because they all contradict each other. Every week after a new episode, the Internet goes nuts. 'It's Frazer!' 'No, it's Campbell!' It comes down to the last episode, and all the Leader's evil plans have paid off. He's finally broken into Anomaly Base, which had always been protected by some kind of time bubble, and it's chaos. There are Vikings and CGI dinosaurs running around. And he corners Frazer and Campbell. And he takes off his mask."

Fred mimes the action of removing the mask, drawing his hand up from his chin and over his face. Alex is rapt. All the episodes his mother's recounted to him, years of bedtime stories, and she's never told him, never revealed the Leader's identity. Alex thought it didn't matter much, but now, about to find out, it matters more than anything.

They're both leaning forward in their chairs, their faces almost touching.

"Who is it?" Alex asks.

"It's their kid," says Fred, leaning back, deflated. "It's Frazer and Campbell's kid. Which doesn't make sense in eleven different ways. He says he came back from the future to split them up, because if they stay together he turns out evil. So if you're worried about turning out evil, stop being evil. Don't go back in time to terrorize your baby self and your parents so they get divorced and you turn out not evil."

Alex is disappointed and confused.

"Then what happens?"

"He zaps back to the future and takes all his Vikings and CGI dinosaurs with him. The show ends with Frazer and Campbell standing in the wrecked Anomaly Base with their jaws hanging open."

"That's it?"

"I told you it wasn't very good," says Fred. "They would have retconned it the next season. Given the track record at that point, they might have made it worse."

"What's *retconned*?" asks Alex.

"It's when a lazy writer goes back and changes something that's already happened," Fred says. "Like 'Oh, no, OuterMan's planet wasn't totally destroyed and everybody didn't die like we've been telling you for seven decades. There was actually a cruise ship full of people from his home planet who survived, and oh by the way they're all douchebags.' It's a cheap writer's trick."

"So it's fixing mistakes?" says Alex.

"It's worse than that. There's a guy who writes for National Comics who does it all the time. It's like his signature move. He's the one who took OuterMan and made him—" Fred stops abruptly. He's watching two men approach the table. One of them is older, not quite grandpa old, and heavy, like a funny cop in a movie. The other one is probably between Fred's age and Alex's mom's age. The heavy one is dressed like a grown-up, with a button-down shirt, the first one Alex has seen at the convention. The other has OuterMan's logo on his T-shirt, an *O* stretched vertically, with a circle orbiting it like a hula hoop. "Shut up, kid," Fred says quietly, although Alex hasn't been talking.

"This is the book I told you about," says the heavy man. He pages through an issue of *Lady Stardust,* but not the way other people have. He's actually reading it. Here and there he points to certain panels. "You ever read this?"

"I never have time to read anything out of universe these days," says the other man, who keeps looking around nervously. "National has me reading all the scripts to check for continuity errors."

"They're sticklers for continuity over there," says the heavy man. "I respect that. Although I've never totally understood it. Who cares if OuterMan's in space in one book and saving Capital City in another? Five fans." He holds up five sausage fingers. "Five fans care, and if they didn't have that to moan about, they'd moan about something else."

"We like to keep things tidy," says the other man.

"I get that. I do. But don't underestimate how much fun it can be to get messy." As he talks, the heavy man is making lots of physical contact with the other man, slapping him on the shoulder and arm. "Look at this," he says, pointing at the open comic book. "The pencils aren't great, but they pop, right? And the story, well, we'll see if they stick the landing, but as it is, there's some holes." Alex notices Fred wincing. "But when I read it," says the heavy man, "I'm not seeing holes. I'm seeing this thing that's crackling with ideas." He smacks the other man on the arm, hard. "What's the last thing National published that was crackling with ideas? Something you didn't write." The other man stammers. "You know what, don't answer that." He shuts the book and sets it back down on the pile.

"You work for Black Sheep?" he asks Fred.

"I'm the writer," says Fred.

"You are?" says the heavy man. "That's fantastic." When he says something is fantastic, you believe that it is fantastic, or at least unusually good. Alex likes him. "Here I was thinking you were the guy who could help me find the guy, when actually you're *the guy*. It's great stuff, really great. Do you know Geoff?"

"I don't think we've met," says the other man, whose name must be Geoff, holding out his hand. Fred, without getting up, shakes his hand, then awkwardly stands up and quickly sits down again.

"I figured all writers knew each other," the heavy man says. "Isn't there some bar where you all go to drink whiskey and mope?" Fred shakes his head feebly. The heavy man turns to Alex and sticks out his big, meaty hand, which Alex stands up to shake.

"Phil Weinrobe," he says. His handshake is firm and vigorous, and Alex feels as if the upswing might lift him right off the ground. "I'm the editor at Timely Comics. They pay me a ton of money to make writers do their jobs."

"Alex Torrey," Alex says. "I'm a writer, too."

"Is that right?" says Phil. "You'll have to pitch to me someday."

"I'd like that," Alex says, although he has no idea what pitching has to do with being a writer.

"This your kid?" Phil asks Fred.

"No," says Fred. "He's a fan."

"Your parents let you read this stuff?" says Phil, surprised.

"I get to read whatever I want," says Alex, deciding that from here on out, this will be true. Phil turns away from him, and Alex knows his role in the conversation, the little cameo adults leave for kids in the beginning of an encounter, is over.

"I used to work for Black Sheep," says Phil, "back in the day. A lowly assistant editor. Back then we specialized in teen romance comics and adaptations of television shows. You ever read the comic book version of *ALF*?" Geoff and Fred shake their heads. "Neither did anybody else. Which is why I no longer work for Black Sheep. Honest to God, when I was twenty-five, I thought people would line up to read a comic about an alien puppet. Who's your editor over there?" he asks Fred.

"Russell Maddox," he says.

"He on your back?" asks Phil. He's talking to Fred, but he's looking at Geoff. "Riding you about continuity, market viability?"

"I've only talked to him twice," says Fred.

"See that?" Phil says. "The lone genius. Free of editorial interference. You know the difference between an editor and a writer?" Phil asks no one in particular.

"Pay grade," says Geoff.

Phil laughs, a loud laugh that shakes his entire body. Alex wonders if there's some connection to Santa Claus that requires all heavy men to be jolly. "That's good, that's good." As quickly as he started laughing, he stops. "The difference is, an editor is not a writer. It's the first thing I tell my editors. *You are not a writer; let the writers write the books.*" Geoff and Fred both nod solemnly, because the way Phil has said this indicates that it is an important piece of wisdom. "You got the time?" he asks Fred.

Fred and Geoff both scramble for their phones, but Alex checks his watch. "Five oh five," he says.

Phil claps his hands together and then slaps Geoff on the shoulder again. "That's excellent. That's excellent news. Me and Geoff here were about to go get a beer." He looks around as if there might be a bar right here in Artist Alley. Geoff is looking around, too, but he seems to be checking to see if he's been spotted.

"There's got to be a bar around here somewhere," says Phil. He turns to Fred and gives him a smile that makes Alex think of Willy Wonka. "You want to come for a beer with us?" he asks.

"Yeah," says Fred excitedly.

"Do you have somebody to watch your table for you?"

Fred looks around frantically. "My artist was supposed to be here an hour ago." He says "my artist" the way you'd say "my puppy."

"Artists," says Phil, and all three of them chuckle. "Some other time, then."

"No, wait," says Fred. He kneels down to get at eye level with Alex. "Kid," he says, "can you watch the table for an hour? I'll give you twenty bucks."

"Sure," he says. Fred takes his wallet out, and as he hands Alex the twenty, he leans in even closer.

"If Brett comes back," he says quietly, "tell him I went for a walk. By myself. To clear my head."

"Okay," says Alex. He won't actually lie to Brett, but maybe he won't say anything. Technically Fred is going for a walk; it's just that he's walking to somewhere and not by himself. Alex can leave all of that out.

As the three of them leave, Phil puts his arm around Fred's shoulders the same way he kept doing to Geoff.

"Kid must be some fan," Alex hears him say.

Once they're out of sight, Alex picks up the first issue of *Lady Stardust* and tries to read it. But his mind is on the *Anomaly* ending. It's not a good ending at all. It turns out it's better not to know who's behind the mask. Until you know, everything is possible. Once a story ends one way, all the other ways it could end disappear. Once it's one person behind the mask, it isn't everybody else.

After a few minutes, Brett comes by, and seems surprised to see him.

"Hey, Alex," he says. "Where's Fred?"

"He went for a walk," says Alex, without adding any other details.

"Huh," says Brett. "He left you in charge?"

"He gave me twenty bucks," says Alex.

"That's surprisingly generous for Fred," Brett says. He sits down next to Alex.

"You guys don't seem to like each other very much," says Alex.

"I like Fred fine."

"He's angry at you because you made him miss the Mad Brit."

Brett smiles. "I knew about that," he says. "I was just about to call him, in fact. I fixed it."

"How'd you fix it?" says Alex.

"I was over at the Black Sheep booth, talking with our editor, Russell. And he's going out for drinks with the Mad Brit tonight, and we're invited along." Brett looks very pleased with himself, and for a second Alex is excited, because it sounds like he's invited, too.

"Fred will be happy," says Alex.

Brett shrugs. "I wouldn't go that far," he says.

"Is he your best friend?" asks Alex. It's a concept that's a puzzle to him, one he's read about more than experienced. Even among the kids he knows in New York, there are very few best-friend pairings. Kids drift toward and away from each other. Alex has friends who are good for swing sets and friends who are good for museum trips. He has going-to-movies friends and going-for-ice-cream friends. None of them is better than the others, and none of them are best.

"I guess so," says Brett.

"How does that happen?" asks Alex. "How did you get there?" It seems right to Alex that best-friendship would be a place you arrive at, after some time.

Brett shrugs. "He was the only person I could talk to about comics," he says. "We kind of got stuck together."

"But now you could talk to anybody about comics," says Alex. "All these people."

"I'd have to meet them," Brett says. "Find out all kinds of stuff about them. Everything we agree on or disagree on. Things about them that bug me. With Fred, I already know all that, so it's easier."

Alex thinks it's exactly the opposite: meeting people is easy, staying friends with them is hard. You'd have to all stay in one place, you and your friends. It's so much simpler to make friends as you go along, then say goodbye to them when you leave. Of course, it's important he believes this now.

# Management

Once she finds him, Val hangs back, taking this opportunity to observe Alex in the wild. He becomes more adult when she's not there. His gestures are broader, more sure. He is taller, maybe, or stands up straighter. Part of it is mimicry: he's taken on some of Brett's mannerisms since Cleveland, most notably a habit of letting his hair fall over his eyes, only to sweep it back dramatically. He is learning to perform adulthood, albeit the adolescent variety of adulthood he's encountering at these conventions, which is eerily similar to the type on ready display in their neighborhood in Brooklyn, or in Tim's, for that matter. Val wonders what adulthood looks like in California and what tics and gestures Alex will pick up in his time there.

But it's also true that Alex is performing childishness for her sake, responding to a need, a signal she must be broadcasting. The past few days at her mother's, she's felt the same pull, the draw of an overacted helplessness as the natural response to her mother's constant message, spoken or unspoken, of *I'm here to help.*

Rather than interrupt, Val seeks out one of the rare places in the convention hall where there is enough cell reception to make a call, and enough distance from the spazzy chatter of the convention-goers. She finds a corner to stand in, surrounded by a miniature tribe of teenagers sitting cross-legged on the floor with their noses buried in comic books, unaware of one another or the thousands of people around them.

Louis picks up on the second ring, consistently. Behind his voice, New York sounds burble in through the open windows of Tim's apartment.

Brooklyn has a pulse and music in deep summer that almost justifies the humidity and the smell. Hearing it, she wants to pick Alex up and run east again. She wants them to spend their summer picnicking in McCarren Park, or on the steps of the public library, instead of trudging inexorably west. It's a momentary want. A pointless thing, so she puts it away.

"How did it go at the place?" Louis asks.

"It was awful," she says. "It was honestly terrible."

"He shouldn't have asked you to do that," says Louis, a rare instance of him taking sides against Tim in anything. "I can't imagine how hard that was for you."

"There are worse things," she says. One of the teenagers grouped around her feet snorts, probably at something he's reading. "How is he?" she asks Louis, expecting his trademark sigh. Instead there's a pause.

"I'm not sure," Louis says, which must be incorrect; Louis knows Tim's moods better than he knows his own. The oppressed must always study the oppressor, he once told her. "Since yesterday," he says, "he's been very . . . positive."

"You make that sound like a bad thing."

"*Unreasonably* positive," Louis says. "You should talk to him."

"Put him on."

She's seen this once before, two years before she found Louis. Tim had become convinced he'd woken up on a particular morning with all his broken parts glued back together. He'd called up Val to tell her about it. He had thought up a new series for her to star in and walked her through three seasons' worth of storylines and plot beats over the phone. They discussed networks that might be interested in the pilot, and the logistics of shooting in New York. Because it was something she wanted so badly for him, for both of them, she'd let herself believe all of it. That afternoon, she got a call from an MTA security guard to come pick Tim up from Fourteenth Street. He'd made it into Manhattan on his own, no mean feat from Greenpoint, but couldn't go any further. The MTA guard had found him curled up under a pay phone, shaking uncontrollably. After that, it was a week before Val could get him out of bed, or even pull back the curtains to let in the light.

"Val!" he calls as he takes the phone from Louis. The word jumps out of him before the phone reaches his lips, causing it to zoom at Val from half-way across the country. "I was thinking of you this morning. I had the weirdest feeling you were running some errand for me. Like I'd asked you to go get me bagels or fastnachts from down the block. Then Lawrence reminded me you were in Chicago, which I knew, and isn't that funny? Thinking you were running an errand for me in Chicago? Pick me up some deep-dish pizzas. Or—Leonard, what do they have in Chicago? . . . No, but what are they famous for? . . . Oh, never mind. Val, how are you?"

All of it spills out of him, manic and breathless. Although she's worried about him, Val can't help feeling angry: she went to see the Woman at his insistence, and he doesn't even remember he asked.

"I'm fine," she says. "Things here are fine."

"I've been thinking about this thing in Los Angeles," he continues. "For the anniversary. Of the show." Tim always avoids speaking the name of the show, just as he never says his wife's name, or the Woman's. "It's a panel? So there'll be other people there. Maybe some of the writing staff? I haven't talked to any of them in ages. And you'll be there. I'd have you there. I think I could handle it. I think I could manage. I've asked Louis to get us plane tickets. I'd rather not fly, naturally, but it's the only reasonable way. Manageable. *Manageable* is my watchword, Val. I am expanding my conception of what I can manage. It's impressive, I think."

Val knows there's no way she can deal with Tim along with everything else in Los Angeles. Shouldn't being in the same room with Andrew, or with the Woman, win her a reprieve from further troubles? Shouldn't she be allowed to lose everything and have that be the end of it? She doesn't want to take this moment away from Tim, this moment in which he thinks he's unstoppable. But she has to stop him.

"There will be *fans*, Tim," she says, pronouncing the word as close to *fangs* as she can. "Hundreds, maybe two thousand *fans*. They'll want handshakes and autographs. Pictures with their arms around you. They'll want a little piece of you, each of them. It's been difficult. Not tensing up when each one approaches me. Not screaming at them to back away. They're so devoted. To us. To *Anomaly.*" She lets the word hang for a second, cruelly. "But there are times all I can think about is how easily that devotion could turn on me. I'm handling it okay." She pauses enough that she could have added *and I'm not insane.* "But you need to think, Tim, about if *you* can handle it. About if you can manage."

It's a terrible thing to do, and she wishes she had the time or the energy to handle this some other way. But she can't have the possibility hanging over her. She can't deal with one more thing. Tim is silent on the other end of the line, except for the smacking sound his tongue makes when it's gone dry. She can visualize the way he must be opening and closing his mouth as if tasting something unpleasant, metallic.

"You might be right," he says finally, quietly. "Anyway, the airports are a nightmare in the summer. Packs of harried parents, brats in tow. Lyndon," he says, holding the phone away from his mouth, "what about a shadow group that controls all the world's airports? Governs them like a city. Yes, I know the difference between a story and a setting. Val," he says into the phone, "I have to go. The help is getting uppity. I'll see you when you get back?"

"Of course," she says. He hangs up before she does and without saying goodbye, which is strange for Tim, who loves goodbyes.

# A Tom Waits Kind of Lame

Gail racks her brains to think of what she might have done to deserve this. She's willing to accept that this must be something she brought on herself. Something this bad could not simply happen. But only a major transgression against God or justice or karma could possibly warrant this level of punishment, and to the best of her recollection, Gail has never killed a nun or kicked a puppy or stolen a clown's wallet.

She's sitting next to Russell Maddox, the editor in chief of Black Sheep Comics, who gave her a proper start in comics, in a bar booth at a piano bar called the Zebra Lounge. It is a uniquely awful bar. Gail's never been to a piano bar before. When Russell proposed meeting up here, Gail figured it could go one of two ways. It could be cool in a Tom Waits kind of way, or lame in a Billy Joel kind of way. It turns out the Zebra Lounge is lame in a Tom Waits kind of way. Every surface is either mirrored, covered in high-lacquer red linoleum, or upholstered in faux zebra hide, giving the entire room a vertiginous array of stripes. The ghosts of old cigars still haunt. At the piano, a kid who probably studies music at UIC growls and grumbles his way through "All My Ex's Live in Texas," followed by a rendition of "Cabaret" that goes all in on male pathos. Tourists stuff twenties and requests into his tip jar, and Gail can only imagine what horrors are being added to the set list.

Worse than the bar is the company. Not Russell, of course; Russell is great. And the kid across from her, Brett, who works either for or with Russell, and his girlfriend, whose eye makeup makes her look like she's been cast as Sexy Zombie #3 but whom Gail recognizes as Ferret Lass from the convention, they both seem all right. Gail's barely been able to talk to them, though, because sitting dead in the middle of the booth, drinking his fifth glass of straight grain alcohol to preserve his purity of essence, and looking more like an unshaved hobo forced into a fancy outfit than the Dark Wizard of Comic Books, is the Magus himself, Alistair Sangster.

She shouldn't use the word *hobo,* probably. It could be considered offensive. *Derelict* is better. *Hobo* implies a bindle, and is particularly American. For all the appellations he's accumulated over his thirty-some-year career, Gail's always thought his early nickname from the comics press suited Sangster best. She's always thought of him as the Mad Brit.

"We're coming to the end of comics," he says, in answer to a question nobody asked. "About time. It's all a fucking chrysalis anyway. Comics are the telephone booths of culture. A mild-mannered reporter steps in and flies out a god." He flutters his hands upward, then slams them down on the table. Ferret Lass jumps. "But once the culture soars off, the booth's no good anymore. Who needs a telephone when you've got telepathy?" He leans back, and Gail is pretty sure he's grinning somewhere inside that beard, immensely pleased at his little wordplay.

"I'll be out of a job," says Russell, who's being ingratiating. Russell's got a dog in this fight, of course. If he could get Sangster to publish something with Black Sheep, it'd be a license to print money. And an easy day's work for Russell, since Sangster reputedly does not allow his scripts to be edited. The only reason Russell would be caught dead in a place like this would be on Sangster's demand.

"We'll all be out of jobs," says Sangster, too loud, too enthusiastic. "We're better off. Whoever said jobs'd be the be-all end-all anyway? Whoever made adulthood a goal? It's bullshit thinking the pinnacle of human achievement is steady employment."

Gail swizzles her gin and tonic, examining the ice cubes. The one small mercy in all this is that when Russell introduced them, Sangster didn't recognize her name. He grunted politely and presented her with a dead-fish handshake.

When she was younger, Gail mostly liked the Mad Brit's work. Some of it was a little too deconstructionist, sure. And his whole late-period Kabbalistic phase had a bit more tantric sex–meets–mystic Celtic woodland creatures than she had the stomach for. But the writing was solid throughout, and excellent at times. His characters had a psychological depth to them that was lacking in ninety percent of comics.

But also there was the rape. Before she'd gotten started in comics, Gail ran a fan site called BrainsOverBreasts.com that took pot shots at the comics industry's retrograde gender politics. When Sangster announced his retirement for about the third time, and every other site fell over themselves to crown him the Greatest Writer in the History of Comics, Gail responded with a thorough rereading of all of Sangster's work, from his early days on *The Savior* at National Comics through his switch to Timely for his *R-Squad* run, and everything in between. What she found was that in every comic book written by Alistair Sangster that ran for more than a hundred pages, there was a rape scene, or at the very least a scene of attempted rape or sexual assault. Every single one. She cataloged dozens and dozens of rapes in the body of Sangster's work. She scanned and posted panels and pages. In the end, she made very little comment, except to say, "Apparently, this is the best our industry has to offer."

Her site had a small following before, but the article on Sangster blew up, beyond the little knot of readers who followed both superhero comics and feminist blogs. The piece on the Mad Brit had run on NerdFeast.com, PanelAddict.com, and a number of other major comics sites. Which was about when the rape threats started. An overwhelming number of them—comments, e-mails, posts on social media. She realized that it was one thing to say something controversial in her little corner of the Internet to a small group of people whom, although she hadn't met most of them in person, she'd come to think of as friends. From the minute the higher-trafficked sites put her words out there, she was attacked with such detailed threats of sexual violence that she began to fear for her safety. Ed and Geoff and a couple of other writers she'd become friends with in her time as a blogger reached out to her in solidarity and explained that they, too, had gotten death threats, but they couldn't understand how this was different.

The obvious option would have been to take down the piece and retreat, but Gail decided to go public with the threats she'd received. She cataloged them just as she had the rapes in Sangster's books. The article ran on almost every site that talked about comics; it got discussed on a couple of morning news shows and NPR. Other women spoke up about harassment at conventions and online. Flummoxed publishers had to field questions about whether or not the comics themselves contributed to this culture of sexual violence. They were asked where the women writers were, or the women artists or editors. And they had no one to point to.

Gail was inundated with interview requests, and the conversations evolved from a critique of what had gone before into a discussion of what should come next. Offhandedly, Gail rattled off possible storylines for dozens of female superheroes, detailing how they would appeal to female readers while not alienating the base—the impossible dream of the marketing departments of every major publisher. A few of her ideas, tweaked and revamped so they were recognizable only to her as her own, made it into the plots of books at National and Timely. But Russell Maddox at Black Sheep was the first one to offer her a job, writing the *Anomaly* miniseries. "Look," he said when he called her up, "none of these publishers realize you've given them a problem and a solution all at once." The threats continued, although they tapered off after she managed, with Russell's backing, to press charges against a couple of her more virulent fans. She got a few calls for fill-ins at National, and when she got offered a regular gig writing *The Speck & Iota*, Russell told her to follow the money. He still threw her work every now and then, licensed stuff she could churn out in a week. Adam Anti spin-offs and adult cartoon tie-ins.

The article itself hadn't led to anyone revoking Sangster's status as Greatest Writer in Comics, nor did it significantly hurt sales of any of Sangster's work, although she noticed that his comeback phase was pleasantly rape-free. It's possible that rather than writing articles in his own defense, Sangster sacrificed a goat or some other piece of livestock to assure that Gail would never rise above the rank of B-list comic book writer. It'd explain her current limbo status at National, among other things. He could have done it from his magician's lair in White Castle or wherever you move after you've made as much money as one person could ever make in comics and then retire to be a full-time professional magus and cultivate the largest beard in any known artistic medium. Look at that thing; you could house a family of sparrows in there. "So you'd stop writing," she says, "in this amazing age to come?"

"I write," Sangster continues, "to bring about that age. To invoke it. Once it's here, the world won't need visionary imaginations." He turns to Ferret Lass. "We'll all be writers," he tells her. "We'll each be epic dreamers of dreams."

"Sounds nice," she says, grinding ice with her molars.

"It won't be a bit nice!" he shouts. "It'll be terrible. Nothing will be stable, nothing will be static. There'll be no more staying in to watch telly or nip down to the pub on a Saturday night. There'll be dragons and ifrits and all sort of mad things about."

"Why would anyone want that?" says Gail.

"Because we'll need it," says Sangster, "to become the heroes we ought to be." He sets his drink down and rises on unsteady legs. "I'm off to the loo," he announces.

"His superpower seems to be staring at my tits," Ferret Lass says to Brett once he's out of earshot. Gail turns on Russell, scowling.

"You set me up," she says.

"I did no such thing," he says, grinning to indicate she's completely correct.

"For kicks," she says. "You set me up for your own sick amusement."

"I thought maybe there'd be spirited discussion," Russell says earnestly. She does feel bad for him a little. Russell is one of those people no one in the industry has anything bad to say about, which he claims is because he's everyone's token black friend. But it's the fact that he's a stand-up guy who's fun to be around.

"Some of what he said was interesting," says Brett, who, again, is probably a nice kid and is trying to be charitable. "About stories being transmitted instead of created? I feel like that sometimes."

"He just wants you to think he's divinely inspired," says Gail.

"He made it sound like a lightning bolt," says Brett. "But it's not like that. It's like tuning an old radio."

Finally, someone at this table other than her has said something intelligent. Because it's like that for her, too, like she's finding her ideas coming though faintly in a vast spectrum of noise. The hard work is in twiddling the knobs exactly right, and translating the little bursts that rise out of the static. For the first time since she sat down, it feels like a conversation is about to start, but before it can get going, a hatchet-faced boy stumbles over to their table, obviously drunk.

"Where is he?" he asks Brett. "Did I miss him already?" He looks around frantically. By his black-suit-with-black-shirt attire, Gail pegs him as an Alistair Sangster fan.

"He's off to the *loo*," says Gail, emphasizing the last word, crooning it.

"But he's coming back," Brett says.

"Loo, loo, skip to my loo," she sings.

"Hey, Fred," says Russell, "you're late. You want a drink?"

"A whiskey," says Fred, sounding as if he's talking to a waiter. "Please," he adds. Russell points around the table. Gail signals him for another; Brett and Ferret Lass take a pass.

"Where've you been?" Brett asks his drunken friend.

"I was having drinks, Mother," Fred says, grinning acidly as he squeezes in next to Ferret Lass.

"I've returned," announces Sangster, standing in front of the table. He takes a head count and after a second realizes the number's right but the parts are wrong. "Who's this?" he asks the rest of the group.

"Your evil beardless twin," mutters Gail.

"Fred Marin, Mr. Sangster," says Fred, standing up and putting out his hand. Sangster looks at it like it might be covered in herpes. "You've been a huge influence on my work."

"Another writer, eh?" he says, scooting past Gail to resume his place at the center of the table. "Writers should be like blue jays: we should each have a patch of territory to ourselves, and we should squawk loud if another writer comes close."

Gail is about to caw in his ear when Russell returns with the drinks.

"You know," says Russell, who must realize he's gotten all the fireworks he's going to out of this, "we'd love to have you do some work at Black Sheep."

"Definitely a possibility," says Sangster. "I wouldn't go back to Timely if Phil Weinrobe sucked my cock while handing me the Hope Diamond."

Gail winces.

"He seems like a nice guy," says Fred.

"He's a figment of your imagination," Sangster informs the young man. "Timely hired him because he's too good to be true. And he's not true. He's just a thing in the dream of a corporation."

"Bad blood?" asks Russell.

"No blood at all. No soul," says Sangster. "I would be thrilled to work with you, Russell. I grew up with mostly blacks," he says proudly. Gail thinks maybe in England that kind of thing gets said all the time. But still, gross. "Not to claim to be part of the struggle," he adds. "The thing is, most of my time now is spent on my magic. Harsh mistress, the dark arts."

"Yeah, magic's a bitch," says Gail.

"I should say, Miss Pope, that I've never actually read your work," Sangster says, turning to Gail for the first time. All of his other responses have been directed to the ether, or posterity or something. Now he glares at her and sips his drink, deftly piloting it to his mouth through the nebula of his beard. "Certainly not with the censorious eye you've taken to mine."

This, she thinks, is where it's going to happen. Alistair Sangster is going to turn her into a newt.

"I'd always wondered if you'd read Gail's article on your work," says Russell, trying to engage the subject in a calm, salon fashion, a marketplace of ideas where Sangster and Gail are both merchants.

"I never bothered," says Sangster. "The French have a saying: The spit of the toad does not touch the white dove."

Gail realizes she was off by one: he's turned her into a toad.

"But I've noticed," says Gail, "that since you came out of retirement, your work's been a lot less rapey. Well done on that, by the way."

"My work was never 'rapey,'" says Sangster, affecting a nasal American accent. "It dealt with transgressive forms of sexuality, which tends to make puritans like yourself uncomfortable. But only through confronting our puritanisms can we be liberated from them."

"So in *R-Squad*, when the Perilous Pentad held down Medea and took turns fucking her bloody," says Gail, straining to keep her voice even, "that was intended to be liberating? Because it seemed to me, at the time, more like wish fulfillment from the kind of kid who didn't see tits that weren't on a page from the time he was weaned till he became the anointed Greatest Writer in Comics."

Gail steels herself for a smiting. She expects Sangster to rise up and expand, his sport jacket billowing out with arcane energies as he strikes her down with a lightning bolt. But he simply looks at Russell calmly and says, "I think, in the interest of civility, that one of us should leave."

"Yeah," says Gail, "I should probably get out of here before someone drops a house on you."

Russell puts a hand on her shoulder before she can get up.

"It's been good to see you, Alistair," he says. "Have a safe trip back."

There is a quiet moment at the table, while the piano plays a maudlin rendition of Billy Joel's "Captain Jack." And as Brett, Fred, and Ferret Lass get up to let Sangster out of their booth, huffing as he goes, Gail thinks that if her man-kissin' days weren't well behind her, she would plant one on Russell right then and there.

# *Anomaly* Finale

His mother is being strange. It's because he didn't talk to her last night, and now it's like she isn't talking to him because she doesn't want him not to talk to her. Alex can't think of anything to say, so neither of them talks. This morning when they checked out of their hotel room, they put all of their stuff into the back of Babu's truck. They're going back to her house for the night and taking the train to L.A. in the morning.

The nice thing about riding in the truck is that he gets to sit in the front seat, but it makes it more uncomfortable that they're not talking. Alex turns on the radio and fiddles with the dial. There's a song he likes on one of the stations. People were playing it in the park back in New York. But he turns it to NPR, because he knows she likes that. The sun is setting as they leave Chicago, the sky full of reds and oranges.

They've been driving for half an hour when Alex reaches forward, straining against the seatbelt, and clicks the radio off.

"Mom," he says, "can you tell me a story?"

She looks over at him and smiles, but it's a sad smile. "You all done being upset with me, Rabbit?"

He's not sure he is. There's still something angry inside him and it hasn't gone away. "Yeah," he says, looking at his shoes.

"How about I tell you one once we get to Babu's?" she says. "Then we can catch up on some cuddles."

"Could you tell me one now?" he says.

"It's tough to story-tell and drive, Rabbit."

It's beginning to get dark, and he thinks maybe she's right. But he decides this is important enough.

"Tell me how it ends," he says.

"I've never told you that one, have I?" She sighs and adjusts herself in her seat. There is always this moment, where she gathers the story, pulls it into herself. But now it's like she is going there, to the place where the story is, and where Alex is waiting for her.

"The last episode," she says, eyes focused on the road, both hands on the wheel, "wasn't planned to be the last episode. There was supposed to be another year. But it was as good a place as any to end it.

"Anomaly is in ruins. The Leader has finally attacked, and it is devastating. He wipes agents out of existence, back to the moment they were born. He zaps dinosaurs into the offices and sets them loose—not huge ones, but the ones that are people-sized and vicious."

"Velociraptor," Alex says.

She nods. "Campbell and Frazer try to fight him, but it doesn't work. He puts Frazer in the hospital with broken ribs, and he steals her baby.

"Campbell goes crazy. He tracks down an agent who's been working for the Leader in secret since season one and tortures him. When he finds out what he wants, Campbell kills him.

"Back at the hospital, the Leader shows up in Frazer's room, with the baby. He gives the baby back to Frazer, saying he only wanted to see him, saying he misses him so much. Then he takes off his mask. You can't see it, but Frazer sees who he is, who he's been the whole time.

"Campbell searches out the Leader's hideout, and the Leader is there waiting for him. The Leader tells him it's already too late: Frazer and the baby are both dead. Campbell shoots him, again and again, and the Leader's mask flies off. Underneath, it's Campbell.

"As he's dying, the Leader tells Campbell it's not too late. The Leader's suit and mask are laced with time-travel technology like Anomaly has never seen. Campbell can take them, go back, and stop all this from happening. The Leader dies, and Campbell picks up the mask.

"In the hospital parking lot, Frazer puts the baby into the car seat. She doesn't know what else to do. She is so scared. Being around Campbell at all would put her baby in danger. He'll be safer if they run. The only way he'll ever be safe is if they run away."

"That's a good ending," says Alex. He knew when he asked that her ending would be different from the real one. The one that was on television, anyway. You couldn't say that one made-up story was more real than another. But driving away is always a good ending, because you can go anywhere. It's way better than people standing somewhere. More than that, it's a good ending because he knows she made it for him, to tell him things she can't tell him any other way. He thinks back on all the other stories she's told him and wonders how many are real and how many she made up for him. It's like the masks the superheroes wear that become more important than the faces under them: the story hides something so it can reveal the thing more clearly.

As the light fails and stars pinprick through the canvas of the sky, Alex thinks about the boy and the robot, and what his story is trying to reveal to him, and what it's trying to hide.

# Secret Origin of Valerie Torrey

*Val checks the time on her phone and again on the clock in the kitchen, hoping maybe they're different. There's no rush, yet. At the little table, Alex eats a heap of Annie's mac and cheese, watching her the whole time.*

*"What time's the play?" he asks.*

*"Not for another hour and a half," she says. She tries to sound casual.*

*"If you need to go, I can be by myself till Debra gets here," says Alex. Lately he's been more strident about his independence. She tries to pinpoint when it started, but it seems like it's been since she took this role. The prospect of a babysitter every night for a month convinced him that supervision is no longer necessary. But there are still nights he wakes up, upset about a dream or just lonely. She can't stomach the thought that he might wake up and find no one there.*

*"It's all right, Rabbit," she says. "She should be here any minute."*

*"Are you all warmed up?" he asks. A baseboard heater wheezes to life. The kitchen is the only room that's stayed warm this winter. They've abandoned the living room entirely. Alex has put all of his Arctic-themed toys in there: a stuffed woolly mammoth on the couch, a tribe of plastic Inuits stalking the cold hardwood floor.*

*"Not yet," she says, checking the clock again. "You want to help?"*

*Alex stands up and answers by taking the neutral stance and pursing his lips. His feet hip distance apart, his hands limp at his sides. Val mirrors him, trying not to grin. The minutes running down toward equity call are forgotten.*

*"I know New York," she says, over-enunciating each sound.*

*"I know New York," he says.*

*"I* need *New York,"* she says.

*"I* need *New York,"* he says.

*"I know I need unique New York,"* she says.

*"I know I need unique You Nork,"* he says and busts out giggling. With some effort, he brings himself under control and resumes his proper stance. Val begins to hum, a light buzzing that shakes her teeth. She moves the sound around in her mouth, vibrating molars and incisors. Then the mirror trick, where they move in synchronicity with each other, neither of them leading the other. The decision to open their mouths, to expand the hum into a low "maaaah" that resonates through the hard palate, is made together; one set of lips pulls almost imperceptibly apart, and the other follows and cracks a little further until they are both making gaping lion yawns, jaws stretching muscles in the neck and along the temples. The sound slowly morphs into "meeeee," teeth nearly together, the breath forced through the nose.

Before they can move into the chest and stomach, the buzzer goes off and Alex shoots away to ring Debra in. He likes his usual sitter fine, as much as a kid can like someone whose primary role in his life is putting him to bed. But he loves Debra. She lived next door to the first apartment Val had gotten for them when they came to New York six years ago. She was finishing a law degree at NYU and would come over to watch Alex when Val was teaching acting classes. Sometimes she'd read him long passages out of whatever textbook she was studying, and for a few months when he was five, Alex would spout off in a weird form of legalese, informing Val that his decision not to clean his room was based on established precedent, or that, because it was based on a magical story, the Alice statue in Central Park was ipso fatso magical.

*"I'm so sorry,"* says Debra as she takes her boots off in the hall. *"I should admit to myself that it's impossible to get out of work on time on a Friday night."* There are snowflakes perfectly arranged on her black coat that twinkle like stars as they melt. When they were neighbors, Val had thought of Debra as a bit of a little sister. She'd been in a constantly harried state,

*usually in pajamas by the time she came over to watch Alex. But this woman she sees now is so poised and composed, Val feels self-conscious about the salty footprints on the hallway floor, and the dishes in the sink, and the fact that she's about to leave the house wearing leggings. By some measure of maturity, Val has been surpassed.*

*"It's fine," says Val. "You're saving my ass."*

*"I told my car service to wait for you," she says, hanging up her coat. "He can get you into Manhattan in like fifteen minutes."*

*"You don't have to do that," says Val.*

*"Please," Debra says, "it's like the only thing I can expense. I call the service when I go out for coffee now. I'm never taking the subway again."*

*"Why don't you like the subway?" asks Alex. He's been leaning against the wall, watching Debra go through the process of arriving.*

*"I'm kidding, kiddo," she says.*

*"Oh," says Alex.*

*"He's eaten," says Val. "And if you want to watch a movie, it's fine, but the living room is freezing. There are blankets."*

*"We'll be fine," says Debra. "You should get going."*

*"You need to pick a night to come see it," says Val. "I'll get comps for you and your boyfriend."*

*"I think it might be a little over his head," says Debra.*

*"It's a little over* my *head," says Val, pulling on her heavy coat. "Rabbit, come here." Alex runs to her and presses his face against her cheek.*

*"Maaaaaahh," he says, and it rings through her whole skull.*

*"You be good?" she says.*

*"He's always good," says Debra, and Val smiles because it's true enough. She grabs a knit hat from off the hook on the wall, the one with mittens tucked into it, and, trying not to look as if she's rushing, rushes down the hallway, down the stairs to the sleek black car collecting snow out front. She climbs into the backseat.*

*"Miss Torrey," says the driver, with an accent that sounds like a tropical beach and feels out of place in the snow and the dying January light.*

"Hi," she says. "I'm going to West Forty-third."

"Okay, Miss Torrey," he says. *The car is warm, and Val begins to take off all of the accessories she just put on.*

"Oh, sir?" she says.

"Jacob," he says.

"Jacob," she repeats. "I should warn you, so it doesn't weird you out. I hum."

"Like a little song?" he asks.

"More like a beehive," she says. "It's a warm-up exercise. I'll probably hum and moan the whole drive."

*She watches him smile in the rearview.* "I've driven in this city ten years," he says. "Humming and moaning's no big deal." *He pulls the car into traffic, and Val leans back into the leather seats, tilts her head back, and begins to buzz, lips together, teeth apart.*

*When they arrive at the theater, Jacob refuses a tip, insisting it's included in the billing. Val can remember when her life was like this, the few years in L.A. when she floated in a moneyless world. All cash transactions were handled elsewhere; cars and drinks and food appeared and were consumed and everyone was properly compensated as if by magic. It always struck her as funny how having money made money obsolete.*

*She checks her phone one last time as she opens the stage door. Forty-five minutes until curtain, fifteen until call. She'd hoped for more time, but the part requires minimal makeup, and anyway, she's here and there's no point regretting minutes that are already gone. The stage manager, Miller, greets her with a gruff* "Valuables?" *before her coat's even off. She checks her pockets and hands over her keys, phone, and purse. He nods and huffs at her. An hour after the curtain's closed, he'll be the friendliest drunk in the city, but before the show Miller exists in a state of constant inconvenience.*

"Should I still sign in?" she asks.

"I'll sign you in," he says, *making it sound like a great imposition.*

"I'm going to have a lie-down," *Val calls after him.* "Ten minutes, maybe?"

"We're about to test the rotation," he says. "Try not to get seasick."

Val throws the rest of her things in the dressing room she shares with the Angel. It's too big for the two of them, but they're the only women in the cast. The Angel plays a half-dozen roles throughout the night, made up and costumed differently enough each time to be barely recognizable. It gives the play a feeling of claustrophobia and coincidence, which is especially important because they're only doing the first half, and many of the storylines don't pull together until the second. Val's got it easy playing Harper. There's not an overwhelming amount of stage time, and she's in house clothes throughout. Three makeup girls are busying themselves with the Angel already, attaching a scraggly gray beard and a fake nose that could be considered anti-Semitic. The fishy odor of spirit gum hangs in the dressing room.

"Cutting it close," says the Angel. It's not a reprimand, exactly.

"My babysitter was running late," says Val. "I'm going to go have a lie-down. Finish arriving."

"See you in a bit," says the Angel, straining her chin upward so the makeup girls can attach strands to its underside.

The stage has already begun to rotate slowly like a drugged carousel. She sits on the floor in the section of the set that will be her apartment. It has a table with two chairs and the fridge that Mr. Lies will step out of. Mr. Lies is also playing Belize in this staging, but that only means throwing a nurse coat on over his slick travel-agent suit and adopting an accent similar to Jacob the driver's. Val lies down, easing her head back onto the plywood. "You have time to run one-seven?" she asks Prior, who's lying on the floor nearby.

"You mean because you flubbed it last night?"

"Don't be an asshole," she says.

"I'm arriving," says Prior, drawing out the word, "but I'll be happy to help with your shortcomings once I get here." Prior got an absolutely glowing review in the Voice and since then has been pretending to be insufferable. He can be very convincing at it.

By thirty out, the makeup girls are done with the Angel and can fix up Val. She's always relieved that they have to dull her down. One day she'll *come in already looking like a Valium-addicted shut-in housewife, and the makeup girls will look at her and shake their pretty young heads. But tonight, they paint bags under her eyes and adjust her costume to give the impression it's been slept in.*

*Miller pokes his head in the door. "Twenty minutes, ladies," he says.*

*"Thank you, twenty," says Val.*

*"So who's coming out with me after?" says Louis, the baby of the cast, plopping into their couch. The men have their own dressing room, but they've decided it's too crowded, so they spend their pre-show in the women's.*

*"How can you even think of going out after?" asks Mr. Lies. "I'm exhausted already. I'm still working through exhausted from three days ago. I'll never catch up."*

*"That's because you're ancient," says Louis. "The theater's no place for relics."*

*"Dear, did you want to go through one-seven?" Prior asks Val. He seats himself on Louis's feet.*

*"What are you doing in my* hallucination?" *says Roy Cohn, who knows everyone's lines by heart. Last night Val said, "What are you doing in my dream?" It botched Prior's next line, which should have been "It's not your hallucination, it's my dream." Prior made a quick recovery, but for the rest of the scene they both sounded wary each time they used the words* hallucination *and* dream, *not sure which was which.*

*"I'm fine," says Val.*

*"You were great in three-three last night," says Mr. Lies.*

*"She always hits her stride in the third act," says Prior.*

*"You know Lookingglass in Chicago's going to do the whole thing this summer?" says Louis. He's paging through his script.*

*"Fifteen minutes," says Miller from the door.*

*"Thank you, fifteen," they all chant.*

*"Christ, how long is that?" says Mr. Lies.*

*"Six and a half hours," says Roy Cohn. "Seven with the intermission."*

*"Speaking of the whole thing—" says the Angel.*

"Don't start," says Val.

"Has someone not signed on for 'Stroika?" says Prior, making a face of mock horror.

"Someone has not," says the Angel.

"Oh, now, Valerie," says Prior, "you can't leave us. Don't you know Grant has a vision?" He says this word so its second syllable thumps down onto the floor like a dead body, exactly the way Grant, their director, says it. "How could you abandon Grant's vision?"

"I'm not sure I'll be up for leaving Alex alone for another run," says Val.

"Bring him to the shows," says Prior. "We're all excellent role models for a kid."

"They run too late," says Val. "He's in bed."

"He could sleep on the couch in our dressing room," says Mr. Lies.

"Er," says Prior, "maybe not on that couch."

"You're disgusting," says Roy Cohn.

"You're jealous," says Prior.

"Ten minutes," says Miller.

"Thank you, ten," they chorus.

"Anyway, you can't leave it half-finished," says Prior. "Imagine your Harper forever in the freezer at the end of three-three."

"Or some other actress getting her grubby fingerprints all over your Harper," says Mr. Lies.

"And you'd miss us," says Louis.

"Terribly," says Prior.

"I've got the contract," says Val. It's been on the kitchen counter all week. "I just haven't signed."

"We'll forge her signature while she's on stage," says the Angel.

"We'll kidnap her and lock her in the theater forever," says Prior.

"'Stroika lasts about forever," says Roy Cohn.

"Whatever," says Prior. "I'll play Harper, too. I'll do the whole play on my own, all seven hours."

"Calm it down, boys," says Mr. Lies.

"Five minutes," says Miller.

"Thank you, five," they say. The five-minute call serves as the death knell for horseplay. Louis and Prior lean over each of Val's shoulders and check themselves in her mirror. Mr. Lies stands and smooths out the creases that have formed in his pants.

In the low thrum of these last minutes of prep, Val lets her mind scatter and diffuse. When she thinks of Harper, she thinks of an abscess, a hole slowly growing at the center of a self, with bits of the person toppling in over its edge.

"Remember," says Roy Cohn, "it's a hallucination, not a dream."

"Places," says Miller. They file out, careful not to touch one another. Each is storing up a charge all his or her own, and any contact now will cause it to disperse. From outside the door of the dressing room, they can already hear the crowd murmuring. They are here to be entertained, or edified, or even changed. And Val is here for something, too: she's here to stay the same somehow, to keep a line of communication open between who she is now and some other version of herself.

When it's over, they all seem lost. The performance is a thing they've expended that will now need to regenerate.

"Run time was three and ten," Miller tells them, reading it off his watch.

"Slack," says Roy Cohn.

"Act two," says Miller, shaking his head. When it goes slack, it's always in act two. "Call tomorrow's at seven thirty, same as it ever was." He hands back wallets, phones, and keys. Val checks her phone immediately: no calls, no messages. Nothing has gone wrong, nothing has ever gone wrong. She exhausts herself some days inventing dangers and hazards so she can experience this relief that nothing has happened. She tucks her phone back into her purse.

"You have to come to the club with me," Louis is saying to the Angel. "Like that. I don't know why I haven't thought of it before. People will lose their shit."

"I'm afraid 'people,'" says the Angel, putting air quotes around the word, "will have to hold on to their shit for one more night."

"It'd be a thrill," says Prior. "Like the moment the clown shows up at the birthday party." He pats Louis on the shoulder. "Adult beverages in the men's for those who are so inclined." He grins acidly at the Angel. "You can wear your wings."

"Oh, Christ, no," says the Angel. She turns to Val. "You coming?"

"In a minute," says Val.

She heads for the women's dressing room to call Debra and check in. Through the open door she can see feet, legs.

Andrew sits in the chair in front of her mirror, elbows on his knees, holding a bouquet of flowers big enough to obscure his face.

"What the fuck—" says Val, and immediately he is standing, holding the flowers out like an offering or shield. He smiles the lopsided grin he uses for his real smile.

"The stage manager let me back here," he says. He shrugs. "He was a fan, apparently."

"He's never mentioned it," says Val. She stands in the doorway, not wanting to enter the room.

"These are for you," says Andrew, thrusting the flowers at her.

"I don't want them," she says.

He sets them down on the dressing room table. "I'll leave them."

"You should take them," says Val, "and go."

"You were great," says Andrew. It's driving her crazy that he can maintain eye contact when she's trying to stare daggers at him. Her face is a stone and he's looking right at it. "I'd never seen it," he goes on. "Even when they did it on HBO with Pacino and everything. I should have, I know." It's such a weird thing to apologize for, given all the apologies he owes her. "I was aware of it, of course. But it's a little over my head."

"What are you doing here?" she asks, to stop him from babbling.

"We were doing some shooting, for the show," he says. "Ted comes to New York to maybe do some theater. It's just the one episode."

"I mean what are you doing here?"

*His smile drops. The scene he'd hoped they'd do together is over. An-*
*other begins.*

*"I thought we should talk," he says.*

*"I said everything I need to say to you six years ago," says Val. It sounds*
*like a line from a hack play, and she oversells it.*

*"You didn't say anything six years ago," says Andrew. "You disappeared."*

*"Exactly."*

*"That's what this is about," he says. What's coming next is obvious, it's*
*been obvious for so long she only wonders how they've avoided this mo-*
*ment until right now. But she tries to put it off a little longer.*

*"You can't see him," she says.*

*"You don't get to say that." He's not getting angry, because he's pre-*
*pared. She's been furious from the moment she walked in, because she was*
*ambushed.*

*"You don't get to show up after six years and demand to see him," she*
*says.*

*"I don't want this to be a confrontation."*

*"You're shit out of luck there," says Valerie. She begins to busy herself*
*with things around the room. She straightens some script pages on the*
*Angel's dressing room table. She picks up her hat.*

*"I've been discussing this with my lawyer," says Andrew, then immedi-*
*ately stops himself. "Okay, see, that's not the direction I want this conver-*
*sation to take," he says. "But you need to know that's a possible road this*
*can go down."*

*"Are you threatening me?" asks Val without turning to look at him.*

*"No, I'm not," he says. He's not lying. She didn't think he meant it as a*
*threat, but it's there, a knife in his voice, a blade in everything he says. "But*
*it's an option I need you to keep in mind. That I have rights, and that you*
*are in a delicate position here, legally speaking."*

*"I'm his mother," she says.*

*"No one is arguing that," says Andrew. "But there is also a viewpoint*
*from which it could potentially be argued that you are a kidnapper."*

"No one would call me that." She wonders if that's what they said about her back then, in Los Angeles. If for six years, she's been the crazy that ran off with her kid. None of her friends from back then have ever called or visited, and she's written it off to the fact that few of her friends from back then were what you'd call close, especially after Alex was born. But maybe Andrew spent the months after her disappearance poisoning the well, protecting himself from other, potentially better-informed opinions on the situation.

"Fuck, fuck," Andrew sputters. He scratches at the spot on his forehead that's lately started to go bald. "That's not what I'm calling you. Can I start over? How is he? Do you have a picture of him?"

She folds her arms over her chest and glares at him.

"I want this conversation to be about Alex, not about us," says Andrew. "Every awful thing you think about who I was back then, as a husband, I'm admitting to. And as a father. I was an asshole, Valerie. But I've changed a lot."

"You know who says things like that?" says Val. "People who haven't changed a lot. People who are still assholes."

Andrew looks at her, pleading, or doing a good impression of someone who's pleading. "I want to be part of his life," he says.

"His life is fine without you in it," says Val. "Vastly improved."

"He shouldn't grow up without a dad," Andrew says. "He's getting into that age. It's right around when I lost my dad."

It's a cheap card to play, the death-of-a-parent card, but it's only been two years now since Val's own dad passed away, and she finds her skin a little thicker on this issue. "I'm not saying this to trivialize your loss," she says, "but there's a difference between losing your dad and never having had one."

"I know," says Andrew. "And I can't make up for the time that I wasn't there. But I want to start now. I'm ready to be a father to him now."

"That's great, Andrew," Val says. She reaches around him and grabs her coat. She wants to exit. If she can find the perfect line, she can walk off stage. "It's great that you're ready. It's great you've had time to figure stuff like that out about yourself. Did you want to tell me all about how you got here, to this point of enlightenment?"

"I didn't cheat on him, Valerie," he says. "I cheated on you and I fucked up our marriage, but it shouldn't keep me from seeing him."

She thinks of the photo, of the moment she knew Alex would never be safe with Andrew.

"He's going to come live with me," says Andrew.

She laughs, a forced, panicked thing. "You're out of your fucking mind."

"Two years," he says, dead calm.

"There's no fucking way."

"It's the custody agreement, Valerie," he says. "We had a seventy-thirty custody split. You've had him for six years. I'm just sticking to the agreement."

"That agreement is bullshit," she says.

"That agreement is court ordered and you've been in violation of it for six years. If we go to court, they'll give me full custody. They'll take him away from you," Andrew says. "I'm not saying you can't see him. You can visit."

"Visit?" she says, her voice breaking a little.

"You could even move to L.A.," he says amicably. "It's not like you couldn't find work."

"I hate L.A.," she says.

"You didn't use to."

"I do now."

"You don't have much in the way of recourse here, Valerie," says Andrew. "I'm offering to do this all without getting the courts involved."

Her anger is spent. It will grow back, she knows, but she needs it now and it's gone. Some practical part of her mind steps up. "When?" she says.

She can see his relief in not having to face her anger anymore. "I'd like to have him settled in before the school year starts," he says. All of his gestures are softer now; he holds his palms up and open. "The place I live, there's a good school nearby. I know a lot of people whose kids go there."

"He's homeschooled," says Val.

"That's great, that you're doing that," says Andrew. He almost reaches out and pats her on the shoulder. She would scream. He pulls his hand back. "But this school is excellent. A lot of resources. I'll send you a link." It's becoming normal already. Links e-mailed, photos shown off. She remembers the little bit of time when the custody agreement was actually in place, the horrible courteousness and civility the court had ordered. It's all creeping back now. "I know you want to look at this like a doomsday scenario, Valerie," he says, "but it doesn't have to be."

"Should I call you or your lawyer?" she says. "With my decision."

"We can make arrangements directly," says Andrew. "It's probably easiest. I worry a little about getting lawyers involved."

"But you spoke to yours," Val points out.

"I spoke to him hypothetically," he says. "There are things about mandatory reporting that I didn't want to run up against."

She feels trapped, checkmated. She wants to have a strategy now, but her mind is a screaming thing.

"I'll call," she says.

"When?"

"Soon."

"I'm in town until the end of next week," says Andrew. "I could come by."

"I'll call when you get back to L.A.," she says. "When you're at a safe distance."

He nods and shrugs. He can afford to look humble now; he's won. He puts on his jacket, leaving it open because L.A. has made him stupid to the prospect of winter. As he goes to leave, she can see again that he wants to touch her or hug her or something. She shies away enough to defuse whatever half thought he's having. In the doorway, he stops and turns back. "So how does it end?" he says. She looks at him, blank. "The play. The second half."

She begins buttoning her coat, paying the buttons more attention than they need. "It ends with all of them talking in Central Park, in the winter," she says. "Except Harper. She flies off to California."

"Huh," he says. "It was great, Valerie. You were really great."

After he is gone, there's no sound in the dressing room, and again she can hear laughter and clinking glass from the room next door. She thinks about having a drink with the rest of the cast, sitting silently in the corner and letting a bit of booze take the edge off. But there's no edge; she feels blunted, like a pencil tip worn down.

# PART THREE

# The Modern Age

I don't really see a need to retire as long as I am having fun.

—STANLEY MARTIN LIEBER

Don't do comics. Comics will break your heart.

—JACOB KURTZBERG

# The *Southwest Chief*

A hundred miles an hour, Alex runs across Iowa, Kansas, New Mexico. He begins, feet planted, hand on the back door of the rearmost sleeper, then takes off, through the sleeper where he and his mother share a berth, through the dining car, through the observation car, bursting with light, and through three coach cars where people too used to airline travel spend the entire trip buckled into their seats as if the *Southwest Chief* will soon undertake a turbulent descent. When he reaches the far end, he turns and does the whole thing in reverse, still managing to move forward at a staggering eighty miles an hour.

His mother granted him his superspeed by giving him an overview of general relativity while his babu drove them to the Chicago train station. As he understands it, while passengers on the train will see him running by at only ten miles per hour, someone watching outside the train would register his speed as a combination of his running speed and the train's traveling speed. Taking a step further back, she explained, someone watching from above the earth would see him barreling along at his own measly ten miles an hour, plus the train's ninety, plus the roughly eight hundred miles an hour at which the earth spins at this latitude. But even that pales when you think about someone observing from farther away, who might see Alex running at more than sixty-seven thousand miles per hour, throwing in the earth's speed as it circles the sun. Which it does within a galaxy whirling along even faster than that.

As he passes windows, Alex slows slightly to see if he can catch anyone watching him from outside, standing by the side of the tracks or floating in orbit. So far as he can tell, he hasn't been spotted.

Time aboard the *Southwest Chief* becomes elastic, due in part to the removal of any enforced bedtime. This is done not by edict but by default. His mother's sleep schedule, which normally dictates his own, has become erratic. She goes to sleep whenever the idea occurs to her: a three-hour nap after lunch, dozing through dinner, only to stay awake from four in the morning till breakfast. Their berth has a cramped feeling Alex associates with confinement, although as a New Yorker he is well adapted to living in small spaces. But his mother never leaves it, for the full duration of the trip. Alex decides early that he is on his own, and while he cuddles up to his already sleeping mother at nine thirty sharp on the first night, by ten he is up again, wandering through the coach cars, where the breathing of dozens of sleepers has settled into unison, and the observation car, where strangers—not just to Alex but to each other—play endless card games. Overhead, the stars sit stationary in a sky that cannot possibly be the same one that hangs over New York: it is so pinpricked with light that the darkness seems the lesser part of it.

Lying on a bench, watching the stars through the ceiling of curved glass, Alex wonders if these distortions in time, and the compression of his mother's days into uneven cycles of eight hours rather than twenty-four, are related to the train's motion across the surface of the earth, or through space. Maybe speed tugs and pushes at time the way a roller coaster stretches your stomach till it's the length of your whole body or presses your face until it feels all smooshed together. Thinking on this, he falls asleep for a while, then wakes up and groggily makes his way back to their berth, where his mother is now awake, sitting in full lotus on the tiny bed, spine perfectly straight. He curls up next to her and sleeps, her knee resting over his hip, her hand stroking his thick hair.

When he wakes up, she is asleep again. Alex stays in the berth, reading *Adam Anti & Houses in Motion* for two chapters, then takes the notebook from his backpack and some trail mix from one of her bags and goes back to the observation car. It is sunny, and the sun has a bigness to it where it seems like it's coming from everywhere at once. The sun is fighting off the air-conditioning that keeps the other cars refrigerator cold. The passengers who have packed only for summer weather group here, away from the enforced chill, and the observation car is crowded. Alex is relieved to spot Gail, who is maybe a friend of his mother but at least is someone he knows from the previous two conventions, and is safe, and, more important, is sitting alone at a table for two. She is hunched over a piece of writing. She looks up at Alex and smiles, tired. He tries to remember if he saw her in here the night before, if maybe she's been here all night.

"Are you done?" he asks.

"Just a break," she tells him. He tries to remember if they've been introduced or he's only seen her, then decides it doesn't matter.

"You're a writer?" he asks. She nods like she's been caught doing something she shouldn't have. "Me, too," he says.

"It's no way to make a living," Gail says, which is something his mom says about acting sometimes. He wonders if that's something you say about things that are important to you. His fingers tap his own notebook as he tries to decide where to start today. He didn't realize this about telling a story, that you needed to figure out where to start again and again. It was easier with Brett, and he even thinks about getting his mother's phone and calling him. Before they left Chicago, Brett gave his mother the number and told her Alex could call him anytime. The Idea Man had said the same thing before they left New York. It's funny, thinks Alex, that his father never gave him a phone number and said "Call me anytime." He wonders how often he would have called his father if he had a number to call him at. But he decides not to call Brett, because Brett is probably working or driving, and anyway, Alex can catch him up on the story when they see each other in Los Angeles.

"Can I ask you a question because you're a girl?" Alex asks Gail.

She takes off her glasses and folds them, placing them on the paper in front of her. "You understand I can't answer for all girls, or for girlkind or anything."

"That's okay," says Alex. He opens his notebook to the last page with writing on it. The boy, the robot, and the shape-shifting girl have left the factory and are at the far edge of the city, where he left them. His concern right now is for the girl. Maybe this is because it was Brett who added her in, but now that she's helped them get into the city, he's not sure what is supposed to happen to her. He's not even sure what she wants to happen. "If you were kicked out of your home," he says, "because you were different or something. And then later you could go back. Would you want to go back?"

Gail leans back in her seat. "That's not an easy question," she says.

"I know," Alex says, rapping his pencil point onto the page, leaving little checkmarks. "I'm stuck on it." He watches her think about it and decides he likes her. He likes that she's taking time to think about his question.

"You think the answer's different for boys than it is for girls?" she asks him. That's not an easy question, either. Though his mother insists girls and boys are the same, he's not so sure. Differences are louder than samenesses.

"I guess it's probably not," he says. "But it's a girl in the story, and I thought since I had a girl here . . ."

Gail laughs at this, and Alex is not sure what he's said that's funny. "You're a real charmer," she says, but not the way people usually say it. It's more like when sometimes he's being stubborn his mom will say, "You're a real pill."

"When I was a kid," Gail says, "I left home because I felt like I didn't have a choice. Because of who I was inside, I didn't think I could stay. But I always wanted to go home. I imagined what it would be like. How they'd welcome me back. They'd kill the fatted calf and all that. Everything would be fixed, and all the things I'd run away from would be gone."

"What's a fatty calf?" says Alex.

"You know, I have no idea," she says. "In the Bible, they're a big deal."

Behind her, weird desert landscapes pass. Outcroppings and gullies and dunes that look as if someone went to the moon and covered it in rust. "You didn't go back?" Alex asks.

"I did," she says, shaking her head. "It took me years. How old are you?"

"Nine."

"I stayed away as long as you've been alive," she says, as if she is daring him to believe it. "And then I went back. It felt strong, going back. I'd made a life of my own. I'd become even more myself than I had been when I left." When she was talking about leaving home, she stared off into the desert, but now she looks at him and registers his confusion. "It sounds hokey," she says, "but it's like there's a person you're supposed to be, and something inside you is always trying to make you into that person, or get you as close as you can get. Hopefully it's a good thing. Anyway, I went home thinking, *Now I'm this complete person and they'll all see that who I was, the person they didn't want back then, was a step toward this person who, really, is quite amazing.*" She shakes her head again and puts her glasses back on. "I sound like a yoga instructor," she says.

"My mom and I used to go to yoga," Alex says. "It's very calming."

"More of a spinning-class girl myself," says Gail.

"So did they see that?" Alex says.

"They tried, I guess. I didn't stay too long. Maybe they would have, maybe not. They still couldn't give me whatever it was I needed from them when I left."

"That sounds sad," says Alex.

"It made me sad for them," Gail says. "That they hadn't changed. I didn't need what they could have given me anymore. I might still want it—I might always want it—but they didn't have anything I needed."

Alex nods and thinks about how sometimes answers are more complicated than questions. He wants to thank Gail, but he doesn't know how, so he looks down at his notepad and writes.

*The shape-changing girl looked around the city, but she was thinking about the desert and how it was quiet and how she had time to practice her magic there. She thought about how they'd taken her name away, and she realized they'd only taken their name for her, and they couldn't stop her from choosing a name of her own. So she wished the boy and the robot luck in their journey, and she put on a face she liked and went home.*

# Los Angeles, I'm Yours

She wasn't lying: the extra room gets great light. Particularly in the morning. Brett worries the shift in time zones will keep him up at all hours. But the first morning in her apartment, in her bed, the California sun reaches into his skull. Reconfigures all the gears in his clockworks. By the time she rolls out of bed, he's been working for an hour. He cobbles together breakfast from the supplies in her kitchen. They eat granola and slices of oranges that are a little suspect. They return to bed giggling. Page three spends the day basking in sunlight, alone and unfinished. He goes back to it later in the evening, under a lamp that makes everything the color of clover honey. But he cannot get back to Proxima Centauri. So in a kind of defeat that is also a victory, he returns to bed. To her.

He was surprised Fred had approved of this plan. And with no protest or snark. He took it as a sign that Fred was finally recognizing Brett's work as something that took time. Couldn't be thrown together in the back of a speeding van. The pencils for the last issue were going to be rushed. But Fred agreed they should use the traveling money from Black Sheep to fly Brett ahead to Los Angeles to finish the pencils for the last issue while Fred brought the van the rest of the way. Monday morning, Fred drove both of them to the airport. Said goodbyes. Promised to meet them at the convention center on Friday. Even kissed her on the cheek, to the surprise of everyone involved.

And now it's Wednesday morning. Los Angeles shakes him out of bed. Coaxes him to the drawing table with sunlight. The pages are white as fresh milk. Asking to be scarred with his pencils. When she wakes up, he doesn't hear her. She has to come in and say hello. Remind him she's there. In this light, she's amazing. Everything is amazing in this light. She looks over his shoulder as he draws. Circles become heads and torsos. She is going to meet her friend Nell for lunch. Nell is a doula. But she's a doula for women who run modeling agencies. It is not quite a contact. Not quite an in. But it's something. Anyway, Nell is buying. She invites Brett along.

It is hot in the apartment. Brett contorts himself so he doesn't sweat onto his pages. When she comes back later in the afternoon, he's glad to take a break. They work together on dinner. A stir-fry. She's vegetarian. Which he did not know. They split a bottle of wine. Then another. He says he should get back to work. Get a few more hours in. But he doesn't protest much.

Thursday morning, he checks his e-mail on her computer to see if Fred's sent the rest of the script, but there's nothing. He's itching to continue. He knows where the story has to go; this far into it, there's a momentum that makes everything inevitable. And after working with Fred for this long, it's not unreasonable to predict what he will do next. Even if he's wrong, he can waste a day working on something unusable or waste a day not working. It comes to the same thing.

She sleeps late. She burns the eggs. The smell pulls him away from his pages. They taste as if they've had bits of crayon mixed in. He excitedly explains a particularly knotted plot thread they introduced back in issue eight, "Hang On to Yourself." He'd been worried they'd never manage to resolve it.

"Lady Stardust captures David's personality, in this case a clown called Beep Beep, and hands him over to Factor Max, the spy agency he used to work for," he says. "They claim they've found a cure for the Persona virus by integrating all of his possible identities. But Lady Stardust realizes that what they're trying to do is turn David into a kind of personality aggregator, to make him into everyone at once. This David would be the ultimate information source for Factor Max, even if it meant David, her David, would be left forever drowning in a sea of personalities. Once

Lady Stardust discovers this plan, she kills Beep Beep and escapes the Factor Max base on Hammurab."

He sounds more like Fred when he talks about *Lady Stardust*. His sentences stretch and entwine.

"All of that implies that David's identities have an a priori existence. I always assumed they blip into being, complete with personal histories, and the universe fills in everyone else's memories of them. But this means that David is becoming people who already are. Which also means that Lady Stardust is not killing off iterations of David, but actual people with real histories and families. I thought of her like a sculptor. Chipping away extraneous pieces to uncover David hidden in a block of personalities. But in fact, she's a murderer, many times over. This being a comic book, we can't let that slide."

They move from the sink to the shower. She washes herself languidly. Vies for his attention. No avail. He is in deep space. Her signals are barely coming through.

"But what if," he says, "what if the penultimate persona, the last faux David that needs to be killed before David returns to himself, is *her*? Is Lady Stardust? Then you could have this spectacular ending where she finds his antepenultimate identity and gets him onto a spaceship aimed at the heart of a sun, the center of Proxima Centauri. She confesses everything. How much she loves him. All the horrible things she's done to get him back. In that moment there's no turning back; she kills the antepenultimate David and then crashes the ship into the sun. A second later, David wakes up in bed with Lady Stardust, exactly where the series started."

She says nothing during these ruminations. After the shower and the fiery death, she shoves Brett onto her bed. Fucks him without looking at him. Stares out the window, even when she comes. He wonders if she fucked him to shut him up. He lies on the bed as she gets dressed. He offers to go with her to run her errands. She says "No, it's fine." She doesn't say where she's going. When she's likely to be back.

He gets dressed. Returns to his drawing table. He fills a bowl with almonds, which he eats over the next several hours. While he works.

It's late when she gets back. She's drunk. Wearing something nicer than when she went out. Something she must have just bought. Her body seems rumpled, while her clothes are crisp. He asks what she's been up to. From the other room she calls something that sounds like *friends*. It could be something else. Sometimes she wants to fuck when she's drunk. But not tonight. She heads directly to the bedroom. Brett considers joining her, even after he hears her hitting the bed still in her new clothes. But he looks at the page he's working on, at the unfinished panel. Lady Stardust destroying the ship's steering mechanism after she's set the controls for the heart of the sun. She stands completed in the foreground. The mechanism has only been sketched in. Brett knows precisely how it should look. He worries he might not remember in the morning. The mental image he'd come back to would be a lesser version of the one he has right now. He adjusts the light and returns to work.

## Secret Origin of the Visigoth

*You assume their gods are weak. Strong gods would never have let their people be conquered. So you spit on their shrines. You behead their statues, as you've beheaded so many of their followers. You shit in their temples, and when, just as you are wiping your ass, one of their feeble gods appears to you, why would you cower? Why would you kneel? Their people are reduced to nothing. Aren't, then, their gods even less than that?*

*But this god with his winged heels, who looks haggard, who may have at one point been in the battlefields among his people, in a way that your gods don't need to, because they are powerful even from the sky, he looks at you. And in that moment he sees in you all of the sins of your people. Every fire set, every town sacked, every woman raped, although you yourself never took part in this aspect of victory. Strange to your comrades, your love for your bride makes you not want to fuck other women, because you find the prospect unpleasant.*

*And he casts you out.*

*You are in a strange place. A place you know is not on your earth, even though you have never considered that there are places other than your earth. Things, great and mighty things, stride above you, tripodal. Around you scuttle armored beasts on six legs. They are like the water striders and crayfish you would snatch at in the creeks near your village as a child. But huge, and metal. You do not yet have the word* alien, *but soon it will be given to you, when the people of this planet, who are like you but colored like grass and with eyes that glow red, place the small worm, the worm of words, in your ear so that you can hear them and understand their jabbering. One of the water striders attacks you, but your sword severs his leg and you are saved. It is only after you have saved yourself that you realize you have also saved a group of the green people's smallings, who were on an outing. You are taller than they. They think your tunic and your helmet are a hard skin. You are a hero to them.*

*The three-legged things, they tell you, are carnivorous. The six-legged creatures are scavengers and ultimately harmless. And the green people who look just like you, only green, with their women who look just like women, call themselves Derridians. And their planet is Derrid. But they have never heard of Earth.*

*Their mages have ideas. To cast you deep into the black, that you might land on your home somehow. Because of course your home is somewhere, out there in the black. They offer to fire you, like a stone from a slingshot, with no target in mind. They have the magic to do this.*

*You know a stone fired at random cannot hope to hit its target. And if there is this world out there, so far away from yours, what worlds might you hit, slung from this one into the ether? You are treated well here, hailed as a protector. Their girls cast their bright red eyes at you in a look you can understand. That look is not so alien.*

*But she is out there. Your bride who allowed you to go to war, to defeat the Romans and their gods so that you could be glorious among the tribe, so your child in her belly could be heir to that glory. And if their mage can fling you out into space with even a hope of finding your way back to her? It is a small risk to take.*

# Ought to Be in Pictures

"It smells like my junior high school out there," says Gail as she steps into the ladies' dressing room. Something apparently went wrong with the air-conditioning at the Los Angeles Convention Center last night, and while it is cool on the convention floor now, this morning when she arrived it was stifling. In the dressing room, the girls are two to a fan. They are all in costume already, except for Val, who Gail supposes is in a costume of a sort.

"It is rank with boy," says Flail.

"It reeks of boy," says Flog.

"Avoid areas with low ceilings," Gail warns them. "It collects. It eddies." She sits down next to Val and hands her a bottle of water, which Val silently accepts. At some point during the train ride here, Gail became a bit of a mother to Val, bringing her food or sending some with Alex when he went back to their berth. Checking in now and then, trying to coax Val out for a walk, or to take some air when they stopped. Gail had begun to think of her in terms of a puppet, not so much one with its strings cut as one from which the enlivening hand has been removed.

This morning, Alex came to Gail's hotel room, asking if she could help his mom get ready. But by the time Gail got to their room, Val was dressed and prepared to meet the public, looking like a copy of herself. Two-dimensional and blurred slightly around the edges. Gail and Alex each took one of Val's hands and, not sure whether or not she needed to be led, guided her down to the dressing room.

"I was hoping there would be more film people," says Spectacle Girl, wearing a baggy sweatshirt over her tights. Her accent is thick, like in a high school production of *Oklahoma!* Gail imagines it is always warm wherever she's from, because she never stops shivering, all of her exposed, tanned skin permanently pricked with gooseflesh.

"Because you're an actress now?" asks Red Emma.

"I could be," says Spectacle Girl, defensively.

"She's got better odds than we have," says the Diviner.

"We could play her lesbian mothers," says Red Emma.

"I'm not dykey enough to play anyone's lesbian mother," the Diviner says.

"That's okay. I'm dykey enough for both of us."

"Look at her," says the Diviner, pointing at Spectacle Girl. "She could play sixteen."

"If she was a man," says Red Emma, "she could play sixteen till she was thirty."

"By thirty she'll be washed up," says Flail.

"By washed up she means doing theater," the Diviner explains to the rest of the room.

"What about you, Writer Lady?" ExSanguina asks Gail. The way she says it makes Gail feel like a superheroine, like the rest of them. Writer Lady, harnessing the power of a thousand word processors. Beware her mighty revisions! "Why don't you write for the movies instead of comic books?" says ExSanguina. "Money's got to be better."

"You know how few women write comic books?" Gail asks. "There's even fewer women writing movies. Of all the movies made, let's be generous and say only three-quarters are about men."

"More like nine-tenths," says Red Emma.

"And of course all of those are written by men," says the Astounding Woman.

"Of that remaining fourth," says Gail, "three-quarters of *those* are written by men, too."

"Leaving us a quarter of a quarter," says ExSanguina.

"A sixteenth!" says Flog.

"Very good, dear," says the Diviner. "Gold star for you."

"So it's hard to break in," says ExSanguina.

"It's nearly impossible," says Gail. "And I've already done the nearly impossible once. I've managed to climb to the middle of my industry. To the point I can pay my rent as a writer, and a couple people read my books. And maybe some of those are girls who will grow up to be comics writers. I didn't have that. All the writers I looked up to were men. If I tried to jump over, I'd be at the bottom again."

"But you're an established writer," says ExSanguina. "That must help."

"I'm an established comics writer. Middle rung in comics is slightly below bottom rung in movies."

"Better working than looking for work, at our age," says the Diviner.

"What difference does age make if you're a writer?" says Red Emma. Gail cannot decide if she likes Red Emma's contrary nature or can't stand it, or just wants to see what's under her trench coat.

"Age makes a difference to everybody," says the Diviner.

"You had to be thirty when you started," says Spectacle Girl to Val, who has been silent this whole time, sipping her water in the corner. She turns as if she's just woken up.

"Twenty-eight, when I started," she says quietly. "Grande dame."

"Ancient," says the Diviner.

"TV's different," says Val. "The box is more forgiving."

"That's going to be the title of my autobiography," says Red Emma.

"Won't be forgiving for long," says the Diviner. "Higher definition means more visible lines."

"Means younger actresses," says the Astounding Woman, as if she is cautioning them.

"Twenty-one-year-olds playing forty," says the Diviner.

"And then they all expect that's what forty will look like," says Red Emma.

"I used to watch you when I was a kid," Spectacle Girl tells Val. "Season four and on. You rocked old."

"I was thirty-two," says Val.

"You were a MILF," says Spectacle Girl.

"I despise that term," says the Diviner.

"Why?" asks Flail. "It denotes a category of sexuality more easily applied to women of an advanced age."

"Don't say 'advanced age,'" says the Astounding Woman.

"It denotes dual purpose," says the Diviner. "'Look at her. She's good for *two* things: bonking and breeding.'"

"I saw you in *Playboy of the Western World*," says ExSanguina. "In New York. Four years ago?"

"You saw that?" says Val.

"I wouldn't have known it was you if I hadn't known," says ExSanguina. "You looked completely different. It was incredible."

"It felt incredible," says Val, as if she's realizing it as she says it. It's the first time in days that Gail has seen her look at all animated. "It was like remembering someone I used to be."

# All Watched Over by Machines of Loving Grace

From overhead, huge machines wage war on the bodies below, battling the heat that rises off of them. The machines are winning for now, but this fight will go on for the next four days. The machines are doomed. Brett imagines that by day two, clouds will form in the air at the top of the hall, weather systems of perspiration condensed by air-conditioning. It will rain sweat, and by then everyone will be so hot they'll be thankful for it. He pictures scenes from a mudless Woodstock of comics geeks, dancing in precipitation they've made themselves.

In the main hall, a dragon's head the size of a compact car looms over the booth for a video game company. Twelve-foot statues of intricate Japanese battle robots twist and bend at the waist, move their sword-bearing arms slowly downward, then back up. If you're close enough, you can hear the strain of the animatronics whirring inside them. On one of the walls, there's a huge banner with the cast of the *R-Squad* movies, and another, smaller and cheaper-looking, with a grinning picture of Toby Melvin, from the sixties television version of *The Ferret*. They look like they belong at a fascist rally. What's impressive to Brett is the absence of comic books. There *are* dealers off in one corner of the room with long boxes and bargain bins. Timely has a booth, with their enormous clock logo floating over it. And somewhere, Russell and Marisha are here with stacks of books and T-shirts with Black Sheep's logo. But calling it a comic convention when there's such a predominance of other things seems a gross misnomer.

Fred finally shows. In a rush. Flustered. Runs right by Brett. Brett hoped for a discovery. A coming upon. He gets up, approaches Fred at the back of the concierge line, taps a shoulder. Fred spins. Actually pirouettes. Quick, with a harried grace.

"You're early," says Fred. "Where's Ferret Lass?" Sounds jilted. This is the bill due. The one Brett didn't have to pay in Chicago. This hurt, this damage.

"We've decided to see other people."

"Is that right?"

"Something like that," says Brett. They start making their way toward Artist Alley, through the crowd.

"I've been a dick this trip," says Brett. "No excuses, just I'm sorry."

Fred mulls. A second longer than he needs to. Theatrical. Overacting.

"It's nothing," says Fred. "Although I could have told you this would happen. If you'd bothered to ask."

"I know."

"You're too trusting," says Fred. There is a moment. Maybe they're supposed to hug. Shake hands and laugh about it. The moment passes. Such an easy reconciliation. Shows the strength of the friendship. Or the opposite. A "nothing personal" aspect to the whole thing. They're more partners than friends. Collaborators. Then what happens after *Lady Stardust* is done? If they start something new, does the counter of their friendship set back to zero? Will it be a different friendship altogether?

"So did you hear?" says Fred on the escalator. "Levi Loeb died last night."

A jolt. He'd been struggling with the last page, before she got home. "Going to bed," she muttered, slamming the door behind her. Brett turned back to the failed attempts at the last page. Blocky. Lifeless. He asked himself how Loeb would draw it. He imagined the scene from an angle he'd never try on his own. Skewed. Hitchcockian. A Loeb angle. And it clicked. It flowed. It was Loeb's, but it was Brett's, too. It was borrowed and original. Pencil scarred page and there they were. Lady Stardust and David. From the beginning, but different. A change not in them or outside them but in the play between. The interface of subject and object. Place where skin meets skin.

In the morning, Brett made coffee. Toast. She seemed genuinely sad when he told her he was going to check in at the hotel near the convention center. Gave him a long kiss goodbye. Her mouth tasted like stale booze and wheat toast.

"It makes me feel bad about missing the panel in Cleveland," says Fred. "A guy that age, you know your opportunities to see him are limited. Still, something seemed permanent about him. Perpetual? And Brewer still looks like he'll dance on our graves. Bathes in the blood of virgins, most likely. I was never that big into Loeb's side of the argument anyway. You want to know who's pulling the weight in a collaboration, there's one test: post-partnership output. Who's the Simon and who's the Garfunkel? Look at Lennon and McCartney. When's the last time you willingly listened to Wings?"

Brett thinks Lennon's post-Beatles stuff is as bad as McCartney's, but he stays quiet as they descend into the scrum of another crowd.

# Inner Circle

It is exactly the kind of restaurant he would like. It is designed with visibility in mind; it answers the question *What if a restaurant was also a zoo?* Seating is divided between two groups: those there to be seen and those there to see them. The latter are in a ring around the elevated platform where the former dine. Even within the raised ring, there are subdivisions. *Just like Hell,* Val thinks as she scans the room. At the very center is a small cluster of A-listers, surrounded by concentric circles of B-, C-, and D-listers. The diners in each ring look enviously inward at the next, and those in the center look warily at the outer circles from which they've come and to which they could easily return. Outward motion is easy. You only have to fail once. To move inward or to remain at the center, you have to succeed every time. Sometimes even that isn't enough.

Andrew waits for her at a table in the inner part of what she judges to be the C circle. *C* for "cable." He stands and pulls out her chair for her.

"I just got seated," he says. "Haven't even ordered a drink." Val had made a calculated guess how late Andrew would be, then showed up twenty minutes later. She felt this would establish something of a power dynamic. Not only does Andrew's nonchalance tells her the effort was wasted, but the effort of performing such a calculation demonstrated how the power between them was balanced.

"You look great," says Andrew as she sits down. He sells the line, and she feels her cheeks flush in a reflexive response to having her appearance complimented, particularly when she knows she does not look great: she hasn't slept more than four consecutive hours in the past week, and today has been her longest uninterrupted span of consciousness since the convention in Chicago. Her dreaming and waking states are blurring together into one long, gray smear of semi-consciousness and half-life. This morning she showed up at the convention without makeup, and the girls performed a team lift to make her presentable, an effort she fears has not held up through the day's heat.

"You look puffy," she says, having no incentive to flatter or appease him. But he laughs at this and orders them drinks, guessing, correctly, that she takes her martinis the same way she did when they were together.

"It's part of the role," he says. "I finally have producers asking me *not* to go to the gym."

"They can't get you a fat suit?"

"They don't want fat," he says as the waitress arrives, lightning fast, with their drinks. "They want puffy."

"You're hitting it out of the park, then," she says. She wants to be all barbs, but she can barely find the sharp edges in herself. She wants to be Dorothy Parker, but after a week at her mother's in Illinois, she feels more like Dorothy Gale. She sips her martini. *Two at most,* she quotes to herself. *Three, I'm under the table.* "How's the show?" she asks.

He shrugs and swallows the better part of his bourbon. She never understood how he could drink whiskey in the summer. "We've been renewed for one more season. That'll probably be it. There's only so many variations on lovable-loser-fucks-women-half-his-age."

She thinks of saying, "He's supposed to be lovable?" But she doesn't want to give the impression she's watched the show, which he probably assumes anyway.

"We need to talk logistics," she says.

"I'm glad you brought that up," he says. "I have this idea." He finishes the rest of the whiskey and signals for another. It is something of a prop for him, in both the theatrical and the emotional sense, but her martinis are no less so. "I've been talking to some people. Very preliminary, but it's gotten to where we're one piece short. What would you think about an *Anomaly* movie?"

She laughs, almost spitting gin at him. "Andrew, I'm sorry to crush your dream on this, but Tim can't write a movie. He can barely write a grocery list. He's been housebound with an in-home assistant for years."

"I wasn't talking about Tim," he says. "I run into some of the old writers every now and then. They've got ideas. And there's studio interest."

"Tim wouldn't allow it."

"It's more up to Tiger's Paw than it is up to Tim," he says.

"You've looked into this?"

"There was no point going forward without looking into it. I put a lawyer on it." Val imagines meetings in smoke-filled rooms. The lawyer she pictures is a cheap private eye from a B movie. "Don't tell me you haven't thought about it," he says.

"I've never thought about it," she says.

"You should," says Andrew. "I'll be straight with you, Valerie." She's always hated it when he uses her full name. "All bets are off if you're not on board. No one wants to see an Ian Campbell solo flick. It'd be good for you, too. Better than these little plays you're doing."

"Little plays," she repeats, pressing her lips together tightly. These are the moments a martini makes an excellent prop: it can be pulled through tight lips, strained through clenched teeth.

"You know I never got theater," he says. It is like an apology in the way a fish stick is like a fish. "It'd give you a reason to be in L.A."

"I can find work on my own," she says.

"It's harder than you think," says Andrew. "It took me three years to land the part I've got, and it's not that great of a part. People only think of me as Ian Campbell. I'm not saying it would be the same for you. I'm saying: this would be work. And near Alex. And the way the show left things, it's not like we'd have to do love scenes. We could even be enemies if you wanted. I'm happy to play the villain." He smiles at her, or maybe the curve of his glass looks like a grin, a half-circle. Val wants to break something against him—not that it could do any damage, but for the sound of it.

"All right, we're not doing this," she says. She bends down, picks up her purse from the floor, and sets it in her lap. She removes the manila envelope and puts it on the table between them.

"What's that?" says Andrew.

"Open it," she says.

Andrew unseals the envelope and pulls out the photo. He looks somber. She can't help feeling a little smug. Her trump card is down.

"Alex can stay with you for the next couple days," says Val. "You two can catch up, throw a baseball around. But after that, he's coming back to New York with me."

"Val," he says, "this doesn't change anything."

"I think it does."

"It's been six years," says Andrew. He puts the picture back into the envelope and sets it back on the table. "I'm not that person anymore. I haven't been for a long time."

Val slides the envelope back toward him. "I'll show it to Alex," she says. "I'll tell him everything. I'll tell him who you are."

Andrew drops his head, folds his hands in his lap. A posture of contrition, classical almost. "You mean you haven't told him already?" he says.

"Of course not," she says. "I wanted to keep him safe from it."

"You can't keep him safe, Val," he says. "If you don't tell him, and if he doesn't know already, he'll find out. Her, the shooting, all of it. He's going to find out, probably soon. Who I was. If I were still that person, Val, I wouldn't be here with you. I wouldn't want Alex back in my life. But I do. I'm ready."

"Why weren't you ready then?" she asks. Everything is emptying out. "What was wrong with you then?"

"I don't know," he says. "When Alex was born, you know, you say to yourself, *I'm a dad now,* and then you expect to feel different. Like, not a little, but completely different. I was waiting for this massive change to drop on me like a ton of bricks. And I was scared. No one told me that, but those first few days, I was so busy being scared of Alex—that I'd break him, or that I'd fuck him up somehow. It was such a relief to go back to work, where I knew what I was doing. And work became more real for me. You and Alex were together all the time, and there was something between you immediately that I didn't have. And I thought about my dad, and I thought, *Maybe this is it. Maybe being a dad is not radically different from not being a dad.* So I put myself into work more, and I drifted away from you, and from Alex. And when . . . she showed up, I was already in this world of fans and fiction. I thought it was a game, or a story. It didn't feel like real life. Nothing did."

"I should go," says Val. "I should be spending this time with Alex."

He stands up immediately, and she wonders if he is going to pull out her chair for her. "Wait," he says. "Wait." She sits back down and then hates herself for sitting back down. She is glad she did not finish her drink before attempting to leave, and does so now. "Tell me about him," Andrew says. "Tell me what he's like."

For a moment, Val forces herself to see Andrew as a father, not as the man she left. It is an overly generous move. He's had no interest in the role for six years, and now he wants notes on how to play it. But she has to remind herself that he isn't awful, and that she is not handing Alex off to a monster but to a man who happens to look like someone she had the reason and energy to hate six years ago.

"He's not like anything but himself," she says. "I used to think he was the best parts of you and me with everything awful sifted out, but he's not. It's like everything you and I ever pretended to be, he is. He's smart. He's so smart. And he is caring. He cares about everything and everybody in a way I've only ever managed to care about him. There's nothing cold in him, Andrew. And if you take that away from him, I'll never forgive you."

Again he has the advantage, because there is something left in his drink. "You're never going to forgive me anyway," he says, and gulps the rest of it down.

"You're right, I'm not," she says. "But *he* already has."

# Takeout

Greedily, Alex devours crab Rangoons, pork dumplings, and shrimp egg rolls. He has ordered a meal of appetizers, all of them gloriously fried. His whole dinner is things that should come before dinner; he is the present dining on the past. Brett made the uninspired choice of chicken lo mein, but Alex generously shares one of everything with him. They sit on the floor of the hotel room, the Chinese food containers laid out between them as if they are planning a great battle.

"So you're thinking," says Brett, with lo mein dangling from the corner of his mouth, "they leave the city of industry and get swallowed by a giant metal worm."

"It's boring if they have to walk again," Alex says. He flinches as the word *boring* gets away from him. It's one his mother strongly discourages, being of the opinion that only people who aren't particularly bright get bored.

"And eaten by a giant metal worm is more exciting," says Brett.

"Not eaten. Swallowed."

"Difference?"

"Digestion. The worm doesn't digest them; he holds them in his stomach. Like he's carrying them."

"All right," says Brett after a pause, "I buy it. So what happens once they get swallowed?"

Alex is happy that Brett has liked everything he's added to the story so far. He was worried Brett would be upset that the shape-shifting girl decided to go home, but he seems okay with it. This next part is riskier, though.

"I thought they could live there for a while," says Alex. "Inside the metal worm. There's light in there, because the worm runs on electricity, and there's food, because of all the other stuff the worm has swallowed." Alex has thought this part out extensively; he has calculated that the boy and the robot could live happily and comfortably there for a year, at least. "They could live there and be friends," he says.

"Doesn't make for a very exciting story," says Brett. It is exactly what Alex knew he was going to say, but it still makes him angry. He wants to throw his chopsticks on the ground, but he doesn't. He holds them tightly, so tightly they're about to break.

"Why does the story have to be exciting?" he says, a little louder and higher-pitched than he wanted to. "Why do things have to happen? Why can't this story be 'They were friends and they had some sandwiches and nothing else happened?'"

By the end he is yelling, which he was trying not to do. His breath is coming in quick, hitching gasps, and his eyes are burning, which is not cool. Which sucks.

"Then it wouldn't be a story," says Brett.

"Maybe I don't want it to be a story anymore," Alex says. "Maybe I want it to stop right here." He crosses his arms with a huff.

Brett puts his hand on Alex's knee, then scoots around to sit next to him on the floor. Alex thinks that this is the first time they've touched in any way other than shaking hands. Alex leans into him and puts his head on Brett's chest, and now the thing he can't stop is that he's crying. It starts out as tears, and he thinks maybe it's okay and Brett won't see it, even if he can feel that now his shirt is all wet, but once Alex is aware there are tears, he starts sobbing, he can't stop. He doesn't want Brett to see him like this, because he doesn't want Brett to think he's a baby—no one wants to be on a co-mission with a baby. He wants to be brave and adult, but he lets Brett hold him as he cries and he thinks, *I made it this far,* which is a brave thought, even if it feels very small.

"It doesn't work like that," says Brett. "Everything changes, all the time. Even if you tried not to change, things would change around you till you'd have to. It's like you're a story, not a picture."

Alex knows this, and he knows about sharks and how they have to keep swimming or they'll die, and how you can't stop moving ever because the earth is moving you through space at ridiculous speeds, speeds that, when you think about the fact you're moving that fast, you feel like a superhero. He knows you can't stop, you never get to stop.

"Every time things change, they get worse," he says.

He can feel that Brett is nodding. "Seems like that sometimes," says Brett. "But I think that's only when you let changes happen and you don't change anything yourself. When you make the changes yourself, maybe things get better."

"Is that what you do?" asks Alex.

"Me?" says Brett, laughing a little. "No, but maybe I should start."

Alex sniffs, a big sniff that pulls the crying part of himself back inside the rest of him and puts it aside. He thinks about scooting away, but he feels good right here, resting on Brett. "Do you ever miss your mom?" he asks.

"She's going to be back in a little bit," says Brett, who must have thought Alex was asking about his own mom and not about Brett's.

"No, *you*," says Alex. "Do you miss your mom?"

"Sometimes, sure."

"When's the last time you saw her?"

"Huh," says Brett. "I usually see her at Christmas. But we came out here to see Debra's parents last year. It's weird when you get older. A lot of times you're supposed to be in two places at once. That was the first year since my dad left that I didn't go home for Christmas."

"Your dad left?"

Brett nods. "When I was a little older than you."

"How come?"

Brett takes a second to think about this. "I don't know," he says. "All he ever told me was 'It's not about you,' which as a kid isn't enough of an answer. Isn't now, really." He stabs a dumpling with the end of his chopstick and eats it.

"Do you ever see him?"

"Yeah," says Brett. "He lives in New York now. Sometimes he calls me up to go have a beer. Sometimes I go."

"Are you like friends?"

"I wouldn't say that," says Brett. "I mean, he's my dad. That doesn't change. Even if you want it to." He looks down at Alex. "My dad's the one that got me into comics. He used to come home from work with them and we'd read them together."

"I have a friend in New York who sometimes reads comics with me," says Alex.

"When I got a little older, he'd take me to the comic book store with him. Every Wednesday when the new comics came out. Even though he had to drive past it on the way back from work, he'd come home, pick me up, and we'd go together."

"What did you do after he left?"

"My mom offered to start taking me, but it didn't feel right. So I would ride down there on my bike after school. It was as far as I was allowed to ride by myself. I think my mom only let me do it so I could keep some kind of routine. It was a way to know time was passing."

Alex thinks about the ways he measures time. He thinks about his watch, which just goes around and around. How do you know time's moving forward? There are pencil marks on the doorjamb in their apartment to keep track of his height, and that's a way to know. But what happens when you stop growing?

"Do you ever call your dad up to go have a beer?" he asks.

"Never have," says Brett. He sounds kind of proud about it.

"So do you see him more than your mom?"

"No," says Brett. "By 'Sometimes he calls me up' I mean like once a year."

"And how long since you saw your mom?"

"I guess it's been a year and a half."

Alex thinks about how long a year and a half is. It would contain two of at least one thing that happens once a year. A year and a half could include two birthdays, or two summers, or two Christmases. "That's a long time with no mom," he says.

"I guess it is," says Brett.

Alex struggles with this state of momlessness, how someone can have a mom who is not there. The primary and undeniable fact of his mother has always been her nearness, her presence. Will she still be his mom if she isn't there to cuddle him, or even to sit next to him on the couch?

"Does your mom know where you are?" he asks. "That you're in California?"

"No," says Brett. "I didn't tell her about this trip."

Alex sits with this thought a minute, that not only would he and his own mother not be together, but they might not even know where the other one was. Any time they spent apart was always defined by place and duration. *I'm going to the store, I'll be back in twenty minutes. I'm going downstairs for a drink, I'll be back in an hour.* It seems impossible to think that soon he will not know where she is all the time, and she won't know where he is, either. His position in space has always been in relation to hers and now, without that, he wonders if he'll be like a boat on the whole ocean, where you can't see land in any direction, and the sun cycles over you day after day.

# No More Stories

The drinks have made everything bright and disconnected. She drives the rental back to the hotel, and L.A.'s legendary traffic is hundreds of pairs of suns burning out of the darkness at her, leaving trails on her retinas. In the lobby, the elevator, the hallway, she is still watching headlights come at her again and again.

She offers to pay Brett, but he declines. He's a good kid. She lets herself hope that he will stay here, that it is love between him and the girl—which one was it? Maybe he will stay here and Alex will have at least one friend, one known quantity in a strange city.

Val thinks about how badly she has squandered her last couple of days with Alex. From the moment they left her mother's, depression has been on her like a thick black cloud. All she can think of is the ending, and it's causing her to lose this time with him, making her unable to pull herself from the deep well that has opened in her chest.

She is sad and relieved that he doesn't ask for a story, because what story could she tell him now? What's the story that comes after the end? In the only way she could, she's told him everything. But now she thinks there must have been episodes she missed, plotlines she left out. All through this trip, she's been listening to the complaints of *Anomaly* fans that in the end it didn't hold together. It went on and on, wandered sometimes for a full season in a direction that didn't make sense. It contradicted itself at times; it changed its past to fit with its present, and when it was finished, there was no resolution. No closure. But why should they expect something of television that life wasn't going to provide? What entitled anyone to reso-lution, and who ever promised closure?

Once in an interview, a fan asked Tim to tell him the answers, and Tim looked at him and said, "You don't want the answers. The answers are 'All of time is a mess, and we plod through our little section of it.' Answers are like orgasms and picnics: they're never as fulfilling as you hope they'll be." She wants more questions between her and Alex, more mysteries for them to solve together, instead of answers that don't amount to anything, or make sense in light of what's come before.

He gets into his pajamas without being asked, performing that incred-ible reversion to a younger self by putting on things that are fuzzy, soft, and overlarge. She asks him if he's ready for sleep and he nods, so they curl up together under the blankets of one of the hotel beds. She hopes he doesn't notice she is holding him too tight, her arms locked around his little body like it might repel itself from her, like a magnet whose poles switch.

In the dark, they are not sleeping. Alex shifts against her and, think-ing he might be wriggling free, she pulls him in tighter, closer.

"Mom?" he says. A sound of upward-swooping birds, a sound headed skyward.

"Yes, Rabbit?"

"You don't have to be upset," he says. "You don't have to be sad."

As he says this, Valerie knows it was never Alex she was protecting from this moment. He is so much stronger than she is. She can remember every fall he ever took and how each time her heart leaped into her throat, and how each time he popped back up and continued on his way as if noth-ing had happened. She wasn't protecting him; she was protecting herself.

"Rabbit," she says, "I have something I need to tell you."

"It's okay," says Alex. "I already know. I figured it out a while ago. I wanted to tell you before, but I didn't know how."

These are the exact words she was going to use. Because the moment to tell him has always been *before*. The right moment is always already past; it is happening right now somewhere else in the geometrical super-solid of timespace. She can point to it from where she is. She can see it flying by her like the headlights of passing cars.

"Everything's going to be okay," he says.

"It is," she says, not believing it. "It's not forever."

"How long for?" he says.

"Two years," she says. "You're going to live with your dad for two years."

"Where will you be?"

She realizes here is her biggest mistake in all this. She's had time; she could have made plans. She spent so much time and energy flailing against what was happening, she never made any proper preparations for when it happened. She wanted so badly to stop it, she never formed a backup plan for if she failed. Which she has.

"I'm not sure yet," she says. "I have to go back to New York, at least for a while."

"Then you'll come back?"

"I'll try," she says. His breath is rapid, as if he might start to cry. If he does, she will take him and run again. They will disappear forever, better this time. They will change their names and not hide in the open like idiot rabbits waiting to be snatched up by something predatory. She'll do it right this time.

"I don't think I like it here," he says. "I want to go back to New York."

"You can't," she says.

"Why not?"

"Because I made a mistake, a long time ago," she says. "I did the wrong thing, and now we have to make it right." She doesn't believe this, even as she says it. The blame is on her, yes, but there's no way of correcting, or if there is a way, this isn't it.

"So if I stay here," says Alex, "that fixes it?"

"It starts to," she says.

He breathes in deep, then exhales. "Okay," he says. "Everything is going to be all right."

He says this with such confidence, and she wants so badly for it to be the truth, that she lets herself believe it. Not just for a moment, but from now on. Because nothing she believes will change anything about the ending, but believing everything will be okay could change how some of the last pages go. So she believes him, lets herself, chooses to.

And a minute later, he is sound asleep.

# Secret Origin of the Astounding Family

*Upon consideration, caring may be the thing the equation cannot accommodate. You sit in what your son refers to as Dad's Wondering Chair and allow your mind to examine, again, the Moment. The cone that winnows all of your possible pasts into that moment, excluding any pasts that don't bring the four of you into that particular jungle on that particular day, that don't lead to you discovering the artifacts that gifted or cursed each of you with astonishing powers. The limits of your causal pasts constricting finally to a point and then exploding outward to include all of your possible futures, an ever-widening array of them. Your daughter, eleven, flits into the living room, the delicate insectile wings on her back flapping too quickly to be seen. She hovers above the coffee table, drops down to select an issue of* People, *brushing aside the issues of* National Geographic *and* Discover *you piled on top of it, and whisks back out of the room. On the floor near the couch, your son, four, makes shapes, tiny homunculi, out of nothing at all, shaping the building blocks of matter into playthings and setting them into herky-jerky motion on the hardwood.*

*You can imagine alternate pasts in which you do not care, in which you are not so insistent that you all undertake these adventures together. You have told your wife you owe it to the children to let them experience everything possible. There is so much that is possible. But it's not the real reason. It's that nothing feels real to you without them there. No experience truly happens until you can see it on their faces. Your caring for them is a desperate, hungry thing, a need bigger than the need to go, to see. And it's that caring that brought you all to the moment, to the incident. If not for your need, your daughter might have gone on to college, happily anonymous, joyfully normal. Your son, whose abilities may have no upper limit, who may know no boundary between desire and reality, could have played T-ball and not been any good at it. Could have learned that he loved to draw and become an artist, the kind who draws greeting cards or illustrates comic books. Your wife could be up for tenure instead of prepping for another talk show appearance that will dwell on the domestic advantages of her extendable, almost fluid limbs.*

*The only one worse off would be you. You would be commonplace and dull, the same normalcy you wish for them weighing on you like a curse. Some days you might look at your children and your wife, and wonder if they were the reason you were so ordinary. If they might have held you back from something better.*

*And then you feel a tug at the cuff of your pant leg. Your son holds up for display a tiny, misshapen man, body like a pear, its arms stretched upward to be lifted. Its little black eyes blink at you, and your son beams proudly at what he's made. In an upper corner of the room, your daughter has abandoned her celebrity magazine for a science journal whose articles are over even your head. The sun falls in through the window and lights up iridescent veins in her wings. And from the next room, your wife calls out. "Honey, there's an article here about a temple in the Urals—you've got to see it." Her arm snakes down the hall with impossible grace and places the article in your lap. There's a photo, taken from the base of a mountain with a telephoto lens. High up the mountain, there's the barest speck, a black dot on a white field, hardly discernible as a man-made structure. The article describes the attempt to reach it, the unscalable mountain, the treachery of the climb. Impossible, the article concludes. But someone must have reached it. Someone built this impossible temple in its impossible location. And now it sits there, unreachable, unreached, unexplored.*

*"Kids," you say, rising from your Wondering Chair, folding the article and tucking it under your arm, "go pack some winter gear."*

# Fan Fiction

If she doesn't move, the day won't have to start. If she can only manage to stay still, the time on the clock will never change, the light will never ladder its way across the floor, and they can stay held in the amber of this moment forever. But then Alex stirs, not waking but considering it as a possible option, and the moment is broken. Val kisses the top of his head, his hair matted with night sweat, the slight hircine stink of his oncoming adolescence lurking behind the boyish, milky smell of him. Sometimes Val would hold him in such a way that she could serendipitously smell the top of his head like this, an olfactory reminder of feeding him as a baby. But this barnyard scent says more about who Alex will be than who he's been.

Val extracts herself from him, removing her arm from under his head and lowering it back onto the pillow. He inhales deeply and, like a flower blossoming in reverse, draws every extremity in tight, condensing a tiny bud of self out of the sprawl he was a moment before.

She is hesitant to leave him alone, even for a second. The thought that he might wake up and find her gone is terrible. But the day is in motion now, and there's little point in fighting it. Val is caught in it like a shoelace in an escalator, drawn to the top, to the end, to the metal teeth that are static, sharp, and impossible to bargain with.

In the bathroom, she strips down and examines herself in the wide mirror. The multiple lights above and around the sink dispel any true shadows but cast leering penumbrae across her like dark grins. She searches her body for one hard angle, something to hold on to among the curves, but today there are only slumps and slouches to her. In the shower, she finds that her skin is buzzing with a painful alertness, and her scalp protests every tug of hair. She turns up the water's heat so it might scald her, but it only hurts, only burns.

Wrapped in towels, she comes out of the bathroom to find Alex sitting up in bed, rubbing his sleep-puffed eyes with one hand and holding her phone to his ear with the other.

"That's great," he says. "That means we'll get to see you soon." Her gut clenches, reminding her how long it's been since she's eaten anything, and she watches Alex's face, his genuine brightness, as he hangs up the phone.

"Who's that, Rabbit?" she asks, sure she already knows.

"Louis," he says, and the thing in her gut relaxes, only to re-exert its pressure higher, at the base of her throat. "He and the Idea Man will be here this afternoon. They'll meet us at the convention."

Val grabs the phone from him too quickly, too violently. He looks at her, afraid he's done something wrong. She navigates the screens, about to call Louis and tell him, "No, turn back, go back to New York and wait for me there on the other side," but then all the energy goes out of her arm. There's no point. No way to stop them when they've come this far. She puts the phone on the nightstand.

"That's great, Rabbit," she says, aware of how unconvincing she must sound. With both her hands, she tries to fix his hair, patting down cowlicks and attempting to unearth the part somewhere under this mess of dark wire.

"How'd you sleep?" she asks.

"Good," he says. "This is a better bed than the one in Chicago. Squishier. How about you?"

"Good," she says, surprised to realize it's true. She'd been determined to stay awake, to catalog every breath and twitch, but sleep took her minutes after it had claimed him.

"You should take a bath," she says, then wonders why. There is the curious question of what condition he should be in when she hands him over to Andrew. It won't prove anything if Alex is presented clean and pressed, and there is a part of her that wants to send Alex to his father with a trace of her presence still on his skin. But he's quick to comply, and before she can rescind the suggestion, the bathroom door is closed, the water running. After a few minutes, she knocks lightly on the bathroom door.

"Rabbit, can I come in?"

"Sure," he says. He has found the complimentary bubble bath, and his body now rests under an iridescent white moonscape. Alex lifts a mountain of it in his cupped hands and blows it away like dandelion seed. Islands of it cling to his shoulders and dot his hair.

"Maybe I should have brought more stuff," he says, concentrating on shaping the bubbles, building towers out of them, then swatting them away.

"Was there something you wanted?" she asks. She almost adds "from home" but stops herself. He considers her question, making the face like a cartoon of someone thinking: brow furrowed, lips screwed into a knot.

"No," he says. "It feels like more stuff would be good. If you're going someplace you don't know. To take stuff with you." He drops a handful of bubbles that fall slowly to the surface and join seamlessly with the others, as if they'd never been divided.

"I'm going under," he says. "Help me rinse after?" And without waiting, he slides down the length of the tub until his head is submerged, his face dipping below the sea of bubbles and disappearing beneath them, floating under their translucent screen but fractured, as if she's seeing him through the kaleidoscopic eye of an insect: his face pixels and facets that are not him but suggest him, as something not whole but of parts, moments, images.

When he is done, they take the elevator downstairs and walk the two blocks to the convention center. With each step, she becomes a little less herself, a little more her character. It's such a gift to have a mask you can hide behind. A skin you can slip into when your own feels threadbare and abraded. As she takes her seat in the booth, she is Bethany Frazer, because Bethany Frazer is the only person she can manage to be right now.

The skin fits poorly and is stiff from disuse. When fans begin to approach, she discovers an old fear. Reflexively, she shies away from them all. She scans the room for danger, for a potential shooter. As if it had been Frazer who was shot at and not Val. Or maybe it's Val's fear and Frazer's vigilance working together. A team up. The thought came to her once: Frazer would have stopped the shooter. It was alien and nonsensical and true. But there are limits to how we can invoke our fictions to protect us, she thinks, even as she sits behind the gauzy scrim of a woman she once helped invent.

She listens to herself greet them, cheery and warm. Her answers to questions about the show are clever and confident. She thinks how easy it would be, from now on, to simply pilot Frazer around, drive her through days like a vehicle that passes less through space than through time. Days are things to be gotten through, traversed. She could sit silently in this corner of herself, pulling levers and flipping switches as Frazer hurtles through time at sixty minutes per hour.

*And thank you, it did change the medium, and yes, they were more like family than co-workers, and no, she didn't think it was a paradox per se, Tim was always good at avoiding those types of things, and it's so hard to pick a favorite, and of course she didn't set out to be a role model for girls, but still that's very nice, very flattering, to meet you, I'd be happy to, that camera there, and how do you spell her name, but no, no she can't imagine there's much chance after all these years and all this time.*

She feels a pressure on her arm that can only be Alex's hand. She's kept the exact measure of its balancing weight against her, constant even as he's grown. How can he be a constant and always in flux? Her little paradox.

He's standing next to her with his book tucked under one arm, his whole body tilted away from her by the weight of his backpack. "I wanted to stay with you for a while," he says. "If I won't be in the way."

She feels her skin tear and rend, the weave of it too weak to hold together through this. And they'll all see. They'll see there's nothing underneath. Like pulling a sheet away from a Halloween ghost to find there's no trick-or-treater, just the air and an empty piece of cloth. She stares at Alex, unsure how to answer.

"Look," says one of the fans from back a bit in the line. "It's Owen. It's Owen all grown up." There are murmurs of agreement, because this is something all of them wanted, all of them needed to know. What happened to Owen? What happened to Frazer and Campbell's child?

Yes, she thinks. He's Owen. Frazer's child. It's a way to keep her skin intact. There are enough stories, enough fictions to get them both through today.

"Yes," she says, quiet, absent, looking at Alex but seeing Owen, who was never Alex but sometimes a crew member's baby and sometimes a doll and sometimes just a weight, something for her body to adjust to.

"Mom," says Alex. He squeezes her arm and the sheet comes off the ghost, the skin splits, but it is a deft motion, like yanking a tablecloth out without tipping a wineglass or candlestick.

She pulls Alex up onto her lap, the weight of him returning weight to her until she is again a thing of mass and substance in the world. She smiles hard and bites his ear lightly, and as each fan approaches, she introduces him again and again saying, "This is my son, Alex. This is my son."

# The Idea Man Cometh

He enters the convention hall as if everyone's been waiting for him to appear, but it's just Alex and his mom, standing in the lobby to greet the Idea Man when he arrives. Still, it's a good entrance, because the lobby is all windows and they're all facing east, so it's like the Idea Man has stepped out of the sun and into the Los Angeles Convention Center. Alex is happy to see him but can't help wishing he'd come at some other time. Alex expects he'll be starving for visitors eventually, in bad need of friendly faces. But today he isn't sure he has enough of himself to share with anyone but his mom.

"There's something about the Los Angeles air that I missed," the Idea Man says. "It's the stink of machines. New York smells like ten million people, but L.A. smells like ten million cars. It's dizzying."

"That's the lack of oxygen to the brain," Louis says.

Alex tries to assess which incarnation of the Idea Man this is, and he's pretty sure it's the one who's like a ringmaster at the circus. This is his favorite version of the Idea Man, although Alex suspects it's also the one furthest from whoever the Idea Man really is. This version has no sadness in it; it's all grins and babbling. It's a performance, for sure, but it's a fun one.

"Val," he says, "how are you?"

"I'm good, Tim," she says, and Alex is reminded that his mother is a performer, too, a professional one. If her acting isn't as over the top as the Idea Man's, it's as convincing in its quiet way.

"Why are we standing in the lobby?" he asks Louis. "All lobbies are essentially the same room. Alex," he says, "I want to go among the mad people. Alice had it all wrong."

He puts out his hand to be led, and Alex takes it. The Idea Man, as a joke, resists, making Alex pull him along, through the gaping entranceway and onto the convention floor. But Alex can still hear his mom talking to Louis behind them.

"I can't do this today," she says. "I can't take care of him. I took the afternoon off from signing so I could spend a last couple hours."

"I know, Val," says Louis. "He knows, too. Honestly, I think he wanted to see Alex one last time."

"Dear God, this place is a nightmare," the Idea Man says, grinning. "The problem is too much and not enough all at once. It's making me wish my eardrums would pop. Can we get it a little louder in here?" he yells to no one in particular.

"He's been like this since we got off the plane," Louis informs Alex.

"Don't file your little reports on me, Lawrence. You're not my nurse; you're my amanuensis. You should be writing down everything I say." Louis pulls out a notebook and stands poised.

"Hi, Tim," says Val, who is behind him by this point.

"Just a second, Val dear, I'm establishing setting." He walks into the room, leaving Val, Louis, and Alex with no choice but to follow. "Look at all this. It's fantastic. A hundred thousand worlds. What I love most, because I'm a hideous narcissist, is knowing many of these worlds are mine. You know what all of this is, don't you? This is the immune system of the human soul. Superheroes, space rangers, time cowboys, they are the T cells of the spirit. They were always here to save us. We made them to save us."

He stops abruptly. "Lazarus, I need coffee," he says.

"I'm not sure that's a great idea."

"It's my idea, and is, therefore, a great idea. Take Valerie with you. Alex and I need to talk."

Alex's mom looks stricken, and Alex doesn't want to part from her, even for a second. But Alex knows from experience that when he's like this, the

Idea Man is a force of nature, and it'd be as easy arguing with a tornado as trying to convince him how important it is that they stay together.

"Come on, Louis," says Val. "Let's be quick about it." The two of them walk away without looking back.

"So what do you think of California so far?" says the Idea Man after they've gone.

"I don't think I like it," says Alex, knowing he hasn't seen enough to judge.

"Give it time," says the Idea Man. "When are you going to your dad's?"

"Tonight," says Alex, looking at his shoes. "Someone's picking me up at six."

"An hour of last things, then," the Idea Man says. "The first thing you need to do is have your dad take you to the ocean. No one can love California until they've seen the ocean." Alex remembers, sort of, something the Idea Man said about the mermaids singing. He thinks it will be good for their first day if he and his dad have something they can talk about, and something they can look at together.

"What can you tell me," the Idea Man asks, "about the boy and the robot?"

"I've got lots to tell you," says Alex. "But it doesn't have an ending yet."

"That's fine. Some of my favorite stories don't have endings."

"How do you know if the story's supposed to have an ending?"

"You ask the story. The story is working with you to figure itself out, to answer its own questions. If it has an ending, it'll let you know."

The question Alex wanted to ask was: What happens if the ending isn't the one you want? What he wants is to be able to step in, before the ending happens, and change it, although he knows the Idea Man would probably say that's cheating and makes for a bad story. But he'd mean for the readers. And Alex knows it's important to give the readers a good story. But what he's wondering is if it's important to make the characters happy, too, if there's something they're owed for coming this far, and for trying so hard. And if both things are important, which is more important? And if he can't make both happy, whom should he choose?

# Walk of Fame

Alex scuttles on toes and fingertips, nimble and insectile. His tail-bone points skyward, his backpack adds to the spidery look of him as he scurries, star to star, between tourists and other passersby. Some stars he skips and others he stops at; there is no indication why some warrant attention. The pauses are the only thing allowing Val to keep up.

"Ee-taf el-Kubra," he says to one star.

"Dub toe-bah."

"Iz-ed zan-rah."

Then off to another, nearly toppling midwesterners as he goes. Under normal circumstances, Val wouldn't allow him to crawl on the ground like this, being convinced that "when we are in public we walk on our feet" is a solid parental baseline for behavior, even if Alex doesn't always see it that way. But she's not going to spend their last few hours chastising him, and she has to admit that, for what he's trying to do, this down-facing, water-strider method is better suited than the chin-to-chest, eyes-to-pavement posture of everyone else on the sidewalk, who constantly bump into one another and mutter apologies.

"Mom," he says, his head swiveled back toward her, "who's Marlene Die-trick?"

"She was an actress in the fifties," she says. "She was very pretty."

"Oh," he says and scampers to another star.

"Mom," he says, "who's Nat King Cole?"

"He was a singer," she says. "Your babu loves him."

"Was he a king?"

"No, that's just what people called him."

"Oh."

At the corner of La Brea and Hollywood, Val feels they're coming up on an event horizon, a last moment when their destination can still be changed—the nature of this outing, these last hours together, altered or salvaged. It's two hours still before the car Andrew's sending—and how like Andrew is it to send a car rather than show up himself—will pull up in front of the convention center to snatch Alex away. They could catch a cab down to the Tar Pits; Alex would love it, and the model elephant, half-submerged in the muck, trumpeting her plight to her family on the shore, would serve as a good parting image. She could remember their splitting like a sinking into blackness, tusks and trunk flailing ineffectively upward even as the bulk of the body is pulled down against its own striving—indeed, because of it. As she thinks this, she understands they are not approaching an event horizon but past it, falling toward their destination, pulled inescapably down.

"Take a right up here, Rabbit," she calls. It's only a couple of steps before she rounds the corner herself and Alex is in sight again. So is the theater, casting its shadow across the boulevard like a fork. Seeing it now, Val is sure she's doing the right thing, or at least the wrong thing for the right reasons. She's thought of what happened here as part of her story, the Story of Val and Andrew, which ended years ago. But it's Alex's story, too. His life was changed here as much as hers, and he deserves to know. More now and here than ever before, Val needs to explain herself to Alex, to be understood by him. He has an understanding of her, but she needs him to have *this* one, the one that grows out of this place and what happened. She wants to apologize to him for what she did and the way his life had to change as a result.

Then there's the other part, the part that's easier to explain to herself but harder to admit. She wants to warn him, to ready him to protect himself. She needs to tell him that Andrew never gave a fuck about anyone but himself, and people have been hurt as a result. People have died, right here.

She needs to know that Alex will be constantly on his guard, will see Andrew as a potential threat, or at least a vector by which harm might come. She needs him to know what happened here so she can feel he's safe.

"Mom, it's a pagoda," he says, pointing at the theater. "It even has dragons." Before she can comment, he's discovered the footprints and handprints in the concrete and is busy comparing the size of his own hands to those of the celebrities commemorated here on the forecourt.

"Rabbit," she calls, "can you come sit with me a minute?" He bounds over to a bench and climbs into her lap. She thinks of the way zoo animals raised by humans sometimes fail to realize they're full-grown and accidentally injure their trainers by applying their adult strength to childlike gestures. What gestures will be unavailable to them in two years, and in what ways will she no longer be able to hold him, even if he's willing?

"I wanted to talk to you about your dad," she says, and she feels his body tense. There is a part of Alex they've never spoken about that wants a father, even if it's an absent one. That part may even *need* a father so that Alex can understand himself and how he fits into the world. Without Andrew there, Alex has constructed him, insubstantial but in a basic way good, a goodness born out of Alex's sense of himself as good. If told about the things Andrew has done, there's a risk Alex will do exactly what Val did years ago and take that badness into himself, constructing culpability out of connection. What does it say about her that she was married to a man like that? Val has spent years wondering this. For Alex, it's the reverse: What does it say about Alex that Andrew, this new, terrible Andrew that Val is about to give him, is part of him?

Here, where her past brushes closest to her present, where there will always be shots firing and Tim screaming and Rachel bleeding out in Val's arms, it should be easiest to slip the poison in. But even here, she can't do it.

"Your dad," she says. "Sometimes he has trouble thinking about other people. Because he was alone for so long and only had to take care of himself. I think, Rabbit, you're going to need to take care of yourself more than you're used to."

She wonders how poorly she's prepared him for this, how taking care of him as best she could might in the end have done him harm.

Without looking up at her, he says, "It's all right, Mom. I can do anything if I have to. Even if I haven't before, I still can."

"I know you can, Rabbit," she says.

"I can take care of myself. And you. And maybe even my dad, if he lets me. I don't know how yet, but I know I can do it."

As was the case last night, his sureness and her desire to believe him, her wanting him to be right, come together, and everything will be all right, if only because the alternative is too terrible to contemplate.

"We should go back," he says. "It's almost time." He stands up and takes her hand and leads her, because he's the stronger of the two of them now, if he hasn't been all along.

# Home, Away from Home

It's a half-hour drive to Hollywood Hills, which really are hills. You can look back and see the city below you, guarded by power lines. They turn into a neighborhood of big houses, one of which must be his dad's. As the car approaches the house, Alex is worried there's been a crime. Trucks and vans clog the narrow street, and on the vast lawn, people bustle back and forth. A woman, sharply dressed and tiny, not any taller than Alex, is coming toward the limo, attempting to wave them off. She comes up to the driver's window, her face level with it, and he rolls it down.

"You can't get through here," she says, louder than she needs to. Alex is impressed someone so small can be that loud. He doesn't think he could do it, although he's never tried. "All the development residents were told we would be shooting tonight. All the waivers have been signed." She clicks both of these off on her fingers, which are also small. "Who's back there?" she asks, trying to stick her head in the window. "What's their name?"

"His name is Alex," says the driver. "He's here to see Mr. Rhodes." Even though they've hardly spoken, Alex has decided there's something protective about the driver. Maybe it's his size that leads Alex to believe he'd be a good protector, if one was needed.

"Oh my God, it's Andy's kid," she says, mostly to herself. "Well, let him out," she tells the driver, a little snappish. "I'll take him from here." The driver puts the car in park, then gets out and opens Alex's door for him. Pulling his backpack onto his shoulder, Alex climbs out of the car.

"Thanks for the ride," Alex says.

"You going to be okay?" says the driver. Alex isn't sure if it's a question or a statement. So he shrugs.

"Where are his things?" the little woman asks the driver. "Are his bags in the back?"

"I've just got my backpack," says Alex.

"But where are your *things*?" she asks him, turning the same intensity she focused on the driver toward Alex. He knew he should have brought more stuff.

"My things are at home," he says quietly. The driver is looking at her as if to say, *Hey, lady, lay off the kid*, which Alex appreciates, and the little woman, noticing the look, appears stricken. Much to Alex's surprise, she swoops him into a hug.

"Honey, I'm so sorry," she says. "These night shoots bring out the fascist in me." Alex doesn't know what the fashion in her has to do with anything, but he is pleasantly overwhelmed by the hug. He has been in need of one, without knowing it. She releases him and steps back, examining Alex for the first time. "My God, you look just like Andy," she says. Alex has never thought of himself as looking like anyone, even his mother, so this is a weird thing to hear. "Come on," the little woman says. "He's going to be so happy to see you."

She grabs Alex's hand and they head off toward the well-lit house. Alex looks back and sees the limo reversing, and it's worse than when the limo pulled away with him in it. That seemed like it could be undone, but this is final. Alex is here now, with no way to go back.

"Have I even introduced myself?" the woman says. "I'm Mandy. I work with your father. And I have heard an awful lot about you." Alex doesn't think there are even an awful lot of things to know about him, but he knows this is something adults sometimes say to people they don't know an awful lot about. "I'm sorry things are in such a state at the moment. Peter, our director, insisted he needed exterior night shots right away. Tonight. So of course everyone has to snap to."

"Is this my dad's house?" Alex asks. It's a big house, not so much tall as wide. There aren't houses like this in New York; there wouldn't be room. But still, it looks familiar.

"Oh, no, no," Mandy says. "It's Ted Kammen's house. Your dad's character on the show."

"I've seen the show," says Alex. Mandy looks horrified.

"Your mother let you watch the show?"

Alex nods. "To see my dad," he says.

"Well, that's . . . nice," says Mandy, although she clearly does not think it's nice at all. "This is the house we use for exteriors," she says. "The inside shots are all on a soundstage. I'm sure Andy will bring you by the set sometime soon."

Alex has the feeling he sometimes gets when they go to a museum and his mother insists they take the tour. Even when the tour guides are super nice and explain lots of things, there's a sense they're also keeping you from something, whether it's secret things in the museum regular people aren't allowed to see or the opportunity to run around the museum really fast.

"Where's my dad?" he asks.

"He's in the trailer getting made up," says Mandy, which Alex thinks is funny. Even now, when his dad's about to become real to him for the first time since Alex can remember, he's still going to be made up. "We probably shouldn't interrupt him. He's getting into character."

Alex wonders if he might be more comfortable meeting his dad in character than out. After all, he's known Ted Kammen for three seasons.

"Can I watch them shoot?" he asks.

Mandy squirms. "I don't think so," she says. "The scene they're shooting is a little grown up."

"Swearing grown up or sex grown up?"

"Sex grown up," says Mandy.

"Never mind, then," says Alex. "I'll wait." Mandy finds him a chair, although he's disappointed it's not one of those director chairs. Even though it's nighttime, there are big bright lights everywhere, so it's easy enough for Alex to read his book. He wonders if they could make it bright enough to shoot a daytime scene at night, and thinks how cool it would be if, instead of lights, there were darks you could turn on so you could shoot a nighttime scene during the day. Probably in Adam Anti's world, there are darks. Flashdarks and darkbulbs. One thing he likes about the Adam Anti books is the idea that there's a whole world, even if the writer doesn't tell you about all of it. You can think of other things, other stories that would happen in that world. Maybe when he's done with the story of the boy and the robot, he'll think of other stories in their world. He'll continue the stories of people they met, or invent stories of people they never met, who live in one of the cities and don't know anything about the boy or the robot but have their own place in the world, with houses and friends and maybe a cat or something. Regular lives but in this strange world.

He drifts off, thinking about this, but then someone is blocking the light in front of him. "Alex," says the shadow. The shadow squats down and it's his dad, who looks like on TV. Which is to say, he looks older than Alex thinks he should be, and in the dark his skin looks like cookie dough that's been smoothed out mostly but is still lumpy. Alex realizes he and his father have the same eyes. It's a weird thing to realize at first, like looking into a mirror and seeing someone who isn't you but has parts of your face. But it also makes him feel connected to something where there was no connection before.

"I'm so sorry I couldn't meet you as soon as you got here," his father says. He is squatting a few feet away from Alex, with his hands on his knees. Every now and then, one of his hands looks like it might reach out toward Alex, but then it goes back to gripping one of his knees. Alex feels like maybe he ought to stand, but he doesn't.

"It's okay," he says. "Mandy explained everything."

"I'm going to wash up real quick," his father says. "Then I was thinking we could grab a burger. Have you ever been to an In-N-Out Burger? Best burgers in the world."

"I like Shake Shack," Alex says, not to dismiss his father's claim about

In-N-Out Burger, but because those are the burgers he likes. It's not easy to find something you like, and when you find it, you should stick with it.

"I don't think we have those around here," his father says.

"There's lots of them," says Alex. "But the good one's the actual shack one in Madison Square Park."

"Well, you'll have to try In-N-Out before you judge."

"Okay," says Alex. Just because you already know what you like doesn't mean you shouldn't try new things, he supposes. But he's skeptical.

"So we'll get you fed," says his father, "then get you home. How's that sound, champ?"

Alex doesn't like being called *champ*, and imagines that over the next few days there will be more of these attempts to fix a nickname on him. He anticipates *pal, tiger,* and maybe even worse things, like *scooter* or *skipper*. He thinks about telling his dad his nickname is Rabbit, but he doesn't want anyone else calling him that, ever. Even if it means no one ever calls him Rabbit again. More important, Alex doesn't like referring to wherever they're going as *home*. But there's no reason to be difficult; it won't fix anything.

"Fine," says Alex.

# Funeral for a Friend

If the bar seems a bit generic when Gail first arrives, it feels much less so once dozens of comics professionals are filling the booths, buying rounds, slapping shoulders, and sketching on napkins, trading the results like baseball cards. Zero to geek bar in ten minutes. But all of it is subdued, the joviality not forced but held in check. No one's called it a wake, but there's no question it is.

Gail, whose social batteries are run down, buys a pitcher with three glasses and sits at a bistro table in the corner, counting on an easy gravity to draw Ed and Geoff over eventually. She didn't run into them at the convention, having spent most of her afternoon walking around with the moderator of the "Distaff Goes the Distance" panel, a woman with a pink-dyed crew cut and piercings who had no right to be straight but probably was. Gail is holding out hope she'll show up here later, although she didn't have the nerve to invite her. There may have been flirting involved. That's the quantum quality of flirting: its existence is provable only in hindsight.

She spots Ed, Geoff, and Fred at the far end of the bar. They're talking to Phil Weinrobe from Timely. Not just talking; in cahoots. There is very obvious cahooting going on here. Gail wishes she were the type of woman who would mutter something like "I'm going to get to the bottom of this," then stomp across the bar and do just that. But if she possesses such a Nancy Drew gene, it must be recessive or dormant. So she tries to read facts and details in their body language from across the bar. All she can determine is that they are definitely in cahoots.

Weinrobe concludes whatever discussion they're having and, drawing himself up to an impressive full height, calls, "Excuse me," in a voice that silences the bar. Gail thinks this silencing is sycophantic, since the careers of most of the people in the bar depend on or could be improved by Weinrobe. But even the booths of civilians quiet and turn, Weinrobe having one of those Moses-like voices.

"We've all suffered a great loss," he says. He speaks like he's the patriarch of the comic book industry, which Gail supposes he is. "No one has been more important to comic books than Levi Loeb. And I'm saying this knowing someone's going to pass it on to NerdFeast and I'm going to get an earful from my bosses tomorrow. Not to mention a certain nonagenarian gentleman who shall remain nameless." This gets a chuckle. "But it's past time someone at Timely said it, so I'm saying it. No one has been more important to comic books than Levi Loeb."

Some people in the crowd lift their glasses in a *hear, hear!* The Brewer-versus-Loeb debate has tended to draw a line between writers and artists, although a fair number of writers, Gail included, side with Loeb. Other people have whipped out their phones, no doubt sending this news tip to one of the blogs or fan sites.

"There was a plan," says Weinrobe, "to have Levi Loeb here in L.A. tomorrow for a big announcement. I bet none of you knew that. Hey, Hampton," he calls to someone down the bar, "we finally managed to keep something a secret." There's a roar of laughter from a knot of what Gail assumes to be marketing or publicity people, her assumption based on the fact that they're dressed like adults. "We're still going to make the announcement tomorrow. Levi Loeb won't be up there on the dais with me, like I always imagined he would. And Hampton and his hacks will have a speech prepared for me that bobs and weaves through a lot of legalese. But, Ham, you're going to cringe now. Spoilers on."

The number of smartphones visible doubles.

"I'm telling you this because it's about the history of what we do. The people who'll be there tomorrow, they're fans. And you know I love the fans. But you all are the makers. You guys. If I was a smarter guy, I'd remember that speech from *Henry V.* The Saint Swithin's Day speech or what you call it. I could rightfully say those things to you. Because I feel that we in this room, here, are a band of brothers."

"And sisters!" Gail yells before she knows she's going to do it. If everyone isn't staring at her, it certainly feels as if they are.

Weinrobe purses his lips. "You know what," he says, "I'm gonna drink to that." He takes a swig of beer. "I always say everyone needs an editor." Gail sits up a little straighter in her chair, and across the room, she and Weinrobe exchange a look she can't interpret.

"Fifty years ago, this company made a mistake. It was the kind of mistake, born of carelessness, born of hubris, that plays a crucial role in the origin stories of so many of our characters. We betrayed, for the sake of money, for the sake of financial expediency, one of the fundamental builders of the Timely Universe.

"Life moved along, we made a lot of money off creations that relied, deep in their DNA, on the imagination of Levi Loeb. So much money, in fact, that when, twenty years later, Levi Loeb sued us for his rights, the money he deserved, it would have been impossible for us to pay him. The company would've been broke. And all our stories would have ended. The Timely Universe, destroyed by its creator. That's not a story Levi Loeb would have wanted us to tell.

"A lot of this has been kept secret. It's been speculated about. But I'm going to pull the curtain back and tell you what happened twenty years ago, when I took over at Timely. I was going over contracts and statements and records. And I was finding the same thing Levi Loeb's lawyers were finding. We were protected, on a lot of fronts. Not saying we were right, just that we were protected. But then there was the Astounding Family. They were the founding heroes of the Timely Comics universe. A brave family that burrowed into the center of the earth and were transformed into superpowered beings by the ancient gods they found there. Brewer and Loeb created these four characters for a company that was so on the ropes, they didn't have the manpower to draw up contracts. And it looked like, because things were done so quickly, with handshakes instead of lawyers, Levi Loeb might be able to destroy the entire Timely Universe. The same one he'd saved by creating the Astounding Family and a hundred other heroes in the first place."

This statement alone would have been newsworthy within certain communities. Timely has always made a point of referring to Levi Loeb only as an artist. He always "draws" characters. The word "create" is studiously avoided.

"So I made a decision. I went to his writers and said, 'I want you to kill off the Astounding Family.' The greatest heroes the Timely Universe has ever known, and they had to die. I tasked Porter Coleman, who was the best guy working at the time, to do it. If you ask me, it's Coleman's masterpiece. People don't think of him as a cosmic writer—they think of the Ferret. But 'Dream's End' is one of the most ambitious stories he ever wrote. The Astounding Family died saving the universe, of course. In more ways than they ever knew. With the Astounding Family off the table, the case between Loeb and Timely was resolved. Everything else was clearly contract work. But we could never publish a comic featuring the Astounding Family again."

This version of the story isn't new, but it's the first time anyone from Timely has ever admitted this is the way things went down. In the official version, Porter Coleman had come up with the story idea months before the Loeb case was decided, and Timely stopped using the characters because they were dated.

"In the years since, nothing has weighed heavier on me than the plight of the Loeb family. And the Astounding Family. It's been my dream to bring both families back into the Timely Universe.

"Two weeks ago, we announced we were restoring Levi Loeb's creator credits to every character he touched. What we didn't announce then, what we were saving till tomorrow, was that we'd reached a settlement on the rights to the Astounding Family. Rights which we signed over to be jointly held by Brewster Brewer and Levi Loeb, or their estates. And that Levi Loeb had agreed to license to Timely, at a pretty hefty fee, I tell you. The old man was a hell of a poker player at the bargaining table.

"It doesn't fix the mistakes we've made," Weinrobe says. "But it means Levi Loeb passed away knowing he had his rightful claim to his creations. And it means the Astounding Family will be returning to comics for the first time in twenty years."

Weinrobe turns and beckons Ed, Geoff, and Fred to come stand next to him, and Gail's whole body tenses. Her head begins to give a little side-to-side shake, involuntary.

"Right here are the three gentlemen who are going to do it. You all know Ed Rankman, because you're reading *Red Emma* every month, same as I am. Some of you might have heard of Geoff Sukowski, who works for our Noted Competition. *Worked* for, I should say. What is it you do over there, Geoff? Talking animal books?" Gail can see Geoff blushing. "But this kid here," says Weinrobe, pulling Fred forward, "maybe you don't know. He's been killing it on a little independent book called *Lady Stardust*. His name's Fred Marin, and he's about to step into some of the biggest shoes there are. Am I making you nervous, Fred?" Oddly, it doesn't seem he is. Fred seems more sure he deserves to be up there than either Geoff or Ed. He bows a little at the waist, not that anyone is applauding.

"I was thinking about this all day," says Weinrobe. "And I was thinking, for me, this is a perfect comic book story. Death's never forever in comics. I wish Levi Loeb was alive to see this day. But his ideas, his work, and his spirit live on. So let's raise our glasses." Pints and wineglasses and lowballs rise into the air. Gail notices hers is empty and hastily refills.

"To a man who was the first and the best. To Levi Loeb."

"To Levi Loeb," echoes the crowd.

Gail has finished the entire pitcher by herself while Weinrobe was speaking. She attributes her overall dazed feeling to that fact as Ed, Geoff, and Fred approach.

"So what do you think?" says Ed.

"I'm sorry we couldn't tell you sooner," says Geoff. "There were non-disclosure agreements."

"Oh," says Gail, "well, if there were non-disclosure agreements . . ." Geoff looks horrified, which makes Gail feel awful for having said it. "It's fantastic," she says, trying to will herself to feel it. "I'm so happy for you guys." Maybe she's sold it better than she thought, or maybe they particularly wanted to buy it, but any momentary guilt they might have felt about keeping all this a secret from her is gone.

"I'm buying drinks," says Ed, slapping Fred on the back.

"No, I've got them," says Gail, getting up on shaky legs. The backslapping around the room goes polyrhythmic and the fog of sorrow lifts, dispelled by the news that he is risen. When she reaches the bar, she looks back to see her table's gone crowded, her friends obscured by a rush of well-wishers, most of whom must feel, somewhere in their guts, the same ember of resentment that glows in hers.

# As I Woke Up One Morning

Alex wakes up alone in the big bed in the big house, and his first thought is to look for his mom. The awful, pit-of-his-stomach feeling that comes with this thought makes Alex resolve that he will not let that happen again, and because thinking might not be enough, he says it out loud.

"This will not happen again."

The words echo in the room, which is entirely bare. Alex has seen movies and television shows where the children of divorced parents arrive at the new home of whichever parent has been displaced and find waiting for them rooms fully furnished, decorated, and stocked with toys. Now, he knows his dad is not that kind of dad. There was talk the night before about shopping trips for furnishings, for clothes, for toys. The days to come, Alex has been assured, will be a spending spree. But he's glad his dad didn't try to choose things for him, extrapolating Alex's tastes from what he was like at three or choosing a collection of items deemed popular for boys like Alex.

Looking for both evidence and breakfast, Alex finds his way to the kitchen. It is, of course, bigger than their kitchen, with cupboards that stretch all the way to the high ceilings and leave much of their contents out of Alex's reach. Even the counters and stovetop are too high for him to make any practical use of unaided. He goes into the living room and finds an ottoman. It looks expensive—all the furniture looks expensive—and probably it shouldn't go in the kitchen in case something spills. But it is the right height for his needs, so he carries it into the kitchen and sets it in a corner for later.

He opens the fridge, noting right away that the milk and orange juice are on an upper shelf and will require the ottoman to be grabbed. But directly at eye level is the holy grail of breakfast foods: bacon.

Alex inspects the package. It is horrible bacon, if there can be such a thing. It is not organic and is almost definitely from a factory farm where the pigs have no room to move or play. His homeschooling group took a field trip to a small pig farm upstate, so Alex knows how much pigs love to play, and how when they have space they're not gross at all. Those pigs ended up bacon, but at least before that they were happy. This is not that kind of bacon. But as with the ottoman, there are compromises Alex needs to make, so he sets about finding a skillet.

The important thing, he remembers, is starting with a cold pan, so, pulling the ottoman over to the stove, he lays four strips out onto the skillet before turning on the burner. It's a gas stove, which he's seen only at the Idea Man's house, but he knows you turn it to the place where it makes the *click-click-click* and leave it there till the blue flame blooms.

After only a few minutes, the kitchen is filled with the smell of bacon, and over the sizzling Alex hears footsteps from upstairs. His mom always says bacon makes the best alarm clock, and at home the whole apartment would be suffused most Saturdays with its salty tang. Alex is surprised the smell can even reach his father's room, upstairs on the other side of the house. Powerful thing, bacon.

In stubble and paunch and a fluffy purple robe, his father stands in the kitchen doorway, rubbing sleep out of his face.

"You're cooking bacon?" he asks, which Alex thought was obvious.

"Uh-huh."

"You know how to do that?" This sounds like a question related to safety, but Alex chooses not to answer it that way.

"It's important to start with a cold skillet," he says. He wishes he'd asked his mom why this was important; it would be a good thing to know.

"Huh," says his father.

"This is horrible bacon," Alex says. "It has nitrates and is probably made from sad pigs."

His dad picks up the package from the counter. "They look pretty happy," he says, showing Alex the picture of a smattering of pink pigs in a vast green field.

"Those pigs aren't real," says Alex. "Real ones aren't pink."

"Good to know."

"Do you like yours crispy or soggy?"

"Crispy," his dad says, sitting down at the small kitchen table. "Almost burned."

"Me, too," says Alex. "Mom likes hers soggy, but she crispifies some for me." He flips the bacon with the spatula and watches with quiet horror as spittles of grease jump from the pan and hit the ottoman, spreading into dime-sized stains on the fabric. He wishes they'd landed on the tops of his bare feet instead. Not yet knowing the rules of this house, it seems as if burns on his feet are less likely to be noticed than stains on the furniture.

"So I was thinking," says his dad, "that maybe today we could go shopping. Get stuff for your room and all. There's a mall about a half hour away."

"Don't you have to go to the convention?" Alex asks. He needs to talk to Brett as soon as he can. A little part of Alex wants to explore the house further. He's only seen the downstairs and his room, and if the house were otherwise vacant, he could possibly collect more evidence.

"Not till the panel with your mom and me tomorrow," says his dad.

"I think we should go to the ocean," says Alex as he lifts charred pieces of bacon out of the bath of sizzling grease. "I feel like I've come all this way and I'm not done going west yet. I feel like I should go as far as I can."

# The Sellout

The official announcement is at the Timely panel in the morning, but everyone knows already. The big comics websites go into a twenty-four-hour news cycle around the conventions, and NerdFeast.com ran the story late last night. PanelAddict.com, always a little more respectful of information embargoes, held it until after it was announced officially, but the story was ready to drop as soon as Phil Weinrobe said the words "The Astounding Family is back at Timely" and the crowd in Hall H, who'd queued up overnight to hear it from Weinrobe's mouth, sleeping on the concrete like unwashed piles of superhero laundry, went nuts.

But Brett wasn't in Hall H, and he didn't read it online. His friends and colleagues, none of them could wait to tell him, the moment he got to Artist Alley this morning. They were buzzing to give him the bad news. It's a sign of where he is in the pecking order, high up enough that people place a value on ruining his day.

Fred approaches. Brett wonders whether his first words will be a shitty attempt to apologize or a shitty attempt to explain.

"I think that once I'm in," he says, "I can bring you in. Like, they let me in through the front door, then I come open up the back door for you."

Brett's never actually punched anyone, though he's sketched a hundred punches. He could consider it research.

"It developed organically," says Fred. Gestures toward the room where the panel was held. "I was out for a beer with them, and they were talking about this project. And Phil said it needed a man-on-the-street angle, so

I threw out some ideas and he liked them. He said, 'Why don't you write it for us?'"

An apology is not coming. Fred has already justified his actions to himself. The only option is to point out some of the flaws in Fred's story.

"The whole time you're out for beers with the publisher of Timely Comics," says Brett, "it didn't occur to you to call me?" Nitpicking about character motivation is pretty standard for comics fans. Most of them understand that smart characters sometimes have to make stupid decisions. For the sake of a good story. It's called *picking up the idiot ball*. But Fred hasn't made a mistake. The idiot ball is in Brett's hands. Fred's clearly given this betrayal a lot of thought. He answers without a pause.

"You know what, it didn't. After you blew off all of Chicago to stay in your room and fuck Ferret Lass? And after you've spent more time collaborating with some kid than with me on the book we're supposed to be finishing? And after you've been generally a whiny little asshole lately about who does the work and who gets the credit? No, I did not feel necessarily inclined to invite you along."

"Nor did you feel inclined to tell me about it all week."

"We were sworn to secrecy," says Fred.

"Did you pinkie-swear? Cross your heart and hope to die?"

"It's called a non-disclosure agreement, asshole," says Fred. "Look, this is a good thing for us."

"It's a good thing for you, Fred. Just you." Brett thinks this would be an excellent line to walk away on. He takes a step to go past Fred, but then stops. "What about the meeting with Black Sheep tomorrow? Are you even showing up?"

"About that," says Fred, looking at his shoes. "They want me at a story summit tomorrow. Me and Geoff and Ed and the whole editorial staff. They rented us a cabin in Big Sur where Kerouac used to go."

"You hate the Beats!" says Brett. This seems like a valid point of protest.

"It's not like we've got the pages," says Fred. "We were going in there to beg for another extension."

Brett is proud of himself that he saw this coming. He brought his portfolio with him. Silently, aware of every second of the pause he is creating, he reaches in and pulls out a stack of twelve pages. Pencils finished. Awaiting the letters. Waiting for the script. He hands them to Fred, who flips through them, frantic.

"When did you do this?" he says.

"Finished the other night," says Brett. "I've been cleaning them up."

"Why didn't you tell me?"

This is a good question. *It was going to be a surprise* would be a bad answer. But it's the true one. Sometime soon, later today probably. Brett was going to whip these out. He'd imagined them spending the evening working on the script. Beers in the hotel room. Bottle of whiskey for when it was done. All these plans made, and none of them shared. No one likes surprises, ultimately.

"It was going to be a surprise," Brett says.

Fred goes through the pages again. Slower now. "These are good. This is . . . I couldn't have come up with a better ending."

"You couldn't have come up with an ending," says Brett.

"Anyway," says Fred. He hands the pages back. "It's your story. Tell Black Sheep I'll give up my writer credit for the last issue." Brett is still glaring at him. "I'll give up my writer credit for the trade. Put your name all over it. It could be big for you."

It's funny how something Fred was once so upset about now matters so little to him. Maybe it's because the last week he's been so close to the work, so invested in the world of Lady Stardust, that Brett is hurt not that he's being stepped over, but rather that the work they've done together, the world they made together, is so easy for Fred to throw away.

"That's very big of you," says Brett.

"Stop sounding like I'm the asshole here. If you'd gotten an offer, you'd have taken it."

"Besides," says Fred, "this is me getting us a foot in the door. After this project, they'll want me on something else. And that's when I say, 'I want to work with Brett Kazan. We're a team.'"

Fred actually holds his hand out for Brett to shake it, and Brett stares at it and laughs. A better liar could have sold it, but Fred misses the mark entirely, and Brett decides that it's the perfect exit line.

# Talent/Agency

Val isn't sure when it happened that cookie-cutter copies of public places began to resonate with one another. Airports are, of course, the worst, forming as they do a massive rhizome that sprouts in the outskirts of various cities but is in fact one huge and singular being. Val hasn't traveled by plane since she first moved to Los Angeles. But for a long time, she's found she can't go into a chain restaurant without the feeling that she's present in all iterations of the restaurant, and that everything happening in each of them will become apparent to her all of a sudden, a palimpsest over the room she's physically in at that moment.

So when Elise wants to meet at a Starbucks, Val is worried. She is aware she's the millionth person to use the word *venti* that day. The cardboard cup, new, fresh, feels like it's been handled by every commuter from here to Portland, Maine, and when they sit down to talk, Val feels wired into a vast network of coffee shops, their conversation quietly broadcast to each of them.

"You," says Elise, "look like hell."

Elise, who is twenty years older than Val, could easily pass as Val's younger sister. She is vibrant and golden, where Val feels drained. She's drinking something that is not coffee, like green tea or maté or chai. Something that you drink when you're thinking short- and long-term at once. Val is drinking coffee, black, large.

"It's a rough day," says Val.

"Where is the boy?" asks Elise, looking around with the hungry eyes of an aging aunt. Elise's two daughters are close to Val's age, and when

Val was still in L.A., Elise took a grandmotherly liking to baby Alex. "I thought you were both coming out here."

"He's with his dad," says Val.

"Seriously?" Because the dissolution of Val's marriage was so closely tied to the collapse of Val's professional life in L.A., Elise was de facto involved in both. She retains a strong loathing for Andrew. "Something we should talk about?"

"No," says Val, "please."

Elise waits another beat in case Val wants to change her mind. "All right," she says. "To business?"

"Please," says Val.

Elise lays both hands on the table. "You need to come to a decision on *Perestroika* basically before you finish your coffee," she says. "And a decision on Royal Shakespeare before we walk out of here."

Val looks out the window, which is heavily tinted. "I'm not ready to decide on either of those," she says.

"Then you are going to lose both," says Elise. "And losing both will make it harder for me to find you something else after."

"What is there locally?" says Val, watching Elise's sepia-tone reflection to see how she reacts.

"Locally here?" she says.

"You knew I was coming," says Val. "Have you asked around?"

"I have," says Elise. Val is waiting for Elise to reach into her overlarge bag and pull out a stack of scripts. That's how Val pictured this going. But Elise doesn't move. "There aren't parts for you right now," she says. "There's one, which I imagine you've heard about."

"Assume I haven't," says Val.

"Tiger's Paw is considering an *Anomaly* movie," Elise says. "There's a draft of a script. It's a smart, low-budget sci-fi piece. And everyone's waiting on you."

"I don't want to do it," says Val.

"Then there's no work."

"Nothing?"

Elise fidgets. Val knows she should have warned Elise that this conversation was coming, but she didn't want to say it out loud, back in Cleveland. Now Elise is struggling for a way to tell Val something she should have already known, or at least suspected. "You know when I say 'people think,' that doesn't include me, right?"

Val closes her eyes. "What do people think?" she says.

"They think you kidnapped Andrew's kid and ran off," says Elise. "It wasn't a story in *Variety* or anything, but that's the widely held opinion."

"Why would anyone think that?" says Val.

"Andrew was here," Elise says, "and you weren't. He was moping around looking bereft. He got a lot of sympathy."

"I bet he did," says Val, but it's been too long, and she no longer has a mental list of the women who might have lined up to offer Andrew their sympathies. But aside from that, even in the face of all the evidence against him, it was difficult to hate Andrew when you were in a room with him. Had she stayed in L.A., seeing him every week to hand Alex back and forth, she would have forgiven him, too.

"I'm not suggesting he painted you in a poor light," says Elise. "But the story that went around was you ran off."

"So nobody wants me?" Val says.

"People are resistant." She begins fidgeting again, as if every step deeper into this conversation is causing her physical discomfort. "Honestly, I think the comeback part would put a lot of people at ease."

"I don't want to do it," Val says again.

"Then let me call up Grant right now and tell him you'll do *Perestroika*," says Elise, relieved. "Let me call up Royal Shakespeare and get you locked in as Gertrude." Val puts her hand over her eyes. She feels as if she's built a bridge, cobbled it together out of scrap wood, and on the other side of the bridge she and Alex are together and safe. And now she's watching the planks of it fall into the gap, one by one. "You're burned here," says Elise. "It's not fair, but you are."

"Why am I burned and he's working?" says Val, too loud. People's heads turn toward her for a second; then they continue with whatever they're doing.

Elise shrugs and sips whatever antioxidant-rich hot beverage she's drinking and gives Val a direct look.

"He stayed," she says.

# Bye, Coastal

The water pushes and pulls at his ankles, moving in and out as if the ocean were breathing. It is not warm or cold, and it seems to find places in between his toes and wake them up, little spots of skin he's never been aware of before now. It feels as if it's bubbling, like soda, but he can tell it's not. Around his feet it's clear, but when he looks out at it, the ocean is exactly the color an ocean ought to be, and it stretches out forever. His back to the shore, Alex stands at the edge of the world.

"So what do you think?" his dad shouts from behind him. For a second Alex forgot about him, and everyone on the beach. Even the gulls were inaudible under the crash of the waves. Now, reminded, he turns his head, but not enough that his dad is in view, just enough to be heard.

"It's pretty awesome," he says.

"Have you ever been in the ocean before?"

Alex turns back to it. "Not this one," he says. There have been trips to Jones Beach, to Rockaway Park. But the ocean there never seemed as vast as this one does. Alex always imagined that if you swam out from the Coney Island pier, you would loop back around to the city somehow, wash ashore in Red Hook or Battery Park. This ocean spreads off to nowhere, pours off the edge of the world.

"Do you want to swim in it?" his dad asks. He insisted they stop at a store near the boardwalk and buy Alex a swimsuit, which looks as if someone took a Hawaiian shirt and made it into shorts. Alex watches a wave crash, twenty feet out. In the moment before it crashes, it creates a tube Alex could easily walk through standing up.

"No," he says. "I'm okay."

His dad puts a hand on Alex's shoulder, still tentative. It's like they're negotiating between handshakes and hugs, and every touch is a question. "So now you've been in the ocean," his dad says. "You've come as far west as you can go." There's a question implied by the statements, a general *Now what?* that Alex doesn't have an answer to. He turns back toward the shore and reads a sign posted nearby.

"What's riptide?" he asks.

His dad follows his gaze, then says, "It's a kind of an undercurrent that can pull you out to sea."

"Oh," says Alex. He wishes he had a notebook to write it down in.

"My understanding is," says his dad, "it basically grabs you by the ankles and drags you out." He demonstrates with his hands, one of them sliding under the other and whooshing out and away.

"Sounds bad," says Alex.

"Yeah," says his dad. They both stare out at the ocean. Alex is glad they came here. The bigness of the ocean almost negates the need to talk about anything. You can look at it and think about it, and the other person can do the same.

"Are there sharks here?" Alex asks after a couple of minutes.

"No," his dad says. "No sharks."

"That's good," says Alex. He tries to think of other things to say about the ocean that aren't stupid or obvious, like *That's some big ocean there,* or *It's too bad we can't drink it,* because ocean water makes you get thirstier instead of less thirsty. Now that they've exhausted the ocean as a topic, there's not much else for them to talk about. Finally, quiet enough so his dad can pretend not to hear if he wants, Alex says, "You never called."

"What's that?" his dad says.

"You never called or wrote or anything," says Alex. It's not an accusation; it's only a fact. What he meant to do was ask why, but his dad answers the question, even though it wasn't asked.

"I figured your mom didn't want me to," says his dad.

"She didn't," Alex says, nodding. "For sure she didn't."

"Does she talk about me?" his dad asks.

"No," says Alex.

"Oh."

"But maybe *I* wanted you to," he says. "To call. Or write."

"Did you?"

"I don't know," says Alex. Because it wasn't an all-the-time want, but a sometimes want. It would pop into his head every now and then, when he'd see a kid with both his parents in the park or on the subway, that he wanted to talk to his dad right then. Usually it happened when he saw dads with little kids—not babies, but before kindergarten. Dads that still picked up their kids a lot, or put them on their shoulders. Alex's mom gave him plenty of cuddles, but when he watched someone being lifted like that, it was hard not to want it, if only for a moment. "A lot of my friends don't have dads," he says, trying to move the conversation from the specific to the general. "We're in a homeschool group. It's mostly moms. Even some of the kids who have dads, they don't see them."

"You know," says his dad, "I lost my dad when I was about your age."

It's kind of the first thing Alex has ever learned about his dad. He thinks that most kids don't have to know things about their parents. They don't know their stories, or their histories. The stories he knows about his mother before he was born come mostly from his grandmother, and are usually about either how wonderful she was as a baby or how difficult she was as a child. They are stories told to him about his mother, but they are really about Alex, in a way, about how he and his mother are similar, and about how Alex's mother and grandmother are similar. But meeting his father like this, as a fully formed person, totally separate from Alex himself— maybe they need to learn things, stories, about each other. Maybe that's the way. "Your dad died?" says Alex.

"Cancer," his dad says. Alex has heard the word used enough to know that it doesn't need any details to come after it. It's just a way people die.

"Then he wasn't *lost*," says Alex, emphasizing the last word. "He was gone."

"Yeah," his dad says. He reaches down and scoops up a handful of ocean water, and for a second Alex thinks he might drink it. But he lets it pour back down.

"You were lost," says Alex. "To me, anyway. There's a kid in our group who doesn't have a dad. Or his dad's not around. He makes up stories about him. Where he's a soldier or a pirate or stuff. It's different all the time."

"That's sad," says his father.

"Not really," Alex says. "He had all these imaginary dads. I just had one." One imaginary dad is what he means, but it feels strange to say this to his real dad. "I watch your show," he says instead.

"Your mom lets you?"

Alex nods. "I insist," he says. "I have some questions."

His dad shifts from one foot to the other. "There's a lot about the show that we can discuss when you're older," he says, which means he thinks Alex has questions about the sex parts. Alex doesn't want to know anything about the sex parts and can imagine a version of the show where they're all cut out.

"Why is he so sad?" says Alex.

"Ted?"

"Yeah. Everybody else on the show," Alex continues, "if they get to kiss one girl, it's a big deal, and they're happy. But he kisses a different girl every show, and he's still sad all the time."

His dad thinks about this for a minute. He scoops water again, this time letting it drop from one hand over the other before it returns to the ocean. "He doesn't love any of them," he says.

"Why not?" says Alex.

"He can't," says his dad.

Alex shakes his head. It doesn't work like that. It's possible to not love a particular person, like when Alex was five and Serenity from his homeschool group fell in love with him and Alex had to tell her that he didn't love her back. She cried the whole rest of the playgroup. But it's not something you can't do in general. "That doesn't make any sense," he says.

"Some people are so broken inside," says his dad, "they can't love anyone."

Alex looks at him, examining him. "Are you like that?" he asks.

"I was," says his dad, "for a long time. I think I'm better now." Alex wants to stretch this answer out so that it explains everything, but all it does is make him wonder where it is they are now, and what either of them should expect will happen.

# More Deadly Than the Male

Gail thinks of lions waiting for one gazelle to fall back from the herd. She hopes this is something that actually happens, although she's never much enjoyed nature documentaries. In her head, a voice, vaguely British or possibly Australian, begins to narrate her actions. *The wily comic book writer lies in wait for her quarry. She is stalking the most dangerous prey: man.*

The trouble is, Phil Weinrobe seems to be a pack animal. A group of editors and writers follow him around the convention floor like a bad smell. Sometimes this group includes Ed or Geoff, and part of her, the optimistic, compassionate part, wants to believe they might be talking her up, putting in a good word for her.

*But there is no room for optimism or compassion in the heart of a mighty predator,* says the British or Australian narrator. *There is room only for the hunt.*

Tomorrow she will kick herself for all of this, for not going through proper channels. A small amount of power can be difficult to recognize for what it is, and Gail has enough clout within the industry that she could set up a meeting with Weinrobe on any day in New York, given a bit of planning. She could be sitting with him in his office next week.

*But the fierce killer thinks not of next week, only of this moment.*

As she stalks him around the convention, she begins to quite like him. He seems like a friendly uncle. He talks to kids and to fans, he smiles a lot. She had initially imagined him approaching Geoff all cloak-and-dagger, in some dark alley in Chicago, like a drug dealer, or Slugworth in *Willy Wonka.* But watching him, it seems more likely he came up and asked Geoff out for a beer. All very chummy. Very bro-y.

When her opening comes, it is exactly this bro-ness that causes it, and Gail sees it moments before it happens. What is the one place the pack will not go together? The one spot they will leave a single gazelle alone?

Gail takes up a spot next to the men's room door, hiding her face behind the latest issue of *The All New R-Squad.* Sure enough, Weinrobe enters the men's room solo.

*The deadly man-eater strikes!*

As the door closes, Gail sneaks in, her hip brushing the doorjamb as she does. She surveys the room. It is brightly lit and empty except for her and her prey, standing at the urinal. She considers options for securing the door, then pulls her hardback notebook out of the back pocket of her jeans and wedges it into the handle. It won't hold for long, but it will hold for long enough.

She stands up stock straight in the middle of the men's room and clears her throat, an abrasive sound that echoes off the tiles. "Mr. Weinrobe," she says, "my name's Gail Pope. I'm a comic book writer. And I have an idea for how we can kill off the Ferret. It'd be a long story, two years from death to return, the way I have it paced out. His death would drive Ferret Lass to the edge. She'd basically be the star of the title for that time. It would reinvent both characters, redefine them in a way that hasn't been done in years. I know that sounds crazy, but I think you should hear me out."

The only sounds in the room are the last few drops hitting the urinal. Phil Weinrobe has been facing the wall this whole time. "Well, you've got my attention," he says. With what Gail thinks is an impressive amount of dignity, he packs his dick back into his pants and zips up. "But since I haven't had my coffee yet, I'm not sure my attention's worth much."

He crosses past her to the sink and fastidiously washes his hands, a sign to Gail that he normally doesn't bother and is putting up a show for her sake. "I don't have a load of time today, as you can imagine," he says. "But let's walk and talk. Somewhere a little less uriney."

"Okay," Gail says, but remains standing in the center of the men's room.

"Do you mind stepping out before me?" he says. "For appearances' sake?"

Gail hurries out, peeking through the door for a second before darting to a spot ten feet away but highly visible, where she waits. Maybe he's using this time to escape. She didn't see any windows in there, but there's plenty she doesn't know about men's rooms. After a couple of seconds, he emerges.

"There's a stand at the far end," he says. "Only passable coffee in the place. Took me years of coming to these things to find it." He gives her an *After you* gesture and falls in next to her.

"I've been reading your run on *The Speck*," he says. "People assume I don't read any of the National stuff, but I do. I read a ton. I haven't read a book without pictures in it in a decade, but comics I read a ton. That's a weird book. Good weird. Real good weird. It reminds me of comics when I was a kid. Where OuterMan's head would turn into a cockroach head for an issue, and then that'd never get mentioned again."

"I had nightmares about that issue," says Gail. "It was never my head that changed; it was always my parents' or my teachers'. When I read *The Metamorphosis* in college, I thought it was a rip-off. When all the comics you read are Kafkaesque, Kafka doesn't seem that weird."

"I hear you're off the book," he says.

"Has everyone heard?"

"Why'd they drop you?"

"Creative differences," says Gail.

"Editorial differences, you mean," says Weinrobe. "Nothing creative about it. That whole thing they're teasing, fridging the girl so the Speck goes dark? It's been done. Change for the sake of change. That should be the motto over there."

Gail wants a NATIONAL COMICS: CHANGE FOR THE SAKE OF CHANGE T-shirt so bad right now.

"We've got the opposite problem," says Weinrobe. "It's the movies. It's a blessing and a curse. Every time a character gets optioned, I say to myself,

'Well, we won't be doing anything interesting with him for a few years.' Like *R-Squad*. Far and away our most boring book right now. In the eighties, we'd change the team's roster every six months. Shake things up. Now they're in the movies every two years, and the team people see in the movies is the one people want to read in the comics."

Gail has heard this argument before, usually from Geoff. But she doesn't buy it. More accurately, the moviegoers don't buy it. If *R-Squad 2* did a billion-dollar box office, why isn't *R-Squad* the best-selling monthly out there? Comic book readers read comic books. And comic book readers go to movies. But moviegoers don't read comic books.

"On the other hand," says Weinrobe, "it brings in money so we can do something interesting somewhere else. The Ferret movie frees my hand to launch three other books that sell below profitability. And we get to let some writer with a good idea turn the applecart over on another character. But until he's off the big screen—"

"No killing the Ferret," says Gail.

Weinrobe shakes his head. "I'd love to kill the Ferret. If it were up to me, we'd off *everybody* every couple years. It's a dangerous business, being a superhero. I'd install a reasonable mortality rate in the Timely Universe. And characters would get old. I'm fifty-five now, and the Blue Torch is still running around like he's twenty-two. Aging, endings: they're what give stories weight. They're what make a character matter. But to the people I answer to, the people who pay me? These aren't characters. They're properties."

Gail begins to wonder what they're talking about. She's pretty sure her pitch has been rejected. Now she's feeling like Weinrobe's shrink. "I should let you go," she says. "You probably get pitched crackpot stories all day."

"I don't get pitched near enough crackpot stories," he says. "You're friends with Geoff and Ed, right?"

At the moment, Gail is not feeling those strong bonds of friendship, but since there's been no formal severing of the ties, she admits she is friends with Geoff and Ed.

"I say this with all the love in my heart," says Weinrobe, "but those guys are hacks. They're talented hacks, but still. People are going to look back on this era of superhero comics and they're going to call it the Competent Age. And it'll be guys like me who get the blame, and we'll say we were following orders. Because that excuse always works."

It is the first time Gail has heard anyone willingly compare himself to a Nazi war criminal. It's surprisingly endearing.

"I've read your stuff for years, and I never once thought of hiring you," he says. "Never thought, *She'd be great on* Red Emma *or* R-Squad. You know what I thought?"

"That I'd be a pain in your editorial tuchus?" Gail says.

"That you'd be a pain in my editorial tuchus," he says. "That on a regular basis, you would be bringing me great ideas that I would have to turn down. And it would break my heart every time. Right now, saying no to this idea you've got for the Ferret? It breaks my heart. Because I want to read that book. But as an editor, you would be giving me tuchus pain, I'm sure of it."

"Thanks?" says Gail.

"Here's the thing. This thing with the Astounding Family. I'm very proud. The books, they'll be fine. You've read those books already, even though those guys haven't written them. But for me, it's big. And for my bosses, I've brought the horses back into the stable. It puts me in the catbird seat, and it frees my hand to try something interesting."

He reaches into his back pocket and pulls out a business card.

"So here's what I want," he says. "I want you to come to me in New York. I want you to call me directly"—he hands her the card and points to the number on it—"and set up a meeting. I want you to bring me something entirely new. The craziest thing you can come up with. Cockroach heads. That's what I want from you, I want cockroach heads."

Gail imagines walking into the Timely Comics offices with a shoebox full of cockroach heads. In her imagination, all the staffers have kitten heads, for some reason. There are Geoff and Ed, adorably licking their paws. Here's Phil Weinrobe, worrying a mouse.

"Can you do that for me?" he asks, breaking Gail's reverie. She's relieved when she looks up from the card and his head is not that of a calico.

"I can do that," she says.

He slaps her on the shoulder, hard. It's the first time a colleague has done this.

"You're no good to me on *The Ferret*, Ms. Pope," he says as he walks away. "I've got hacks for *The Ferret*."

# The Return of Ferret Lass

She's the last person he wants to see. So naturally, here she is. Of all the gin joints.

Ferret Lass is at the bar Brett's picked, at random, to get shitfaced in. She's in her civilian clothes. Still wearing dark makeup around her eyes. Surrounded by a chorus of other stunning women and girls. Many of them still in costume. It looks like her natural habitat.

"Hey, you," she says. Comes up and kisses him. On the lips, but maybe only friendly. Whatever it means, it makes him feel awful.

"So here's the boy," says the Diviner. "We thought she was hiding you away somewhere."

"Her little fuck puppet," says Flail. Slurs the *f*.

"Dick in a box," says Flog.

"Ignore them," says Prospera. "They're drunk."

"Ignore them regardless," says Red Emma.

"So you're crashing our hen party?" asks the Astounding Woman.

"That term is a patriarchal diminutive," says Flail.

"I'm glad you're here," says Ferret Lass. Brett gets the feeling he's here at her request. But it's her ability to make the best of any situation. To accept givens and work with them. "The perverts at this bar are only buying drinks for the girls in costume."

"Get it while you can," says the Diviner. "If I dress like this next week, they'll lock me up."

"I am so glad to be out of that tail," says Ferret Lass. "I swear I'm burning that thing tomorrow night."

"You'll lose your deposit," says the Astounding Woman.

"What are you both drinking?" asks Iota. "I'd rather buy a round than have another of these guys breathing down my shirt." Ferret Lass asks for a beer, and he asks for the same.

"So what's your trouble, kid?" says the Diviner. "Most guys would be a little cheerier with her on their arm."

"I would," says Red Emma, throwing Ferret Lass a wink.

"Fred signed with Timely," he says.

Ferret Lass looks at him. Sweet. Caring. "I don't know what that means," she says.

And Brett, who came in to drink alone, tells the whole story. To her. To all of them. It does make him feel better. They rub his shoulders. They pat his back. They make sympathetic noises. They say awful things about Fred. He's been in conversations like this with groups of guys. Commiserating. One or the other of them complaining, usually about a girl. The base attitude of those sessions falls somewhere between competition and annoyance. *Yes, your heart got broken. But mine got broken, run over by a bus, and then burned. Life sucks. Wear a helmet.* Maybe he imagines it, or has been programmed to think of women as inherently sympathetic. But as his story ends and others chime in with accounts of their own betrayals, there's no sense of one-upmanship. They are trying to get at something. Find a common thread that can, if pulled painstakingly, unravel the entire thing. Soon he's had several drinks. Is, for the most part, not talking. Not even planning to talk. Not attending to someone else to glean a jumping-off point or rebuttal. A rein he can seize to steer the conversation back to himself. He listens, and it is an all-consuming thing to do.

"A few years ago, a friend and I were going to launch a fashion line," says Ferret Lass. Her turn has come around. "Which, I know, in L.A. is a stupid idea. But we were young."

"Not the wizened hag you are now," says the Diviner.

Flail, who has been nodding off, looks up. "Fashion is—"

"Shut the fuck up," says Red Emma.

"It feels like a similar thing," says Ferret Lass. "She took a job with Rodarte. Used designs we'd worked on together for the interview. She never even told me she was going for the job." She drinks from a fresh beer. A boy with trouble keeping his eyes in his head had timidly approached Red Emma and ended up buying all of them, Brett included, a round. He was then dispatched back to his table.

"So what'd you do?" asks Brett. What he needs is a plan. A revenge plot. Some hell-hath-no-fury stuff.

She shrugs. "Got over it, I guess. It ruined the fashion thing for me. I never went back to it. But that might have been for the best. It's different than with you. With us, she was the talented one anyway. It was a shitty thing to do, but she's making some nice stuff now. I bought one of her dresses last year."

Brett will never buy any of Fred's comics. May boycott Timely altogether.

"You can't let this stop you from drawing," she says. "Maybe it's a sign you need to start writing your own stuff. You were practically writing the book anyway."

The only advice Debra ever gave him was to get out of the business. Which, probably, was good advice. He wants to kiss Ferret Lass. The whole time Prospera is talking about how her boyfriend slept with her sister while she was away at NYU, Brett wants to kiss her. There are probably blinking lights over his head that say WANTS TO KISS YOU. After another beer, the intensity of it fades. Her arm is around his waist. Hand rests on the edge of his pocket. If he looks at her, he'll want to kiss her. So he looks the other way.

A couple of tables from them, he sees Alex's mother. Obviously upset. A friend is consoling her. Brett recognizes her as Gail Pope, who used to write *The Speck.* He takes Ferret Lass's left hand in his own. Removes her arm from his waist. Misses it immediately.

"There's a friend of mine over there," he says. Their faces so close. "I'm going to go check on her."

"Okay," she says. Smiles. Not sure what he's doing or how he's managing to do it, Brett walks away.

# Anomaly S05E14

Alex is so tired. So tired he could stay awake all night. So tired he should never, ever go to bed again. He knows this place. It is where being sleepy and being wakeful, as in literally *full of awake*, blur into each other, his body's and his brain's signals getting so crossed that they're entangled and inseparable.

"So goodnight," his dad says at the bottom of the stairs, Alex halfway up. Alex looks at him, quizzical.

"Aren't you going to tuck me in?" he says. He didn't last night, but last night Alex wouldn't have asked, and might not have let him.

"You aren't too old for that?" says his dad.

"Maybe," says Alex. "But I still like it."

His dad follows him up the stairs and into his room. He stands in the doorway with his back turned while Alex changes into his pajamas. When Alex climbs into bed, his father pulls the covers over him and sits on the very edge, and Alex thinks he must have his butt really clenched to keep himself from falling off.

"Is this . . . ," says his dad, gesturing to the whole room. "The bed and everything?" He presses down on the mattress. "It's fine, right?"

"It's fine," says Alex.

"Good," says his dad, standing up. "Okay, then." He starts to leave.

"Can you tell me a story?" Alex says.

His dad looks like he's been caught by the police. He freezes in the doorway. "You don't want to read or something?" he says.

"I might later," says Alex. "But a story would be good."

"I don't have any kids' books," his dad says. He looks around like maybe he's left some kids' books somewhere, or they're in his other pants.

"Not *read* a story," say Alex. "*Tell* a story."

"Off the top of my head?" says his dad.

Alex pats the bed next to him and his dad sits down again, a little closer now. Still not cuddling, but that's okay. Alex isn't sure he's ready to cuddle yet. "Mom tells me about episodes of the show," he says.

"How does that work?" asks his dad.

"I pick a season," says Alex, "and she tells me one." None of this is working out right. The light is still on, so Alex won't fall asleep during the story. And his dad is still sitting up, which means that Alex feels like he should sit up. So he props himself against the headboard.

"Okay," says his dad, rubbing his hands together, "pick a season."

Alex considers. "Five," he says.

"Which episode?" says his dad. Of course, this is not the way the game is played. But his dad is still within the rules as Alex laid them out, so Alex should be the one to adjust.

"How many are there?" he asks.

"Twenty-two a season," says his dad.

Alex spins a wheel in his head. "Episode seven," he says.

"Huh," says his dad. "That's funny."

"I like the funny episodes," says Alex.

"No," says his dad, "it's funny because that was my first episode back to shooting after you were born." Alex feels like he has picked a lucky number between one and twenty-two.

"What was it about?" he says.

"They had to write Frazer out for a while," says his dad. "So Tim had her kidnapped by the Leader and hidden somewhere in time."

"He did that a lot," says Alex. It was never clear to him what the Leader's plan was, but he carried it out mostly by kidnapping people and hiding them somewhere in time.

"He did," says his dad. "For a couple weeks, Campbell—" He checks with Alex. "That was my character, Ian Campbell."

"I know," says Alex.

"Oh," his dad says, looking happy to hear it. "Campbell was looking for her all the time. But she was right in the middle of Anomaly headquarters, stuck in a time loop."

"What's a time loop?" says Alex.

"She was out of sync with everyone else," his dad says. "Living the same ten minutes or something over and over again."

Alex thinks this could be great or terrible, depending on the ten minutes.

"And no one could see her?" he says.

"She was out of sync," says his dad. "She was a half second ahead. Campbell was searching for her all over the past and the future, but she was right there, stuck, like a record skipping. Except he couldn't hear it."

Alex tries to imagine it but can't. Someone right there next to you whom you can't talk to or see. Then he thinks about it the other way: being right next to someone and they can't see you. Waving your arms like you were stranded on an island and a plane was flying overhead, knowing that if they saw you for a second, you'd be saved. Except the plane was right there, so close you could touch it, except you couldn't.

"But he found her?" says Alex.

His dad has to think about this for a second. "On the show he did," he says finally. He pushes the hair back from Alex's forehead and kisses him softly above his left eyebrow. He puts his hand on Alex's chest for the space of one breath, a rise and a fall. Then he gets up and shuts off the light. He pauses in the doorway, a shadow, a shape of a dad. Then he's gone.

# Our Celebrity Guest

Between the two of them, they're not making things any better. In fact, since the kid came over, Val's stopped talking about Alex altogether, which Gail thinks is probably a bad thing. The conversation has taken on the quality of a talk show interview, with Gail and Brett as the guests and Val as the obliging host. She seems happy all of a sudden, but it's a Stepford-wife kind of happy, robotic or painted on.

"What got you started reading comics?" she asks.

"If you could meet any . . . comics person, real or fake, who would you want to meet?"

"What's it like to make someone up?"

As much as she wants to keep the conversation focused on Val, it's hard not to be engaged by this dynamic. There's part of her that's mentally rehearsed this interview for years. A monstrous little creature inside her that has been privately practicing for when she becomes famous. She imagines everyone has this creature in them, but she's got no evidence to back that up, just an intuition. Certainly Brett sounds like he's been prepping. She's surprised how similar their answers are, particularly when Val asks, "If you could work on any superhero, who would it be?"

"The Visigoth," they both say at once.

"Are you serious?" says Gail. "Timely hasn't published a decent *Visigoth* since before we were born."

"How old are you?" Brett asks.

"A lady never tells."

"Levi Loeb's stuff on *The Visigoth,* right before he got fired, is some of the most amazing stuff," Brett says to Val. "Space gods that can straddle planets. Sentient stars. But it's all told from the point of view of a third-century barbarian."

"Except in the eighties, Ryder Starlin brought him back to earth," says Gail, well aware that they're nerding out on Val. But a positive feedback loop has been created, and the nerdier Brett gets, the nerdier Gail has to respond. It's an infinite nerd cycle. "So he was just this big shirtless lunk who said *thou* instead of *you*. Why anyone ever let that man write dialogue is beyond me."

"I always thought he should go into space looking for a time portal back to when he came from," says Brett casually. "Do a sort of Odysseus thing."

"But he's pissed off some space god, who's trying to keep him from getting home," says Gail, musing. She notices that Brett has started to sketch on his bar napkin. She can detect a long tunic and one of those helmets that've always looked to her like metal breasts. Underneath the helmet, the face begins to take shape, a prominent brow and square jaw. Eyes that look like they're drilled right through the napkin.

"But Timely doesn't do cosmic stuff anymore," says Brett. "It's too bad. They've got a lot of crazy toys lying around out in space."

Gail excuses herself to use the ladies' room, half hoping that, in stereotypical female behavior, Val will follow. But she has no such luck and spends her time in the restroom tallying a list of the crazy toys Timely Comics has lying around in space. It would be years' worth of stories, easily. With an overarching narrative structure like the *Odyssey*, it'd practically write itself. All she'd need is the right artist. Someone who could visualize that level of crazy.

Coming out of the ladies' room, she runs into Red Emma, who's wandered away from the flock.

"Hey," says Red Emma. "The writer lady."

"Yes," says Gail, and then sort of waits to come up with something to add. Again, no such luck.

"Do you smoke?" says Red Emma.

Gail smokes, occasionally, but she is not a smoker. Just as she dances, on occasion, but is not in fact a dancer.

"I smoke," she says, which seems somehow not to answer the question, even as it directly answers the question.

"You want to step out and have a cigarette?" says Red Emma. "Not a single one of these girls smokes. For all the terrible life decisions they're making, their lungs are pink and fresh."

"Sure," says Gail, who finds that she wants a cigarette very much. She follows Red Emma out the front and around the corner of the bar to a narrow alley. Red Emma leans her back against the brick wall of the building, props one foot against it. She draws a pack of cigarettes and a lighter from the inner pocket of her trench coat, places two cigarettes in her mouth, and lights them. Then she hands one, lipstick-stained, to Gail. It's the coolest thing Gail has ever seen.

"You live in New York?" Red Emma asks.

"Queens," says Gail.

"Appropriate."

"You?"

"Manhattan," says Red Emma. "My girlfriend works for Goldman Sachs. When people talk about how the rich are ruining New York? That's us they're talking about."

Gail has not been big on the dating scene, and her skills are a little rusty. But she suspects the mention of a live-in girlfriend this early in the conversation doesn't bode well. "That's the way of our people," she says. "Always finding new ways to ruin the neighborhood." Red Emma smiles at her, smoke seeping from one crooked corner.

"You know not one of those girls in there is gay?" she says.

"Not even Flail and/or Flog?"

"Oh, God, those two are the straightest of the bunch," says Red Emma. "Watch out for the ones who talk a big game."

"What about their gimp suits?"

"Underneath that leather is pure white cotton, I guarantee it," says Red Emma.

"So what are you doing here?" Gail asks, meaning in equal parts *here in Los Angeles* and *here in this alley*.

"Me? I'm a fan," says Red Emma. For a second, Gail wonders which version of her question has been answered. "In our ridiculous Manhattan apartment, I have an entire room devoted to my comics collection."

"That sounds like a dream come true," says Gail. She almost mentions that her own comics collection lives in her closet, but it seems like too obvious a setup.

"Ultimately it's like those kept wives who collect Precious Moments figurines," says Red Emma. "But, you know, it's different because it's mine."

"So you wouldn't call it a hobby."

"Annie calls it my hobby. To piss me off, mostly."

"And she doesn't mind that you're out here, dressed like this?"

"No more than I mind she goes to work every day dressed like Hillary Clinton," says Red Emma. "We are who we are to each other, and we are who we are to the world. Love one, leave the other the hell alone."

"And you're a *Red Emma* fan."

She nods and stubs out her cigarette against the wall, flicking the butt deftly into a sewer grate. "When I was in college, my girlfriend at the time got killed. Shot waiting for the G train on her way home. I was not, back then, a person who could process her own anger. Who could own it. The whole thing left me destroyed. I started going to this grief therapy group, which for the most part was awful. But this guy, he brought me the first four issues of *Red Emma*. And I loved it. It fit right where the empty part of me was, and it propped up my anger inside of me so it was something I could use."

"I figured all of you were supermodels," says Gail.

"A couple of them have aspirations. I don't think anyone's holding their breath. But when someone offers to pay you to play dress-up? That's a plum gig. I was going to dress like this anyway." She adjusts her fedora, which has been slowly rotating like the big hand of a clock. "You should come talk with us," she says. Gail winces. "I don't want to break up your incredibly sad little party."

"I can't," Gail says. "My friend is having the worst day you could imagine."

"It's her kid, isn't it?"

"Yeah."

"Fuck. You're a good friend for helping her out."

"I should probably get back."

"All right. But we should get together, once we all get back. Annie worked as a bartender while she was doing her M.B.A. She makes a mean cocktail. And I have the best comic book lending library in the city."

"I'd like that," says Gail. She and Red Emma head back into the bar, and Gail thinks about grabbing another drink, then decides she should check if Val or the kid needs anything first. But when she looks over to their table, they're gone.

# Just Call Me Angel of the Morning

There should be a word like *waking* that means *giving up on a long and failed attempt to sleep.* That's what Brett does when he hears the knock on the door. He looks at Valerie at the far edge of the bed. Arms folded across her chest like a mummy. Eyes fluttering like she's either fighting for sleep or fighting against it. There's a second knock, and she doesn't move. So he sits up. Smooths a few new wrinkles out of his clothes. He wonders about the propriety of answering a woman's hotel door in the morning. But she's not going to answer it. So.

Gail stands in the hallway. Hands on her hips. Like his mother when he'd come home from high school parties late, drunk.

"You, young man," she says, "are a scumbag."

Brett's addled brain can barely process this accusation. He looks at her blankly. Aware of what a slack-jawed expression he has on his face, but unable to adjust it.

"Get out here," she says. He steps out into the hall. Gail spins him around so she can step toward the door. She puts her foot in to keep it from shutting. "I thought you were a decent kid," she says. "For you to take advantage of her in that state—"

"I didn't," says Brett. Glad that synapses are beginning to fire. "She took advantage of *me.* I mean, she didn't. Look." He indicates the state of his clothes, but he's unsure what aspect of them he means. That they're on? That they're mostly unwrinkled? Somewhere here is proof of his innocence. It's clear Gail doesn't know, either. What can he say? She'd asked him to take her back to her hotel. She hadn't asked him to come to her hotel. There was a difference there, and he understood it. They'd walked back, and she talked about Alex. How she was glad Brett had met him. How he was a special kid. When they got to the hotel, she asked if he would walk her up to her room. Even when he paced through it in his head, it sounded like he was lying. None of it sounded innocent, but it was. There had been something ghostly about Valerie when she asked. Something not there. "She said she couldn't be alone," he says. "But we just lay there in the bed. No touching. We didn't even talk much. I think she needed someone to be there for her. Literally there."

Gail softens. Becomes shorter, even. Brett's not sure he's convinced himself. He searches his memory for a moment when sex was a possibility. Something he said wrong. A look that was supposed to beckon. Can't think of anything. "What's going on with her?" he asks.

"You spent the whole night with her and you didn't ask what was going on?" says Gail. Brett had wanted to. A few times during the night she started crying. A soft, hitching sound. Like she was trying to keep it to herself. He asked, each time, if she was all right. Each time she said, "I'm fine," and stopped crying. She pulled in a deep breath and stopped.

"It didn't seem like she wanted to talk about it," he says.

"You might not be a bad guy," says Gail, "but you are most certainly a guy." Brett can accept this judgment. "And no funny business?"

"No, ma'am," says Brett.

"For the love of God, don't call me ma'am," she says. Gail turns around and opens the door a crack wider. Peers in. "How is she?"

"She's lying there," says Brett. "I don't think she slept."

"That's no good," says Gail. "How does she look?" This seems like an odd question. Especially since Gail is in her pajamas. Or maybe is the kind of person who goes out in public in clothes that look like pajamas.

"I didn't check," says Brett. "But she probably looks like she hasn't slept."

Gail sighs deeply. "She's got a big day today. It's the tenth-anniversary panel for *Anomaly*. People are probably already lining up. She can't look like she came home from a one-night stand."

"We didn't—" Brett says.

She cuts him off. "I know. I'm saying, I don't know that I can be of much help in this area. I'm not a wizard with the makeup, you know?"

"Hold on," he says. He takes out his phone. Surprised at what he's about to do. She must be mad at him. She must have seen him leave with Val last night. There's no way she'll agree to it.

"Hey, you," says Ferret Lass. Like she's happy to hear from him. How wonderful it must be to live in a world where everything is okay all the time. Where everyone is already forgiven.

"Can I ask you a favor?" says Brett.

"Sure, what's up?"

"How are you with makeup?"

"I'd be insulted," she says, "but my mother says the best makeup job is one a boy doesn't notice." This makes sense to Brett. He's only ever noticed makeup when it's egregious. "You thinking of doing drag?" she asks. "You'd look so hot in drag."

"It's a friend of mine."

"Your friend from last night?"

He tries to determine if there's any malice in the question. Can't find any. "Yes."

"She is so nice," she says. "There's the thing for her show today, right?"

"Yes."

"You didn't leave her covered in hickeys, did you?"

"No, she's—"

"Hickeys aren't your thing, are they? Although I remember a few bite marks."

"I didn't—"

"Relax," she says, laughing. "Your lady friend needs some makeup assistance before the thing for her show."

"She's not my lady friend."

"You can tell me all the sordid details later over a drink. You do realize you'll owe me a drink for this?"

"I will?"

"Possibly multiple. Depends on how badly you've ravished her."

"I didn't—"

"There's an after thing at Harlowe tonight. The girls are all going to be there. They liked you. You want to go?"

Brett has no idea what conversation he's having. Only that it's not the one he set out to have. He's not sure if it's better or worse.

"Sure," he says.

"Let me throw some stuff in a bag and I'll see you in a bit," she says. He gives her the room number and hangs up. Stares at the phone a minute as if it had crawled into his hand.

"What was all that?" asks Gail.

"We have a crisis," he says, "so I called a superhero."

# The Last City

Alex is somewhat impressed. His father seems like he knows everybody here. The convention floor is packed with people, but at each of the booths for a movie studio or a television channel, the people who are working stop everything to say hi to his dad. People who are there for the convention ask for autographs or high fives or pictures. He's sure it's probably like this for his mom, too, but they never got the chance to just walk around. It makes Alex feel like he's secondhand famous.

But Alex is here today on a mission, and he has no time for distractions. He's got to get free of his dad, at least for a little bit.

"Can I wander around a little?" he asks his father.

"Did your mother let you wander around?" his father asks. The use of the past tense bothers Alex. His mother is still alive, can still let him do things, or forbid them. He wonders how long this will go on: his requests met with questions of precedent. It would be an easy system to take advantage of. *Did your mother let you ride a motorcycle?* Yup. *Did your mother let you eat nothing but pizza and ice cream?* Sure did!

"I'm allowed," he says.

"I think you should stay with me," says his father. "It's too crowded in here." His father is shying away from contact with anyone, as if they're carrying some disease.

This does not fit with Alex's plans. "I've got people I need to talk to," he says.

"You've got people?" says his father. "You're a big Hollywood player already?"

Alex does not like the tone and does not have time for this. "I'll see you at the panel thing," he says, counting on the fact that his father hasn't developed the clairvoyant *Oh no you don't* skills his mom has. He uses his invisibility powers. He uses his superspeed. In seconds he is out of sight of his father. He's running full bore through the Los Angeles Comic-Con, through its streets and down its alleyways, and for the first time he thinks maybe he will keep running. For the first time, he cannot think of a reason to stop.

He runs down Artist Alley and sees Brett bent over his pages, and Alex thinks of running right by him, but he stops, skidding on his heels in front of Brett's table, panting, cheeks flushed.

"Are you busy?" he asks.

Brett hesitates before he answers, which makes Alex worry. "I am, a little. What's up?"

"We have to finish," says Alex.

Brett sighs, and his face scrunches up into a face he's never seen Brett make before. It's a face Alex's mom makes that means an excuse is coming.

"Is there any chance we can finish later?" Brett asks. "I've got a meeting in a half hour, and I have to do the dialogue and captions on these." He holds up the page he's working on. It shows whatever you'd call a car chase if it happened with spaceships. A space chase? A fleet of spaceships chase one solitary ship from the upper left corner of the page to the lower right.

"I'm not sure I'm going to be here later," Alex says.

"That sounds dire," says Brett.

"What's *dire*?"

"Desperate," says Brett. "Bad."

"I'm trying not to think about it like that," says Alex.

"Something you want to talk about?" asks Brett. And it is. It's something Alex has wanted to talk about for a long time, and there's been no one for him to talk about it with. Not his mom and not the Idea Man, and then who else is there? He wants to tell Brett everything that's happening, but there's no time anymore.

"We have to finish," he says. And maybe it's the way he says it, but Brett says okay and puts away the stuff he's been working on and takes out his sketchbook.

"Where'd we leave off?" says Brett. "They'd been swallowed by a giant metal worm."

"It was a train," says Alex. "It was always just a train." He sounds disappointed by this realization, but the story is changing behind him. The Golden City is becoming only Cleveland after all, and the shape-shifting girl was Brett's girlfriend, whom Alex has never even met, or maybe the girl with the tail. If it weren't written down and drawn in Brett's drawings, all of the magic would be draining out of it. Alex has to get the rest of it told while there is still magic in it.

"So where did the train take them?" says Brett.

"To the last city."

"What's the last city like?" Brett sits with his pencil held above the page. Whatever Alex says now, whatever city he creates, will become real.

"It's like New York," says Alex. "It's a lot like New York, only it's still being built. The Empire State Building and the Brooklyn Public Library, everything is still being built. But the Astounding Tower and the Brooklyn Academy of Magical Fundamentals, they're being built, too."

His heart has not slowed down since he stopped running; if anything, it's beating faster. He's racing again, standing here in one place. On the page, scaffolding forms around the Astounding Tower.

"There are people," he says, "not like in the Golden City. This city is full of people. And they go to work, but not all the time. They have time to play in the park and ride bikes. In the summer there are pools and fire hydrants that spray out water for kids to play in, like the movies." And there are the kids, jumping around in the spout of a hydrant, and behind them other kids are on bikes, cruising toward him as if they're about to jump out of the page.

"It sounds nice," says Brett.

"It's not perfect, but it's nice," says Alex. "And there are heroes. Not like

Captain Wonder or the Ferret, not superheroes. But regular people who are heroes. Only it's not the same people all the time. They take turns."

Brett flips to a blank page.

"So what do they do, now that they're here? The boy and the robot?"

"They walk around," says Alex, "and everyone knows them. Everyone's seen them before, but they won't say anything. They're all so surprised. They guide the boy and the robot to the center of the city."

Alex stops, out of breath. He doesn't want them to be here. He doesn't want them to come to the center of the last city, but it's time. It's time for the boy and the robot to come home.

"Tell me what's there, Alex," says Brett.

"There's a statue," he says. "Of the boy and the robot, together. It's not a golden statue, because the people all made it themselves. It's made of car parts and toasters and bits of aluminum foil and toys that weren't even broken, but the kids wanted them to be part of the statue even if it meant they could never play with them again. It's a beautiful statue; it shines like it was gold. It shines better than gold, because every part of it shines differently, all together.

"And there's a plaque that explains it all. There was a terrible battle, and the boy and the robot, it was their turn to be heroes. They won the battle and they saved the city. They saved everyone. But to save them all, the boy and the robot had to forget. They had to forget everything, even that they were heroes.

"And at the bottom of the plaque is their names. Both their names."

Alex is tired and he wishes he were home. He wishes he could curl up in his bed in his room and listen to the city noises with his eyes shut until he fell asleep.

"What are their names, Alex?" says Brett.

"I don't know," Alex says. "You can give them names if you want."

Brett puts his pencil down, and for the first time, Alex looks at this last drawing, the boy and the robot surrounded by all of their friends, looking up at the statue they've built for them. "I don't think I need the story anymore," says Alex. "I think I only needed it to get me here. I don't need to know their names. If you do, though, you can give them names. It can be your story from now on."

Alex opens up his backpack and takes out the rolled-up drawings he's been carrying around for the past two weeks. They are like maps, and one by one he takes them out of his backpack and lays them on the table in front of Brett.

"But who were they battling against?" Brett asks. "And what happened to the shape-shifting girl? How did the boy know how to fix the robot?"

"Those are all good questions," says Alex.

Brett grins at him, and Alex knows there's a part of this that Brett doesn't understand. Brett grabs him by the shoulders. "When we get back to Brooklyn," Brett says, "I'm going to come to your house and shake you until you give me the answers." To prove he's serious, he shakes Alex back and forth and side to side. Alex lets himself feel all kinds of discombobulated, and when the shaking stops, it takes a second before he can see Brett's face clearly again. Brett's face has gone all blurry.

"I'd like that a lot," says Alex. He shakes Brett's hand, because he's not sure you're supposed to hug at the end of a co-mission. It's a good handshake, though. Then Alex turns and, using his superspeed, runs away at sixty-seven thousand miles an hour.

# Contract Negotiation

For some reason, the kiosk in the convention center that sells phones is lined with mirrors. It's important, Val supposes, to see how it will look held up to your cheek, or how you will look gazing down into it. No less important than with a necklace or a top, and you expect jewelry and clothing stores to be mirrored. But every time she sees her reflection, she's surprised she doesn't look as haggard as she feels. As if the coat of makeup the girl studiously applied, chattering the entire time about Val's cheekbones and the strength of her jawline, is blocking Val's exhaustion, shielding it from the world.

The phone she settles on is brown, like an extra-shiny chocolate bar. She can picture it against Alex's cheek, and the way it will resonate with his eyes, making them seem unfathomably dark and deep. She worries he might look brooding, or that when he's older his eyes will give him a monkish appearance. But it's only a phone, and by the time he's old enough to brood, it'll be at least outdated, or more likely obsolete, and he'll have replaced it with another. She pays for it and, stepping out of the kiosk, cracks the plastic shell of its packaging like a lobster claw. She hesitates before throwing away the instructions, but kids never need instructions for pieces of technology like this. It's all built to match some intuition that only appeared in the population a generation after Val's. With great care, as if a typo would form a permanent disconnect between them, she programs her number into the phone and labels it VALERIE TORREY. She immediately corrects this to MOM.

She tucks the new phone into one pocket and pulls her own phone from the other. For a moment she examines it, noticing for the first time that the color, a fire-truck red, must look like an angry wound against the pale of her skin. When she gets back to New York, she will buy a new phone. One that matches her eyes. When she gets back to New York, she will buy any number of new things, she will become the kind of woman who shops, who treats shopping as a primary or even sole activity for a day. Maybe it won't stick, but she can try it out. When she gets back to New York, she will buy a new Val. One that matches her eyes.

She programs Alex's new number into the phone, the 310 area code seeming like an obvious error. When she's done, she checks the time. Tim is late. Tim is always late, on the rare occasions he leaves the apartment. He never used to be. It was a running joke among the *Anomaly* crew that turning the lights on in the morning was strictly a union job and Tim was violating contracts coming in as early as he did. But now Tim is unaffiliated with time, the two having little use for each other. Louis tries to keep him on schedule, and Tim is generally obedient. But it's only that he understands he's supposed to be somewhere when expected, not that he feels any push to do so. He's shrugged off the burdens of letting people down and created for himself a world where nothing is expected of him, and anything that's given is treated as a gift.

Val sits on a bench. She wants to call Alex, but she knows it would only ring to the phone in her other pocket. She thinks of calling Andrew's phone, but the thought of having to ask to speak to Alex is so hateful it pushes away even the desire to talk to her son. She finds herself hoping Alex will use this phone only to call her, never program in another number, not even his father's. The phone will be like the hotline between the White House and the Kremlin. Private. Secure. He can keep it under glass, for emergencies, and he'll never say *Hold on, Mom, I've got another call.* A direct line, flimsy tether.

When Tim arrives, ten minutes late, below his average, he looks dapper. *Remarkable,* Val thinks, *that we're all bringing not our best selves to this, but selves that are better than us, more polished and better mended.*

Maybe the panel will be a series of meltdowns, veneers dissolving into crying jags and screaming fits.

"You look terrible," he says as he sits down next to her. "Not that exactly. But you look like you're doing terribly. Have you slept?"

"No," she says, unsurprised that Tim's clairvoyance has seen right through her. From the moment Andrew made contact again, told her the terms he was exacting, Tim has been her only confidant. Now she's regretting her choice, unsure how much he remembers of what's going on, how much of their confidence he's retained. She doesn't have it in her now to explain it all to him again, but she needs someone she can talk to who doesn't need recaps.

"You should," he says. "Sleep. Most important meal of the day. And the beds at the hotel are very nice."

"Squishy, Alex said," she recalls. She's amazed how quickly she's switched to the past tense for him, some grammatical demon in her already letting him go.

"Yes," Tim says brightly. "Squishy. That's right. He's good with words, your boy."

"He's not my boy anymore," says Val.

"Well, that's nonsense," Tim says. As if he knows sense from nonsense. As if Val hasn't listened to him babble on at length, or helped Louis prune the leaves of the Book that no one would want, that would make people question why they'd come there at all. You invest ridiculous efforts in raising a child, with some always unspoken hope that he'll reach a point where he'll be grateful, but where did her efforts on Tim's behalf go? Were they thrown into some hole in the past that he can't bring himself to remember? Or has she spent all these years shoveling clouds into a ditch, hoping to fill it even though her efforts evaporate the moment they leave the spade? And if that's the case, can she count those efforts wasted?

"They want to do an *Anomaly* movie," she says. "Andrew. Some of the writers from the show. A producer somewhere, I don't know."

"Why would they want to do that?" he asks.

"There's money in it," she says, more a question than an answer. "All they're waiting on is me."

"Are you keeping them waiting?" he says.

"I didn't want to do that to you," says Val, putting her hand on his. She hates the little part of herself that feels proud for saying it, but that little part breaks up when Tim says, "Do what to me?"

She's turned the thing over and over in her mind and tried to find a way to say yes that isn't selfish. But so far, she's been unable. It always boils down to hurting her friend to keep her child, or not even keep him but retain him. Stay with him. She's tried to take herself out of the equation, weighing only the benefit to Alex against the harm to Tim. Even in that, she has to think of the actual benefit to Alex of having her around and not its reverse. She's come into this conversation without knowing how she wants it to end, which is always a dangerous thing with Tim, who prefers scripts.

"Take your creation from you," she says.

"Do you want to do it?" says Tim. "This movie?"

There is nothing in her that wants it, not for herself. It is a means to an end and nothing more. "It'd be a reason to stay in L.A.," she says.

"It seems to me you already have a reason to stay in L.A.," says Tim.

"But there's no work," she says. "No one here wants Valerie Torrey unless she's playing Bethany Frazer."

"That could change," he says. "You'd have to give it time."

"I've got offers," she says. "In New York, and in London. Alex would love London."

"Louis said something about Gertrude," says Tim.

Val laughs. "I'd be leaving my son to play one of the worst mothers in theater."

"That could be your gimmick," says Tim. "Follow this up with Mama Rose and Jocasta. Maybe *Psycho: The Musical*."

"Will you write it for me?"

Tim smiles at her, and it's an old smile. It's the one he gave her when he cast her, the one he gave her when she told Tim and Rachel she was pregnant. It's a smile that affirms everything and forgives everything.

"There's nothing wrong with wanting something for yourself," he says. "I think parents forget that their children want to see them happy."

"Their children also want to see them," says Val. "I don't think I can give him up and go back to New York to live my life."

"You also can't give up your life to stay here," he says. "If you want my blessing, you've got it. I'm just not certain you want it."

# Freedom of the Press

Gail skips the greenroom and heads right off the front of the stage at the National Women in Comics Panel. She doesn't put her head down and barrel through, although she wants to. She takes her time and takes compliments and shakes hands, until, of course, she gets to Geoff.

"What the fuck was that?" he says, not angry so much as panicked.

"Was I wrong?" she says. She puts her hand on his back and pulls him along with her through the crowd, meaning they're attracting twice as many fans and moving half as quickly. It also means their conversation has to be carried on in staccato sentences between greeting well-wishers.

"I'm not saying you were wrong," Geoff says, then stops to answer one quick question about the Astounding Family announcement. "But." Signs an old issue of *OuterMan*. "Why now?"

"I had an audience," says Gail, autographing the first issue of *The Diviner* she wrote. "They asked."

"I can fix this for you," he says. He poses for a quick picture with a fan dressed as the Blue Torch. "I'll call Breverton."

"I don't want it fixed," says Gail as they step out of the lecture hall and onto the main convention floor. Security has cleared a space to allow this room to empty before the *Anomaly* panel, which is in a half hour. Twenty feet away, a horde is waiting to get into the room. The staff is going to open up dividers and make the room four times bigger, at least. The math works out.

"Let me call him," Geoff says, and before Gail can protest, he's gone, probably to find cell phone reception so he can save the day. Gail runs her hand back through her hair. She's sweating like Nixon. She wants to drink ten beers and run a lap around the outside of the convention center and curl up in a ball and cry. Preferably in that order.

She sees that Brett has walked around the edges of the line, which snakes back and forth through a maze of velvet rope such that it's actually a square of people about the size of a basketball court. He seems like he's looking for someone he knows who will let him cut the line, but panel queues are like breadlines in pre-glasnost Russia. There are no friends here, only stony-faced comrades. He comes over when he sees her, then pauses.

"Are you okay?" he says.

"I'm not sure I am, actually," says Gail.

He points at the room, which is still emptying out. "This was the women-in-comics panel, right?"

"National Women," she says.

"Aren't you pretty much the only woman who writes for them?"

"Not anymore," she says, raising her eyebrows like Groucho Marx.

"They hired someone new?"

"I think I quit," she says. Then she says it again, to hear it out loud. "I think I just quit National." She hasn't said the words, and Geoff was right: it can probably be fixed. Not by her, mind you, but Geoff can still fix it.

A girl who looked like she was probably an undergrad at one of the UC schools had asked a pretty straightforward question. "As a woman, do you feel like you have creative freedom in your job at National?" And Gail decided she would give a straightforward answer.

"Oh, not at all," she said. "But it has nothing to do with being a woman. It's the nature of working as an intellectual-property generator for a mul-tinational corporation. But as a woman, as the only woman writing for National at the moment, I'm pretty well insulated."

"Insulated how?" asked Joy, one of Gail's editors, who was moderating the panel. But Gail couldn't tell if Joy was offering her an out or egging her on to tell the whole truth. There could have been a mischievous glint in Joy's eye, or it might have been a reflection of Gail's own.

"If National fired me," she said, "they'd have to hire another female writer within, I'm going to say, three months. As long as I'm the token woman writer on staff, I'll be okay. Like right now, they're replacing me on *The Speck & Iota* with Ryder Starlin. Who, shockingly, is still alive. They told me this at the same time they asked me to come out and wave the diversity flag for National all summer. Which I thought was a little tactless. But, wait, what was your question?"

Everyone laughed, maybe a little uncomfortably. Gail tried to read Joy's expression, but Joy avoided eye contact for the rest of the panel. Which was probably all the information Gail needed to determine the steaming pile of shit she'd stepped in.

"I probably didn't quit altogether," Gail says. "I just don't have an immediate job right now."

"Me neither," says Brett.

Gail punches him lightly on the shoulder. "You have your drag-queens-in-space thing," she says. She picked up the first three issues from Fred yesterday, and they were good. They were more fun than most of what she's read recently. They didn't have the same feeling of being written while wearing mental handcuffs.

Brett shakes his head. "Just submitted the last issue," he says.

Gail wants to congratulate him, but his face says he's not up for congrats. "So now what?" she asks.

"No fucking idea," says Brett.

"Me neither," she says. She checks the time on her phone. The panel starts in twenty minutes. "You know that thing you were talking about last night," she says, "with the Visigoth?" He shrugs. "That was a good idea."

"It's like an idea for an idea," says Brett, as if that's a bad thing. As if that's not where things start.

"You and what's-his-name should work on it," Gail says. "Pitch it to Timely. He's got an in there now."

"Fuck him," says Brett.

It's a hard-sounding statement, anger tempered by resignation. Not the kind of thing you get over. "I was wondering if that was a *Fuck him* situation," she says.

"I should quit," says Brett. "I should go back to New York and get a real job and make up with my girlfriend back home."

Gail laughs. "What the hell's a real job?"

"I don't know," says Brett. "One where you wear a suit."

"Sounds awful."

"It does."

They both contemplate a job where you have to wear a suit. One that you have to go to every day. One that doesn't follow you around and live in your head.

"It wouldn't have to be the Visigoth," she says, almost to herself.

"Huh?"

"I mean, why play with someone else's toys?" she says. Something is picking up speed, coming together. "We could write an epic space-opera-type thing and not have it be a Timely character or a National character. We could make something up."

"We?" says Brett.

Gail scratches her nose and shrugs. "You got a job?" she says.

"No."

"Me neither." It's not quite an idea, but it's an idea for an idea. There would be a lot of logistics to work out. It would be a collaboration, which is not Gail's thing. She hates to admit it about herself, but she likes having an artist she can treat a little like an employee. This would be more like a partner. Still, she's seen the kid's work. He sure can generate intellectual property.

"You going to Val's thing?" she asks.

"I was thinking about it," says Brett. "But the line looks nuts."

"I'm on the list," says Gail. It's one of the coolest things you can say. She thinks about polishing her nails on her shoulder after saying it.

"There's a list?" says Brett. Gail turns to the woman with the clipboard, who is about fifty and works for the convention center. She clearly doesn't give a single fuck about what's going on. At Chicago and Cleveland, all the staffers were also rabid fans. This woman looks like she can't wait until these geeks clear out and make room for the boat show.

"Gail Pope," says Gail. "I'm on the list, right?"

"Yep," says the woman, who does not think "I'm on the list" sounds as cool as Gail thinks it does.

"Do I get a plus one?" says Gail.

The woman gives her a long, withering stare. Gail prays that when she is fifty, she has a stare like that in her arsenal of stares. "Honey," the woman says, "I couldn't give a fuck."

"Perfect!" says Gail, clapping her hands excitedly that she guessed the number of fucks the woman would be willing to give. "We'll go to this," she says to Brett, "and then we'll grab a drink after and discuss."

The woman lets them both into the hall, where dividing walls are being beaten back into their holding pens. The room is vast now, as if it wants to remind them both that the most popular comic book on the market is read by a fraction of the number of people who watch the worst-rated network television show.

"I'm supposed to go to this other thing with . . ." Brett trails off.

"Ferret Lass?" says Gail.

"Yeah," he says.

"Can't say I blame you," says Gail. "She seems like a good egg." Gail's not sure exactly what she means by this, having never used the term "good egg" before. What she'd like to communicate is that the girl is cute and seems smarter than she lets on. But to the best of her knowledge, there's no word for that. "What about the make-up-with-your-girlfriend-back-home part of the plan?" she asks.

"That was more of a long-term plan," says Brett as they take their seats in the front row. What he means is that it was more of an admitting-defeat-and-becoming-someone-else's-idea-of-a-grown-up plan. She wonders if, like herself, Brett measures himself against some imaginary parental scale according to whose measurements he is permanently unfinished, immature.

"When I started writing *The Speck*," she says, sounding a little like a seasoned veteran offering advice to the wide-eyed rookie, "I had ten years plotted out. I only got to write three." She thinks about those dead stories, stories she would have loved to write. Then she files them away, next to ideas about killing the Ferret, or a story where Red Emma learns that her husband faked his own death, arranging the deaths of their children to do it. There's the one where the whole R-Squad lose their powers and they all leave the R-Estate and take on day jobs. In the end, it's a trap designed by Labrinthyne, but the book is months and months of Medea trying to get a modeling career going and Computron working a shitty job in middle management. She hates Computron so much. "I don't believe in long-term plans," she says. "Ferret Lass, you think she'd mind if I was there and we talked shop for a bit?"

"Probably not," says Brett.

"Well, then," Gail says, "let's make some short-term cosmic plans."

# The Future of *Anomaly*

Val stands at the edge of the stage as they begin to let the crowd into Hall H. Tim is late. Andrew is late. As she watches people find their seats, Val imagines that it will be only her on the stage; questioned, scrutinized. From somewhere behind her, she hears the busy noises of Tim arriving, a flurry of questions and corrections. But at the same time, she sees Alex and Andrew enter through the back of the hall, hand in hand. They're walking together, neither leading the other, and although fans wave and tug at Andrew, he stays leaned over toward Alex, bent like a flower toward the sun. It's a tropism they never teach you, a way to stay in earshot with someone so little, so low to the ground that his words have trouble rising to adult ears. Val scans Alex's face for harm, for sadness, but there's only a bit of worry. Andrew sits him down in the front row and squats down on his haunches to talk to him, eye to eye. She strains forward as if she might be able to hear what he's saying, but the room is full of buzz and chatter, and Alex's face is eclipsed by Andrew. Val can see his hand resting on Alex's shoulder, right where it meets his neck. Something is passing between them that Val is not a part of, and when Andrew stands and Alex's face is revealed, the worry is gone. She wonders what Andrew might have said, and then wonders what she might have said, if it was her there. What words might change that face? As Andrew makes his way up to the stage, Alex spots her peeking from the edges and waves with a frantic happiness, but stays pinned to his seat.

The moderator claps his hands. "Oh good, we're all here," he says. He pulls Val back from the edge of the stage and arranges them all in a line:

Andrew, Val, Tim. "I'll bring you out one at a time," he says. Then he steps out onto the stage and buzz and chatter focus into a roar.

It is hard to remember who you were six years ago, because it involves thinking about who you are right now and carefully subtracting everything that's happened to you in those six years. As Val sits on the dais between Tim and Andrew, waiting for the panel to start, all she wants is to leap over the table, grab Alex, and hold him until everything else falls away. But something Val knows now that she did not know six years ago is that you keep your promises, one way or another. You keep them willingly or you keep them with blood in your mouth and a pain in your stomach that doesn't abate, only spreads.

So she is doing this thing she agreed to. She will be, for a little while, a younger version of Valerie Torrey, one who was inextricably linked with a fictional woman named Bethany Frazer. Val thinks about how much their lives dictated each other's, how Valerie's pregnancy caused Frazer's, how the infidelity of Frazer's partner and lover, Ian Campbell, equally fictional, bled into the real world and destroyed Valerie's marriage. How in the end they both chose to run, Frazer disappearing completely into wherever it is a character goes when her story ends. Val disappearing ineptly, only for a time, and then washing up on shore here like something broken.

She flips a switch in her head and six years disappear and she is thankfully not in this moment anymore. She cannot even see Alex in the audience, only the fans in an undifferentiated mass.

When the questions begin, it becomes apparent that Tim has found the same switch somewhere in the cluttered maze of his own head. He is charming and funny and fierce. He's the person he used to be, and for a second she thinks how unfair it is that this is the version of Tim that Andrew gets to see, the one he'll walk away thinking is real. But the thought fades, and despite herself she is enjoying being here with both of them again.

"Can you explain how timespace works?" a fan asks.

"Yes," says Andrew flatly. This gets laughs.

"Timespace works however Tim says it works when the cameras roll," Val says. This gets more laughs.

"I'm a very powerful man," Tim says. More laughs. The tone is set: they will all quip their way through this. They will smile and be clever, because clever is safe. They field several questions this way, playful with the audience and with one another.

"Where do you think Bethany Frazer is right now?" someone asks her. Val tries to come up with a quip, but the question sticks with her. She thinks Frazer may be in her head, that maybe an actress carries all of her characters inside herself like dresses in a suitcase. Or maybe she's six years ago in a direction Val can't point to. She thinks about Gail, who must be in the audience somewhere, and that maybe Frazer is in her now, or out in some space of pure idea and story that people go to whenever they need something from it. The answer she gives, of course, is simpler than all that.

"I'd like to think she's peacefully raising her child somewhere. But that doesn't sound like Frazer to me. I imagine she's fighting. For her past, or her future. Or for her child."

This does not get laughs, but solemn nods. Someone asks Andrew the companion question, "Where is Ian Campbell right now?"

"Assembling an evil army to invade the past," he says without pause. It cracks them up, partly because of the contrast with her answer. Six years, and one thing has not changed: Valerie is still playing Andrew's straight man.

A fan asks what was going to happen in the seventh season, and Val and Andrew both defer to Tim.

"It was always supposed to end with Ian dropping back into the past, into that cow pasture in Kansas, his mind addled, remembering nothing. It was always going to end where it started. To my mind, there are only two valid endings: death and return. And they're the same. I like our ending better, though, because all of you have written your own seventh season in your heads. You started from the moment the sixth season ended. In your heads, Campbell and Frazier are having adventures and discovering things I never could have come up with. We stopped when everything was still possible, and I always liked that."

"Speaking of death," says one audience member, "what do you think about the death of Constance Robinette, who hanged herself in her cell early this week?"

The name drops into the room like an anvil onto a mirror. Andrew looks as if he's been slapped, and Val moves immediately to put her arms around Tim, as if this could protect him. For six years, the name has not been spoken around him, and she's scared that hearing it now will break even the pieces of him to pieces.

She searches through the garbled mess of their conversation in the cell to find some clue that this was coming. She tries to look at that moment through the lens of Constance Robinette's death. It should be an easy thing to do. She can look at her life, or Tim's or Andrew's, through the lens of Rachel's death. But the time she spent in the cell with the woman who murdered her friend has nothing more to reveal. Only ramblings about time and love and freedom, nothing that means anything.

She's stunned when Tim pulls the microphone closer to himself and begins, softly, to speak.

"Stories infect us," he says. "They enter through our brains and they cross the blood–brain barrier until they are in every part of us. Generally it's benign. It's an infection that keeps us alive, keeps our hearts beating. Somehow this story that we all loved, that brought all of you here, turned malignant in Constance. It mixed itself with other stories in her blood and changed into something terrible. There must have been so much pain in her. So much hurt and damage. I can't blame myself anymore for what Constance did. I can't blame her, either. That's all in the past, and we're not. Not anymore. Next question."

Val looks at Tim to make sure he's not too badly shaken. He looks pale, drained. Andrew looks tired as well, but more specifically, he looks careworn. It's a look she's seen staring back from many mirrors, after nights awake worrying about some tiny thing with Alex that turns out to be nothing, a stomach bug or a sniffle. Or some vast generality of him, future abstractions that, to stay up fretting about them now is what her mother calls "borrowing trouble." Val wonders what it was for Andrew, what pea under his mattress kept him tossing and turning. But she also takes a little comfort, knowing now that Andrew must care enough about Alex to lose sleep.

She wishes they could end the panel right here. They are all so tired. They've all come so far to be here.

Another fan raises his hand. He is about Val's age and looks familiar.

"Trevor!" says Tim excitedly. The color comes back into his cheeks. "Ladies and gentlemen, this is Trevor Whitly. He was one of the writers on *Anomaly*." The audience applauds, and as Val remembers Trevor from back then, one of the few writers Andrew was close with, she realizes what's going on. He's a plant. Andrew put him in the audience to ask about the movie. Even with Tim here. There's some sort of plan here, something Andrew's worked out. At the very least, it puts Val on the spot. She thought she had more time, but what gave her that idea? Everything is ending right now.

"How about *Anomaly: The Movie*?" Trevor asks, as if it's only now occurring to him.

"Not for me," says Tim. "I said goodbye to all that years ago. You could write it, Trevor." She looks at Andrew, and he's struggling to contain himself. He couldn't have asked for a better answer. And then Tim continues. "Of course, I'd rather see you come up with something on your own than comb through our old production notes for salvageable ideas. It seems like the only good of it would be nostalgia. A pull to return. If I could go back, yes, I would love to go back to the set with you, Trevor, and with Val and with Andrew. With everyone. But it wouldn't be everyone. It wouldn't even be me—not that me, from back then. And that's who I want back. Part of that me calls out to this me. That's what you're feeling, Trevor, I'd bet on it. But if that pull is strong enough for you, then you've got my blessing." He looks at Val as he says this.

"I'd be all for it," says Andrew, jumping in. Val imagines he's been champing at the bit, wanting to cut Tim off so he can say *Yes, yes, I'll do it, it's happening.*

Val is aware that everyone's looking at her now, expectant. Andrew raises his eyebrows at her, encouraging her to affirm it, make it so. Val finds Alex in the audience, pushing the crowd back so they're only a curtain behind him. He's making his thinking face, his mouth screwed into a tiny knot and his head tilted to one side. There is no nostalgia for Val about those times; she's spent years drawing the poison out of the years that came before, like sucking venom out of a leg that, other than being snakebit, is a perfectly good leg. She's tried to keep that time pristine and unsullied by what came after. If she goes back, she'll have to bring everything with her. But if there's no pull backwards, there is a fear that she doesn't know the way forward from here. She can have a past she doesn't want or a future she doesn't know. She looks at Alex, who smiles. She will find a way to be with him, to be there for him. But Bethany Frazer is not his mother, even if in some sense she's the woman who gave birth to him. His mother is Valerie Torrey, and there's no place for her here anymore. She can't go back to being that other woman; it would be as bad for her as it would be for Alex. She'll find another way. She smiles back as she leans toward the microphone.

"No," she says, feeling lighter as the word comes out. "I don't think that's something I'd be interested in doing." In the corner of her eye she sees Andrew deflate, and she can feel some power move from him into her, a strength created by negation, the energy released when an idea, unwanted, dies.

# The Magic Words

The city made up of things is ending. His parents argue about visitation, about him coming to New York for holidays, and how many days, and how many weeks. His father says "agreement" a lot, and his mother says a number of times that she is Alex's mother, as if this could be what they're arguing about. Alex thinks that maybe this argument has been saved up, held like air in a balloon with the neck pinched by their separation, and now it's all rushing out in one long stream. But what he thinks is that all these years, their silence has acted like a shout, one long, deafening shout across an entire country, from one side to the other. One continuous scream of *no*. *No* is a powerful word, he thinks, and not always bad. Not always bad and sometimes magic.

They are walking the streets of the city made up of things, streets that are coming apart, breaking down into space. Vendors who have already dismantled displays of four-colored stories and pixelated dreams fold up tables, and one aisle widens to swallow the next. It feels like Alex and his parents are leaving nothingness in their wake as they stalk through the city this last time, his parents taking strides so long that Alex now and then has to run to keep up.

His father's face is red, and his mother's eyes are red. *Angry and sad*, Alex thinks. He suspects they think they are determining who will win and who will lose. But that's because they think they're telling the story of them, when it's his story. It has been all along.

Once there was a boy who was born in Los Angeles. He had a mother and a father, like everybody else. There was a man who was like a grandpa, maybe, or an uncle, who told amazing stories, and a woman who painted, and took care of the boy sometimes. But something bad happened and the woman who painted died, and the boy and his mother had to run away. They ran for years and years, so even when they were standing still they were running. And then it was time to stop running, so they came back.

This could be Alex's story. He knows only part of this story, and there are gaps and inconsistencies. If this was going to be his story, it would be one someone would tell to him, and it would be different depending on who told it. He would have to dig for facts, and then maybe that would be his story, a story about a boy who goes searching for clues about where he came from. He thinks about what the Idea Man said: that sometimes the way to end a story is to return, to go back. But even that isn't as simple as it looks. Where you go back to depends on where you started.

Once there was a boy who lived in New York with his mother. They went to the park on days it was sunny and ice-skated in the winter or stayed by the heater in their little apartment, telling each other stories. They rode the subways, sometimes not even to go anywhere but because the boy liked moving through the earth like that, and the idea that people a hundred years ago had dug these tunnels and laid these tracks and crisscrossed underneath the whole city without ever breaking the skin. They visited his friend, who lived in a castle because he was hurt. They went to plays and to movies and to bookstores, and they practiced math and did science experiments. One day they decided to take a trip that would take them all the way across the country. They started out in a car, and then they were in a van, and then they were in a train. The boy got lost in the woods and found his way back. He met a friend, and together they figured out a story. They made a story. The boy met his father, and if it wasn't the first time, it felt like it was, which matters just as much. Then they were all together, everyone, in a city that was dreams and stories everywhere.

That was another story, and it could be Alex's, too. Then the ending would take him back to New York, because he'd started the story there. This is part of what Alex wants. It's the *where* of the ending he wants, but there are things that can't fit into that *where*, and he still wants them. It's the trouble with writing stories. Everyone deserves to get everything they want, but it can't work like that. It should, but even if you're writing the story, there are rules you can't change. They're there before you start, and they have to be there at the end. Even if the story doesn't end, the rules are still there; they go on as long as the story does.

Alex and his mother and his father stand together as the city disintegrates. Parts of the city dissolve like a sugar cube in water, becoming gradually less there until they are gone. Others break apart like ice floes, large chunks coming loose and drifting away. Still others are carefully deconstructed and packed in an exact reversal of how they were assembled, so that the process can be repeated somewhere else and later. People take off their masks and are only themselves again; fairies and robots and dozens of alien species vacate the room. Screens that were windows to other planets go dark, and the apparatuses of a thousand dreams and fantasies are loaded into trucks and vans that will disperse them into the larger world, where they are needed. If Alex stands here long enough, it will all be gone, and he and his mother and his father will be in a cave, bare but brightly lit, walls of concrete that would toss back at them anything they said, if they said anything at all.

This is the first time this has ever happened. Firsts are always powerful, always magic. A story when it starts can go anywhere it wants, and that is a powerful thing. The problem, he's realized, is that he's been thinking of this moment as an ending, and endings are inert, spent things. They are stories that have gotten tired of their own telling. So this is the first part of the magic he does: he turns an ending into a beginning. This is not the last time they will all be together; it is the first.

The next part is harder, because the next part is the trick itself, and requires the magic words. If he's off by one sound, one syllable, it will fall apart and become an ending again. He can't rush it, because he has to get it right, but whoever speaks first, it'll be their magic that works, so he has to hurry. He will have to be brave right now.

His mother and father are opening their mouths. Alex is not sure he has the words, and he has spent all this time trying to find them, but here now there is no time—there is a fraction of a second to step into between the ending and the beginning.

Alex closes his eyes and opens them again, and he knows in the way sometimes he knows things that the trick is going to work. The story starts here.

# Acknowledgments

When this book was still a rickety draft, my wife Heather sat me down and told me it was time to quit my job at the bookstore and focus on my writing. "Take a year," she said. "We'll be okay." It is a rare kind of bravery and generosity, and I am beyond lucky to be on the receiving end of it. Thank you also to Alex and Story for putting up with my times of (physical and mental) absence while working, and for understanding that I am in fact working, even on days I don't necessarily leave the house.

This book was lucky enough to find a brilliant advocate in my agent, Seth Fishman. That he occasionally appears to have Jedi powers is only evidence of the fact that he's worked tirelessly on my behalf, and I can't thank him enough.

Andrea Schulz is the kind of editor one dreams about finding, one who will call you out on every lazy bullshit line in the book until it is the best possible book it can be. She is a savvy reader who is quick with the scalpel, and has extended amazing trust to me as an author to fix problems once she's spotted them. I am exceedingly grateful that she took the book on, that she has helped me distill it down until its true heart shone through, and that she brought me with her when she became a Viking.

This book was drafted in residency at the Constance Saltonstall Colony for the Arts, and I've returned there multiple times to work on revisions. Thank you to the Foundation, to its amazing Executive Director Lesley Williamson, and to Connie's spirit, which resides and resonates in the upstairs writer's apartment.

Without the support of the New York Foundation for the Arts, I would still be schlepping books for a living. Their fellowship program provided not only necessary financial support, but vitally changed my estimation of myself as a writer. And look: public support of the arts pays off. For real!

I am indebted to Aaron Kuder, a gifted comic book artist who repeatedly made himself available for pestering "how does that work?" questions about the comics industry. Likewise to a gifted actor, Karl Gregory, who walked me through what an actor does to prepare and basically wrote the "Secret Origin of Valerie Torrey" chapter for me over the phone.

This book didn't have a lot of readers in draft, but those who read it provided invaluable assistance and advice. They include Heather, Stephen Frug, Rob Costello, Sarah Jefferis, Scott Brown, Aimee Lehman, Billy Cote, Nancy Gossett, Scrap Wren, and Jim Rutman. Thank you all for your time and comments.

Everyone at Viking, and at PRH has been fantastic, and their enthusiasm has filled me with renewed faith about the state and future of publishing. I'm certain I will forget people here, but: publisher Brian Tart has been thoughtful and generous, and when you see the amazing endpaper illustrations in this book, please note that was his idea. When I was simultaneously searching for a title for the book and a name for my daughter, Emily Wunderlich swooped in and saved the day (with the former). She also offers to take the blame when I forget to do things like write the acknowledgments, and occasionally braves the northlands to attend David Bowie-themed dance parties. I generally consider myself pretty sharp on grammar, but Beena Kamlani's editing at times made me cringe at my own idiocy. Everyone in publicity and marketing has been inspired in coming up with ideas for how to get the book into your hands, and they've been incredible to work with. Also thanks to Andy Dudley, who I have known since ages ago and has put the elbow on the other folks in sales to read this thing.

Thanks to the folks at Gernert Co. who have helped me navigate the waters of being a first-time author. Andy and Flora, thank you for making sure my family didn't starve due to my inability to, say, correctly transcribe an account number.

Thank you to my dad, who stopped off at the comic book store every Wednesday on his way home from work with my little Post-it notes of the floppies I "needed" that week, and to my mom, who never threw any of my comics away. Even the ones that I left in a garbage bag by the back door that time. Seriously, those can go.

Last off, thank you to an impossibly long list of comic book writers and artists. This book is, among other things, a love-letter to a medium that's been dear to my heart since I was a kid, and now stands at a cliff's edge. From here, it can stand, safe in the fading dreams of life-long readers like me, or it can leap forward to give vast and diverse new audiences the thrill, hope, and solace it's given me. I have no doubt that if it takes that leap, it will fly.